The Case of

Kindall, K.

Books in the Kindall K series

#0 The Ninao Incident

#1 The Case of Kindall, K.
#2 The Redemption of Kindall, K.
#3 The Deliverance of Kyle Kindall

The Case of

Kindall, K.

Renee Nielsen

Callaei Books

Published in New Zealand by Callaei Books (independent publisher)

callaeibooks.com

Second edition.

First published 2019.

The Case of Kindall, K. (Kindall K series, Book 1)

ISBN-13 (paperback): 978 0 473 47876 6

ISBN-13 (hardcover): 978 0 473 63051 5

ISBN-13 (Kindle): 978 0 473 47877 3

ISBN-13 (ePUB): 978 0 473 56213 7

First printed in the United States of America

For Katy

KINGDOM of ARKALA

Key: 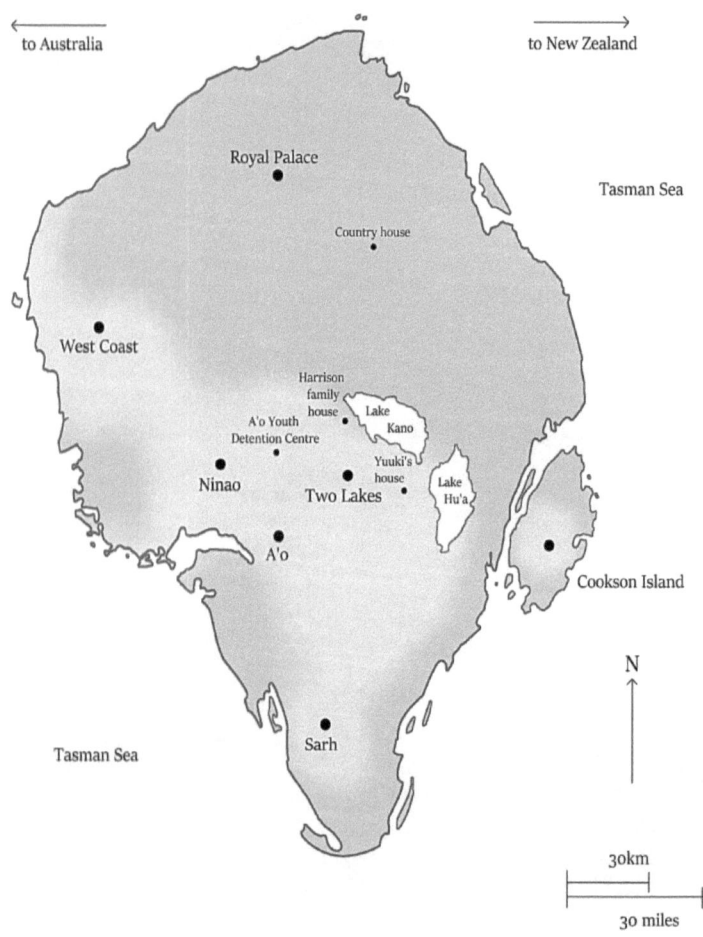 Native forest
Urbanisation

to Australia

to New Zealand

Royal Palace

Country house

Tasman Sea

West Coast

Harrison
family
house
A'o Youth
Detention Centre

Lake
Kano

Yuuki's
house

Ninao

Two Lakes

Lake
Hu'a

A'o

Cookson Island

N

Sarh

Tasman Sea

30km

30 miles

Letter Addressed to Takahashi, Y.

Date: 4th July, Thirteenth Year of Taularh's Reign

Greetings, Takahashi.

As I have stated in my previous letter, it has been brought to my attention that the defendant at a recent trial may not have had a fair trial. The defendant's youth advocate is at present working to submit an appeal. This may take some time.

Please find below a summary of Kyle Kindall's trial. You are by no means obliged to accept this position. Before submitting your response, please read the trial information carefully and take adequate time to consider your potential role and what it would entail. A formal title of the position will be decided should you choose to accept.

If you have any queries, please send them direct to my email or call me.

Kind regards,
Harrison, Timothy

RENEE NIELSEN

Judge of Arkala Kingdom Youth Court
Harrison, T.

Case #2310   Offense: *Manslaughter*
Defendant Person/s: *Kindall, Kyle (17)*
    Youth Advocate: *Smith, Charlie*
Victim/s: *Wilson, Daniel (17) – deceased*

Date of Trial: *2nd July, Thirteenth Year of Taularh's Reign*

Notes:

Location: Village Park, Two Lakes.

Incident Reported: (cell phone) 7.08pm, 29th June. Witness reported observing Kindall in a state of insanity. Peace Forces arrested Kindall on site (held at A'o Peace Force Station until trial).

Kindall, K. charged with manslaughter. The victim, Wilson, D. was found at the scene of the incident with the weapon (knife) protruding from his abdomen. Wilson died at the scene. Residents in the area reported hearing shouting within minutes of the incident. Peace Forces found Kindall's fingerprints on the knife. Wilson was found to be heavily intoxicated and it is thought that Kindall may have been provoked. Kindall's retaliation is nevertheless extreme.

School records and foster care families report Kindall as 'violent', 'volatile' and 'hot-headed'.

THE CASE OF KINDALL, K.

Place of Trial: *Arkala Kingdom Youth Court (A'o)*

Judge: *Harrison, Timothy*

Defendant Pleaded: *Not Guilty*

Outcome of Trial: *Guilty*

Defendant transferred to A'o Detention Centre.

Imprisonment Duration: Two months*

Imprisonment Type: Isolation

*Subject to revision

This information is confidential. If you are not the intended recipient, please return to Arkala Kingdom Youth Court immediately. Failure to do so will incur penalties under the Revised Crimes Act (03) ss17-21. If you are the intended recipient, for further information please request a meeting with administration at your District's Court. Thank you.

1

What am I getting myself into?

He's still plagued by doubt. In a few hours Yuuki will be voicing his final decision, and though the meeting with Timothy is casual, the subject is far from it.

For the twenty-eighth time that morning, he weighs up the consequences of if he says yes and if he says no to looking into Kyle Kindall's case. Again, Yuuki reassures himself that it's okay to say no to the position; Timothy had written that letter the way he did specifically so that Yuuki won't feel guilty about it if he does.

But the weight behind those words 'won't feel guilty' dawn on him and wrench his heart. He'd stayed up all night thinking about it.

And what if this Kindall guy is innocent, like he says he is? What if the trial really was unfair and he's being kept in prison – in isolation *– for something that wasn't even his fault?*

It's why Yuuki's mind is made up to say 'yes.' No matter the doubt. No matter how much self-preservation urges him to reconsider. He can't bear the idea of denying this young guy a second chance all because Yuuki decided he wasn't worth the time and energy. He can't do that to the kid, guilty or not guilty.

There's a knock on the bathroom door. "Yuuki," his flatmate, Lee, calls. "You all good?"

Yuuki runs some water and splashes his face, trying to make the lines beneath his eyes not so conspicuous. It doesn't have much effect. "Yeah," he mutters into the face towel. "I'll be out in a sec."

"I'm sure you've thought about it a hundred times over," Lee says, "but you know you don't *have* to do this. The trial's already been held. Whether you take up this job or not isn't going to change much."

Yuuki frowns. He tosses the towel onto the bathroom vanity and pulls the sliding door open with a little more force than necessary. "It might," he counters.

Lee doesn't step away from the doorway. "You don't know that, though."

"You're right, I don't. But what I do know is that nothing's going to have a chance at changing unless I give it one."

Reluctantly, Lee takes a step backwards, allowing Yuuki to leave the bathroom. Yuuki tries not to express his frustration but he's not sure if it works. He's too tired for this.

"Yuuki."

"No, don't say it."

Lee's brow creases. "I'm going to say it, whether you like it or not. Think about what you're doing. You have enough going on in your life already. Cut yourself some slack."

There's an uncomfortable burning in Yuuki's chest. It's fierce. It's instinctive. Yuuki's health be damned, this could be Kindall's last second chance. He has to do this – for the sake of this kid's freedom.

"Yuuki."

Continuing to ignore his friend, Yuuki grabs a decent t-shirt from the bedroom and shakes it out in front of him. He shoves his head through the shirt and wrestles it on. Giving the hem a quick tug, he sidles past Lee and heads back into the living room to pack his bag.

"Yuuki," his flatmate murmurs, following him. "I'm worried about you."

"I'm fine. Don't be."

"You're not. You haven't been since Ninao."

Ninao. Yuuki grits his teeth against the wave of fresh emotion overwhelming his mind. No, he will not think about that. *Cell phone. House key. Wallet. Timothy's letter. A pen, just in case I need it for whatever reason.* He will not think about it. *Right, and I need a jersey. Back into the bedroom.*

"Do you think you need to see someone?"

Yuuki's getting really sick of this. Lee cares, he gets it, but it's really starting to get on his nerves and he doesn't know why. Maybe it's because Ninao happened a year ago and all Yuuki wants to do with the memory is forget it.

If only that were possible…

"I am seeing someone," he retorts. "His name is Timothy Harrison."

Lee gives up. "Fine. Fine. Just…take care of yourself."

This isn't an argument Lee's able to win and he knows it, but Yuuki feels no triumph in the matter. If anything, his friend's silence only makes the relentless pain in his heart bitterer. Ever since Ninao, their friendship has been strained. Yuuki blames himself for that: if he was able to get a better handle on his PTSD, maybe they wouldn't be fighting so often these days.

Yuuki decides on his thicker jacket since it's only just gone sunrise. He also takes his warden uniform, carefully folding it up and putting it in his satchel. Timothy often decides things spontaneously; so it's better to go prepared.

Neither Lee nor Yuuki say anything for the next half hour. Yuuki eats breakfast and finishes making himself presentable while Lee absent-mindedly reads through teaching material on his tablet. It's close to eight o'clock when Yuuki slips his satchel strap over one shoulder and heads to the door to put on his shoes.

"I'm off to meet Timothy," he says, even though Lee already knows where he's going.

"I'm going to my mate's place tonight. I'll be home late."

Yuuki nods. "'kay. I'll, uh… I'll see you later, then," he says, opening the door.

Lee answers with a wave of his hand and a forced smile. Yuuki ducks in his head in goodbye and shuts the door behind him.

It's an hour's train ride into the city and from there a fifteen minute walk to where he's meeting Timothy. Yuuki gets off a couple of stations early.

The fifteen minute walk turns into one that takes forty minutes. Buying a coffee at a nearby vendor, he spends those forty minutes thinking and attempting to walk off the anxiety swimming in his gut. The air is crisp, but due to the overnight rain they had, it's thankfully not freezing. The warmth seeping through cup is nonetheless comforting.

Yuuki thinks about what Kindall will be like. He wonders if he'll be one of the more difficult ones. He wonders if his PTSD will get in the way of talking to him, maybe even make things worse – for himself, not so much Kindall. Maybe for both of them.

By the time he reaches halfway, he's consumed half the coffee and he's not so stressed, but Yuuki can't shake off the anxiousness. Belatedly, he realises it has more to do with the area in which he's walking than any thoughts regarding his potential involvement in the case: the streets are narrow and the second-story housing throws the pavement in shadow; it's not a dodgy area of the city, but there's lots of corners and shortcuts where dodgy people could be hiding; and then there's the way his footsteps echo in the quiet of a winter's Sunday morning, echoing, echoing and sounding like someone else's footsteps coming up behind him.

Yuuki grimaces and walks a little faster. Being vigilant and situationally aware is one thing; being hypervigilant because you're still on edge about something that happened a year ago is another.

"Do you think you need to see someone?"

Maybe he does, but he doesn't want to. Yuuki's never been good with talking about himself so he has no idea how he'd go about it. He doesn't understand his issues well enough to be able talk about them anyway, so he reasons that even if he did go to see a counsellor or a psychiatrist, he'd have too much trouble trying to describe what he was going through for such sessions to be of any use.

Timothy is the only person he trusts enough to be able to talk about it. Yuuki knows what Timothy's about and Timothy knows what Yuuki's about, all without him having to verbally explain himself. Part of that's because Timothy was directly affected by what happened at Ninao, and involved in more ways than one. Though they haven't been friends for long, they trust each other completely.

It occurs to him that Kindall probably doesn't have anyone like that in his life. If Yuuki's conclusion is correct, then the only person who spoke on Kindall's behalf at the trial was his youth advocate. No one else did. If the kid had any other support, they weren't present. Even his foster family spoke strongly against him.

Something about that doesn't sit right with him. There seems to be a strong bias in the words used to describe Kindall, all giving the connotation that the kid is some sort of hot-headed mess. Who's to say the people describing him are even reliable sources in the first place? Who's to say Kindall's behaviour wasn't misinterpreted or provoked to begin with?

Thinking about that, he understands why Timothy called him up about this case now. Yuuki's no judge, but he's had plenty of experience dealing with misinterpretation issues such as these. He's been a warden long enough – even if what he mostly does now is paperwork – to know it's more than an occasional problem.

It didn't escape Yuuki's attention last night, though, that the word 'isolation' was listed as Kindall's form of imprisonment. Isolation. Solitary confinement. Kept in a locked room, just himself and his shadow. It might be a concerning punishment for someone who might not even deserve it and it might be something that Yuuki hates to think of someone possibly not guilty being subjected to, but he has to be careful how much he lets himself get involved in this investigation.

Yuuki knows what Lee's warning is about. What happened at Ninao still haunts Yuuki, and the setting of an isolation cell might end up being too much. While that's true, where Yuuki had people looking out for him, searching for him and fighting for a way to get him back, Kindall has no one. Not now, not when the incident at the park happened and seemingly not even before.

Yuuki hadn't been alone when he was kidnapped. Timothy had with him, helping him finish setting up the Youth Rehabilitation Trust fund. He was there when Yuuki had been abducted from the Ninao office, and he would've been kidnapped himself had it not been for his son Joshua's quick action.

The unidentified pro-Taularh people had taken Yuuki to a shed and left him there to die.

Of all people to have an idea of how Ninao impacted him, it would be Timothy, and Timothy wouldn't suggest working on reviewing this case with him if he thought that it might prove to be too triggering. Yuuki trusts Timothy's judgement, and that alone is enough for Yuuki to be convinced and assured that Kyle Kindall's case deserves to be looked again.

Timothy and Joshua had rescued Yuuki. If Kindall's innocent like he says he is, then Yuuki hopes that he'll be able for Kindall what Timothy and Joshua had been for him.

Ten o'clock rolls around fast. Yuuki only has to wait five minutes before Timothy's car pulls into the carpark. They order and find a spot in one of the corners where they can talk in relative privacy.

"Alright," Timothy says, hands clasped where they rest on the table. "Before you give me your answer, I want to make sure you know what you're dealing with. You're already a warden, so it's not as though you haven't interacted with any of the kids before, but to Kindall I'm going to need you to be a counsellor and possibly a mentor to him also." He pauses, watching Yuuki's reaction carefully. "Are you prepared for that?"

Yuuki breathes out slowly and leans back in his seat. "If I'm to be honest, I…I'm not sure. I don't know if it's something that can really be prepared for, I guess. But my answer is yes, regardless. I want to give him a chance."

"I figured you'd say 'yes'." Timothy says, mouth quirking. "Just know that you aren't alone in this, okay? If it gets too much, there's no shame in pulling back."

"Thank you. I appreciate it. I just…I feel like this is something I must do, you know? If Kindall really is innocent, then I'd hate to think what two *months* of isolation is going to do to him – on top of being accused of taking someone's life."

"You're kind to a fault, aren't you? But, Yuuki, if things don't work out with Kindall, don't beat yourself up over it, okay? Or at least try not to."

Yuuki smiles. "You know me too well."

They break off conversation when the waitress brings over their coffee. Timothy acknowledges her with a thanks as she steps back and walks away. He takes a moment to sip his coffee and gather his thoughts while Yuuki waits for his own to cool.

"Have you got any questions?" Timothy asks eventually.

"I do. When will I be meeting Kindall?"

"Today."

Yuuki opens his mouth to automatically say he can't but Timothy only grins.

"No need to worry. I sent Mitchell the contract details before I sent you the letter with the case details on it. He said you're all good to start work after you've met with Kindall."

"Good thing I brought my uniform, then," Yuuki murmurs. "Mitchell's not worried about how it's going to affect my hours? I'm surprised he hasn't just replaced me, for all the days I've had to take off."

"He's reworking your schedule." Timothy crosses his arms over his chest. "You probably won't be doing your usual work while working on this, at least not to begin with, but Mitchell still wants you around. I know work's been hard for you since…since Ninao, but you're an invaluable member of the team, Yuuki. Since the change in legislation, there's not many who would be willing to give out second chances. It's going to take every person we have to keep fighting for fair justice."

Since Taularh took over the Arkala kingdom, the rules became stricter and the punishments harsher. One chance is all most people get. If a person is wrongfully convicted, the compensation is minimal. While it isn't anywhere near as bad as medieval penalties were, it's still a far cry from King Fahlu's ideals. There's no way King Fahlu would have allowed a seventeen-year-old to receive a punishment of two months in isolation for something he may not have even done.

Timothy unzips a jersey pocket and pulls out a folded piece of paper. He puts it down in the centre of the table and smooths it out. It's a photograph.

"Here," Timothy says, sliding the photo closer to Yuuki. "This is Kindall."

Yuuki spends a minute familiarising himself with the teenager's appearance. His features suggest he's of Arkala'ana ethnicity, or at least partly. The contrast between dark brown hair and too pale skin is concerning – that and the purple-tinted shadows in the corners of his eyes. There's no hint of malice in his expression.

In fact, the longer Yuuki looks, there's no hint of anything in his expression. He looks…empty. It's like getting arrested destroyed the last sliver of hope he had left and after that he just…gave up on life.

The coffee's cooled enough for Yuuki to drink. He savours the bitter aftertaste as he mentally prepared himself for the challenge that lies ahead. His heart hurts for a person he's never even met before.

"You personally believe he was telling the truth when he said he wasn't guilty?" he asks Timothy.

Timothy raises an eyebrow. "You know that I'm not allowed to say. What I can say, though, is that I believe he was poorly represented and it basically came down to his word against everyone else's. There was sufficient evidence to suggest he may have been guilty, but none to suggest he wasn't. What I want to know is if there actually *was*, and if so, for what reason it wasn't presented at Kindall's trial."

Yuuki nods. Timothy may not have articulated which side of the fence he's on, but Yuuki can hear it in his tone. It's also clear in his actions of asking for another perspective on the matter.

"I will do my best, sir," Yuuki says firmly.

Finishing the last of his coffee, Timothy smiles and shakes his head. "No need to be formal here, Yuuki. Now, you said you brought your uniform along with you? Finish your coffee, go change and then we'll head over so you can meet the one at the centre of all this."

*

Since the Ninao incident, Yuuki hasn't been in his warden uniform often. The royal blue seems duller than he remembers, the material lighter, and when he shrugs off his jacket on entering the heat pump warmed building, it makes him feel more vulnerable than it should.

He and Timothy wait in the meeting room as requested, Timothy standing off to the side and Yuuki sitting at a table with a vacant seat opposite him. He's nervous now. Though he studied the photograph in the car on the ride here, Yuuki knows it'll be much different meeting Kindall in person.

Yuuki's anxiousness builds again. He hasn't really been involved in anything outside paperwork for over a year now. What if his interacting skills aren't up to scratch? What if he ruins all of Kindall's chances of a retrial because of his own incompetence? What happens if Kindall says something that triggers Yuuki's PTSD, and though he wants to keep helping Timothy, he can't because his head's such a *mess* –

"Yuuki."

Timothy's watching him stress himself out from where he's leaning against the wall. He's smiling softly, though there's a crease in his brow. He's about to say something when then the door opens.

Yuuki's nervousness dissolves into concern at the sight of the youth.

Kindall shuffles in, eyes downcast, shoulders slouched. His wrists are hand-cuffed in front of him, secured to a belly chain wrapped around his waist. The orange prison uniform makes him look ill. The shadows beneath his eyes are like bruises. His expression is blank.

"Take a seat," Mitchell orders, guiding him to the chair opposite Yuuki.

Kindall sits. He leans heavily against the back of the chair.

"This is Officer Yuuki Takahashi," Mitchell says gruffly. "He's here to help. All goes well, your time of imprisonment may be reduced a few weeks or you might even be offered a retrial. If that's going to happen though, you're going to have to cooperate. Understood?"

Yuuki hopes the boy will look up so they can make eye contact, but he doesn't. He just...sits. It's like he doesn't have the energy to function properly anymore. Yuuki tries to recall how many days it's been since the trial and his stomach starts churning.

Hasn't it only been a few days?

Unfortunately, Mitchell interprets the behaviour as flat-out disrespecting a warden. He gives him a sharp nudge in the shoulder.

"Answer me, Kindall."

The teen's throat moves as he swallows. He murmurs something, but it's too low to hear.

"Kindall!"

"Yes, sir," Kindall says, louder this time but voice still husky.

Yuuki studies him carefully. Kindall's eyes are void of emotion. His body language is that of someone defeated, of someone who's given up. Someone who's been given up on.

But not by everyone. Yuuki takes a deep breath and asks, "Name's Kyle, right?"

The question is met with silence. Yuuki's afraid Mitchell's going to reprimand him again when Kindall replies with a small nod. Yuuki lets out a relieved breath.

"My name's Yuuki Takahashi," he says. "I'm a warden here...well, off and on, these days. I've read about your trial and I've heard that you may

15

not have had as fair a trial as you should have. I want to help change that."

Kyle's eyes flick to where Timothy stands at the side of the room. He glances up at Yuuki briefly before dropping his gaze to hands. His voice is barely a whisper. "Why?" he asks.

Yuuki opens his mouth to reply but the words catch in his throat. *'Because I want to help'* isn't going to be very convincing to someone who's in his position. He's probably heard it a hundred times over only for the same people who said it to give up on him. Yuuki pauses for a few seconds to think, aware of the silence stretching out longer.

"Because I believe in second chances," he says. "May I ask you something?"

He waits for a response. Kyle shrugs.

"It's recorded that you pleaded not guilty. Do you still stand by that, Kyle?"

Kyle's gaze hardens then. His brow furrows and his frown deepens into a scowl. He closes his eyes, nostrils flaring. "What does it matter?" he mutters. "It doesn't matter what I say. If they say I'm guilty, then fine, I'm guilty."

"But are you?"

Yuuki fights the urge to lean forward. The action might be an inquiring one, but it's also one that'll impose on Kyle's space. Maybe if Mitchell weren't standing at Kyle's back he would because he wants Kyle to look at him.

Kyle does look at him. The intensity of his glare is scolding and painful all at once.

"I'm not asking you to tell me what you think everyone else thinks,"

Yuuki says. "I'm asking you what you think."

The heat dies in Kyle's eyes, leaving only a deep-seated loneliness and an anger born from injustice. At least, that's what Yuuki makes of that expression. He knows other people see it differently, but Yuuki's not here to see Kyle in the same light as everyone else.

"What do *you* think?" Kyle asks. There's a challenge to those words.

Yuuki shrugs, forcing himself to hold eye contact. "I don't know. The only information I have on your case is generalised, and I'm glad it is because I want to decide for myself what I think. But you're going to have to help me. There's a number of people who I could ask for their opinion on whether you're guilty or not, but I want to hear your side of the story."

"For all you know, I could be lying. What's my word worth?"

Yuuki feels a small smile tugging at his lips as the challenge redirects itself. "And why would you try to succeed in lying if you knew all the evidence was going to be against you anyways?"

The scowl eases back into a frown. Kyle considers Yuuki warily. *He's fighting himself*, Yuuki realises. *I'm giving him hope, but for all he knows that hope isn't going to last. At this stage, it's still his word against everything else.* It occurs to Yuuki then that even with his added perspective, it still might not be enough. Judging by the way Kyle doesn't seem to be overly excited about the opportunity, he's already realised this.

We've still got to give it a shot, Yuuki thinks resolutely. "So," he says, leaning forward this time. He extends a hand across the table. "Will you let me help you?"

Mitchell's posture changes slightly, as though he's preparing for Kyle to grab Yuuki's hand and yank him over the table. Yuuki ignores him and remains as he is. He keeps his expression neutral. No fake smiles. No trying to convince the kid he's as honest as he is when he says he wants to help. That's all for Kyle to decide.

For a long moment, Kyle just stares at Yuuki's hand as though waiting for him to withdraw it. But Yuuki waits patiently. Kyle grunts, sits up slowly and awkwardly accepts Yuuki's hands in his hand-cuffed ones. There's a drop in tension in the room.

As they both sit back in their respective seats, Kyle remarks, "I suppose I have nothing left to lose."

Yuuki doesn't understand how much weight those words carry.

"Alright," he says, "Officer Mitchell here is going to sort out a schedule for us to meet a few times during the week, starting from...uh..."

"Starting tomorrow," Mitchell supplies. "Half an hour every three or four days to start off with."

Kyle doesn't react.

Yuuki frowns. "Is half an hour long enough?"

Mitchell grunts. "He's lucky to have even that. The terms of isolation mean no contact."

Kyle's eyes have gone dull and lifeless again. *Talking about him as if he's not in the room. Treating him like he's not deserving of healthy social interaction.* Yuuki forces himself to control his anger. Mitchell's not the one who made these rules – Taularh did. Expressing his anger at how much he resents this kind of punishment is not going to change them.

For now, Yuuki agrees to the terms. Kyle has no choice but to do so.

With the purpose of the meeting achieved, Mitchell takes Kyle by the arm - Yuuki doesn't miss how Kyle flinches - and escorts him back to his cell. Yuuki's gaze lingers long after the door shuts, a sense of helplessness overwhelming him. It's Timothy who stirs first.

"Yuuki?" he asks quietly. "Are you okay?"

It's hard to breathe. Anger turns to a sharp pain behind his eyes, and before Yuuki's able to get a grasp on his emotions, he's crying.

He thinks of Kyle being forced back into isolation this very minute and memories of what happened at Ninao flood his mind. The darkness. The hopelessness. Losing his mind. Minutes stretching into hours that felt like days with nobody coming to rescue him. He thinks of Kyle going through that, accused of something he may not have even been entirely responsible for. He thinks of Kyle having to go through what he did.

Timothy's strong arms wrap around him as he begins to hyperventilate.

"It's okay," Timothy murmurs. "You're okay. Just breathe, Yuuki. You're safe. You're not there anymore." The door opens but he ignores it, continuing to rub Yuuki's back. "We're going to do all we can to help Kindall, okay? We'll do all we can to get him out of there."

Yuuki nods, fighting for control of himself.

"He's going to be fine. Okay? We'll see to it that he is."

If Yuuki wasn't a hundred percent on board before, he is now. Taularh's rules or not, he's going to find a way to make sure that Kyle is out of there as soon as possible – guilty or not guilty.

2

Yuuki launches into the investigation the moment he gets home. He barely registers the sound of Timothy's car reversing down the driveway due to the roaring of questions inside his head.

It's a good thing Lee's not home. Yuuki's hands wouldn't stop shaking the entire car ride home. He noticed that Timothy noticed. The shaking still hasn't stopped, making Yuuki have to re-enter his laptop password twice after hitting the wrong keys by mistake. If Lee finds out about the panic attack, Yuuki will never hear the end of it.

His phone buzzed in his pocket just before he got out of Timothy's car. As suspected, it's a message from Lee, but Yuuki doesn't have the energy to deal with lying right now.

He's got a truth to work on finding out.

What his gut's telling him is that both Kyle's pleading not guilty and the evidence piled up against him *is* all truth, but it's the stuff that's been automatically assumed that Yuuki's after: the points that weren't covered and the parts that were omitted.

Yuuki wonders if racism might have a part to play in Kyle's case, too. The Arkala'ana, whom Kyle appears to be affiliated with, have a history of being discriminated by the Arkala, mostly for their preference of living down in the valleys of the island in the Great Caves and also for their pale skin tone. While the lingering racial tensions between the two native Arkala tribes have died down since the arrival and immigration of multi-national people, it's still seen floating around from time to time.

Even if Kyle Kindall isn't fully Arkala'ana, it wouldn't be far-fetched a thought that maybe his ethnicity is one of the reasons why no one wanted to properly represent him in court. All it would take is for one of the witnesses to harbour racist thoughts towards the Arkala'ana and just like that Kindall's case could be swayed by bias.

Whatever the reason, Yuuki swears in his heart he will find out why Kyle Kindall insists he's innocent even when everyone else says he's not.

Before he loses himself in his thought processes, Yuuki checks the door's locked. He opens a window in the lounge to let in some fresh winter air, but everything else he keeps shut out of paranoia.

What happened at the office in Ninao isn't going to happen here.

Logging into the work server, Yuuki scours the documents he's acquired. His stomach growls. He ignores it. He brings up the trial transcript Timothy sent him and reads it.

> *Case #2310 (Charge: Manslaughter)*
> *Judge: Harrison, Timothy*
> *Defendant: Kindall, Kyle*
> *Youth Advocate: Smith, Charlie*

Yuuki skims over the formal introductions and guidelines to

proceedings.

Judge: Kyle Kindall. You are charged with the death of seventeen year old Daniel Wilson. How do you plead?

Defendant: Not guilty.

Judge: Before the incident happened, did you have any intention of taking Wilson's life?

Defendant: I didn't.

Judge: If not, then why did you have a knife on you?

Defendant: I didn't! I was just sitting at the park doing nothing when –

Judge: Kyle, I request that you control your emotions or else your advocate will need to answer for you.

Defendant: I was at the park. Doing nothing. Daniel came up to me, with the knife.

Judge: How do you explain your fingerprints on the knife handle?

Defendant: I didn't do it!

Judge: Second warning.

Defendant: He made me do it. He forced me to put my hand on the knife and wouldn't let go and I freaked out and he still wouldn't let go and then I stabbed him, on accident.

Judge: You could've walked away. Why did you chose to retaliate?

Defendant: He gave me no choice! He attacked me! I was just trying to get away!

Judge: I apologise, Kyle, but I am going to have to ask Mr. Smith to speak on your behalf. The Court has the permission to restrain you if necessary should your emotions escalate further. You have had your third and final warning. Mr. Smith. Does Kyle's account to you of what happened match his answers?

Youth Advocate: It does.

Judge: Do you believe his account to be mostly true?

Youth Advocate: I do.

Judge: How would you describe the reason behind Kyle's actions?

Youth Advocate: I believe his retaliation was no more than a means of self-defence, if not perhaps on the extreme side.

Defendant: He was holding me down!

Judge: Court, you may act in accordance.

[Defendant muted]

Judge: Court, we will proceed. Evidence supporting the charge of manslaughter include, but are not limited to: witness reports of shouting, a key witness seeing Kyle with Daniel at the scene and Kyle's fingerprints found on the knife handle. Peace Forces have ruled this as sufficient enough evidence to support the charge of manslaughter. Mr. Smith, do you have anything to say against this?

Youth Advocate: I have nothing to say that will counter this evidence.

Judge: Kyle, though you pleaded not guilty, as you can see there is substantial evidence to suggest that you are. For the record, even upon hearing this do you still plead not guilty? Nod if you do.

[Defendant nods]

Judge: Alright. You are hereby sentenced to two months of imprisonment on the charge of manslaughter. That time may change. You are eligible for a retrial should evidence supporting your claim come to the Peace Force's attention. You will accept these charges. Due to your volatile nature, you will be subjected to isolation for the safety of those around you. Mr. Smith, have you anything to say to Kindall before he leaves this room?

Youth Advocate: I will continue to support you, Kyle. Don't lose hope.

23

Judge: Court, you may proceed with the defendant's transfer. All rise.
[End of Transcript]

Yuuki reads over it until the words become so familiar to his head voice that his brain switches off analysing them. Rubbing his eyes, he stops and sits back to think.

Questions start popping up in his mind immediately.

There was a knife involved in the incident. Who did that knife belong to? Is it even the same knife some of Kyle's old school reports said he had confiscated off him a couple of times?

Yuuki taps his finger on the side of his thigh, frowning. He fetches a notepad and pen to write the question down on.

The only information given about Daniel Wilson being intoxicated was a note from his autopsy. Why wasn't the matter brought up in court? Did the Peace Forces decide that Kyle's fingerprints on the knife were incriminating enough?

How did Kyle's fingerprints end up on the knife? ...especially if that knife isn't his and he isn't guilty?

It was reported that people in the neighbourhood heard shouting. How many voices were heard shouting? Who shouted first, and what was the nature of their tone?

At the trial, Kyle said that Daniel approached him. To what extent is this true? Did he have any prior knowledge suggesting that Daniel might come after him?

Yuuki taps the pen on the notepad. He glares at the laptop screen, heart beating fast.

Are Kyle's fingerprints the only ones that were found on the knife?

Pause. Tap tap tap.

The key witness saw only Kyle and Daniel. Were there any others at the scene? –

see shouting.

Did Daniel's family know Daniel was drinking that day? What were his drinking habits?

How far away is Village Park from their homes, school, friend's places, common haunts....?

And lastly, in bold, scribbled handwriting, *Why were these things not asked during the trial?!?!?!*

It's unlike Timothy to not question these things. It's unlike Timothy to speak to anyone the way the transcript said he did in Kyle's trial. But Yuuki understands that when he's at work, Timothy must act with indifference to his own feelings, so then maybe there's nothing really out of the ordinary there in that regard.

Yuuki still finds it suspicious. Timothy must've been under some kind of pressure to have the trial outcome decided that day, else he would've ruled that they needed more evidence before coming to any conclusion. Maybe he had to satisfy the Peace Forces. If they found Timothy to be 'too soft' under Taularh's new rules, then he'd be called unfit for his job and get kicked out of it, or worse.

They can't let that happen. He did what he could for Kyle given the situation he was in, and now it's up to Yuuki to take the baton from him. With it, Yuuki vows to do the best he can.

The afternoon passes. Yuuki eventually caves in to his hunger and takes a break from his searching. The muscles in his right hand ache from all the writing. His head aches, too, but it's a pleasant kind of ache. It's been a while since he's been involved in non-PTSD related deep thinking, so he's enjoying getting back into his old work mind-set.

Ever since Ninao, he thinks, *I…*

Just like that, Yuuki loses his appetite. He has to force himself to swallow down the mouthful of toast. The rest of the slice is returned to the plate. With a grimace, he brushes the crumbs off his hands, grabs his phone from the table and takes himself outside to distract himself.

It's cold, now that the sun's minutes away from setting, but it's stress-relieving. The cooling air on his forehead is a profound relief. Slowly but surely, the oncoming wave of flashbacks recedes.

Yuuki sits on the slope of the driveway watching the colours of the sky fade into dusk. Seemingly out of nowhere, he suddenly remembers he hasn't checked his phone since he got home. Yuuki slips it out of his jacket pocket, squinting against the screen brightness.

You have one (1) unread message:
Lee, 12.35pm
How did the meeting go?

He tugs the sleeves of his jacket further over his hands, otherwise ignoring the sudden drop in temperature that's now got him shivering.

Oh, it was great Lee, Yuuki thinks. *I accepted the position like you didn't want me to. We went to the detention centre and I met Kyle. I think he's hurting. I don't like it. Guilty or not, he shouldn't be kept in isolation. I'm worried it's going to do more harm than good. I had a bit of a flashback episode – I'm okay now. Actually, I lie; I'm not. Kyle's not. I'm going to do what I can to get him out of there.*

There's no way he could text that and expect Lee to understand. Even if Yuuki spoke those words to his face, he'd still insist that Yuuki's ignoring his own health to help Kyle. But nobody else is helping Kyle, convincing Yuuki that he might very well be, along with the scarce few people who believe the trial was unfair, the last line of defence standing between Kyle and his loss of freedom.

Yuuki noticed the asterisk on the case summary. *Subject to change*, it said. Not the isolation part but the duration of imprisonment. In other words, there's nothing stopping the higher-ups from extending and extending that time period. In other words, the supposed two month sentence could very well end up being a life sentence.

Kyle's seventeen, for crying out loud! Yuuki wants to shout. *He could be my younger brother in another reality.*

Perhaps that's something else that makes Kyle's situation all the more real to him. Yuuki's only seven years – and however many months – older than him. That's not much of an age gap. Yuuki turned twenty-five a few months ago, free, and here's Kyle Kindall looking like he's going to be spending his eighteenth birthday in prison, possibly even for something he didn't do.

And what of the fingerprints? Yuuki's not sure what he ought to think. If the Peace Forces found Kyle's fingerprints on the knife's handle, and the charge was recorded as manslaughter, then… either Kyle *is* guilty and he tried pleading otherwise, or else he's not guilty, just as he said he is, and he was set up.

Yuuki feels in his gut that it's the latter. As he'd said to Kyle earlier that day, what good would it do him to plead not guilty in a court room full of people saying that he undoubtedly is? Kyle doesn't strike Yuuki as being the kind of guy who would go to all that trouble.

That means it's just as Timothy said – Kyle had to have been merely poorly defended. It's quite possible that only evidence supporting the idea of him being guilty was presented.

But that only raises yet another question of why, and it makes Yuuki's head spin trying to figure it all out.

Tomorrow, Yuuki reminds himself. He's going to have his first official meeting with Kyle tomorrow. He can start his investigation then.

Yuuki doesn't sleep. He tries, but he can't.

Knowing he's got to be up early, he even attempts just napping on the couch. It doesn't work. He's exhausted; he should be able to sleep, but the second he closes his eyes the flashbacks come. And with it, imagination.

Under the Revised Crimes Act, an amendment Taularh made to King Fahlu's set of justice legislation, isolation can mean a number of things. No contact with others is an obvious. Restricted contact with anything is another, and that can even mean the sight of the corridor outside the cell.

He imagines Kyle sitting in his cell. Alone. Bored. Chest aching. Throat void of sound. No one to talk to. Nothing to listen to. Mind blank. Head foggy. He wonders how much room there is to move around. If Kyle busies himself with exercises every now and then. What he thinks about the most. What the bed's like. What food he's being given.

Yuuki wonders if Kyle's sitting in darkness right now. There should be a light in the room at least, right? If there isn't, is that darkness cold? Is it silent to the point of suffocating? What happens if Kyle needs help? Can he ask for it, or does the term 'isolation' mean exactly that – complete isolation?

Two months…

What is that going to do to Kyle's mental health being locked up like that for so long?

The door to the house clicks opens.

Yuuki snaps back to reality. He's breathing fast, heartbeat pounding. His fingers clutch at the pillow he's holding tightly to his chest. He realises he's been staring wide-eyed at the black television screen for who knows how long. The digital clock reads *21.03pm.*

He sits up and finds himself confronted by a very displeased-looking Lee.

"Yuuki," Lee says evenly. "I sent you a message on my lunch break. You didn't reply."

Yuuki hunches his shoulders. "Uh…sorry? I figured I'd wait till you got back to tell you."

With a drawn out sigh, Lee drops his bag on the floor and pats Yuuki on the shoulder. "Well? How'd it go?"

Yuuki hesitates. Once, PTSD or no PTSD, he would've told him everything. But Lee's not known to have much patience when it comes to controversy, and Yuuki putting his health on the line for the sake of this case is pretty much that. As much as Yuuki understands and appreciates the concern, Lee's just not seeing the full picture: Yuuki's not the only one whose mental health is at stake.

Because what if Kyle wasn't even responsible for that other kid's death? What if he's innocent and he's being punished on the basis of other people's assumptions?

Lee watches him carefully. "You said yes, didn't you? I know that face you're making."

"I did say yes," Yuuki declares. "I meant it, too."

"So what's the plan? I'm guessing you and Harrison arranged some kind of regular meeting schedule with the kid?"

The undertone of distaste in Lee's voice has anger flaring in Yuuki's chest. He gets to his feet and decides to busy himself making a cup of coffee before he snaps.

Dimly he's aware that this sudden irritation could be affiliated with his post-traumatic stress, but what's going on in his head is too confusing and it's too stressful trying to understand it. He's at war with himself, something that Lee isn't aware of and often misinterprets.

Such as now. He can feel his friend's eyes on him, scrutinising him, and it makes the hair on the back of Yuuki's neck rise.

I've probably just driven another rift between us, he thinks, *but that can't be helped. If he can't see how much danger Kyle is in, then that's his problem. I will not make it mine.*

"I met him today," Yuuki says as casually as he can. "His name's Kyle." He flicks the switch on the jug and moves to the other side of the bench to ready the plunger. "Seems like a nice kid, once you get to know him. He's quiet. Wary of people and all, but I mean who can blame him? He said he's not guilty and only one person defends him – his youth advocate. He's got to be at least a little bit cynical."

Lee walks into the kitchen behind him. He reaches into the pantry for a clean cup, grabs a tea bag. Yuuki has his back to him but the frustration in Lee's movements is palpable. The cup comes down on the benchtop with a little more force than usual, the lid on the tea bag container screwed open with a yank as opposed to a gentle turning. Yuuki narrows his eyes at the fresh grind of coffee he's just poured into the plunger.

"You've read his case files, haven't you?" Lee slams the lid back on the container. "Do you really think he's not guilty?"

"Timothy gave me the full transcript of the trial. I saw plenty of evidence to suggest he was involved but none to confirm it."

"I read Harrison's letter after you'd gone to bed last night. It was saying they found fingerprints – Kindall's – on the knife that killed Wilson."

"You're right. It did. But did anyone actually *see* Kyle stab Wilson?"

"If I remember correctly, the notes mentioned that the person who called in the incident saw Kindall in a craze."

Yuuki grunts. "Wouldn't you be in a 'craze' too, if you accidently killed someone?"

"Ah," Lee says, the hint of a smile in his voice. "Remember, that's still classified as manslaughter."

The jug switches off. The water keeps bubbling wildly.

"But how can they prove that he did it if *no one saw him do it?*"

"Fingerprints," Lee says easily.

Yuuki grabs the jug handle. As he pours the hot water into the plunger, he accidently scolds himself on the steam. With a hiss of annoyance, he sets down the jug on the bench and sticks his hand under the tap.

"If no one saw him do it and Kyle says he's innocent," Yuuki grits out, "then fingerprints are not significant enough evidence to prove – *without a doubt* – that Kyle did kill Wilson."

"Then how do you explain the fingerprints, the knife, Wilson, and Kindall being the only other person at the scene? Do you hear yourself?"

"He could've been set up."

"By who? Wilson?" Lee laughs darkly. "You're blaming the victim now?"

Yuuki turns off the cold water, finishes preparing his coffee, grabs a cup and then turns to face Lee square on, feet planted shoulder-width apart on the linoleum.

"I'm trying not to blame anyone at this stage," he says tightly. "You said you read the letter. Did you happen to see the note that said Wilson was drunk?"

"Even if that Kindall kid was provoked, he still didn't have to use his knife."

"I didn't read anything to say that the knife belonged to Kyle."

"Are the fingerprints not enough evidence for you?"

Yuuki shrugs. "Guess not. You see, what kid would stand up in court and say he's innocent when *he knows* there's evidence saying he's not? That part just doesn't make sense."

"So… the Peace Forces didn't do a good enough job proving he's guilty? Is that what you're saying?"

"No. What I'm saying is that they didn't do a thorough enough job to prove he isn't."

"Is that not the same thing?"

Yuuki takes his coffee back to the lounge. He's already had enough of this arguing, but he knows it's necessary. This is what he's going to have to do if he's wanting to defend Kyle. As much as he doesn't like arguing with Lee, this is a serious issue that needs to be discussed and Yuuki needs the practice saying what's on his mind.

"There's too many blanks. Too many questions that seem to have been filled in with assumptions. Take the incident itself, for example – did anyone actually *see* Kyle stab Wilson with that knife? Did anyone *see* what happened in the seconds leading up to it?"

Lee pours his cup of tea. He's staring at the tea bag as though it's the one he's having a heated discussion with, not Yuuki. "I know I keep coming back to this," he says, "but what of the fingerprints, then?"

Yuuki raises his hands. "I don't know. I don't have the answers to that. No one does but Kyle. If he is adamant in saying he didn't do it even though he knows his fingerprints are on the knife, then there's more to this story than the jury were willing to hear. I want to hear it."

"Kindall could lie about it."

"He could, yes. He even said that himself when I told him I wanted to talk to him about it. But it won't do him any good to lie, so I'm hoping he'll stick to the truth and maybe let out some details he may not have given at the trial."

"Who said he wasn't lying at the trial?"

"And why would he bother when he's already convinced no one's going to be standing up for him anyway?"

Lee puts his elbows on the bench and leans his head in his hands. He threads his fingers through his hair. "I just don't see why you're so invested in this," he says. "You're dealing with enough stress in your life right now, Yuuki. You don't need more."

Yuuki's gut twists. He closes his eyes, cheek twitching. "Do you have any idea how stressed I'd be if I gave up? How responsible I'd feel, knowing that I had the chance to help this kid only to deny him the one last opportunity he had to be free again? And for what – a little less stress to my life? I'd be just like everyone else. I can't do that to him. So much for setting the Youth Rehabilitation Trust if that's what kind of a person I am."

"Alright, well…" Lee says, straightening up. "I'll leave you to it." He takes his cup of tea and disappears down the hallway.

Yuuki sinks into the couch cushions, exhausted. It seems there's a lot more at stake with this case than he originally thought there would be.

Is that a risk I'm willing to take, though?

Yes.

Outside the barred window, it's dark. It's been dark for hours. Shortly after sunset, the sole light bulb flickered out and nobody's come to replace it.

Like they care…

Kyle wonders how far through the night it's been. When the morning will come. Maybe it won't. Maybe he'll die in this darkness, and his ghost will be looking on through his body when that guy, Yuuki… whatever his last name was, comes to talk to him tomorrow.

He still can't decide how he feels about that meeting today. Can Yuuki actually help him like he says? Kyle highly doubts it. He'll give up on him eventually, decide he's not worth the effort. Just like that guard he'd been handed over to earlier who'd shoved him back in his cell without taking his handcuffs – still linked to the belly chain – off.

Kyle wonders how long it'll be before he loses the last bit of a grasp on himself he has left, how long it'll be before he no longer knows himself as Kyle Kindall.

Something tells him it won't be long at all.

3

When Yuuki wakes, Lee's already gone. Morning classes, probably, and possibly a mind made up to avoid having to talk to Yuuki for a while. There's no new messages on his phone so he guesses it's got to be at least partly the latter.

Yuuki's beginning to feel the strain in their friendship now. He considers flicking Lee a text, but the apology he wants to give isn't one that he really means. He wants to be able to find some middle ground between them, but putting aside the investigation into Kyle's case and his own misgivings about Kyle's conviction isn't something Yuuki's willing to do to achieve that.

Standing his ground means extra stress, however. There's a tension in his shoulders that won't go away. He's losing the state of calm he used to be able to keep in these situations. Self-blame is starting to eat away at his optimism and doubt starts creeping in, too – the dangerous kind. It asks him if this is even worth it. It asks him if he's willing to give up what he has with Lee, one of the few friendships he has now, and for a case investigation that he might not even be able to have any influence on nonetheless.

But it's not really about the case, is it? It's not about being right or wrong, and it's not about whether or not Kyle is guilty. This is about that kid's health and wellbeing. Lee can try to protect me from heaping a whole lot of stress on myself all he wants, but who's going to do the same for Kyle?

When he went missing, Yuuki had had people looking out for him. He had people, namely Timothy and his son Joshua, who were actively doing something to find him, to get him back. They refused to give up searching for him and it's that which saved his life.

He can't shake off the feeling that Kyle's going to end up in a bad place if no one does anything about his situation. If no one had done anything about Yuuki's being kidnapped, then it would've been the end of him.

Yuuki lets out a shaky breath, tears the covers off his legs and gets out of bed. *Now's not the time to be thinking about that,* he thinks, but it's not like his brain will give him the choice. He doesn't have flashbacks voluntarily. The only thing he can do to make them less intense is limit his exposure to triggers, which is…difficult, to say the least, especially when dealing with a case involving isolation as a punishment.

He'll admit he's worried about what might happen to his health if this investigation proves too much. Panic attacks. Flashbacks. Increased hypervigilance. Nightmares. Self-preservation says he be more cautious. A voice sounding suspiciously like Lee's agrees.

He said he's not guilty and he still says he isn't, Yuuki argues back. *Something's up with that. I can't just ignore that.*

Judging by the transcript, Kyle was denied the right to speak, too. Timothy wouldn't go through with that protocol unless the act of not doing so put Kyle in danger. In other words, Timothy only did that to protect Kyle.

But from what?

A thought Yuuki doesn't wish to entertain enters his mind. Could Kyle have somehow unknowingly wound up involved in something associated with the same people who kidnapped Yuuki at Ninao last year? It's a thought that makes his blood run cold. Timothy must suspect this, too, and maybe that's probably why he allowed Kyle to be imprisoned so quickly. If locking Kyle away from the world means simultaneously keeping him safe from whoever set him up, if that's what Timothy's indeed quietly suspecting, then it might not have been such an outrageous idea to have Kyle imprisoned after all.

So why Kyle? Did he hear or see something he wasn't meant to? Does it have anything to do with the yet-to-be-identified men behind the Ninao incident?

Yuuki's thoughts flicker back to the knife. He has so many questions surrounding that one object because, if it didn't even belong to Kyle in the first place, it's possible that Daniel Wilson had actually been the one in possession of it. If that's true, then it's possible that he'd either tried to kill Kyle, and the plan had backfired, or that Wilson had gone in there with the intention of setting him up, and possibly on the behalf of someone else – that someone else potentially being Yuuki's kidnappers.

Only Kyle has those answers. Some of them anyway, if not all. If Yuuki's train of thought is correct, then Kyle's in a lot more danger than he originally thought.

He needs to act carefully, then. Be careful who he talks to and how much he conveys. He should watch how much he tells Lee, too. While Yuuki doesn't think his friend would speak to anyone about what Yuuki's working on, since he knows it's confidential, there's still a chance he might accidentally slip up and their suspicions be overheard.

Maybe parting ways with Lee is for the best, in more ways than one.

They've been friends for a while, him and Lee, but if they're going to go their own ways, then what better time to do so than now. It's been the elephant in the room ever since Timothy first contacted Yuuki about the case. With Lee so opposed to Yuuki investing himself in helping Kyle and with Yuuki's frustration over the matter becoming closer to anger, it's nigh on time to have that conversation.

While he prepares the first coffee of many he'll be consuming today, Yuuki runs several sentences over in his head to text Lee and settles for a non-complicated *'we should talk.'*

The jug couldn't boil any faster, could it?

Yuuki ends up leaving the house a couple of minutes later than usual. He misses the train. There's a twenty minute wait for the next one, bringing him into the start of the Monday rush hour and the start of a long morning riddled with small panic attacks.

The crowds that aren't really 'crowds' unsettle him. All the people standing around set him on edge. The train ride makes him anxious. It's too claustrophobic. It gets worse when he remembers that, since he's late, he's going to have to take the train all the way to the terminal.

All the way to Ninao.

There's not enough time for his usual get-off-two-stations-early-and-walk trick this morning. He'll be late if he does that, and the only way he's going to get onto the connecting train is if he rides this one all the way.

Yuuki tries not to look suspiciously nervous. He's not sure it's effective. At Ninao station, he doesn't take his time. He walks, fast. Just shy of a jog. He'd run if it didn't make him look like a criminal. He steers wide berths around the corners. He doesn't trust the shadows.

At the Northern A'o Line platform, he waits at the far end and digs his clammy hands into his pockets. Thank goodness it's winter, else he'd be getting some mighty strange looks from people. A warden all nervous when all he's doing is standing at a train station?

It's a good thing his jacket does a good job at hiding the uniform.

Yuuki waits, impatient. Tries to distract himself but it's hard to do. There's so many shadows and people at this hour of the morning. Shadows are good places for people to hide in. Shadows are what those people hid in before they kidnapped him at the Ninao office a year, a month, and a day ago.

Get a grip, Yuuki. You're not there anymore.

No, he's not, but he's nearby where it started.

The train comes and Yuuki steps in. The adrenaline doesn't fade. A woman sitting a couple of metres away from him regards him warily and shifts a little further away. It's not until the station is out of view that his heart rate begins to settle down. He closes his eyes, takes a deep breath. Holds it, for four seconds, give or take. Lets it out. Takes another, slower this time. Holds it. Lets it out.

He's fairly sure that, despite the cold, his shirt's all sweaty under the arms. As much as he hates what life has become for him now, it's not something he can blame himself for. Rather, it's not something he should blame himself for at all, and yet somehow he still ends up doing so.

He's able to breathe a little easier once he arrives at his stop. Yuuki signs in at the A'o Youth Detention Centre's office five minutes later, fighting off emotional exhaustion. He's on time, thankfully. Early, in fact.

His stress quickly morphs into something else, however, when he learns that the guy who escorted Kyle back to his cell yesterday didn't take his handcuffs off.

Mitchell hands him a freshly brewed coffee from the nearby café and Yuuki gratefully accepts it. He sips it, welcomes the slight headache it brings while he processes the truckload of emotion roiling inside of him.

"So," Yuuki mutters. "Are you telling me that he's been in them all night?"

The new guard whose name he doesn't care to know gulps. "Y-yes, sir."

"Why?"

Mitchell takes a careful step in Yuuki's direction.

"No," he says sharply. "I want to know why. What did he do to deserve to be unnecessarily kept in handcuffs for –" Yuuki checks the time and does the math. "– for twenty-one hours?"

He's letting his emotions get to him, he knows that. But it's also so much more than that. What happened to him at Ninao is something that'll haunt Yuuki for the rest of his life. The fear that he might have to watch Kyle go through a similar experience terrifies him – the kind of terror that Yuuki can only allow himself to express as anger.

If it weren't for prison protocol, he'd be letting Kyle sit through this meeting they're about to have with his hands free. There's a risk to that though, especially when he barely knows the kid and doesn't know what he's capable of. It's for that reason, of course, that he must be the responsible warden and ensure that Kyle is handcuffed when out of the cell, but…

Yuuki hates it, but the only way Kyle will be permitted to meet him without the handcuffs on is if Yuuki meets him in his cell. Maybe not even then, depending on what other conditions his imprisonment's been given.

"He's been out of them for the last two and a half hours, Yuuki," Mitchell says softly.

Yuuki glares at the guard who still hasn't answered him. "Oh, my mistake. *Nineteen* hours, then."

"Takahashi."

"Let's just…get this meeting underway," he mutters.

"You're dismissed," Mitchell says to the guard. "I'll get Kindall." After the guy leaves and the door to the office shuts, Mitchell heaves a sigh. "Yuuki, I know you're dealing with a lot, but I do need you to take a moment to calm yourself down before you speak with Kindall. Is that clear?"

"Yes," Yuuki murmurs. "It is. I'm sorry, I just…"

"It's alright. Take your time." Mitchell nods at the half-downed cup in Yuuki's hand. "Do you need another?"

He chuckles at that. "You trying to get me drunk on caffeine or something?"

"As if that'll ever happen with you. The amount you drink…"

"Maybe after the meeting. Thank you, though."

Mitchell gives him a supportive pat on the shoulder. "Finish that, take ten minutes. I'll go and get Kindall for you after that."

"I'd like to ask you some questions. Before we start, do you have any questions that you'd like to ask yourself?"

Kyle narrows his eyes slightly and his lips purse. Yuuki waits patiently while Kyle finds the words he needs. Yuuki's not fussed if he doesn't ask anything, but judging by Kyle's expression, there seems to be something that's been bothering him.

"By law," Kyle says eventually, "I am allowed to defend myself, aren't I?"

Yuuki frowns. "Of course."

"Your friend doesn't seem to think so."

"My friend?"

Kyle scowls. "The judge."

A sense of guilt and concern wash over him and stab him in the gut. Did Timothy say something to Kyle at some point that got misinterpreted? Yuuki thinks back to the meeting they all had yesterday, wondering if Timothy had done anything Kyle might've found offensive, but he can't think of anything. Timothy's not the sort the sort person to disallow someone from –

Then it clicks. *'Defendant muted.'* Yuuki shifts in his seat and swallows. He gets the impression he's not going to like finding out the answer to what he's about to ask, if Kyle's accusing glare is anything to go by...

"Kyle..." Yuuki begins carefully. "What did they do to you in the court room?"

"Decided I'm guilty, apparently."

Yuuki makes sure to keep his tone even. "No, not that. I'm not referring to that. I... I wasn't able to see the recording of your trial, but I had access to the transcript. I'm guessing that's where you're coming from? The judge gave you a series of warnings and then…?"

Kyle's gaze has turned steely. The tips of his ears have gone red.

"What did they do to you, buddy?"

"What they had to."

Yuuki's heart sinks. Kyle's refusing to look at him. Instead, his eyes are fixated on a spot on the wall behind Yuuki, but he's not actually looking there. He's looking somewhere else. At his memories. At the faces of the people in the court room.

"Kyle," Yuuki says, quiet but insistent. "What did they do to you?"

There's a long pause during which Kyle's cheeks light up and the stillness of the room becomes choking. It's something he would rather not voice, words too foreign on the tongue and a subject too taboo to speak of.

"They gagged me."

The two of them stare at each other intensely. Kyle's gaze is challenging, angry. Deeply disturbed. Yuuki meets it steadily, working his jaw. Kyle upper lip quivers. It's not a snarl.

"Don't you know how *humiliating* that is?"

Yuuki grimaces. "Actually, I do."

"As if you…" Kyle's anger shorts out abruptly. "Sorry?"

"Ninao."

Yuuki's voice pitches on the last syllable. Kyle's eyes flash. They both sit a little stiffer in their seats. Kyle's rubbing his thumb over his knuckles and Yuuki's fighting off memories. The silence between them is tense, as though it's expecting a polite 'sorry to hear that' from Kyle that never comes. Yuuki's grateful it doesn't. He doesn't need it, and the atmosphere of empathy is more than he could ask for.

A few precious minutes pass before anyone speaks again. It's Kyle who does. "You said you believed in second chances," he murmurs. "What makes you think I'll get one?"

Fair question, Yuuki thinks. "Well, did you do it?"

"Do what?"

"Did you kill Daniel Wilson like everyone else says you did?"

Kyle's eyes flick over Yuuki's face, as though trying to decipher whether he's being led into a trap or not. Yuuki watches him consider all the possible intentions behind that question and the different ways he could answer it.

In the end, the decision Kyle settles for is not to answer, so Yuuki tries again.

"Kyle," he says. "Be honest with me. I don't care what came out of the trial. You can lie to me if you want, say that you did kill him when you didn't or that you didn't kill him when you did, but let me get this one thing straight – I have the chance to change your situation here. I have questions I want to ask you about the incident that weren't asked or answered at your trial. There seemed to be a lot of assumptions made and I want to clear those up. Even if they still decide you're guilty at the end of it, who knows, maybe we can lessen your time in here or change the terms and conditions of your stay here. Can't be any worse than it is now, right?"

Kyle's scowl is a deep frown now. He stares down at his hands, his handcuffed hands, seemingly weighing up the options. Yuuki waits for him. He waits as Kyle processes all he just said.

"And what if does get worse?" Kyle whispers. "What if they find more supporting evidence and decide to make things worse for me?"

"Did you kill Wilson?"

Kyle winces. "I…my hand…it was on the knife when it…so…"

"Did you kill Wilson?" Yuuki repeats, voice softer this time.

Kyle wrings his hands. His throat moves but he doesn't swallow and he doesn't speak. He glances up at Yuuki for a brief second before tearing his eyes away. The frown contorts as Kyle fights to keep a lid on whatever emotions are threatening to surface.

With a strangled noise, Kyle whispers, "I didn't."

Yuuki is tempted to ask for his version of the story right that second but decides it's probably better not to. He's probably overwhelming Kyle too much already, forcing him to accept the idea that there's someone that's willing to go the extra mile for him when everyone else has given up.

Wanting to give Kyle a little more time process it, Yuuki instead simply offers him a smile. "Then you've got nothing to worry about, then."

He wants to reach out and give Kyle a reassuring pat on the shoulder, but he's not sure if Kyle would welcome that. Judging by the way he reacted when Mitchell touched him yesterday, he's most likely not particularly fond of the idea. Yuuki wants to respect that.

"So what are you going to do?" Kyle asks once he's recovered his voice.

"Well," Yuuki says, habitually folding his arms across his chest. "First I want to fill in the blanks. To do that, I'm going to need to hear your side of the story. Every last bit of detail you can give me, I want to hear it. It'll help to cross-reference with whatever other information I can gather. I'll talk to your youth advocate at some point, see what additional information he can give me…

"Basically, I'll be asking the questions they didn't and looking for a way to prove that you're innocent. I want to believe you, but I need the rest of the world to be able to, too."

Kyle's scowl returns. "But they already have evidence to say that I'm guilty."

"Yeah, but I'm not here to prove that you're guilty. I'm here to prove that you're innocent, just like you said you are."

"But they...*how* are you going to do that? It's pretty much just my word against theirs."

"You're right, it is. But how much of their word is based on assumptions, do you think?"

Kyle's eyes flash again and Yuuki meets them with a knowing half-smile. Kyle's finally recognised that Yuuki's serious about trying to find him a way out. That he gets the situation he's in and the unfairness of it.

Maybe now is a good time to start asking the important questions, after all.

Yuuki clears his throat. "I know that one of the 'key points of evidence', as they say, is that your fingerprints are all over the handle of the knife. Everybody thinks that's evidence enough, but I know for a fact that there a number of possible ways they could've gotten there. Can you tell me what you started saying just before?"

"You mean about how my hand got on the knife?"

"Yeah."

"I...Daniel did it." Kyle's gaze shifts as he remembers. "I was just sitting at the park like I always do, and then he comes out of nowhere with this knife and pushes me over and then *pins me there*. Then before I can do anything, he's putting the knife in my hand and forcing me to..."

Kyle's eyes have gone dark and…scared. Haunted. Yuuki knows that expression well. He's become quite acquainted with it in the past year when he looks at himself in the mirror.

"What was he trying to force you to do?"

Kyle studies his hands. "He was…he wanted me to get me to cut my own throat."

Yuuki's blood chills. The notes said Daniel was drunk, but…

"H-he…I don't know why. He said *something* about hearing something so I had to die or something, but I have no idea what he was talking about. I think…I think he was trying to make it look like it was an accident. As in, that he didn't do it kind of 'accident'."

Yuuki's glad he's got a recording device tucked away in his pocket and that this room has decent surveillance. This meeting is evidence.

"I was freaking out," Kyle continues. "He wouldn't let me go, so I…the best thing I could do was get the knife away from me. I managed to get it so that the blade was facing away from me, but Daniel still wouldn't let go of my hand and I was freaking out and I just…tried to thrash my way out of there, I guess." His face pales considerably. "He still wouldn't let go. I was starting to get free but he wouldn't let me let go of the knife and as I tried to yank my hand out of his grasp, it…it ended up in him."

"I'm guessing he let go of you then?"

Kyle grunts. "Yeah." He takes a shaky breath. "Not immediately, though."

Yuuki doesn't want to imagine what that must've felt like. He can see Kyle visibly attempting to calm himself in an all-too-familiar way and Yuuki's concern increases. Too much time alone with nothing to do but think about these things can't be doing Kyle well.

But if Yuuki wants to get him out of here, then he needs to focus. As much as he wants to see Kyle free or at least with a less severe punishment, he can't be impatient about it.

As he takes mental notes and considers the details carefully, there's a knock on the meeting room door. Five minutes remaining.

"The knife," Yuuki says. "Was it yours?"

Kyle frowns. "No."

He's consistent in what he says. Doesn't have to stop to think about it either, which is a good sign. "And Daniel. Now, I'm not accusing you while I'm asking this, I just want to know...how is it that the report fails to mention his fingerprints also being on the knife handle?"

"He was wearing gloves."

That haunted expression is back. Yuuki watches Kyle's expression carefully for any sign of faltering. Anyone could've added that little detail in there to cover themselves. But it's also winter. Gloves aren't a strange sight in winter. Neither are jackets, and jackets have plenty of room to keep a knife out of sight in. If Daniel really had headed to the park, drunk and with the sole purpose to get rid of Kyle...

It's too plausible. But there is one key bit of information missing from that scenario.

"Kyle. You said Daniel came after you because you overheard something. Can you think of what that is?"

"Like I said," Kyle grits out. "I *don't know*. You don't think I've been stressing out about that since he said that? I honestly have no idea, and it really bugs me because none of you are ever going to believe me unless I can give you a satisfying enough reason to believe that Daniel would want to kill me. After all, it seems *so* much more likely that the kid with the discipline issues is going to be the one to cause trouble, not Daniel Wilson."

If anything, Kyle's stress is genuine. Yuuki can taste the underlying tones of it in the air. Some of it's familiar, some of it only vaguely so, but still something he understands. He can also empathise with how everything must be from Kyle's perspective.

While he can see how easy it would be to misjudge Kyle, it hurts to think about the possibility that much of his current situation is due to people not giving Kyle's version of what happened a decent amount of consideration.

The door opens. Mitchell comes in, leaving the door wide open.

"It's time. Finish up."

Kyle tenses. Yuuki winces at Mitchell's gruff tone.

"I'll be back in a few days," Yuuki says, sitting forward. "Thank you for what you've given me. I'll be able to start doing some investigating. In the meantime, Officer Mitchell here is going to make sure that you don't get left in those handcuffs overnight again, so you don't need to worry about that happening twice.

"I want you to really have a think about what Daniel said. Anything. It might've been something that never occurred to you to be important. Just…can you do that for me?"

Kyle's expression is unreadable. He nods.

Mitchell comes forward. Kyle is standing before Mitchell can grab him. Yuuki stands, too. Kyle maintains eye contact with him as Mitchell leads him away. He only looks away when he's shuffled through the door.

Yuuki stays as he is. It occurs to him then that the expression on Kyle's face was one of hope. Real hope, even if it was only a trace of it.

He can only pray that it won't be disappointed. His gut instinct says it won't be. As of today, Yuuki has one conclusion he is ninety-percent sure of: everything Kyle told him today was the truth.

From what it seems, Kyle isn't guilty.

4

Sam Harrison's nonchalant clomping down the stairs comes to an abrupt halt. Her Dad's laptop is unattended. Her heartbeat picks up and she tiptoes down to the bottom of the staircase.

She listens. Mum's not here since she's at work and Dad… is nowhere to be seen. Sam tightens the straps on her backpack and glances around, just to make sure, then makes her way over to the benchtop.

The screensaver goes on so she gives the mousepad a touch. A document full of legal jargon pops up. If it were science or tech jargon, Sam would be able to understand every word of it, but this…this is insane formal English. The most she can make of all the words is that it's about various terms and conditions of youth imprisonment. The name of the file printed on the first tab open reads '*Kindall, K. Tria…*'

Something to do with that case he's working on that he won't tell me about?

A door shuts. Sam lets out an involuntary squeak, skips into the kitchen and shoves her head into the refrigerator.

"Mornin', Samantha."

Sam makes a show of rummaging around in the fridge. "Hi Dad."

"Not sitting down for breakfast today?"

She shrugs, grabs an apple and closes the door. "Meh. Not hungry."

Apparently her little sneak peek has gone unnoticed. Her Dad sits calmly on one of the stools, mulling over the complicated document. Then again, he is a judge and it's the Arkala usurper-in-charge-of-the-Kingdom era. He's too situationally aware; she can't fool him.

"Whatcha working on?" she asks as nonchalantly as possible.

Timothy sighs. "Same old. I've got Yuuki helping me out now, so hopefully we'll make some progress."

"What's the case?"

"You know I can't divulge that information to you."

Then I'll hack into your computer and get it myself later. "Can't you at least tell me what the problem is? You've been stressing out about this one particular case like crazy. There's got to be some wrong with it if you're still looking into it. It's closed already."

Timothy raises an eyebrow. He regards Sam carefully. "'A suspected unfair trial' is all I'll say. Don't go snooping."

Sam smirks. "It won't hurt them if they don't know."

"*Samantha.*"

"What?" She trots out of the kitchen and gives her Dad a reassuring pat on the shoulder. "You need supporting evidence? I'll help you get it."

"You're not authorised. I am *not* having your case to deal with alongside this kid's."

The distress that flashes across his face catches Sam unawares. The grin falls from her lips. *An unfair trial, huh. Must be pretty unfair if Dad's getting this emotional about it.* Not that that deters her in any shape or form, of course. If anything, it compels her.

Kindall. The name sounds familiar but Sam can't picture him. Something

52

tells her she should be able to but she can't. Maybe she knows him past the acquaintance level, which means she'd be used to referring to him by his first name and not his last. He wouldn't happen to be someone she knows from school, right? Someone she might not have classes with that often?

Unfair trial. Someone who I might know. Hmm…

"Samantha," Timothy warns.

Sam blinks, shoves her pondering aside. "Yeah?"

"I can hear you thinking."

"Right, you can. So what conclusion did I just come to?"

Timothy frowns. "I know you want to help. But I can't allow you to do it illegally."

The corner of Sam's mouth upturns. "Oh? Who said I couldn't help legally? Don't worry – I have friends. If it's about the thing that happened at Village Park a week ago, they might know a thing or two. They live in the area."

With a defeated sigh, Timothy shakes his head. "I know I can't stop you. Just…stay out of trouble, alright? Please?"

Sam gives him the thumbs up. "I can do that. At any rate, I'm off to meet Avi. Pair assignment."

Timothy waves her off with a tired smile. "Have a good day."

"You, too!"

Taking a bite of the apple, Sam haphazardly buttons up her coat and walks out the door. She's hard-out thinking before the chill of outside has first hits her in the face.

'Unfair trial' could mean a lot of things.

*

Ninety-percent sure isn't enough. Yuuki's word alone isn't enough. All it shows is that Yuuki believes that Kyle is telling the truth, and while instinct still plays a significant part, Kyle needs evidence not intuition. There's legal processes to go through, stubborn people to satisfy and people's assumptions to combat. Yuuki can argue all he likes in Kyle's defence but nothing's going to happen unless he can prove Kyle isn't guilty.

To do that, he's got to start from square one: Village Park, where it all started.

The weather seems far too fine to be true. Yuuki shrugs off his jacket and plonks himself down on the park bench. There's no one else around but that's not unusual for this time of day on a weekday. A pigeon sits on a nearby lamppost, observing. It doesn't seem bothered by Yuuki's brooding and almost appears to be brooding with him.

Yuuki used to frequent this park. Before Ninao happened, he would often go for runs along the lakeside trail. This park used to be his exit point before he turned around and ran all the way back home. It's uncanny how it so happened to become Kyle's exit point, too.

It's like the whole legal system is working against Kyle. Yuuki finds that somewhat unsettling. It's like they're not willing to risk giving him a chance to prove his innocence. Yuuki plays the scene out in front of him, the one Kyle told him, and finds it all too likely.

Someone definitely set him up.

He's asked Kyle to do his part in trying to remember who or why that may be. Now Yuuki's got to continue his part in backing him up with evidence.

The first thing that catches Yuuki's eye is the layout of the park. It's located at the end of a cul-de-sac, a small strip of land connecting the street and its houses to the lakeside trail. Access to the park is via the street or the trail, both at opposite ends of the park. Houses border the south-west and north-east edges. Those houses all have trees growing in their backyard or on the park-side of their fences, giving them privacy.

Few people use the trail after dark. Even fewer hang around in the streets. Kyle only had one witness. It's not hard to see why.

"I was just sitting at the park like I always do..."

Yuuki frowns at the pigeon. He wants to ask it if it knows why on earth Kyle would want to stay out in the cold and the dark. There must be a reason. Two Lakes gets chilly at night, and since it's winter, there's really no reason to be lingering outdoors any longer than necessary. Maybe he didn't even want to be out, but lingering in the park was a better option than...than what? Going home? Yuuki adds that to the many questions that still need to be asked.

He's wondering what Kyle's home situation was like when the hair on the back of his neck rises. His stomach dips. His heartbeat picks up.

Someone's watching him. It's not the pigeon.

"Yuuki!"

He flinches. But it's a voice he knows and the relief is immense. He turns to face the street, albeit a little shaky with the burst of adrenaline.

Timothy's daughter jogs across the grass towards him, schoolbag swinging back and forth across her shoulders. There's a huge grin plastered on her face. She flings herself at Yuuki in a rough embrace.

"Haven't seen you in ages!" Samantha exclaims. "How've you been?"

Yuuki smiles wryly. "I've been better...I think. Aren't you meant to be in school?"

"Uh, no? First of all, it's the holidays –"

"Here we go."

" – which is great and all, but then our physics teacher decides to give us all an assignment to work on over the two weeks which requires us to use the lab equipment, meaning that we have to go into school to work on it, even though I already have what I need at home." Samantha finishes her spiel and huffs in annoyance. "Just finished the practical stuff. Gotta do the write up now. That aside, what brings you to the neighbourhood?"

Yuuki shrugs. "Just enjoying the sun." It's not a lie, not entirely.

"You meeting Dad or something?"

"No?"

"About that case you're working on?"

Yuuki raises an eyebrow. Samantha grins.

"He has a habit of leaving his laptop in plain sight," she says, as though that's a perfect explanation as to how she's gotten information on a confidential case. "Don't tell him I saw."

"You know you shouldn't be snooping."

Samantha raises her hands in the air. "I wasn't snooping. I was just curious. Dad won't tell me anything – anything at all – and it was bugging me. He left his laptop unattended and I happened to be passing by while the screen was still on…"

Yuuki sighs. "I'm not allowed to tell you anything, so don't get any ideas."

"Wasn't going to." The glint in her eyes says otherwise. "You know," Samantha says. "There used to be this guy who I always saw in the park every day I walked home after school. He'd be just sitting there, contemplating life or something. He looked lonely. I never had the courage to go up and talk to him. What's he like?"

Yuuki doesn't have the heart to keep his expression neutral. A shaky breath escapes him. He puts his elbows on his knees and leans his face into his hands. *"He looked lonely."* And he's literally alone now, too. Locked up in isolation for something he didn't even do.

"Yuuki?"

"Sorry, Sam. Can you give me a sec'?"

"Sure thing."

The Harrisons are sharp. All of them. Yuuki could really use Timothy's help with this case, but like they've already discussed, they have to be careful with how much they interact. Timothy must remain a neutral party. As the judge in this case, the best he can be is a mediator.

"Dad's working from home today, if you need to talk to him."

Yuuki stills. He lifts his head and stares out at the park. Yeah, he's really not getting anywhere on his own. Regardless of his PTSD affecting his capacity to think, he needs someone else's perspective on all this. He knows Sam's not just meaning talking to Timothy about Kyle's case, too, but Yuuki's too stubborn and confused to like the idea of talking to anyone about the daily grind of his struggles with post-traumatic stress.

"Is he busy?" Yuuki asks.

Samantha shakes her head. "Not if he's not in the work office."

He needs more information. The transcript Timothy sent him is vague and the letter with the case overview too sparse on detail. If Yuuki has any hope of proving that Kyle's telling of the story is true like he's sure it is, then he needs the more detailed version – the one that Timothy has full access to.

Timothy's got to know something, surely, he thinks. *This is more than an unfair trial. It's got to be. He wouldn't have assigned me* after *the trial, otherwise.*

"Alright," Yuuki says, standing up. "I might go see him then. Which way are you going?"

Samantha points in the direction of the local train station. "Technically that way, but I need to go back and get my laptop charger. I'll come back with you."

As they walk the ten minutes to the Harrisons', Yuuki can't help but wonder how much of an odd sight they make: a young guy in a warden's shirt and a high school student walking down a suburban street at eleven thirty in the morning. If Joshua were here, he'd probably make it into some kind of joke.

"Sorry, I forgot to ask you," Yuuki murmurs, "are you going by Samantha or Sam these days?"

Joshua, her older brother, had always called her Sam for short and she hadn't liked it too much, but recently Yuuki's heard Timothy starting to refer to his daughter as Sam instead of Samantha, and so he'd wondered.

"I've started going by Sam," she says, flashing him an appreciative smile, but the smile soon morphs into a forced one. "You know, just since Ninao, I…"

They lapse into a solemn silence. Ninao changed them. Not just Yuuki, Joshua and Timothy, but their families as well. While for Yuuki, 'family' kind of only counts as Lee, for the Harrisons it's their entire household that's been affected. Even their old dog, Ginger, had begun to hang around more to socialise before she passed away last summer.

It's with a slight bitterness in his heart that Yuuki thinks about how the family have drawn nearer to each other through the trauma. He and Lee have been torn apart by it. The Harrisons have been a major support for Yuuki in his physical recovery and the PTSD that came thereafter. They've said he's welcome to stay with them anytime he needs, but Yuuki feels too guilty to be able to even think about taking them up on the offer.

He doesn't deserve that much kindness. He's intruded on their family enough already as it is.

"So," Sam says after a couple of minutes, interrupting his thoughts. "You never ended up answering my question. What's he like?"

Yuuki frowns. "Joshua? Oh, right, you mean Kyle?"

Sam stops in the middle of the footpath. "*Kyle?* As in shaggy-hair, emo guy Kyle?"

"Uh…I guess that's one way to describe him."

"You've got to be kidding."

She mutters a curse under her breath. Yuuki's too curious as to why she's reacting like this to be bothered by the language or the fact that he just confirmed her suspicions. Sam catches him staring at her and shakes her head. She starts walking again, though there's a hint of anger present every time her heels hit the ground.

"Do you know him?" Yuuki asks, catching up.

Sam's brow furrows. "No. Not personally."

"Same school, then?"

"Yeah, something like that."

Yuuki considers how best to word his thoughts. Obviously, she's bothered by the connection between Kyle being the guy she saw at park all those times and Kyle being the guy caught up in the case Yuuki and Timothy are working on. He wants to ask her to elaborate, but he's also keenly aware that they're still out in public. There's only so much he can say, and the fact that it's becoming increasingly likely that Kyle was set up nearby, Yuuki's got to be really careful.

He decides to drop it for now. He can ask her again later. Maybe she's just upset that someone she knows, someone who she wouldn't have thought capable of killing someone, is involved. Yuuki wonders exactly how much she saw when she looked at Timothy's laptop screen, but that's yet another thing he can't talk about while walking down a street like this.

Who knows who could be accidently eavesdropping?

When they get to the house, Sam slips in first to announce Yuuki's arrival. Yuuki takes his shoes off and follows her in. Timothy's sitting at the dining room table surrounded by papers, manila folders, his laptop and a scattered collection of post-it notes.

"Timothy," Yuuki says, admiring the mess. "It's good to see you."

"Yuuki. How are things?"

"Going alright. But we need to have a talk."

Timothy sighs, slipping a hand beneath his glasses to rub the shadows under his eyes. He looks up with a tired smile. "We certainly do."

5

Once Yuuki's accumulating stress is satisfied with a triple shot Americano from the Harrisons' coffee machine, he pulls a chair aside and settles down next to Timothy. Interestingly enough, Timothy's got the exact file on screen that Yuuki wants to discuss.

Yuuki nods at the laptop. "Kyle was incredibly upset that you did that to him."

"I know," Timothy mutters. "And boy, let me tell you how much I hated having to do it."

"Having to?"

Timothy gives Yuuki a warning glance. He leans forward, scrolling up to arrive at the beginning of the document. "Did you read this?"

Yuuki grunts. "The formalities? You know me."

"Right. Well, before you go pointing finger at me, I suggest you read over the names again. Properly."

Taking a sip of his coffee – still a little too hot – Yuuki does so. He frowns deeply when he comes to the name of the Peace Force officer in charge of leading the investigation. Timothy's right; he shouldn't have read over the formalities so quickly.

"Commander Jeff? What's he doing involved in a youth case?"

The corner of Timothy's mouth twitches. "Precisely."

"You didn't question it?"

"Believe me, under normal circumstances I would have, but Jeff doesn't like negotiating. If he says he's leading the investigation, that's that. I don't have a good enough reason to argue. It would only raise suspicions."

"You do now," Yuuki points out. "Have a reason, that is."

"Yes, but that was then and this is now." Timothy's gaze is severe, conflicted. "Regarding having to prevent Kyle from speaking, I had to do what I could with what I had available at the time. I can't say I'm proud of it. But I was worried, Yuuki – Kindall was putting himself more and more in danger with every word he spoke. If he so much as said the wrong thing…"

As a judge, Timothy is allowed to ask such questions in court like asking about Jeff's intentions in leading an investigation for a case he wouldn't usually have taken interest in. Since the result of the investigation showed evidence strongly suggesting that Kyle is guilty as charged, it's not so far-fetched a speculation to say that it's almost like Jeff *wanted* Kyle to be put away.

Yuuki takes a deep breath. *So I was on the right train of thought.* He's beginning to see why Timothy's trying to go about questioning things with caution. He frowns as a thought occurs to him. "Did you see something?"

"You know what I'm getting at, then," Timothy murmurs.

"I do. But Kyle – he has no idea. I've asked him to think about it, but what if he can't remember anything that could've gotten him set up like this? I mean, if there's higher authorities involved in the case, then they basically still have some control over what happens to Kyle. I'll need to cross-reference with his youth advocate, of course, but the way Kyle was telling me what happened makes it sound like someone sent Wilson after him. What if they were…?"

"Let's not get ahead of ourselves. I can't be a hundred percent certain that anything was going to happen at the trial, but I had a darn good gut feeling that something had…been arranged. The prosecutor had a certain vibe about them."

Deciding it doesn't matter if the coffee scolds his tongue or not, Yuuki drinks half the coffee. *This is a lot to think about.*

"You believe him?"

Yuuki looks Timothy in the eye and nods. "Yeah."

Timothy smiles softly. "Well, that makes three of us fighting for him. Kyle's got hope yet. We just have to make sure we don't compromise it."

"Say that Kyle remembers something…how do we protect him?"

"We'll cross that bridge when we come to it. For now, we need to gather as much information as we can. However," he says, pausing to ensure Yuuki knows the implication, "we need to be extra vigilant in how we go about this. There could be far more at stake here than we think. I suspect that whoever set Kindall up had a fairly good reason for doing so. They wouldn't have gone to such lengths otherwise.

"We don't know who we're dealing with and we don't know why. It's possible that Kyle does. It's also possible that he does, but he doesn't realise that he does. Hopefully it's the former, for our sakes. It'll make getting him out of prison a lot easier, for one.

"As for how we can make sure he's safe in the meantime, well…" Timothy grimaces. "I'm afraid there's little we can do if we want to stay under the radar and not draw any extra attention to ourselves than we already are."

Ninao. They don't need to say it aloud to know that they're both thinking it. Their kidnappers still haven't been caught. No one knows who they were and it's something that haunts Yuuki wherever he goes. He thinks of how he felt someone watching him back at the park and suppresses a shiver.

What if it hadn't been Sam? What if it had been someone else?

"We've just got to be on our guard," Timothy says. "Be careful of who we talk to. I'd advise that we meet here from now on. My office could easily get bugged and we don't want to be discussing these things out in public."

Yuuki nods. "I agree. Only talk in person too, right?"

"Yeah. We'd better."

"Could we come up with a code? For if we can't talk face to face?"

"You mean a program?"

"Nah, just…a signal or something, for if something urgent comes up."

"Hmm, good thinking. But it needs to be subtle, like a minor change in tone. Something that will remain undetected by everyone else, otherwise we waste the point in even having a code."

Talking about the weather would be too obvious. Key words could easily be picked up on if anyone were to intercept their communications. Someone like Jeff would be able to decipher their messages at first glance, so on the presumption that he's involved in Kyle's case, they need something that'll appear accidental or innocent even to someone picking the words apart.

They settle on using an intentional wrong auto-correct if Yuuki's the one giving the signal and incorrect grammar if it's Timothy. To distinguish between signal and typo, they won't correct the mistake if it's an intentional one.

With the issue of communication discussed, Yuuki and Timothy lean back in their chairs. Yuuki quietly finishes his coffee and Timothy stares absent-mindedly at the transcript on the laptop screen.

Neither of them notice Sam slipping out the door.

Four thirty and the sun's on its way to setting. Not wanting to be out after dark, Yuuki leaves Timothy's to catch the train home before the street lamps come on. He arrives at the front door of his and Lee's house as they do. He never used to mind the early nightfall, but after Ninao last year the extra hours of darkness only make him edgy. It's why he doesn't sleep well in winter and why he looks forward to summer so much.

Lee's already home from work. Yuuki steps into the house quietly, easing the door shut behind him.

He clears his throat. "H-hey, Lee. I'm home."

Yuuki waits. Judging by the fact that the windows are still closed (Lee likes fresh air, as does Yuuki), Lee's only just got back. Yuuki tries to suppress the nervousness rising up inside him, tries not to think about how he'll react if Lee doesn't want to talk to him.

A tired but easy reply comes from the bathroom and he lets out a breath of relief. "Hi, Yuuki."

Lee emerges from the bathroom, looking worse for wear. Yuuki shoves his clammy hands in his jacket pockets and stands awkwardly as he is by the door.

"How was work?" Lee asks.

Yuuki feels the tension melt off his shoulders. Lee's not angry. So long as he doesn't mention anything that might trigger an argument on the whole 'Yuuki-you're-going-to-make-your-health-worse' issue, things should be okay.

"It's good," he says. It sounds like an automatic answer, so he elaborates. "I'm making good progress working out what needs to be looked into and so now I just need to start looking for evidence that supports that."

Lee nods, shifting his weight onto one foot. "I see."

"Kyle's cooperating," Yuuki continues. "That certainly makes things easier. Timothy's been a big help, too, gathering what evidence he can."

"Yuuki, it's okay. You don't need to worry about justifying yourself to me. I…I'm sorry for the way I've been lately. I'm sorry for getting angry at you. I'm just worried, that's all."

Yuuki grimaces. "Yeah, I can understand that."

"I just don't want to see you stressing yourself out like this."

The quiet that settles between them isn't tense so much as it is solemn. They both can feel their friendship falling apart. Yuuki blames himself for it, even though he knows that having PTSD is completely out of his control. He can heal, slowly, but he can't stop it affecting his and Lee's friendship no matter how much he would like it not to. Yuuki's not the same person he once was and there's nothing he can do about it.

Yuuki's forcing himself to put the thought aside before unwelcome thoughts and feelings manifest from it when his phone pings. He slips the phone out of his pocket and brings the screen up to his face. There's an email come through from Mitchell's email address.

Witness statement, it says.

"Lee," Yuuki says, staring at the notification in disbelief.

"Hmm?"

He double taps the screen and the email pops up in full.

We had something that might interest you come through from Two Lakes Peace Force Station this afternoon. The PFS received a witness statement from a resident of the area in which the incident happened. They asked to remain anonymous, but I can give you a summary of their statement.

[Anonymous] reported seeing Kindall at Village Park an hour prior to the incident occurring and said it was not unusual to see him there at that time of day. They were concerned when they saw he didn't frequent the park anymore and, on putting two and two together, decided to approach local authorities. They don't believe there to be any connection between Kindall's visits to the park and the incident occurring there.

I hope this is of some value to you.

Yuuki has to take a deep breath and gather his thoughts. His heart flutters with hope. "We have another witness," he says.

6

Kyle shivers. He hasn't stopped shivering since night fell. He pulls the thin blanket tighter around his shoulders but it's to no effect.

He's always been prone to the cold but he's never had to endure anything like this. Night after night ever since he got here, his muscles have been tensed up to the point of hurting. Tonight the pain is particularly bad because it's colder than it has been. He won't stop shaking.

He wants to ask for a blanket, but isolation means no contact. The door is also sound-proof. Maybe it's in case he goes insane like that witness said he had at Village Park. The officers on duty here will still be able to hear him, but at least it would be muted.

No matter how hard he tries, he can't sleep. He's too cold. It's too dark. The silence is too deafening. The worst of it all is knowing there's no escape from it. This is going to happen again when the sun sets again tomorrow, and the day after that, and the day after...

Kyle wishes Yuuki would hurry up. It's only been a couple of days since the first met, but he's not sure how much longer he can handle being in here. If it were just the isolation then maybe he could do it; he's used to being alone, be it in a crowd or when he's by himself. But there's everything else that goes with being kept here, and it's that which is overwhelming.

The night, of course, is the worst.

The tightness in his chest chokes him. The silence makes him feel like he's about to go insane. The cold is unrelenting and in the darkness the memories of what happened at the park – the reason why he's in prison – are all the more vivid.

Whether he closes his eyes or not makes no difference, not when it's pitch black. Sometimes he hears things like someone fiddling with the lock and opening the door, only to wait and find that no one was ever around in the first place. Sometimes he sees things too, shapes forming in the dark that aren't actually there.

Even worse and more unsettling are the flashbacks. Kyle's hand twitches involuntarily with them. He can feel the shape of the handle pressed into his palm and the gloved hand locking his fingers around it. The tension in his neck, the adrenaline washing over him when Daniel forced the knife to his throat. He remembers the panic in vivid colours, the terror in his shouting, the way Daniel wouldn't let up, the moment he was almost able to tear his hand free when Daniel slammed it back down…

Kyle's breaths become quick and shallow. He tries to block out the feeling of when the knife found leverage in his wild, panicked attempts to escape, that brush of material on the back of his hand – Daniel's jacket – after the knife lodged itself in Daniel's stomach.

He digs his fingernails into his palms. It's not enough to ground himself.

He's losing it.

He's losing it.

Kyle chokes on a sob. He doesn't get it.

He doesn't know why Daniel came after him. He didn't do anything. The only 'why' he can think of is that Daniel had a personal hate for him since Kyle got into a fight with his twin brother, Ben. But that happened back in middle school, so unless it was something Daniel had refused to let go of all these years, then gotten drunk one afternoon while thinking about it and decided enough was enough, then...

That's not a good enough excuse. It doesn't have enough reason. Yuuki asked him to think of whatever he could that could help explain the why, but this is all Kyle's got and it's not enough. The only thing he knows is that Daniel went to Village Park with the sole intent of killing him.

The thought is terrifying because he *doesn't know why*. Maybe if he did he would've had a better chance at defending himself. It's almost like the Peace Forces *wanted* him in prison. Even the judge seemed to. It's not fair, any of this, and it's overwhelmingly confusing.

Kyle clings to the hope that Yuuki can get him out of here. It's the only thing keeping him *alive* right now.

Morning comes. Kyle's fallen into an exhausted sleep when it does.

He wakes in time to eat breakfast before the guard he doesn't like comes in to take the tray away. A short time after that, he's brought lunch. He barely has any appetite, but he forces himself to eat that, too. If he falls asleep without doing so, it'll be taken away from him before he gets dinner. The meals are small enough as it is. He can't afford to skip one.

Exhaustion weighs heavy on Kyle's mind. The day passes slowly. He does a few stretches, takes a nap, dissociates, comes back to himself and tries to think like Yuuki asked him to. There's three days until the next meeting, meaning that there's still time, but now he's getting desperate. He racks his brain for anything – *anything* – that seems out of place from memory, something that he might be missing.

Dinner comes before the day is over. Kyle doesn't manage to finish it. He drinks all the water he's been given, sets the tray aside and goes back to zoning in and out of thinking.

His thoughts keep dragging him back to a few hours before the incident at the park. On his way back from school, a couple of guys had glared at him as he walked past the bar they were talking outside of.

Maybe he'd startled them? They'd seemed to be in the middle of a conversation, but the topic hadn't struck him as being dangerous or strange at the time… only weird. It hadn't seemed important, so he hadn't bothered to remember it. Something about a princess?

The jingling of keys in the lock interrupts his thoughts. Kyle tenses.

The door opens. Mitchell comes in to collect the dinner tray and the half-eaten food. He keeps Kyle in his peripheral as he bends down to pick it up. Kyle watches him warily.

Now's my chance to ask about a blanket, he remembers suddenly. But the words don't come fast enough, and before he can catch Mitchell's attention, he's on his way out. Kyle's heartbeat picks up. Hastily gets to his feet, reaching out to –

The tray drops. Mitchell pivots and uses the momentum to slam Kyle into the wall. The hand he'd been reaching out with is wrenched up behind his back. Pain shoots through his wrist and up his forearm.

It's the same arm he pulled muscles in trying to escape from Daniel.

"Don't try me, Kyle," Mitchell growls in his ear.

Kyle's trying hard to breathe through the panic and throbbing pain. His face is pressed against the wall. He's pinned down. Like before. Like when Daniel attacked him. He wants to fight back but he know he can't. He can't. He mustn't.

"Are you going to tell me what that was about?"

He thinks he feels Mitchell's harsh grip ease a little, but he's too tense to know for sure. The consequences will be far worse if he moves. He knows from experience, and so he stays still, as still as he can manage while he's fighting to steady himself.

Kyle swallows. "I-I just wa... it's c-cold, so I, I was gonna ask if I could... if I could have another blanket? Please?"

There's a moment of silence, then Mitchell releases him. Kyle doesn't move from the wall. He doesn't trust the officer's expression. One minute he's angry and the next he looks...sorry?

But then Mitchell's gone, the cell door shut and locked on his way out. Kyle suddenly doesn't have the energy to stand. His legs are weak. He sinks down to his knees, feet sliding out from under him until he's sitting on the cold cell floor. He slumps back against the wall.

No one believes anything I say.

No one but Yuuki has even tried to. His youth advocate might have, but he had to since it was job to. Yuuki didn't have to but chose to anyway.

Everyone's so quick to pass their judgement. They never asked Kyle for his side of the story. Did his youth advocate even *care?* He said he wouldn't give up on him, but...Kyle's heard that far too many times to dare to believe. He's putting a great amount of energy into hoping that Yuuki will be the exception.

He should get up. The cell floor is stealing his warmth. The bench that is his bed isn't warm per say, but at least it doesn't suck the warmth from him like this. He should get up, but he...

The lock clicks open. Kyle tenses all over again. Mitchell slips inside, a folded blanket in his hands.

"Here," he says gruffly.

Kyle doesn't move. Mitchell grimaces, deposits the blanket on the bed and leaves.

Ignoring the flare of pain in his forearm, he forces himself to his feet and makes his way over to the blanket. He nearly tears up at the texture of it beneath his fingertips. Picking it up, he watches as it unravels.

It's a large blanket, not thick enough to insulate him as well as he needs, but it'll stop him shivering so hard at night. Kyle clutches it to his chest, raises his face to the ceiling and lets out a shuddering breath.

He's got to be breaking fast to be losing control of his emotions so quickly. He thought he could hold out longer, hold onto his sense of self for at least another couple of weeks. But this isolation... it's killing him from the inside out.

Kyle curls up on the bed, huddling under the precious warmth of the blanket. It's only been five nights so far. He won't cry yet. He's too stubborn for that.

He can do this. He's just got to be patient.

Yuuki will get him out of here soon, right?

Just a little while longer...

He can do this.

"Hey, Logan," Avi says. "You doing alright over there?"

Sam smirks from her seat beside Avi. "You missing your partner, are you?"

Logan blinks. *Oh, I totally zoned out again.* He's been staring out Avi's bedroom window for who knows how long. He comes back to himself, back to the assignment instruction sheet in his hand. Avi and Sam have scribbled notes all over theirs. Logan's looks like it just came out of the printer.

Usually he can focus better than this, but…

"No, I'm not," Logan snaps. "And yes, I've got this. Thanks, Avi."

Sam hums. "Really? Doesn't seem like a lot's happening over there."

"Yeah, well, some of us aren't as brainy as you when it comes to physics, okay?"

Avi glances between the two before his gaze settles on Logan. He raises an eyebrow. "Seriously, man," he says. "You look a little stressed. What's up?"

What Logan wants to say is that it's nothing, he's just having trouble working on this assignment all by himself. It would be a perfectly acceptable answer. It's a pair assignment, after all. His classmate's still away and she hasn't been in contact with him to say when she'll be back so, yes, he is a little stressed.

But that's not the truth and Avi knows it. Even Sam has dropped the joking around.

Logan sighs and slouches further. "I've just been having trouble sleeping lately. You know, after what happened at the park. When I close my eyes at night, all I hear is the shouting."

Sam winces. "Your house is right next to the park. I'm sorry, I forgot."

He shrugs. "It's not like you guys come to mine often. It's too cramped to work on something like this anyway."

"Yeah, and it's hard to concentrate with so many people around."

Logan grunts. "That too."

"Did you actually see it happen?" Avi asks. "What happened at the park, I mean?"

"No. There was a lot of shouting, then the police showed up and went knocking on doors in the neighbourhood asking if anyone witnessed the fight. They said someone got murdered. My room's on the second story so it overlooks that park. If I'd looked out my window, I would've seen someone – someone I know – get killed. I…it disturbs me."

Avi murmurs, "It's a lot to process, huh."

Logan fidgets with the hem of his shirt. He nods.

"It's weird not seeing Daniel around school anymore," Avi says. "Kind of brings a sense of reality to what happened, eh. Come to think of it, haven't seen, uh…what's his name around much either. Wonder what's up with him."

Logan looks up. "You mean emo guy?"

"That's not his name, Logan."

Sam, who has been quietly listening and not saying anything, frowns. "You know Kyle?"

Logan scoffs. "I don't *know* him. We're like rivals, kind of…not really. He's always trying to one up me in track and field, and he's always just *slightly* ahead of me when it comes to grades and it really annoys me."

"You know he's in prison, right?"

The room falls dead silent. Avi and Logan exchanged horrified glances. Avi pales. "As in...*prison* prison? Kyle Kindall?"

"He –" Logan feels too hot and too cold all at once. *That was Kyle?*

"They *say* he killed Daniel," Sam interrupts, "but there were a lot of assumptions made in coming to that conclusion."

Logan's brow furrows. "Assumptions? I heard shouting *right outside my window.*"

"Who was shouting, Logan?"

Logan opens his mouth to reply but stops himself. He'd assumed it was Wilson – key word: *assumed.* Sam is watching him carefully, but not with scorn.

She's worried, he realises. *She's worried about Kyle.*

"Was your Dad the judge?" Logan asks.

Sam nods. Her eyes flash behind her glasses.

Avi frowns. "But if Kyle's in prison, then it means that your Dad found him to be guilty, right? Timothy wouldn't put him away unless he was."

"I don't know what's going on exactly, but Dad won't leave that case alone. He won't talk to me about it, either, which makes me think that something's up." Sam clicks her pen. "I haven't seen him in this kind of stress since he was searching for Yuuki when he was still missing."

Logan leans against the wall. "You mean when he and your Dad and your brother were kidnapped?"

"Yeah," Sam says.

"Oh, man. So what happened at the park – did Kyle do it or not?"

"What do you guys think?"

Avi and Logan exchange questioning looks.

Logan frowns. "I don't know. Kyle doesn't exactly strike me as the kind of guy who would do something like that. Even if he was provoked."

Avi raises a finger in conjecture. "Uh, don't you remember how he decked Wilson – Ben, that is – back in eighth grade?"

"Yeah, but that was eighth grade, Avi, not senior year. Kyle's had plenty of opportunities to deck me, the number of times I've purposefully annoyed him. Did he ever do it? No."

"Hmm, okay. What about you, Sam?"

Sam grunts. "From what it sounds like, the only evidence that was brought up was evidence supporting the claim that he did it. It's like they were avoiding giving any possible evidence to say that he didn't."

Avi hums in thought. "So…sort of like in experimenting, when you only sample the areas in which you *know* are going to give you the results you want."

"Precisely."

"So we're talking bias?" Logan says.

Sam nods. "Yeah. I reckon the evidence provided at the trial was heavily biased."

Avi clears his throat nervously. "You don't happen to know what said evidence was, do you?"

"No, I don't. Even if I did, I wouldn't know how much of it is true or not. There were a lot of assumptions made; it's possible there were lots of details missed out, making the truths only partial. It's too suspicious. Someone has to have set Kyle up."

Avi smiles. "You sounded like your Dad just now."

"Look, guys," Sam says. "While we're here enjoying each other's company, free to walk out that door whenever we want to, Kyle's cooped up in some cell and he doesn't get a choice. It rubs me the wrong way. So if you guys can think of anything at all that would help his case…"

"You want us to report in or something?"

Sam nods. "Yeah."

Logan exhales sharply. "You already have, haven't you? This is serious."

Sam is never this quiet when she's insistent. She's genuinely worried about Kyle being in prison. Logan gets the feeling he should be, too.

On the way home from Avi's, it's all he thinks about. Sam must be thinking about it, too, because she doesn't say a word as they walk the familiar streets homeward. They pass by a school hockey field that their school uses for practice. Ben Wilson is there training with his team. He draws both Logan and Sam's attention, but not for the typical reason: he's Daniel's twin. It's impossible not to think about what happened to Daniel while looking at him.

"Rose, on your six!"

His voice is so similar to what Daniel's sounded like. If Logan closed his eyes and Ben and Daniel were standing side by side, talking, he wouldn't be able to tell who was talking when.

But neither of them have or had the husky undertone that rang out in the night when the incident happened.

Logan's heart drops into his stomach. "Oh…"

"Didn't think you were into hockey," Sam mumbles. "Or any of our school's players, for that matter."

"No, not that. The shouting I heard at the park that night?"

"What about it?"

"Kyle was the one who was screaming."

7

"Yuuki, are you sure you want to do this?"

Yuuki knows he's taking a risk, but it's a necessary one. He's dealing with sensitive information – the dangerous kind. The fact that someone wanted Kyle dead for overhearing something says as much.

He nods. "Affirmative. Don't worry, I trust him not to try anything."

There's a flash of…something in Mitchell's eyes that he can't decipher. It almost looks like guilt.

"Besides, you'll be right down the end of the hallway, right?"

"It's not Kyle I'm worried about," Mitchell says gruffly. "It's you. Think about what you're about to do. Carefully."

Yuuki works his jaw. He's been trying not to think too hard about it. The flashbacks are inevitable, he guesses. He is, after all, about to lock himself in a prison cell.

Four walls. Not much space.

He has the keys, but he'll have to lock the door. Trapped.

Closing his eyes, Yuuki takes a deep breath. "I'm doing this for Kyle. I can't let my own issues get in the way. It's not fair on him."

"Yuuki, they're not just issues and you know it."

"I know. I know, it's just…"

"You care for him. You care about that kid."

Yuuki fights the overwhelming emotion back down his throat. "Yeah," he murmurs. "I do. He's got no one else."

Heaving a sigh, Mitchell nods. "Alright. You sure you trust him, though?"

"Yes."

"I still don't think this is a good idea."

"Neither do I. But I've been given a job to do and I'm going to see to it that I do it well."

Mitchell regards him carefully. Something's different about him today. His expression is softer, lacking the dubious frown it used to have whenever Yuuki would speak of the idea of Kyle being innocent.

Yuuki wonders what's changed.

"Alright," Mitchell says. "Go have your meeting, then."

The cell is just down the hallway from the main office, since 'isolation' comes under the high security tag. There's only two of them at A'o Youth Detention Centre. Only one of them is occupied. Yuuki would've been able to see Kyle sitting in there if not for the fourth wall being a sealed one.

No bars. Just a wall and a soundproof door.

Yuuki's stomach churns. *This is a bad idea.* He hesitates at the door, foldable chair in one hand and key card in the other. He doesn't have to hold the meeting in the cell. They could have it in the designated meeting room as they have the last couple of times.

But no. Timothy's right, they have to be extra vigilant from now on. This information is what put Kyle's life in danger in the first place. It's the reason why he's locked up in prison for something he didn't do.

I have to do this. He knocks on the door three times, swipes the key card and opens the door.

Kyle's sitting on the narrow excuse for a bed, knees tucked up under his chin. Both arms are wrapped around his stomach. He looks up at Yuuki tiredly.

"Hey," Yuuki says, forcing a smile.

The door shuts behind him. His body fills with adrenaline.

No. Not now.

Distantly, he can hear Kyle calling out to him but his body won't react anymore. His eyes still see the pale walls of the cell and Kyle in his orange prison clothes, but Yuuki's mind is trapped in darkness. Stifling darkness.

"-ki?"

You're not there right now, he tells himself. *You're with Kyle. You're not there anymore.*

He remembers the moment when the door opened and the harsh light from outside the room burned his eyes.

"Yuuki! Hey!"

But the terror is still so real, the hopelessness –

The door bangs open. The rustling of clothes and fast-paced footsteps come too close, too soon, and Yuuki knows who they're going for and he's not allowing it.

He steps in front between Kyle and Mitchell, breathing heavily.

Mitchell stops in his tracks. It's too late for Yuuki to hide the fright in his eyes or the way his hands shake. It's too hard to get the words out to say that it wasn't Kyle's fault, but his intervention seems to be enough. The guard accompanying Mitchell – the same one as last time – takes the hint and stands down.

"We heard shouting," Mitchell says.

A glance over his shoulder reassures Yuuki that Kyle's not panicking. At least, not as visibly as he is. He waves a hand at Kyle to reassure him that he'll handle this.

"It wasn't him," Yuuki says, turning his head back to face Mitchell. "He didn't do anything. I just...I had a bit of a flashback, is all."

The guard knows his place and doesn't say anything, but the twitch in his cheek makes it clear that he's unconvinced. Mitchell, on the other hand, doesn't look surprised, and asks, "Are you alright?"

Yuuki swallows. He fights back the wave of still unprocessed emotions and nods. He shuts his eyes for a few seconds to try to recollect himself. With a deep breath, he opens them again.

"Yeah," he says thickly. "I'll be fine. It's just...PTSD...stuff. Don't worry about me. I'll be fine."

Mitchell regards both Yuuki and Kyle carefully. "Alright, that's fine." He fixes his gaze on Kyle behind him. "Regardless of that, you're going to need to have these on."

He holds a pair of handcuffs in his hand.

Yuuki frowns. "Is that really necessary?"

"Protocol."

Yuuki grimaces as Mitchell proceeds with the handcuffs. There's a pinch in his gut as he watches Kyle shrink into himself, pressing himself as far up against the wall as the wall will allow him to. Kyle seems to fighting to control his breathing and trying to hold it at the same time. Yuuki wonders what that's about. It's worse of a reaction than the previous time he saw Kyle flinching. It's like he's having a flashback of his own.

"Alright," Yuuki says when Mitchell has finished securing Kyle's hands behind his back. "I'll take it from here."

Thankfully Mitchell understands the cue to leave them to the meeting again. The guard casts one last look at Kyle before following.

Breathing out slowly, Yuuki sets down his foldable chair and sits down opposite Kyle. "Sorry about that," he mutters. "I... that was very unprofessional of me."

It's not like Yuuki can help that he has PTSD. It's not like he can control how he reacts to certain things either, but he wishes he could have a better handle on his emotions. What happened to the calm, collected and easy-going Yuuki Takahashi that he was before?

Why did the Ninao incident have to affect him so badly?

"Am I allowed to...can I hug you?"

Yuuki looks up at Kyle, startled. No...he heard those words right. Kyle's shoulders are hunched forward a little, as though he's expecting to be reprimanded for asking such a ridiculous thing. The sincerity in his gaze is so overwhelming, and Yuuki knows it's not an act.

It takes a solid minute for Yuuki to respond, during which Kyle's gaze flits about the room, anxious. Yuuki swallows his pride and nods.

Kyle rises from his seat hesitantly. He takes two slow steps forward, watching Yuuki cautiously, then he leans over and hugs him. It's rather awkward since the handcuffs don't allow Kyle to spread his arms in a proper embrace, but Yuuki's already past the point of crying and Kyle's careful half-hug is so much more than he could ask for right now. He loosely wraps his arms around him, returning the hug yet being cautious so as not to make Kyle feel like he's trapped. Whatever Yuuki had been expecting from his meetings with Kyle, it certainly isn't this.

Neither of them are aware of Mitchell watching them through the security feed.

"You okay?" Kyle asks quietly, moving away to sit back down on his bed.

Yuuki grunts. "Yeah, I, uh…I will be. Thanks."

Kyle pulls his knees up to his chest again. "Why are you helping me if your PTSD affects you so much?"

"You know, I've been asked that many times, actually." Yuuki remarks. "My answer is this: because I don't want the same thing that happened to me happen to you."

"…what happened to you at Ninao?"

"Yeah."

"You were…they kept you…" Kyle's face falls. "Oh."

Yuuki's kidnapping had been on the news. Three days after he disappeared, the search team finally found him locked in a garden shed at an abandoned property. He'd thought no one was going to come for him, and at first no one did: Timothy and Joshua, who had managed to escape the vehicles before reaching their destination, had lost all trace of him.

But Timothy had never given up searching for him. It had saved his life. While Yuuki hopes that the situation doesn't end up becoming that dire, he wants to be that person for Kyle.

"So," Yuuki says. "Have you thought of anything that might give us an idea of why it was that Daniel went after you?"

Kyle shrugs. "Not really."

"Okay, well 'not really' means at least something's crossed your mind, right?"

"I don't know."

Yuuki can see the walls going up. "It's okay if you think it's stupid or unlikely. We've got to consider everything we've got here which, to be frank, isn't a lot. Besides, something that may seem silly to you might be code for something dangerous to someone else."

Kyle's brow furrows. "I may not have heard it right."

"Let's just go with what we've got for now. Anything is better than nothing."

"Well, I couldn't think of much. It's been hard to think lately. I…the only plausible explanation I can think of is that Daniel had a personal hate towards me."

"Can you tell me where that might've come from?"

"I got into a fight with his twin brother a few years back. Daniel never seemed to want to let it go."

Hmm. But it seems odd that a grudge would spiral so out of control like that, especially if Daniel hadn't acted on it for several years.

"What was the story re that fight?"

Kyle averts his eyes. "I punched him."

"Why did you punch him?"

"Ben was being a jerk."

Yuuki waits for Kyle to elaborate. When he doesn't, he says, "Okay. Whether he started it or you did, it doesn't matter. I'm only trying to understand the reason for Daniel Wilson's grudge against you. Would you be able to tell me how it started?"

Kyle mutters something beneath his breath, scowling. "He was being a jerk, like always. I got the class in trouble for running late and Ben got really annoyed at me, started saying stupid stuff to get on my nerves and I just – snapped. He wouldn't shut up. It got to me."

One thing Yuuki's noticing is that Kyle has a tendency to shrug and avoid eye contact, as well as try to make the topic at hand seem like not much of a big deal, when he doesn't think the person he's talking to is going to care. Yuuki's been finding himself doing the same gestures lately when people ask him how he's doing.

But he gets the feeling that this 'stupid stuff' is personal. Trying to get Kyle to tell him the kind of things Ben was saying would be crossing the line. Yuuki decides to respect that boundary.

"And I'm guessing Ben and Daniel are pretty close, huh?" he remarks. "Being twins?"

Kyle nods. "He beat me up a couple of times for it."

So Daniel *had* previously acted on the grudge. "How long ago was the last time?" Yuuki asks.

"Back in middle school."

So not recently at all…

It seems rather extreme for Daniel to all of a sudden want Kyle dead. Yuuki decides there must be some other explanation for what happened at the park.

On to the next question. "Okay. I'll make a note of that," Yuuki says. "But can you think of anything else? Remember, I don't care how stupid you think it sounds."

This is where, if Kyle were that sort of person, he could start making up lies and fooling around with Yuuki's questions. Obviously that would get him nowhere, but he could still do that for entertainment. But Yuuki already knows deep down that Kyle isn't that sort of person, and he thinks it's that level of trust he's willing to have with him that allows Kyle to open up the way he does.

"The day it happened," Kyle says slowly, "I had these two guys glare at me. I was on my way to the park after school. One of the streets I walk down has a couple of pubs. There were a couple of men sitting outside one of them, their backs to me, and as I passed they suddenly stopped talking. I was wondering what their deal was, so I turned and they were glaring at me. I kept walking, but...I don't know. It was weird."

Yuuki's heart rate picks up. The palms of his hands grow clammy.

"I didn't really hear what they were talking about, anyway, so I don't know why they were so annoyed."

"Did you hear anything at all?"

Kyle grunts. "I probably didn't hear it right. I wasn't really listening."

"You think I'll think it's stupid?"

"They were talking about a princess."

Kyle looks at him through half-lidded eyes, waiting expectantly. But Yuuki doesn't laugh. He doesn't scoff. Instead, he considers it carefully.

"Princess?" Yuuki murmurs. "You don't think they were talking about the Arkala princess?"

"But why would they want to kill me over that? Taularh had the royal family assassinated thirteen years ago."

"Probably some political scheme they didn't want anyone hearing about then, I'd say." Yuuki pauses, a thought occurring to him suddenly. "Do you know if Daniel associated himself with pro-Taularh groups?"

The corner of Kyle's mouth quirks. "He was rather vocal about it."

"So it's not out of the question that he possibly had a connection to those two men. That could explain why Daniel came for you only a few hours after those guys glared at you."

Kyle stares at him, eyes wide. "I…I never thought of that."

There's a knock on the door. Five minutes.

Yuuki can't resist grumbling. "Half an hour is not enough time."

"I, um…that's all I could think of. Sorry it's not much."

"No, Kyle – it's given me an answer to a lot of questions. Of course, that only raises *more* questions, but I think we're getting somewhere. Hopefully it won't be long before we can get you out of here." Yuuki's nods in the direction of Kyle's arms behind his back. "In the meantime, let's at least get you out of those."

Kyle doesn't flinch backwards like he did with Mitchell. Instead, he turns to the side and holds out his hands while Yuuki takes the specialised pin from his pocket and pokes the release mechanism. As Kyle goes to pull his wrists free, his right hand gets caught and he lets out a hiss of pain.

Yuuki frowns. "What's wrong? Did you hurt yourself?"

Kyle keeps his eyes down. "I just pulled some muscles, is all. I'm fine."

'I'm fine.' Yuuki knows how that lines works now. "Remember how we shook hands about a week ago? Your arm wasn't sore then. What happened?"

Kyle doesn't answer. His expression has gone hard.

"Kyle?"

"Officer Mitchell."

Yuuki decides he doesn't need to ask further. Mitchell has a tendency to presume the worst situation first, especially when it comes to judging character. While it's not a bad thing to be cautious in this line of work, there's a point at which judging someone like that only makes winds up hurting people.

"I'll be back," Yuuki says. "I'm just going to get you something for your arm."

Anti-inflammatory cream would be the most ideal, but they don't have any of that here. Yuuki doesn't have enough time to go and find some either. He's only got a couple of minutes if he wants to stay under the radar.

He ducks into the office, ignoring Mitchell's questioning glance. He feels the moment when that glance turns into a remorseful one, when Yuuki leaves the office with a roll of bandage in one hand.

At least he understands now that he shouldn't have judged Kyle like that, otherwise Yuuki would be having a word with him.

"Here," Yuuki says, unlocking and reopening the door. "Where does it hurt?"

Kyle looks at him strangely. "I, uh…" He gestures, with his other hand, from his wrist to his elbow.

Yuuki holds Kyle's hand carefully in his as he starts winding the bandage cloth around Kyle's wrist.

"About Mitchell," Yuuki says. "Try not to get on his bad side. You don't want to be getting in any trouble here, intentionally or not, if you want to be able to go back home soon-ish. Mitchell's not one to –"

Apparently that was the wrong thing to say. Kyle's gone completely closed off to him. He lets Yuuki finish bandaging his arm, but his expression is edged with anger and duller than it was a few seconds ago.

"Kyle?"

"I understand."

Yuuki tears the roll of cloth and tucks in the end. Kyle immediately withdraws his hand.

"Thanks," he says curtly, refusing to meet Yuuki's eyes.

The abrupt silence leaves Yuuki feeling utterly displaced. His time's up anyway, so he needs to take this cue to leave, but he hates it. He wants to talk to Kyle, find out why there's so much hurt burning in his eyes and what it is he said that made Kyle so upset.

Instead he quietly stands back, folds up the chair and takes it under one arm. "I...thank you for what you've given me today, Kyle. It'll be very useful."

Kyle stares at the wall, unblinking.

"I'll be back in after the weekend. I'll see you then."

Yuuki lingers a moment longer before taking his leave.

8

He's not himself all day. The terror he felt during the flashback he had in the cell still hasn't left him. It's like it's warning him of some impending danger that never comes, warning him that it *will* come if he so much as happens to let his guard down for a few minutes.

Yuuki spends the afternoon notetaking, mind-mapping and trying to work out how all the pieces of the puzzle fit together. The problem is that he doesn't have all the pieces and he doesn't even know what the full picture looks like.

All the thinking eventually exhausts him, and Yuuki falls asleep on the couch before Lee gets home from work.

Yuuki nightmares. He's back in the cell, having a meeting with Kyle. Things are going well and Kyle's about to tell him a critical piece of information that'll bring this whole case around when the cell wall with the window set in it explodes inward.

Bricks crumble. Dust and dirt and smoke cloud the room. Before Yuuki can recover, several masked figures swoop in. They grab Kyle by the arms and drag him out through the debri. He kicks and yells but can't get free. There's fear shining in his eyes. Yuuki gets up and dances between mess of bricks and steel rods and cladding. But Kyle's already gone.

Someone lays a hand on his shoulder and Yuuki jerks out of their grip, tries to run after Kyle, but it's no use. He has no idea where he is. He has no idea where he's being taken. He can't find Kyle. He can't find –

"Yuuki."

He wakes with a gasp. Lee's standing over him, hand on Yuuki's shoulder. Yuuki pushes himself upright, breathing fast. *It was just a dream. It was just a bad dream. It wasn't real.*

"You held the meeting in the cell after all, didn't you?"

Yuuki frowns up at him, caught off guard. "What? Yeah, why?"

"I warned you it would take a toll on you."

"Y-yeah, I know. I…I'm fine. It was just a bad dream."

Yuuki gets up and fetches a glass of water from the kitchen. Lee waits until the fright has died down in Yuuki's eyes before wrapping him up in a hug. There's no further arguing as of yet, but Yuuki can't relax. There's still a wall he can feel between the two of them. A strained, exhaustion-built wall.

Lee pulls away, and with a tired sigh, looks Yuuki square in the eye.

"I know how much this case means to you," he murmurs. "But is it really worth putting your health at risk like this?"

"This is nothing compared to what Kyle is having to deal with right now. I'm not giving up on Kyle."

"That's not what I'm asking."

"No," Yuuki mutters, "but the way you're putting it makes it sound like you want me to choose. I…there is more at stake here than my health. It's probably more than Kyle, too, and he doesn't even get a choice in the matter. You don't have to babysit me, Lee. I can handle this."

Lee raises an eyebrow. He stares at Yuuki a while longer before letting taking a deep breath. He breathes out slowly, carefully.

"Yuuki," he says. "It's killing me to see you hurting like this. You might be able to handle it but I can't. I think it's best if we went our own ways."

Yuuki struggles to process exactly what that means.

Lee spells it out for him. "I'm leaving."

The weekend comes and goes and Yuuki gets nowhere further on the case.

He can't concentrate. Over and over, he questions whether that's his own fault. Kyle's depending on him. Now is *not* the time for Yuuki to let something personal aka friendship drama interfere with his work. Kyle needs him to focus.

It doesn't happen, and by the time the weekend's over, Lee's moved out entirely.

Yuuki's meeting with Kyle again tomorrow. Until then, he's got nothing. He's beginning to wonder if it's not just a coincidence how difficult this case is to work on. It's like someone's messing with him, making it impossible to pull together enough evidence to sway the result of Kyle's trial.

That...wouldn't be surprising, really.

Yuuki thinks of his conversation with Timothy the other day and their discussion about the Peace Force commander who was present at the trial, Jeff. Yuuki's gut instinct tells him that guy's involved somehow. It's too unusual that he would appear in a youth case, even more unusual that Timothy would be unnerved by the very memory.

Timothy must've seen something at the trial. There was a reason why he mentioned something not seeming right. Timothy's situational awareness is exceptional. If he thinks he saw something then it's most likely that he did.

No wonder he took measures to prevent Kyle from accidently saying the wrong thing.

There might be something bigger happening in the background, then, something that Kyle isn't aware he knows about. If that's the case, then he's a liability to whoever set him up.

Yuuki's heart skips a beat. A liability. That means that Kyle has the power to expose them. *That's why they wanted him dead. That's why the sentence forced upon him was isolation when the plan to kill him failed.*

Abandoning his pacing around the living room, Yuuki plonks himself down on the couch, grabs his notebook and hastily scribbles that in. His heart rate picks up as he thinks of something else.

They don't plan on letting Kyle leave.

He thinks of Kyle alone in the cell, far more alone than Yuuki is in the house right now. It nearly undoes him. *They don't plan on letting Kyle leave.* Yuuki digs the pen into the paper and scrawls, *WHO IS THEY?!?*

He slaps the notebook onto the arm of the couch and leans back with a loud sigh. How is he supposed to figure out anything if he doesn't know who and what he's dealing with?

Of course I'm getting nowhere. 'They' don't want me getting anywhere. Not only are there stricter laws to work around, the record of all the evidence gathered for Kyle's case was probably tampered with too.

Kyle's not going to last two months. Yuuki doesn't have that long and he certainly doesn't want to take that long, either. If he does, no doubt the duration of imprisonment will only be extended. He didn't miss the asterisk saying Kyle's time is subject to change.

Yuuki's determined to get him out of there. He's not giving up on Kyle, no matter how much it feels like he's losing traction. He just has to be patient and not rush this investigating.

His phone rings. Yuuki frowns at it. It's not exactly late, but… Yuuki picks it up and swipes the screen. "Hello? Yuuki Takahashi speaking."

"Ah, hi there! It's Charlie Smith, young Kindall's youth advocate!"

Yuuki sits up straight. "Yes, hi. I, uh…how are you doing?"

"Been better," Charlie replies, still in a lively tone. "And how's it with you?"

"I'm doing alright, thanks."

"Good, good. I apologise for not getting into contact with you sooner, Takahashi. Family business called me out of town and I only just got back today."

"It's not a worry, really."

"So, anyways… I was wondering if you're available to catch up sometime this week?"

Yuuki rubs his forehead, relieved. "Yeah, I am. That would be great." *I might be able to piece a bit more of the puzzle together with this man's help.*

"Okay, well…how does Thursday sound to you?"

"Thursday? I think I've got a meeting with Kyle in the morning, so maybe after that?"

"So Thursday afternoon then?"

"Yeah, if that works with you?"

"Yes, that's fine. Shall we say one o'clock for now?"

"That's good for me. Where…?"

"I'll come over to you. If you don't mind waiting a bit after you finish your meeting with Kyle."

"I can do that."

"Alright, I'll see you then."

"Thanks. Bye."

Kyle's youth advocate. The only one who actively defended Kyle during his trial. Yuuki lowers the phone and falls back into the couch cushions behind him.

It's not impossible. There's a way to get Kyle out of this mess, but it's going to take more than just what Yuuki and Timothy can bring to the table. A desperate part of him hopes that maybe Charlie has all the remaining answers Yuuki needs.

Just be patient. Things will work themselves out.

The thought doesn't quite make it to his heart.

Yuuki needs solid proof that Daniel attacked Kyle. He doesn't have it. It's likely someone doesn't want him to have it and is working behind the scenes to make sure he doesn't get it.

The issue lies with the first witness – the one on the scene. Since they were the only one of the reported witnesses to have *seen* anything, it's their word over the rest unless Yuuki is able to find some sort of evidence significant enough to outweigh that statement.

And where on earth am I meant to get that from?

It seems helpless, this situation, but then Yuuki remembers the person who stopped by the station the other day to give a statement in favour of Kyle and his heart stirs. It bothered them, not seeing him at the park anymore. There *are* people out there who care, people who can help in ways that Yuuki can't.

He takes a deep breath, closes his eyes. Opens them.

He's just got to be patient.

9

Monday comes quickly and with it, the next meeting with Kyle.

Yuuki's not doing a good job of hiding how tired he is. Even Mitchell notices something's up, but he doesn't press, allowing Yuuki to continue pretending his parting with Lee doesn't affect him as much it does.

Thankfully Kyle isn't still upset at him. In fact, he looks just as exhausted as Yuuki is. They share an acknowledging look as Yuuki enters.

"Hey," Yuuki murmurs, the cell door swings closed behind him. "How are you doing?"

Kyle shrugs. "I don't know."

"How's your arm?"

"Better, I guess."

Yuuki notices a strip of white poking out from under Kyle's pillow and wonders how long he left the bandage on for. "Is it still sore?"

"It's fine."

Yuuki sets down the foldable chair, but instead of sitting down, he pulls out the pair of handcuffs Mitchell insisted he take. It makes his stomach churn, especially in light of having his own hands bound behind his back for three days during his kidnapping, but he follows protocol and Kyle doesn't comment.

"I'm sorry about this," he says as he fastens the cuffs. "I do have the authority to decide whether or not these are necessary, but I don't want us to get in trouble if anyone else comes in here. You've got enough trouble surrounding you as it is."

Kyle leans back against the wall. "It's fine."

"It really isn't. I don't think you should even be in here in the first place."

"Everyone else thinks I should be."

Yuuki sits down in the chair. "No. Not everyone."

"Mostly everyone."

"Yeah, but that means there's still a few people who haven't given up on you. I'm one of them. Timothy's one of them. Your advocate, Charlie, is one of them. We're doing all we can to figure out what exactly is going on here. So, Kyle? Don't give up on yourself just yet. We're going to get you out of here."

Kyle breaks eye contact and fumbles with the metal binding his wrists. He mumbles something indistinguishable.

"Sorry, I didn't hear you."

"I said, 'do you really think that's possible?'"

Yuuki waits until Kyle glances up at him, then gives him a firm nod. "I will make sure of it," he says. "I *will* get you out of here."

The intensity in Kyle's gaze is unsettling, the otherwise expressionless way he stares at him even more so. Yuuki recognises that pain. He *knows* it. It's the kind of hopelessness that hollows you out. The kind of pain that numbs all ability to feel any kind of emotion in a last ditch effort to survive.

Kyle's bleeding on the inside – not blood but life. There's definitely no way he's going to last the entire two months like this.

"I've gotten in contact with Charlie," Yuuki tells him. "We're meeting on Thursday, after our meeting, so hopefully he'll be able to give us a bit of extra insight. In the meantime, is there anything else you've thought of that might give us a lead?"

Kyle leans his head back against the wall. "No."

"Alright. That's okay. I'm a bit stumped myself, to be honest."

They sit in silence for a few precious minutes. Yuuki feels his anxiety rising again, the four walls of the cell pressing in on him, but then he focuses on Kyle's presence, his unimposing demeanour and the steady rhythm of his breathing, and it grounds him.

Kyle clears his throat. "Say you did figure all this out. What happens to me then?"

Yuuki frowns. "What do you mean?"

"Where do I go from there?"

You get to go home, he automatically goes to say and then stops before the sounds leave his tongue. Kyle got rather upset the last time Yuuki mentioned anything about going home. It almost sounds like Kyle's now wondering if staying locked up in prison is a better alternative to what waits for him outside.

The case summary in Timothy's letter. *'School records and foster care families report Kindall as 'violent'…'*

Oh.

"We'll sort something out for you," Yuuki says, then winces when he realises it sounds like they're just going to shove him back into the foster system. "First and foremost, we need to get you cleared, and then we can decide what's the best option available to you. How long until you're eighteen?"

Kyle's brow furrows. "Um… a few months. My birthday's in October."

So not quite soon enough, in other words.

"You're not going to send me back there, are you? I don't think they want me back."

"Who?" Yuuki asks. "Your foster family?"

Kyle grunts. "Hardly a 'family'."

"In answer to your question, no – you won't be sent back there. Once we clear the case, Timothy, Charlie and I can start looking for a place for you to stay until –"

"No one will want me staying with them. No one ever does. It's going to be even worse now that I also happen to have a criminal record."

"One that you shouldn't have. One that was forced upon you."

"Maybe I deserve it."

"No, Kyle…"

Yuuki curses inwardly. He knows how quickly thoughts can spiral. One minute he's fine and then something triggers him and he's not. Kyle has had over a week imprisoned in both a cell and his own mind; he's had plenty of time to convince himself that it's his own fault he ended up here. Self-blame is something Yuuki's familiar with.

"Kyle," he murmurs. "You don't deserve *any* of this. It doesn't matter what you did or what others think you did. We're human. We mess up all the time. If we constantly got what we deserved, there'd be none of us left.

"Besides, what happened at the park wasn't your fault. Sure, had you not walked down that street past those men who were having that weird conversation at the pub, or had you not gotten in that fight with Daniel's brother, maybe things would've turned out differently? Maybe they wouldn't have. Regardless, you being here is not your fault. That's why I'm here. To convince the world of that."

Kyle exhales sharply. "And what if you can't?"

"I will. Someone may have built up a wall of lies surrounding you, but I'm also a 'someone', and I'm going to take it down, brick by brick."

Kyle closes his eyes. He doesn't say anything for a couple of minutes and neither does Yuuki. Yuuki's words settle in the room – a truth, a declaration. Kyle breathes it in and Yuuki feels his confidence rising again.

The five-minutes-left knock sounds on the door.

Yuuki sighs. "Time already, huh." He looks up at Kyle, who quickly averts his gaze before Yuuki can read his expression properly. When Kyle doesn't speak what's on his mind, Yuuki takes the pin out of his pocket and nods in the direction of Kyle's hands. "I can take those off for you now."

Kyle wordlessly extends his arms back and Yuuki releases the mechanism on the cuffs. It's as he goes to return to his chair that Kyle grabs onto one of his hands and grips it tightly in both of his.

Yuuki drops the handcuffs in shock. Kyle's hands are shaking. He stands as still as he can, perplexed. "Are you…what's wrong?"

Kyle's face screws up. He ducks his head to hide behind his hair, but Yuuki hears his breath hitch a little on the inhale. He clutches at Yuuki's hand like it's the only thing keeping him together.

"Kyle? What's wrong?"

Stupid question, really. Yuuki doesn't wait for a reply, only sinks to his knees and wraps his free arm around Kyle's shoulders. Kyle leans forward and buries his face in Yuuki's shoulder and Yuuki holds onto him a little tighter.

"I'm going to get you out of here, okay?" he murmurs. "I know it seems like forever, like it's never going to happen, but I promise you – I'm not giving up you, Kyle. No matter what. If they try to keep the truth from being spoken, I won't stop until it is." Yuuki rubs his free hand over Kyle's shoulder blade. "I'll get you out of here. Just hang in there, okay? I'll get you out of here."

He's so close and yet still so unbearably far. Time might yield the answers that he's searching for but it doesn't yield any comfort for Kyle, only more suffering.

It breaks Yuuki's heart when he pulls away from him, conscious of the thirty minute time limit about to tick over. It isn't right, leaving Kyle like this. It goes against every human instinct Yuuki has in him. But he has to do it, or else they'll likely start drawing dangerous unwanted attention if they haven't already.

"I'll be back," he whispers before he pulls his hand free of Kyle's grasp.

Kyle reluctantly lets go. The most he can manage is a weak nod. Yuuki takes a deep breath, picks up the chair and the handcuffs and pin he dropped, and walks over to the door. Instead of saying goodbye, Yuuki forces a smile. Kyle doesn't return it.

Somehow Yuuki manages to fake being okay the entire hour it takes from closing the cell door to closing the house door when he gets home.

Before the door's even fully shut, the tears are flowing freely.

10

"Uh, Laura?" Avi says from the other side of the table. "You alright over there?"

Logan laughs as his assignment partner tugs her hood further over her head. Her long hair doesn't all fit so the ends of it poof out in front of her face.

She huffs out a breath of annoyance. "Does it look to you like I am?"

Sam smirks. "Absolutely."

"I just don't understand why the Lakes has to get so freezing *now*," Laura grumbles. "Couldn't it have done so while I was away? I was gone for a whole week. There was plenty of time for this extra chilly weather to come and go then."

Logan tilts his head to the side. "Maybe you're the Snow Queen."

Laura's face turns a couple of shades paler than her Arkala brown. She starts wringing her hands as she looks away.

"Um…are you okay?" Logan asks, frowning.

Laura fakes a smile. "Oh, it's not that." She stuffs her hair down inside her jacket hood and turns her attention back to the assignment they're working on. "I, er... I just have a lot on my mind right now. Sorry."

"No need to apologise. You've been busy dealing with family stuff."

"Yeah..." Laura bites her lip. She's avoiding making eye contact now, and the abrupt drop in mood catches even Sam's attention.

Time for a change in subject. "Hey, Sam," Logan says. "Have you heard any more from your Dad about Kyle?"

Avi's eyes widen. "Oh, that's right! You went into the station on...what day was it? Friday last week?"

"Yeah. Gosh, I was so nervous! There's some scary Peace Force guys out there, I'm telling you."

"I told my Dad what you said, too," Sam says. "Just in case your statement doesn't get to Yuuki any time soon. It got to Monday and he still hadn't heard anything from them, apparently."

"That's weird."

"Not just weird, a little suspicious if you ask me."

"What did your Dad think when you told him?"

Sam frowns deeper. "Honestly? He looked so relieved. I know he's the judge and that he's the one who declared Kyle guilty, but I don't think he reckons Kyle did it. He and Yuuki have been working so hard on this case..."

Avi raises a hand in interjection. "Does Laura know what we're talking about? Just saying. She...you look a little lost."

It's then that Logan realises Laura's gone uncharacteristically quiet. She's gripping her pencil so tight Logan half expects it to snap in two.

"I'm presuming you're talking about the incident that happened at the park nearby your house?" she says. "The one involving Kyle Kindall?"

Sam narrows her eyes thoughtfully. "You know something about it?"

"Oh, I know very well about it. I was there."

The four of them fall into a tense silence. Logan looks between Sam and Avi, stunned. "You mean you saw it happen?" he asks.

"I didn't see it happen, but I saw Kyle there with Daniel as I was walking home. I don't live too far from you and Sam, remember?"

"Laura…"

"It's fine. I didn't see anything terrible. I just…I fear I've made a huge mistake."

The three wait quietly for Laura to gather her thoughts. Some of her hair escapes her jacket hood and poofs in her face again, but no one laughs this time.

"I thought Kyle had gone mad. I thought he'd gone crazy. So when I saw he'd *stabbed* someone, I…" Laura takes a deep breath and closes her eyes, frowning. "I didn't realise…no, I didn't stop to think about asking the question of *why* he was freaking out. It never once crossed my mind that he may have been freaking out because he was scared."

Logan hums in thought. "So what you're saying is, given to time to think about it…?"

"I was racist," Laura says bluntly. "You all know that my parents were killed when I was very young. The people who took their lives were Arkala'ana, descendants of the cave dwellers, and when I was old enough to understand what they did I swore I'd never forgive them. I see now the kind of damage it's been causing. Begrudging like that… it caused me to see Kyle in the same light."

"Because of Kyle's Arkala'ana heritage?"

She nods. "I was wrong to judge him like that. And now you all are talking about the idea that Kyle's innocent in all this, I…I'm sickened by how quick I was to presume that he intentionally took Daniel's life."

"Laura," Logan murmurs. "Yeah, you made a mistake, but it's not too late to do something about it. How about we go down to the station and you can make an alteration to your statement? They won't be mad at you for getting the details a little wrong. Sometimes people remember things later, just like I did."

Laura flashes him an appreciative smile. "Yeah. I plan on doing so. My relative who I live with, he's Kyle's youth advocate. Since realising how wrong I was to just assume Kyle's behaviour like that, I've felt so ashamed. I can't help but feel like I've let him down."

"Then let's go do what we can to help him." Logan turns to Avi and Sam, who have been listening closely. "You guys free to go down the station with us tomorrow?" he asks.

Avi shakes his head. "Sorry, I've got to help my Dad out at the garage. Otherwise I'd definitely be there. Actually, depending on when you go, I might be able to…"

"I'll come," Sam says. "What time?"

Logan glances at Laura. "Morning?"

Sam groans. "Not too early, please."

"We'll go late morning. That suit? Laura, you said that you live near me and Sam. How about we meet at the park at ten?"

Laura smiles wryly. "Village Park?"

"I just figured it was an easy meeting point…and a kind of symbolic one, you know?"

"Alright, then. Which station are we going to, might I ask?"

Sam exchanges a warning look with Logan. "My Dad's going to be working at the North Two Lakes Station tomorrow," she says. "I say we go there. We don't want this update getting lost in space."

Laura grimaces. "I agree."

"Cool," Logan says. "North Two Lakes Station it is."

Avi gives them all the thumbs up. "Good luck, guys."

Eventually they get back to working on their pair assignments, but it's not science that's on their mind, it's Kyle – him and the constant wondering how this all happened. And Laura, unable to concentrate at all, can't shake off the feeling that she is the reason why.

Something smashes inside the house and Ben Wilson freezes, hand hovering over the door handle. His thoughts flash to what happened to his brother and his instincts kick in.

He flings the door wide open. "Mum!"

Adrenaline. Listening for any kind of suspicious noise. A hand gripping on his hockey bag, ready to use his equipment if necessary. But it turns out he was just over-reacting: his mother is standing in the kitchen with a dishtowel in one hand and the dishwasher door is open.

Oh. She accidently dropped something again. Ben sets down his hockey bag and goes into the kitchen to assess the damage. A broken plate lies cracked on the floor. His mother is crying.

"I'll get this cleaned up for you," he murmurs, heading to the cupboard to grab the dustpan.

His Mum doesn't answer. She still hasn't said anything five minutes later when Ben has disposed of all the broken bits of plate. It worries him.

"Hey, is everything alright?"

She shakes her head. With a trembling hand, she digs her fingers into the dishtowel and points to the knife block.

"I don't understand. What about it?"

"We're missing a knife," she grits out.

Ben's throat tightens. He swallows. What kind of a guy was Kindall, he'd thought, to pretend he's innocent although he was clearly the one to use a knife to stab his brother?

The growing horror doesn't go away. It just sinks deeper and deeper into his gut as the pieces of the puzzle connect.

Daniel's heavy footsteps pounding up the stairs. The slamming of his bedroom door. Rummaging in his drawers, cursing. He's clearly drunk, so Ben doesn't bother him, but he catches a glimpse of thick gloves in his brother's hands as Daniel marches back down the stairs.

Footsteps entering the kitchen and then leaving again straight after.

Kyle's fingerprints were on the knife. Did he really think that anyone would believe him?

The door slams shut.

That guy's got to be out of his mind to think anyone would believe he didn't do it.

The next Ben sees of Daniel is his dead body by the ambulance.

Ben had been sure that Kyle had killed his brother. As of now, though, he's no longer so sure.

Yuuki hits the send button and sits back with a sigh. *This isn't enough.*

It's only been a week and a half since he started looking at the case, but there's been nothing concrete to support Kyle's side of the story, no matter how much Yuuki searches for it. It seems like Timothy's having no luck either, which brings him back to the suspicion that information is indeed being withheld from them. It's something they seriously need to talk about again.

Since they haven't yet met up again in person, Yuuki hasn't yet told Timothy about the two men Kyle saw at the pub. He made sure not to even allude to it in the progress report he just sent. If even one person in the know intercepts the report, there's no telling what might happen to Kyle. There's no telling what might happen to them.

Lee always said that Yuuki worries too much, that something akin to the Ninao incident isn't likely to happen again. But Yuuki's not so sure, and it's not just the PTSD talking. If it's happened before, it can happen again. Last time took him completely by surprise – he's not letting that happen again.

Tonight, in particular, Yuuki's a little more anxious than normal. He's alone in the house, now that Lee's packed up and gone. Now would be the perfect opportunity for someone to –

Stop it, he scolds himself, though it's easier said than done when hypervigilance has his heart racing despite it being quiet and peaceful outside. *It's fine. You're safe. No one's out there.* But how does he know that?

Yuuki battles with his mind for thirty minutes before deciding he needs a distraction. He makes a coffee and then goes and sits down on the couch to watch a movie.

He settles on *The Lord of the Rings: The Return of the King*. Yuuki imagines Kyle watching it with him and wonders if this is his kind of movie. Who is his favourite character and what is his favourite thing to quote? Is he the type to watch in silence or someone who points out all the missing details like Joshua and Sam do?

He wonders if they all could be friends. Found family.

As the story reaches its climax, Yuuki finds his determination rising. He watches as the protagonists press on despite all odds and he feels a new sense of courage.

None of their efforts are for naught. Good still prevails.

And so will he.

11

All encouragement Yuuki gained from the movie last night is gone when he gets up. He tries to stay positive but his confidence is slipping.

Whoever set Kyle up are doing a darn good job of continuing their work, he thinks. *But there's no way I'm going to sit back and let them win. I'm not going to let them have their way. This is a fight I will not give up.*

A spark of hope flares in his chest again, but as soon as it does there's self-doubt telling him that his efforts won't be enough. Self-blame too, telling him it's his fault Kyle's still locked up since he hasn't been able find any substantial evidence that'll get him out of there.

Just be patient, he tries to tell himself. *It'll come. We'll find it.*

And what if it doesn't? What if we can't?

No. There's got to be a way around this. There has to be.

Yuuki hopes the fresh air on the way into work will help his state of mind. It doesn't. It's freezing outside and it only makes him miserable. The train ride is somewhat dull, what with the sky being grey and the people being cold and the train itself not being very warm in spite of it being late morning already.

Yuuki gets off the train silently praying he'll find it soon. He's been there, at the end of himself, and he's worried about how much longer Kyle's going to be able to endure all this. Kyle's been in prison for just shy of two weeks now, not including the three days he was kept at the station before the trial. Yuuki was stuck in isolation for seventy-eight hours and look what that did to him.

The circumstances might be different, but how different are they really? Going by what he and Timothy are finding, it could be said that Kyle was kidnapped under the guise of his imprisonment for manslaughter.

He arrives at the detention centre fifteen minutes early but goes in anyway. Inside it's warm. Yuuki feels a shiver run through his body as he signs in. Mitchell walks past with a grumble.

"Morning, Yuuki."

Yuuki blinks. "Uh, morning? Is something the matter?"

Mitchell grunts. "What do you think?"

"The cold is bothering you?"

"That kid's acting up."

"Who, Kyle?"

"Who else? Refused to eat breakfast and ignored everything I said when I asked him to clean up for your meeting."

Yuuki frowns. "That's weird. He's never been that stubborn."

"Well, this morning he is. Probably hasn't moved since I went in just now to get him up."

"You said he didn't eat. Did he last night?"

"Not much."

"Alright," Yuuki murmurs, a little perplexed. "I'll handle it... Did you ask if he was okay? Maybe something's wrong?"

Mitchell raises an eyebrow. "You think he answered me? And no, don't worry, I didn't raise my voice at him. I've seen how sensitive he can be. "

"Still seems a little strange though, don't you think? I'll talk to him."

"I figured you would."

Yuuki's brow furrows. He reluctantly takes the pair of handcuffs Mitchell hands him and makes his way down the hall to Kyle's cell. As he leaves the office, he notices the drop in temperature in the hallway.

A great sense of unease washes over him. *If I'm cold and I'm dressed in a thick winter jacket… how's Kyle handling this weather?*

Yuuki knocks on the cell door. "Kyle? It's Yuuki." No response. He waits a few seconds, but there's not even a gruff acknowledgement. "Kyle, I'm coming in, alright?"

He opens the door and his breath catches in his throat. Kyle is curled in on himself as much as he can manage, still as a rock. Something's got to be wrong if he's leaving his back exposed like this.

"Kyle?"

Before he steps into the cell, Yuuki flicks the light switch. Nothing happens. He tries it again and swears. If the light hasn't been working then the heat pump hasn't been either. At all.

The lack of difference in temperature between the hallway and the cell only confirms as much.

"Mitchell! We have a problem."

Yuuki doesn't wait for him. He tosses the handcuffs aside and moves to crouch down beside the bed. Kyle's facing the wall, so Yuuki lays a hand on his shoulder and carefully rolls him onto his back.

His lips are blue.

"Kyle," he says, tapping his cheek. "Kyle, can you hear me?"

Kyle's eyes stay closed. Yuuki can see him breathing, his chest rising and falling, but it's shallow. His skin is cooler and paler than it should be, but it's the fact that he's not shivering which sends alarm bells off in Yuuki's head. When he feels for a pulse, it's weak.

Get help, is his immediate thought. Then he remembers Timothy's warning and his heart sinks. Getting help means entrusting Kyle's life to someone else. If that someone else has any kind of connection to whoever set him up, to whoever allowed *this* to happen...

Mitchell appears in the doorway. His frustrated expression quickly changes when he sees whatever emotions Yuuki's got on his face.

"You're supposed to be checking on him," Yuuki says, voice tight. It's almost a growl. "It's been freezing this week and this is all he has?"

Kyle's only defences against the cold are the two blankets he's been given, one of which is barely thick enough to actually call a blanket in this weather, and the thin material of his short-sleeved prison clothes. There's no way that's insulating enough.

Yuuki sits down on the edge of the bed and pulls Kyle up into his arms. His head lolls back on Yuuki's elbow. It takes a lot of strength to his composure.

"I had Robert on most of the nightshifts," Mitchell says. "He reported in every shift..."

Yuuki holds Kyle closer as he slips his phone out of his pocket. "Who's Robert?"

"One of the two men on night shift. The guard who left the handcuffs on him."

Robert's actions sound deliberate. It's too suspicious to ignore, but

Yuuki can't worry about that now. There's more urgent matters to tend to.

He dials Timothy's number – the priority call number. Keeping Kyle's head supported on one arm, he brings the phone to his ear with his other hand. It's ringing.

Yuuki's heart beats faster. "Mitchell," he says. "Can you get another blanket, please? A decent one?"

Mitchell leaves. Kyle doesn't stir.

The ringing cuts out. "Yuuki?"

"Timothy. We have a situation."

A pause. "Give me a second." There's the sound of talking in the background, and movement, then Timothy is on the phone again. "What's going on?"

"Kyle. He's…I can't leave him here. He's hypothermic, unconscious. I just found out that the cell has had no heating for I don't know how long, and the light doesn't turn on either."

"We can organise a medical team to go in and –"

"*Timothy*. We can't do that."

"Why not?"

Because we can't afford to trust anybody. "Because," he says slowly, "there's not enough time. Kyle doesn't have that long." Yuuki closes his eyes a moment. "I…is there any way you can get him out of here?"

Legally they wouldn't be able to let Kyle go to hospital. Relocate him to another room until he's well enough to go back into isolation, yes – by which time the problem with the heat pump and the lighting will have been sorted out, yes – but that doesn't fix the underlying problem.

This place, this *treatment*…it's draining Kyle's life out of him.

117

"Timothy?"

Mitchell returns with the blanket Yuuki requested. He helps Yuuki tuck it around Kyle's body, wrapping it around his shoulders and folding the ends around his feet.

"Hang on a moment, Yuuki..." Timothy trails off, sounding preoccupied.

Yuuki's not sure how to take it and the uncertainty of what's going on is starting to get to him. He tries his best to stay calm, tries his best to keep himself steady. He readjusts his hold on Kyle so that he can hear Yuuki's heartbeat.

"I'm not leaving here without you," he whispers. "Just hang in there, Kyle. Please." Yuuki's voice pitches. He swallows. His eyes start burning and his legs start shaking, whether due to the cold or fear or both, he's not sure. "Just a little longer. I'll get you out of here."

The calm shatters. His throat constricts and he's crying. A crushing weight slams into his chest as a voice that haunts him says, *and what if you can't?*

Mitchell lingers in the room. Under normal circumstances, he would've called emergency services or at least, under Kyle's circumstances, gotten someone in to help. But Mitchell seems to understand where Yuuki's coming from, now that he's seen what Robert did – or rather, didn't do.

It's a long, painful five minutes before Timothy speaks again. Thankfully in that time Kyle's started shivering again, but he's not showing any signs of coming back around anytime soon. Yuuki's still crying.

"Yuuki, you there?"

He sniffs. "Yes. I am."

"You're clear."

Yuuki's expecting a long spiel. He waits, but those two words are the only thing he hears.

"You're clear, Yuuki," Timothy repeats. "Get him out of there."

He exhales sharply. "Y-you're serious?"

"Yes. I'm at the station just across the complex from the detention centre. Are you able to meet me there? Bring Kindall with you."

Yuuki doesn't trust the stab of hope in his chest. He doesn't understand how. He doesn't –

"Yuuki, stay focused. I know you're probably feeling overwhelmed right now, but so is Kindall. I need to write up an emergency discharge form but in the meantime, bring him over to the station. The heaters are on but it shouldn't be too hot for him. And don't worry about explaining to Mitchell – I'll handle that."

Timothy hangs up. Yuuki stares blankly at the wall for a few seconds before lowering the phone.

"What's the plan?" Mitchell asks.

Yuuki tries to answer but he's speechless. He shakes his head as he slips his cell phone back in his pocket, and then slides his arm under Kyle's knees.

"Yuuki?"

Kyle's dead weight puts a strain on his arms, but he's already moving. He stands and sidles past Mitchell, carrying Kyle out the cell door.

"Where are you going?"

"Timothy."

"With Kyle."

"Timothy said he's clear."

119

"He what?"

Yuuki's reaction exactly. "He said he's clear." *No time to think, just keep moving.*

As they pass through the heated office, Kyle's breath hitches. Mitchell hurries ahead to open the door for them, trusting Yuuki's word. Yuuki gives him a curt nod and then they're out.

Kyle's out. He's free. There's no walls surrounding him, only the three blankets and Yuuki's arms carrying him across the courtyard. Yuuki's eyes sting as he finds himself crying again.

He lets out a breath that billows out in front of them. "You're gonna be okay," he whispers. "Though I bet that's pretty hard for you to believe right now, huh?"

The administration foyer is flooded with warmth. Yuuki's surprised to see Sam standing by the desk with three friends, two who Yuuki recognises and another who he doesn't. The taller guy's face pales a little. Even Timothy, in spite of being warned, is visibly alarmed.

Someone lets loose a string of curses.

Yuuki lowers himself down on a bench by the wall, careful not lose his grip on Kyle. He slips his arm out from under Kyle's legs, tugs the blankets back in place. One of Sam's friends takes off her beanie and offers it to them wordlessly. Yuuki flashes her a forced smile and gratefully pulls it over Kyle's head. There's a pompom on it and it looks ridiculous, but it's the functionality Kyle needs, not the aesthetics, and he needs all the insulation he can get.

"We had a call come through," Timothy explains. "From the Wilsons. There happens to be a knife missing at their house. We also just received a statement from Miss Laura Smith, here. Long story short, we now have enough for a retrial."

Yuuki rubs his hand over Kyle's back. He's warming up, slowly. Shivering badly now, but that's a good sign. "I didn't think there would be," he murmurs. "I couldn't find anything…"

"Samantha," Timothy says, handing her a set of keys. "Go unlock the car for them. I'll be there in a second."

Sam takes the keys and heads out the door.

"Do you need any help?" the taller guy asks.

Timothy shakes his head. "Not right now, thanks, Avi."

Sam's friends take that as their cue to leave. Laura Smith stays behind to finish giving her details.

As patiently as he can, Yuuki waits. Kyle's shivering increases and the blue tinge on his lips fades. He stays unconscious, but after five minutes he groans. Yuuki can't put words to his relief.

"Alright, Yuuki," Timothy says. "You go ahead and get him in my car. Just look for Sam and you'll find it. I've just got to run this letter to Mitchell and I'll be right with you."

Yuuki picks Kyle up again and Timothy heads out of the building with a sheet of paper in his hand. As Yuuki goes to follow him out the door, he turns to Laura Smith and thanks her.

"Oh, it's…I'm glad I could help," Laura says. "Also, keep the beanie. Kyle needs it more than me right now."

He nods in acknowledgment. "Thank you. I'll return it to you via Sam when I get the chance."

It doesn't go unnoticed that she used Kyle's first name. Yuuki wonders if she knows him, from school or something. Sam had mentioned that Kyle went to their school. Whatever it is, all that matters right now is that she's one of the reasons Kyle doesn't have to stay here any longer and Yuuki couldn't be more grateful.

He finds the car easy enough with Sam and her friends waiting beside it. The doors are all closed, presumably to keep the cold air out.

"A bit longer than a second, isn't it?" she mumbles.

The shorter guy looks like he's about to add something, but then his gaze falls of Kyle's shuddering form and he stops himself.

Sam smirks. "You were about to say something stupid, weren't you, Logan?"

"It's cold, alright!" Logan protests. "I just…it feels wrong complaining about it when he's…"

Avi opens the back door and Sam and Logan shuffle aside. "I'm presuming you want to stay with him?"

Yuuki nods. "Thanks."

It takes some manoeuvring, but with Avi's help he manages to get Kyle settled in the back seat long enough for him to slip inside. He sees Timothy coming towards them from the other side of the carpark so leaves the door open.

"We weren't sure about whether or not to put the heater on," Avi apologises. "Didn't want to accidently turn it up too high."

"It's fine," Yuuki says. "We'll be away in a moment anyway."

Avi nods. "Good, good."

Behind him, both Logan and Sam have their worried gazes fixed on Kyle.

"Alright, you lot," Timothy says. "We're going to leave now. Thanks for sticking around."

Sam gives the thumbs up. "No problem. Do you want me to call Mum?"

"If you could. I'll ring her when we get home if she hasn't got back to me by then, so don't worry if you can't reach her."

"Okay."

"See you later on."

Timothy takes the keys from Sam and walks around to the driver's side. Since Yuuki's got his arms around Kyle, Avi closes the back door for them. Yuuki flashes him a small smile.

"Hang in there, Kyle," Timothy says as he gets in. "We're almost out of here."

Yuuki draws the seatbelt over himself and holds Kyle close against him. Timothy starts the engine. He puts it in gear and then they're moving, leaving behind the detention centre and the cold of the prison cell Kyle just finished two weeks of isolation in.

As they hit the road, Timothy glances at Yuuki in the rear view mirror. "How's he doing?"

Kyle's shivering has reached his face, his teeth chattering and eyebrows twitching every now and then. As far as Yuuki's aware, he's still yet to regain consciousness though.

"Better," Yuuki answers.

"And how are you?"

"Huh?"

"How are *you* doing?"

"Yeah," Yuuki says quietly. "I'll be fine."

123

He's well aware that his face is a mess of fresh and dried tears, but he hasn't given it much thought. He's still trying to comprehend the fact that what's happening right now is real and not just some kind of hopeful dream. The reality of it has yet to sink in. He doesn't think it will until he's heard the full story of how Timothy came to the conclusion that he did, that the evidence they had gathered in Kyle's favour so far is sufficient enough for a retrial.

As if reading his mind, Timothy clears his throat. "I know this is a lot to process for you already, but I'm going to have to warn you, Yuuki – the case isn't over yet. Once word spreads about the retrial…"

"I'm not letting anyone make him go back there."

"It might not be our choice."

"Then I'll fight for him. I didn't start the *Youth Rehabilitation* Trust for nothing."

"Ninao didn't happen for nothing, either."

Yuuki works his jaw. The next few minutes are tense. Both he and Timothy knew the stakes when they went into investigating Kyle's case. Those stakes are much, much higher now – for all three of them. Yuuki and Timothy have shown that they can win and Kyle's shown them that he can survive.

But they're prepared this time. Ninao caught them unaware, but this time they'll be on the lookout. Whatever happens, Yuuki will do all he can to keep Kyle safe.

"No matter what," he murmurs, "I'll keep fighting the good fight."

Timothy hums. "Remember you're not alone in this anymore. There's… something I need to talk to you about later. I had a talk with

Charlie earlier in the week. He said we might have a chance of turning this whole thing around."

Yuuki knows Timothy's not just talking about the case. He's talking about the injustice of the entire law change. "What…what do you mean?"

"Later. Let's just worry about getting Kyle settled first."

It's sensitive information, then. Something they can't risk speaking of aloud in case Timothy's car's bugged and the Harrisons, intelligent as they are, haven't found the bug. But if they've really got something big, then they might have something bigger than Kyle's case that they're looking at.

"Yuu…?"

Yuuki's heart skips a beat. Kyle's eyes are open. "Hey," he says.

Kyle mumbles incoherently. His brow furrows, eyelids slipping shut again.

"Just rest, okay? You're safe now. You're going to be okay, Kyle. You're going to be okay. You're not in that cold, dark place anymore and you don't have to go back there. Timothy and I are going to make sure that you don't."

He's not sure if Kyle hears him or if the words are just sounds floating around in Kyle's mind. Either way, Yuuki means what he said.

They're going to make sure that today is the last Kyle ever sees of that prison cell.

12

By the time they arrive at the Harrisons', Kyle's drifted into a restless sleep, still shivering and brow furrowed. Yuuki keeps him close against his chest until the car stops.

When Timothy gets out and opens up the back door, offering to give Yuuki a hand carrying Kyle inside, Yuuki's too afraid to let go of him.

"No," he says, shaking his head. "I can do it."

Timothy nods and steps back to allow Yuuki room to manoeuvre both himself and Kyle out of the back seat.

Kyle's no longer limp in his arms, but the way his head falls back over Yuuki's arm still has him worried. Despite having been cocooned in blankets, a beanie, Yuuki's jacket and a twenty-five minute car ride worth of warm air conditioning, the tension has yet to leave his muscles and he hasn't said a word since mumbling Yuuki's name earlier.

Yuuki's gut twists. The wind's picking up outside and there's patches of blue sky starting to show, the warmth of the Harrisons' house in cosy and comforting and the living room smells faintly of coffee, but all he can think about is that Kyle could've – probably would've – died today.

As he sets Kyle down on the longer of the Harrisons' two couches, that's all that's on his mind. The orange prison clothes Kyle's still wearing is a constant reminder of where he's come from, the too-pale shade of his face a reminder of how he could've ended up. It's shaken Yuuki in a way that he struggles to get his head around.

Timothy can see it. He's probably feeling it too. As soon as he shuts the door behind them, the first stop he makes is the coffee machine. It whirs and growls and fills the stillness of the house with noise. Kyle doesn't seem to hear it.

Holding Kyle with an arm around his shoulders, Yuuki begins rearranging the cushions on the couch. Once he's satisfied that Kyle won't get a sore neck or back from it, he lies him back down with his head and shoulders elevated by the cushions. Kyle's head rests against the arm of the couch, Laura Smith's beanie slipping off his head. Yuuki decides he should be alright without it now so just spreads the three blankets out over him a bit more.

"If you want to get him some more comfortable blankets," Timothy calls from the kitchen. "There's a pile of them in the linen cupboard down the hall. I'll go up to Joshua's room and grab some socks and clean clothes in a sec."

Yuuki frowns. Kyle needs more than just clean clothes – he needs a shower. His hair's greasy and tangled at the ends, and quite frankly he smells. The detention centre should've let him shower at least twice a week, but given the condition he was in when Yuuki went into the cell this morning, Yuuki wouldn't be surprised if all Kyle was given to wash with during his stay was a flannel and a bucket of cold water.

I should probably ask Mitchell about that Robert guy, he thinks, but Kyle is number one priority right now and Yuuki doesn't have the energy to be stressing any more than he is now.

"He'll probably want a shower first," Yuuki says. "It'd be nice for him to have a nice hot shower before changing. We can ask him when he's lucid. Don't want to cause him any more stress where it's not needed."

Timothy murmurs in agreement.

Yuuki's not fazed by the idea, but Kyle very well might be. If their roles were reversed, Yuuki certainly would be, what with how modest he is, not to mention that the two of them barely know each other. Those are boundaries that shouldn't be pushed past without permission, not unless the situation is dire.

Soon there's fresh cups of coffee on the table in the lounge, a glass of water and a steady hand on Yuuki's shoulder.

"He's going to be okay," Timothy murmurs.

Yuuki doesn't move from his seat by Kyle's side.

"He's gone from there. He's out…and we're going to fight for him." Whether Kyle hears it or not, Timothy says it loud enough for the three of them.

In the quiet, a cell phone rings. Yuuki flinches. It's his.

He looks up at Timothy with wide-eyes as he slips the cell phone out of his jacket pocket. Timothy frowns, but gestures for Yuuki to answer it and folds his arms over his chest, ready and waiting.

It's from an unknown number. Yuuki takes a deep breath and answers it. "Hello?"

"Takahashi, hello!"

The relief is palpable. "Mr. Smith, hi."

"Ah, Charlie is fine," the voice on the end of the line says. "I'm just making sure you were still good for our meeting today? I was just looking at the time, you see, and it's fifteen minutes past the time we arranged to meet at the other day."

Yuuki blinks. He shoots a glance at the clock on the wall and winces. "I am so sorry. I should've contacted you sooner. Something came up, so I, uh, I won't be able to make it."

"Is everything alright?"

Yuuki looks at Kyle out cold on the couch. "It will be. Listen, regarding Kyle, he – "

Timothy makes an urgent cutting motion over his neck, shakes his head and makes a phone gesture with his hand. There's a flash of warning in his eyes. *Not over the phone.*

"Yuuki?"

"Yeah, sorry," Yuuki says quickly. "I've got to go. Can I give you a call later?"

There's a pause. "Yes, that's fine."

"Sorry, Charlie."

"No need to worry! Talk to you later."

"Okay…bye."

Yuuki hangs up and lets out a sigh. Breathing in the aroma of the coffee waiting him, he gets up and takes the cup in his hands, frowns at it a moment and then downs half of it at once.

"You're all good, Yuuki," Timothy says, taking a sip of his own. "We're just going to have to be careful who we talk to and how we go about correspondence from now on."

Yuuki nods. "Yeah, no – thanks for the reminder. We don't know who could be listening."

He doesn't want to think too hard about it. The more he does, the more anxious he gets, what with flashbacks of what happened at Ninao flitting through his head.

They hadn't seen it coming. They still don't know the who or the why, only that Yuuki had gone into the Ninao office to meet Timothy and Joshua, and then, next minute, four masked guys had come barrelling through the door and knocked them both out. Joshua had managed to save Timothy but they'd gotten away with Yuuki.

Yuuki had woken up bound and gagged in an old garden shed, left there to die.

The only sense they've been able to make out of Yuuki's kidnapping last year is that when Yuuki established the Trust, he declared that he did not agree with Taularh's justice system. It nearly cost him his life, and Timothy's. Now, in freeing Kyle, they've just gone ahead and painted targets on their backs again.

The difference this time is that the people whose plans he just screwed up by setting Kyle free… they want to hide something they don't want anyone else to know about. They didn't want that information getting out. They didn't want *Kyle* getting out, and now he is, which means only one thing: at some point or another, they'll be coming for him.

How are they meant to prepare for that if they don't even know who they're up against?

"Hey, do you need to take a few minutes?"

Yuuki comes back to himself. He's been staring wide-eyed at a random spot on the floor, unblinking. When he glances back at Kyle, Timothy sets down his coffee cup and takes Yuuki's from his hands to set down beside it.

"I'll look after him. Go outside and take a breather."

Yuuki nods numbly. "Sorry."

"It's okay."

With a resigned sigh, he goes out onto the deck and just stands there, detached from the world, the weather and the birdsong. He's still trying to process the last hour. The shock of it all. The fear.

Yuuki looks out into the Harrisons' garden and counts five different things he can see. He thinks about four different things he can hear. Three he can feel. Two he can smell. One he can taste (which, as always, happens to be coffee).

He's got to believe that they'll all find a way, somehow, to succeed in making sure that whoever's after Kyle doesn't get to him. If they don't find a way, they'll just have to make one. Such optimism doesn't do anything to reduce Yuuki's apprehension, but it's at least reassuring to know that Kyle's not alone in this. Neither is Yuuki, for that matter, and neither is Timothy.

The question is, though, are they enough? It's one thing to say they'll fight and another to be strong enough to put up a decent one. Yuuki guesses only time will tell. He tries not to linger on the thought of how stressful the anticipating's going to be.

When Yuuki walks back inside, he finds that Timothy's replaced the three detention centre blankets with two much more decent and comfy looking ones. A pile of clean clothes wait next to the discarded blankets.

Kyle's awake. He stares at Timothy perched on the edge of the couch, not really registering who he's looking at. Then his gaze flicks sideways, seeking out Yuuki. As soon as he sees him, he keeps his eyes fixed on Yuuki's. Timothy gets up to give them space.

"Hey," Yuuki murmurs, coming around the coffee table to kneel beside him. "You warm enough?"

Kyle's lips part, as though he's trying to say something, but no words come. He just stares at Yuuki through tired eyes. Yuuki slips an arm beneath Kyle's shoulders and gently pulls him up against him, moving to sit on the edge of the couch as he does so. Kyle slumps against Yuuki, making no effort to move and probably not having any energy to actually do so. He's stopped shivering though, a major improvement.

"I know you probably don't feel like it, but do you think you can drink some water? You'll feel a bit better afterwards."

Taking the glass of water Timothy hands him, Yuuki brings it around in front of them so that Kyle can see it. Kyle stares at the water like it's nothing interesting, or that it's a task too energy-consuming to do, but Yuuki hears the low whine in Kyle's throat. He takes that as an answer. He carefully leans them back against the arm of the couch, enough so that Kyle's head is tipped back enough to drink, and then he raises the glass to his lips.

It's painful to watch. Kyle struggles to keep the water in his mouth long enough to swallow, and even then getting it down seems a mission. The first two mouthfuls make it down alright, but on the third Kyle makes the mistake of accidentally breathing in.

Timothy takes the glass from Yuuki as Kyle chokes and splutters and coughs, the water in his mouth spilling over his chin and soaking the edge of one of the blankets. Yuuki sits him up straighter and rubs his back in slow circles as they wait for the coughing fit to pass.

"You're okay, Kyle," he murmurs. "You're okay."

Kyle coughs some more and hangs his head with a groan.

"You want to lie back down?"

A small nod. He's out before his head hits the arm of the couch.

Timothy doesn't say anything and neither does Yuuki, but they're both appalled. They're both angry and they're both worried sick. Timothy gets a text message from Susan saying she's on her way but it doesn't do much to relieve their anxiety. They'd succeeded in getting Kyle out today, but what happens now? Between the two of them, and Charlie, they'll definitely be able to sort out some kind of living arrangement for Kyle, but in regards to the people who put him in isolation in the first place...

Yuuki looks down at Kyle and pulls the blankets a little further over his shoulders. They'll figure all this out, and in the meantime they'll make sure Kyle knows he's not alone.

13

The house is quiet with thought. Yuuki takes the opportunity to let his mind drift. Timothy offers to make him another coffee after he finishes the first and Yuuki doesn't say no. Kyle sleeps, completely out to it and colour easing back into his cheeks.

He turns to Timothy, frowning. "So... how did you manage to clear us so quickly anyway?"

"With what you wrote in the report," Timothy says, "plus my own findings and the several witness statements that have come in since the trial, it was enough to raise a question of doubt."

Yuuki blinks. "Several?"

"We had two separate anonymous statements in that past week and a half, plus Miss Smith's and the call I just got from the Wilsons. It's not yet enough to clear Kyle completely, but it's sufficient for a retrial."

Yuuki can't resist a smile hearing Timothy talking in his work voice. It means he's confident in his ability to argue what he's got and he's confident in his ability to argue it well.

They're a force to be reckoned with.

Twenty minutes later and a rumble sounds outside. Timothy gets up from his seat on the other couch to open the door for his wife. As soon as she's out of the car, Susan makes a beeline for Kyle, pausing only to place a hand on Timothy's shoulder. She's seething. Yuuki has only seen that set in her jaw once before, the first time she'd visited him at the hospital and seen the condition he'd been in after the kidnapping. It stirs a great warmth in Yuuki's heart seeing that she'd feel the same fierce love for Kyle.

She speaks in low tones, easy and reassuring. Kyle doesn't respond to anything she says, but he doesn't flinch at her touch either, meaning he's either fast asleep or Susan's presenting herself as someone trustworthy and kind. Yuuki thinks it's likely a combination of both.

In a couple of minutes she's lifted one of Kyle's arms to lie on top of the blankets, taken his temperature, pulse and blood pressure, and is moving on to set up an IV for him. Timothy fills her in with the other details of Kyle's situation, from finding him freezing in the cell to what Mitchell mentioned about him having not eaten anything substantial for at least a day. Susan nods and takes it in silently, eyes alight with concern as she disappears down the hall to fetch supplies.

After she's finished setting up the drip and assessing Kyle's condition, only then does she step out of the medical mind-set of her work. Without a word, she walks over to Yuuki and gives him a friendly pat on the back.

"You did good," she murmurs. "You and Tim, you…" *You saved his life.*

Yuuki ducks his head. He casts a sideways glance at Timothy, who's equally as unsettled by those unsaid words as he is.

"Thanks for coming, honey," Timothy says.

The smile she gives is a tight one. "All good. Although I am going to have to head back to the uni now," Susan says, looking at the clock. "I have a three hour lecture to teach. You'll call me if things start to go south, you two? I sure hope they don't, but if you need me back here sooner than four, I'll come."

"We will."

With a sigh, she takes her keys out of her pocket. "Sam will be back soon with pizza. I've warned her not to make too much noise, but you know what she and her friends can be like."

"I'm sure they'll be fine," Yuuki says. "We saw them on the way out, so they know the situation."

Susan nods. She glances at Kyle, checking one last time that he'll be fine while she's gone, then takes her leave.

The day passes by slowly. Yuuki watches over Kyle while Timothy gets to work on writing an official document for his 'temporary' release. To distract himself from worrying about all the things that could go wrong, especially now that Kyle's out of prison when some people don't want him to be, Yuuki plays a game of chess against his phone on difficult level. The distraction unfortunately isn't as effective as he'd have liked, and he finds himself battling his mind more than the computer in the game.

At about one, Sam brings home pizza. The lively chatter between her friends dies down quickly as they enter the quiet of the house. Logan casts a worried glance at Kyle as he helps Sam with the boxes of pizza.

"How's he doing?" he asks, putting Timothy and Yuuki's lunch down on the kitchen bench.

Yuuki nods and Timothy gives the thumbs up, but the lack of smiles is enough to make their apprehension known. Logan takes in Kyle's sleeping form and the IV connected to his hand as though that's the reason for Yuuki and Timothy's nervousness, but that's not even the half of what

Yuuki and Timothy are stressed about. Ninao is still on their minds, but they don't have the energy to explain that to the others so instead remain quiet.

Laura and Avi wait patiently in the entranceway. They can't see Kyle from where they're standing, but they're polite and remain where they are. Avi holds a couple of boxes of pizza in his hands waiting to be shared between the friends. Timothy locks eyes with Laura for a moment in a wordless exchange Yuuki doesn't understand.

When they have the house to themselves again, Timothy finally gives up the pretence. "Yuuki," he says, leaning his head into his hands. "I'm worried."

Yuuki, side-tracked from the game of chess, forgets about the knight waiting on the side of the board and loses a bishop to it. "Me too."

"No, you don't understand. Not fully."

"What…what do you mean?"

Timothy has never looked so stressed in his life. Yuuki's nervousness grows. "I know something; I figured something out earlier today, from your report. But you've got to understand, this is dangerous knowledge. I want to check a few things before I tell you, just to make sure I don't put you in any unnecessary risk, but…"

"Timothy?"

"All I'll say is that the stakes are much, *much* higher than we thought they were. Much higher. The less you know the better at this stage."

Yuuki doesn't like it, being kept in the dark, but he knows Timothy's only protecting him. If what Timothy's talking about is the same thing that Kyle supposedly know, then… "Okay, I understand," he says slowly. "I trust you to do what you think is best. But...what does this mean for Kyle?"

Timothy takes a deep breath. "I'm not sure."

Several emotions pass over his face, but it's hard for Yuuki to decipher them. It's likely that Timothy's still trying to process everything himself. Yuuki trusts his judgement, but he's worried about the weight of burden he's taking on by himself like this.

"Are you okay?" Yuuki asks quietly.

Timothy grimaces. "I just don't want to put you in the same position as Kyle."

"This is dangerous knowledge," he'd said. Yuuki had figured as much, but what Timothy seems concerned about involves a whole other thing to think about. Surely, though, if they continue going about this investigation in a quiet and legal manner, there won't be any necessity for Peace Force intervention – for Peace Forces to investigate the investigation themselves?

But who said that whoever's responsible for setting Kyle up is going to play by the rules to get what they want? If they're serious enough about their business that they'd go to such lengths as trying to kill someone and then later frame then when that failed, then they'll take whatever action they find necessary to ensure they achieve whatever it is they're trying to achieve. It doesn't matter how much we stay on the legal side of things.

All Yuuki can think of is Ninao.

Susan insists Yuuki stay the night with them and he gratefully accepts. They move the coffee table to the side of the room so that Yuuki can sleep near Kyle and so that, should Kyle wake in the middle of the night, he can find Yuuki easily.

The evening passes. Kyle does wake, shortly after Sam gets home at seven, needing to use the toilet. He clings to Yuuki's presence, eyes refusing to leave him, so Yuuki's the one who helps him up and helps him walk with stiff legs down to the bathroom. The IV stand won't fit when the door closes, so Yuuki leaves the door open and stands guard around the corner of the hallway.

Once Kyle's finished, he only manages to flush the toilet and wash his hands before he's too tired to take another step. He calls for Yuuki, who finds him bracing his hands on the vanity, arms shaking under the strain of keeping himself standing vertically. Yuuki hurries to his side to let him lean his weight against him, and the two hobble slowly back into the living room.

He almost suggests using this opportunity of Kyle being up and awake to get him into a fresh pair of clothes, but Kyle's looking ready to collapse any second so Yuuki dismisses the thought. As long as it isn't upsetting him, the fact that he's still wearing prison garments, there's not really any issue in letting him sleep in them. Kyle can shower and change in the morning, once he's rested.

Susan's finished setting up a makeshift bed for Yuuki by the time they return to the living room. It's a simple fold-out mattress laid out on the floor with a couple of blankets and a pillow, but Yuuki's so tired he'd be happy to crash right now. The thought is tempting, but he wants to stay up a little while longer to make sure Kyle's alright before he hits the hay.

As soon as Kyle's settled and sure that Yuuki's not going to be leaving him, he's back asleep again. Susan checks over the IV once more and then bids them good night.

It's only nine when Yuuki settles down for the night. He doesn't expect to fall asleep so quickly, but it doesn't take him long before he does.

Timothy leaves the kitchen light on when he goes to bed a few hours later, and the entire family, Yuuki and Kyle included, sleep soundly though the night.

Everyone except Timothy.

14

Kyle wakes to the sharp stinging in his hand being removed. There's a gentle hand on his, someone speaking kindly and in a quiet voice.

"Did you sleep alright?" the woman asks.

He stares at her, albeit a little blankly. He doesn't know how he should respond and he doesn't even know the answer to that question. The woman doesn't seem to mind though. She just smiles softly and presses a plaster on his hand where the IV was.

"It's okay," she says. "You don't have to push yourself to talk if you don't want to. I understand you've been through quite an ordeal. It's okay if words are hard."

Kyle's distracted by the sound of footsteps coming down a staircase. He tenses. It doesn't matter how exhausted he is – if he needs to run, he will this time. But the footsteps reveal themselves as belonging to someone he knows and he can't suppress his surprise.

"S'm?"

It clicks. Last night, Yuuki said something about this being the Harrisons' place, so this must be Sam's house. The woman must be Sam's mother and the wife of Timothy, the judge of his case.

Sam's eyes light up. "Kyle!"

As she comes over, her mother gets up from kneeling on the floor beside the couch and that's when Kyle catches sight of Yuuki. There's a mattress on the floor and Yuuki's passed out on it. Sam's mother steps over him as Sam sidles closer in the small gap left between where Yuuki is and the couch Kyle's lying on.

"You're looking better," she says, ducking into a crouch.

Kyle's caught off guard by the concern written all over her face. He doesn't know what expression he's making, or how bad he looks right now – he couldn't make himself look in the mirror when he went to the bathroom last night – but...

He fidgets with the blanket. "Hmm." He doesn't think it's necessary that she crouch down for him, but then again it does feel a little less intimidating, especially since he's lying down.

Beside them, Yuuki groans. Both Kyle and Sam glance over in time to see him raising his head from the pillow, hair ruffled and blinking wearily. The confusion clears from his face and becomes a relieved smile when he sees Kyle awake.

"Mornin'," Yuuki murmurs.

Kyle mumbles an automatic greeting in return and decides that a half-asleep Yuuki looks like a completely different person to warden Yuuki. He wonders what he's like outside of work mode.

"Morning, Sam," Yuuki says. He yawns. "Don't mind us, barging into your house like this."

Sam grunts. "You owe me coffee for all your snoring."

"What? I don't snore."

"Just kidding. Pretty sure Kyle would've told you if you had been." She turns to Kyle and grins. "Right?"

Kyle swallows. Hearing his name being spoken so casually is a shock to the system. Thankfully, Sam seems to notice that he's not up for much conversation and turns her attention away from him.

"So you guys are going back to yours, eh, Yuuki?" she asks.

Yuuki nods. "That's the plan."

"What time? Avi was going to make soup and maybe bring it over about ten."

Kyle has no energy to try to figure out the time let alone look for a clock. He's still trying to get used to the warm colours and comfy couch he's lying on…and the blankets – they're so warm.

He zones out to whatever they talk about, not really listening when Timothy walks in and starts talking to Yuuki about technical stuff and Sam and her mother talk about getting some of Joshua's clothes ready. Kyle's not sleepy enough to nap, but he finds it so hard to focus that he might as well be.

After a while, Yuuki gets him up to eat something, but Kyle can't find any appetite to get anything down. Maybe once he's woken up a bit more he'll be able to. Considering it's been a couple of days since he's eaten anything solid, he's a little reluctant to without knowing how his stomach will react.

Kyle ends up dissociating the entire morning. He doesn't have the energy to do anything but sit slumped in his chair at the dining table, just trying to breathe and try not to be overwhelmed by everyone's kindness. He tries to absorb the comfort everyone is offering him but it's like he's incapable of it.

They're acting like he's part of their family and not some guy who's been in prison the last two weeks. They're smiling at him even though he can't smile back. They're letting him just be without scolding him for scowling and not paying attention and not looking anyone in the eye but Yuuki and Sam.

He doesn't even know…

"Hey, Kyle?"

Kyle comes out of his daze and shifts his gaze from the sleeve of his prison shirt to Yuuki.

"I'm going to take you back to mine now, okay?" Yuuki says. "Well, Timothy's going to take us. He's the one with the car."

'Okay,' is what Kyle tries to say, but the words get stuck in his throat. In the end, he just nods.

Sam's mother – Susan – nods at the blanket he's got wrapped protectively around himself. "You can take that with you if you like," she says. "We have plenty spare and it might be nice to have something to hang onto while you recover. Something you can call yours."

"Besides prison clothing," Timothy adds.

Kyle frowns at that. "You're really not going to make me go back there?"

It's the longest thing he's said since…whenever the last time he had a meeting with Yuuki was. He expects there to be a hasty reassurance that he's not, or that Timothy will tell him that yes, he will be going straight back to that cell once he's well enough to.

He doesn't expect the hug Yuuki gives him. The arms around him are strong, sure and protective.

"No," Yuuki murmurs, leaning over in his seat and pulling Kyle closer.

144

"You are not."

Nothing more is said. Kyle doesn't move and neither does Yuuki, and when it's clear that Yuuki doesn't intend to let go – doesn't intend to give up on him that easily – Kyle lets out a shuddering breath and drops his head on Yuuki's shoulder.

A chair shuffles across the carpet and Yuuki's able to hold him better. He rubs a hand over Kyle's back, slowly, gently, like he did when they were on their way here. Kyle might've not been all that conscious then, but he remembers the touch that grounded him and pulled him out of the darkness.

More chairs shuffle as the others quietly leave to give them space.

"Kyle," Yuuki says.

He says it like it's him. That it's not the name of a prisoner, of a case. That he's a person, not a throwaway.

"No matter what happens, I will fight for you. Timothy got you a retrial. We were able to pull together enough evidence in your favour for one.

"People are going to fight against us. Bad people – the people who sent you there in the first place. But we will stand up against them, Timothy and I. We'll fight for you no matter what. You don't deserve what you've gone through and we're going to find out what exactly this is all about so that the whole world knows that too."

Kyle is having trouble understanding that those words are reality. They sound so far removed from the situation he's ended up it. If he could remember how to cry, he'd be doing so right now. Instead there's just an intense ache in Kyle's chest, a kind of force desperately trying to reach his heart. He knows it's a good feeling, but he's stopped feeling altogether and so it doesn't go further than his mind.

It reminds Kyle of how empty he's become.

Yuuki slowly releases him, watching him carefully. Kyle keeps his eyes downcast. Movement begins to creep back into the space around them. Sam says something about Avi taking longer than he thought he would and soup being delivered later. Timothy says something about Joshua's clothes and Susan replies back, and then Yuuki's helping Kyle to his feet and guiding him out the door.

Out the door.

It shouldn't affect him this much. It's just a doorway. There's nothing unusual about that. But it's a door that's *open* and he's free to go out it. It doesn't close when he approaches it. No one slams it in his face. No one forces him through it either. The fresh air rushes out through to meet him and Kyle finds himself so close to losing the small bit of composure he has.

The socks on his feet stop the gravel from hurting so much, keep the cold from seeping through. It's only a short walk to the car and Yuuki helps him the whole way. Kyle's throat closes up at the thought of being shoved in a car and taken back to the detention centre, but when Yuuki climbs in the back with him, his fear lifts a little.

Trusting Yuuki might end up being a mistake, but so far it hasn't turned out to be. It's not like he's got anyone else or anywhere else to go anyway.

Kyle spends the car ride to Yuuki's home staring blankly out the window. Everything's recognisable – the streets, the shop names, how this side of the city looks at this time of year – and yet it's all so foreign at the same time.

Trees look like 2D objects messing with his mind. People look like they're part of some simulation and he's not a part of it. He could vanish and no one would notice. He could be locked up in prison for the rest of his life for something he didn't actually do and no one would care.

Maybe Timothy and Yuuki should just send him back there. It's not like he belongs in this world and besides, he –

Yuuki's hand comes down on his shoulder. Kyle flinches, but Yuuki's expression is kind. Worried, even. Caring.

"You're gonna be okay," Yuuki murmurs. "We're going to get through this. Together."

Together? Oh, that's right. Sometimes Kyle forgets that Yuuki's dealing with stuff too. Somehow it makes the daunting task of remembering how to feel again a little less overwhelming.

15

They soon arrive at the small single story house that is currently where Yuuki lives. While Timothy gets the box of Joshua's clothes from the floor of the passenger side, Yuuki walks with Kyle to the house door.

It's hard to tell what Kyle's feeling right now, he's so expressionless. Yuuki's guessing it's going to be a while before the emotional numbness wears off. He hopes he'll be able to help Kyle through the chaos of it when it does.

When he opens the door, the first thing Yuuki does is walk in first. Until he has to move out now that Lee's gone, this is his house and Kyle's welcome to come in at his own pace. This isn't another prison cell. It's already a habit to open the windows as soon as he gets home, but Yuuki makes a point of opening all the windows he can. He pulls the blinds back the whole way and lets the light and fresh air stream in freely.

Kyle steps inside hesitantly. Yuuki notices how he pulls the blanket a little tighter around his shoulders, the way his eyes flit about the room, wary. He flinches when Timothy brushes past him with the box and finds the nearest wall to put his back against.

Hypervigilance, Yuuki realises. His stomach dips. There's a chance Kyle could develop PTSD from everything that's happened. Yuuki's not sure he's ready to see his own reactions expressed by Kyle.

"So this is where you'll be staying for now, Kyle," Timothy says, putting the box down on the table. "Yuuki's a good guy. He'll take good care of you, and I'll be around some time to check in with you both and see how things are going."

Kyle nods slowly. "It's…it's just you?"

Yuuki's not sure what side of that meaning he's on and it makes him nervous. "Well, my friend used to live here with me but we kinda parted ways last week, so it's just me now. Is that…is that okay with you?"

Kyle nods again, relaxing slightly.

With a sigh, Timothy glances between them both. "Alright. I'm going to head on back now. Got some work to catch up on and some official letters to write." He gives Yuuki a hug and pats him on the back. "Call me if you need anything."

"Thanks," Yuuki murmurs. "For everything,"

"No worries at all."

Timothy says bye to Kyle on his way out, shuts the door behind him and then it's just them.

The quiet is somewhat awkward, if not tense. "Okay, well," Yuuki says, "we've got a change of clothes now, so do you want to choose what you like, maybe take a hot shower before you change into them?"

Kyle just stares at the carpet and shrugs.

"It's up to you when you want to. You might feel a bit better once you're out of those clothes, that's all."

"Jus' wanna sleep," Kyle murmurs.

"You'll probably get a better sleep if you're in clean clothes."

"I jus'…I don't think I have the energy to. Sorry."

Yuuki's brow creases. "It's okay. You don't need to be sorry. Do you…would you like me to help you? It's totally fine if you say no. I want to be clear on that."

It's hard to decipher Kyle's initial reaction, but after a few moments of careful considering, he nods.

"Alright. Let's find you a change of clothes and then I'll show you where the bathroom is, yeah?"

Yuuki has no idea what Kyle's preferences in clothing are, but he doesn't seem fussed. They find a comfy-looking grey shirt and a pair of loose-fitting black trousers. It's warm inside the house, but if they're going to open the windows again after Kyle's had a shower, then he'll probably want a jersey as well as the blanket he's still clinging to. Kyle picks out an oversized one with Joshua's senior tutor class and year of high school graduation printed on the back of it, and then with a new pair of underwear that Susan bought from the department store on her way home from work yesterday, they head into the bathroom.

Yuuki wishes they had a Japanese bathroom, one with enough room so that they could both sit without any awkward trying to avoid getting water everywhere. They don't, of course, but they do at least have a shower with a bathtub as its base so they're not completely at a loss.

"Shower or bath?" Yuuki asks, the thought suddenly occurring to him that if Kyle's lacking energy then he's probably not going to have enough energy to stand.

Kyle stares into the bath, eyes unfocused. He clutches the blanket tighter and swallows. "Is it okay…?" He risks a nervous glance at Yuuki's expression. "Is it okay to have a bath instead? If you want to save water, I..."

"Of course it's okay," Yuuki reassures. "Don't forget, I offered." He puts the clean clothes on top of the vanity and then gets the warm water running in the bath. "I'll leave you to get ready. You can hop in whenever you want. I'll come back in another fifteen minutes, so take your time. Also, if you need to use the toilet, it's the room the next door down the hallway."

Kyle nods, blanket still wrapped around his shoulders. Yuuki almost asks if he can take it for him, put it in the lounge to avoid it getting wet. He doesn't, though. It's like an extra layer of protection for Kyle, a shelter, and he needs to be the one to decide when it's safe enough to put it aside.

He leaves the bathroom door open when he exits. While he's conscious of Kyle's privacy, he's also aware that that door is the only exit; just like the cell, the bathroom only has one way to come in and out of. The last thing he wants is to make Kyle feel trapped all over again and send him into a panic attack.

Yuuki waits in the lounge. There's enough time to boil the jug and make a coffee, so he does. He intentionally makes more sound in the kitchen than he usually would, wanting to reassure Kyle that he's not about to be snuck up on.

The whole time, Yuuki can't help but be anxious about how he's going about this whole thing. Is he doing it right? He's not being weird, right, asking Kyle if he wants help washing himself? Of course Kyle is going to have to do the more private areas, and there's no way Yuuki's going to be looking, but...what if Kyle thinks it's weird and uncomfortable?

There's more important things to worry about right now, though: Kyle needs to know that someone cares for him. Yuuki doesn't really know what he's doing, but he can do the best he can regardless – and that he will, even if it feels rather awkward and nerve-wracking at times.

Fifteen minutes passed, Yuuki leaves his half-finished cup of coffee on the bench and returns to the bathroom. He knocks on the wall outside the door before entering.

"Kyle, is it okay to come in?"

The water's not running anymore, so Kyle must've turned it off already. A mumble of a reply answers from around the corner where the shower is. Yuuki finds Kyle sitting slumped against the side of the bath, one of the towels Yuuki got from the hot water cupboard over his lap. He's staring at the water, arms around his knees, detached from himself.

Yuuki kneels down on the tiles with a flannel and a bar of soap in hand. "Is the water warm enough for you?"

Kyle hums. "'s good."

"Go ahead and run some hot water if you start getting cold, okay?"

"'kay."

"Okay. Now I won't touch anything sensitive, but is there anywhere that you're particularly sensitive about besides the obvious areas?"

"You're fine."

Yuuki dunks the flannel and the soap in the water. "Alright then. Just tell me if you want me to stop, okay?"

Kyle nods.

Yuuki starts at the shoulders. He works the soap and the warm water over Kyle's back with a gentle massage. Kyle lets himself relax and Yuuki doesn't rush. After he's done washing all he can, he hands the rest over to

Kyle and gets started on washing his hair.

It's an oily, tangled mess. The isolation unit is meant to permit two showers a week, but now Yuuki's wondering if Kyle was let out of his cell at all. Just because he was permitted to be escorted to the shower room doesn't mean he was – he was likely just given the second option of a bowl of water, a tiny bit of soap and a towel. Yuuki makes sure to give his hair a thorough clean. He needs it, both physically and emotionally.

Once he's done all he can for Kyle, Yuuki leaves him to soak and get out when he's ready.

Time drags on. There's the odd swish of water every now and then, reassuring Yuuki that Kyle's okay. He's probably lost in thought, Yuuki thinks, and finds himself zoning out to do the same. With his PTSD though, it turns out to be the wrong thing for him to do.

He's paranoid. Yuuki finishes his coffee and makes another, some strange adrenaline flowing through his veins for no apparent reason. He looks out the window and thinks he sees a shadow that's not a shadow. He listens hard for any sounds of anyone approaching the door – which is locked – but hears only himself and the occasional sound of Kyle's quiet presence.

The problem is that he doesn't know how much of this is situational awareness on 'be vigilant' mode, or if it's just that his anxiousness is beginning to wind up his PTSD. He's overthinking, he knows, but he's scared of being caught off guard like he was at the Ninao office.

He's afraid for himself, but more importantly, he's afraid for Kyle.

The afternoon passes both slowly and quickly. When Kyle finally emerges from the bathroom, he's still a shell and is too exhausted to do anything but sleep. Yuuki offers him his bedroom with the arrangement of Yuuki sleeping on the couch later on, but even with the small window in the room, Kyle finds it too much like the cell and refuses to take one step inside the doorway.

Yuuki understands it. He went through the same troubles readjusting last year after being released from hospital. Kyle is willing to sleep on the couch because there's space all around him to move. He can't be cornered. There's no doors that'll lock him in. If someone approaches him, he has room to move away. The open plan of the living room also has very little reminiscence of that isolation cell.

Before Kyle settles down, Yuuki shows him where everything is and tells him he can help himself. Of course, Kyle's not been able to do that for a couple of weeks, so he's not expecting him to feel comfortable doing so. Yuuki gets him what he needs until he can: a pile of blankets, intentionally more than Kyle will require and puts them down beside the couch; a glass of water out for him and puts on the coffee table; when he offers to make him lunch but Kyle declines, saying he's not hungry, Yuuki takes a couple of muesli bars from the pantry for when he is.

Once they're both finally settled, Kyle sinking into the couch wrapped up in the blanket again and Yuuki sitting comfortably on the floor, Yuuki puts on a movie once they're both settled. Twenty minutes in and Kyle's fallen asleep, curled up against the arm of the couch. It doesn't look all that comfy but Yuuki doesn't want to disturb him. He's still asleep when the movie finishes.

By that stage Yuuki himself is ready for a nap, and so he has to debate whether or not stay out in the lounge for this first night, or go head off to bed like he usually does.

In the end he decides the latter, seeing as Kyle knows where he'll be if he wakes and wonders where Yuuki went or needs him for something. It'll also give Kyle a bit less to be on guard about, not having another presence in the room to be monitoring.

Yuuki closes the windows and draws the curtains, turns the light on and leaves it on so that Kyle's not drowning in darkness when he wakes. He leaves the hallway light on, too, so he doesn't have to worry about hunting down the light switch on the way to the toilet if he needs it.

With one last check on Kyle, Yuuki heads to bed. It's earlier than the time he'd usually sleep but he's had it. Looking after someone like this is a whole new experience and a draining one at that. The few days are likely to continue to feel that way, but Yuuki hopes that at some point he and Kyle will be able to be friends, even brothers, and that this period of time in which Kyle's staying with him will be at least good starting point in Kyle's recovery.

That, he decides, is worth all the exhaustion the world could throw at him.

16

For the third time that night, Kyle wakes, only this time it's not because of hunger. His stomach feels weird. He sits up slowly, breathing deeply, and then his mouth starts watering as he looks at the empty muesli bar wrappers on the coffee table.

Oh no. Thank goodness Yuuki left the hallway light on.

He chokes on the desperation to keep quiet, to not wake the household which is Yuuki, but that only makes it worse. The sounds he makes are hideous. Kyle's still on his knees and retching when Yuuki comes in, but there's no grumbling at him or asking him to shut up or go outside if he wants to vomit. There's just gentle hands moving his hair away from his face and holding it out of the way for him.

"It's okay, Kyle," Yuuki murmurs. "Just get it all up."

He does. It takes a good ten minutes afterwards before his stomach settles, but at least there's nothing left to irritate him.

Yuuki grabs a length of toilet paper and hands it to him. "You feeling a bit better now?"

With a wary glance over his shoulder, Kyle nods. He wipes his mouth with the toilet paper and tosses it in with the rest of the mess.

"Don't worry about flushing the toilet; I can do that for you. Why don't you go and get a drink of water?"

Kyle nods again, on the brink of tears. He can't understand why Yuuki hasn't snapped at him yet. It's the middle of the night and Kyle clearly woke him up. He shouldn't be imposing on him like this as it is, not when Yuuki's already doing so much for him. And yet it's like Yuuki *wants* to help – he wants to help *him*. It's a little too much for Kyle to get his head around.

Yuuki helps him to his feet and ushers him away from the stench. Kyle wanders into the bathroom to wash his hands, miserable, and nearly trips over his prison clothes that he left dumped on the floor after the bath he took yesterday. With a groan, he stumbles over to the basin and washes his hands in the semi-darkness, the light adequate enough to see by but not enough to see himself in the mirror by. Kyle doesn't want to see the person he's become just yet.

Whether he wants to or not, that choice is nearly taken away from him when Yuuki comes in to wash his hands too and turns the light on.

Dark hair in his peripheral. Off-colour white. Kyle flinches violently and jumps away from the mirror before he can see the expression in his own eyes. Yuuki frowns at him, brow creased, but Kyle's heart is beating too fast. He's too full of nerves to wait around to hear what Yuuki has to say to his over-the-top reaction. Hastily drying his hands, Kyle leaves.

It's overwhelmingly confusing. It was just his reflection. Why is he so jumpy over seeing his own reflection? Hugging himself, he speed walks back down the hallway, snatches the empty glass off the coffee table, goes to the kitchen and downs a cup of water.

He's shaking with adrenaline and frustration and confusion and a tidal wave of emotions threatening to tear him apart. Kyle curls his fingers around the glass, gripping it tighter and tighter. He hears Yuuki's footsteps growing closer and his skin pricks with anger, fear and more confusion at why Yuuki would be so *kind* when Kyle's done absolutely *nothing* to deserve it.

It's too much. He can't take it anymore. High on adrenaline, he whirls around and smashes the glass on the floor.

Yuuki steps out of the hallway as it happens.

Kyle's eyes stretch wide. He's breathing too quickly. He's angry – why is he angry? He shouldn't be, he can't be, because Yuuki will realise he should've believed everything everyone said about him – all the statements saying Kyle's a discipline case, saying he's violent and temperamental and has anger issues and needs to learn some self-discipline and should be locked up in prison for something he didn't even do –

Stepping carefully over the broken glass, Yuuki approaches quietly and pulls him into a hug. "It's okay."

Kyle stiffens. Waits for the lecture. Waits for the backlash, a punishment, a hit on the back of the head, or at least a warning. It never comes. There's just Yuuki, holding him carefully, breathing slow and steady. Kyle growls low in the back of his throat, eyes burning, almost daring him to react, but Yuuki's body language doesn't change.

"I know you're hurting," Yuuki murmurs. "You're hurting far more than you realise. These…reactions that you're having…they're going to keep happening for a while. I don't know how long – it might only be a few days or it might be weeks – and it's going to be confusing and frustrating and scary… but know that I'm here for you when it happens."

Kyle's throat constricts.

"If you want to be alone for a while, that's cool. If you need someone to talk to or just need a hug, I'm here. Just give yourself time to process everything, yeah? Don't rush it – take as much time as you need."

What does he say…? *I'm sorry? Thank you?* But it turns out Yuuki's not expecting an answer and he's not mad that Kyle doesn't give him one. It takes Kyle a moment to realise why: Yuuki's been here before. He's been here in the terrible confusion and the over-exaggerated startle reflex and the hyper-awareness that Kyle will learn is called hypervigilance. He *understands.*

After Yuuki's helped him clean up the broken glass and wipe the small puddle of water up off the floor with a towel, Kyle goes to sit on the couch. Before Yuuki joins him, he finally remembers to put the washing machine on, so there's a load of clothes and Kyle's prison ones going through now. The hum is a soothing addition to the quiet.

Kyle tucks the blanket further around himself. "I just don't understand why this is happening to me."

Yuuki is quiet, listening, taking in, thinking. "I know."

"I don't even remember what I used to act like before…this."

The clock ticks past three in the morning.

"Yuuki?"

"Hmm?"

"Is this what your PTSD is like?" Kyle hates the way his voice breaks on the last words. He hates himself for sounding so afraid.

Yuuki clears his throat. "The first stages of it, yes. But anybody who's gone through bad trauma is likely to be on edge for a while after whatever it is that happened to them, so…while I'm not trying to invalidate what you're going through, there is a chance that you'll be okay after a while. PTSD takes a lot longer to work through. A lot longer. Sometimes it can take months or even years before it's even recognised. You just have to take one day at a time, each moment as it comes, PTSD or not."

He pauses, and though Kyle's not looking in his direction, he can feel Yuuki's gaze on him. "Can I...do you mind if I ask you about your foster family situation before all this?"

Kyle's nostrils flare. "Why?"

"Have you heard of Complex Post Traumatic Stress Disorder?"

"No."

"It's different from PTSD itself in that it's developed over a much greater period of time, not just a one-off shocking event. The symptoms are similar but they're different too. I'm only speaking from what I've heard, but...it's just something to think about. If how you were treated at the detention centre is something you've experienced before and for an extended period of time, then you're likely to experience healing from such trauma in a different way to what I am.

"In other words, if you see me having reactions that you don't, don't – in any way – invalidate yourself. People react differently to different trauma and also deal with it in different ways."

Kyle's not had enough rest to be able to fully understand what Yuuki's saying, but the words 'don't invalidate yourself' stick with him. He struggles with the idea of allowing himself to think that way though, since nine times out of ten he *did* deserve all the lectures and the punishments he received – at least, that's what his brain tells him.

It's because of that way of thinking that Kyle's not ready to tell Yuuki

160

about what his foster home was like. Half of that is because he doesn't know how to. No one's ever asked him if he was being treated well there, not even the child protection services who placed him there.

The conversation peters off there and doesn't pick up again. Kyle wants to ask about Yuuki's coming to terms with his post-traumatic stress, but he's too tired to focus enough to do so.

They sit in silence for a while, both of them too awake to sleep. The washing machine beeps and Yuuki gets up to replace the clothes with a load of towels. After he's hung the washing on the clothes horse, he boils the jug and makes them both hot drinks which they drink together on the couch. Yuuki's falling asleep before he's taken more than two sips of his coffee and Kyle's finding the hot chocolate in his hands equally lulling.

They're back to sleep, Yuuki having retreated back to his bedroom, before the dawn comes.

Kyle comes awake to voices. He tenses, keeps his eyes closed and listens.

"Yeah, Avi says he's really sorry. He thought he had all the ingredients he needed to make it, but he apparently didn't, so…that's why it's late. I hope you guys didn't starve."

Yuuki laughs softly. "It's alright. We managed. Thanks, Sam."

So that is *Sam's voice.* Kyle forces himself to relax and pushes himself upright. The digital clock on the TV reads 10.45am.

"Ah, sorry, Kyle," Yuuki says. "We didn't mean to wake you."

Kyle covers his mouth with a hand to hide a yawn. "'s fine."

He turns to see Sam grimacing apologetically, hands dug into her short pockets. Yuuki ducks his head. Kyle blinks.

Yuuki nods at Sam. "If you see Avi, tell him we say thank you. I'd completely forgotten he'd offered to make something for us."

"Will do," Sam says, giving the thumbs up. "I've gotta head over to his place to finish a group assignment we've been working on all holidays, so, uh… I'll definitely see him."

Not really interested in their conversation and feeling out of place listening to it, Kyle takes himself off to use the toilet. He still refuses to look at himself in the mirror afterwards. At least he was able to sleep off a lot of the nervous anxiety that had filled him last night…this morning.

Kyle takes a deep breath as he leaves the bathroom. He hopes he doesn't have to experience that again anytime soon, no matter what Yuuki says about it probably happening again.

When he gets back to the others, Sam is standing over the couch getting ready to leave.

"How's Timothy doing?" Yuuki asks as Kyle slips in.

"Yeah, he's a little stressed. Won't tell me why, though." Sam fidgets with the cushions leaning against the back of the couch. *"Anyway*…I'd better get going. Got to finish this assignment off to hand in on Monday."

"Tell your Dad to be careful not to burn himself out, will you?"

Sam smiles wryly. "I'll try."

"Bye, Sam."

Kyle feels himself relax when it's just him and Yuuki again. He trusts Yuuki, he realises. He's not sure about Sam because he doesn't know her all that well. He may have been more trusting when he was still a little out of it, but now's a different story.

"So," Yuuki says, including his head towards the bowl on the table.

162

"This lemongrass soup smells pretty good to me. You hungry?"

Kyle frowns. He mentally questions his stomach and his appetite and decides he is.

The soup is good and settles well. It's the best food he's tasted in a long time, such a long time that he finds himself tearing up at how good it is. It's like he can *taste* that the soup's been made with care, with love, by someone who cares about what they're putting into it and about who will be eating it.

Kyle only knows Avi as a classmate from school, and vice versa, and yet he'd go to this length to make something nice for someone he didn't even know.

His heart struggles to understand how these people can be so *kind*.

Yuuki smiles softy but makes no comment.

Between them they finish off half the soup, since Yuuki's not been eating all that much recently either. Kyle is able to keep the food down, which is a big plus, and it does a great deal for his mood.

...until there's a loud bang on the door.

Yuuki freezes, hand on the refrigerator door he's just closed. Kyle sits ramrod straight in his seat at the table, heart pounding. They exchange a wide-eyed glance and Kyle sees his own fear in Yuuki's eyes.

That wasn't just a knock.

"This is the Peace Forces! Open up!"

17

The house is dead silent for a heartbeat. Then Yuuki crouches down low and gestures at Kyle to do the same. "Get away from the windows," he hisses.

Kyle's blood runs cold. He scrambles off his chair and crawls over to hunker down in the kitchen with Yuuki.

Another bang, this time on the door handle. "This is your second warning. Open up!"

Yuuki reaches up to one of the drawers and quietly slides it open. He takes the handle of a knife in his hand. Kyle tries his best not to have a panic attack right then and there. A kitchen knife is what Daniel Wilson tried to use on him.

A smash. The lock breaks.

Kyle swallows. "Yuuki..."

Something happens then, before the door bursts open. Kyle sees Yuuki's white-washed face. The bone-deep fear in his eyes. The way the knife shakes in his hand. But he also sees the fierce determination in the crease of Yuuki's brow, in the way he's crouched, ready to spring, ready to *defend* and *protect*....

Kyle's going to do the same for him.

Three men barge in. Kyle and Yuuki come out of hiding and launch themselves at them.

Two go for Yuuki. Kyle lands a kick on one of the guys' knees. The third man grabs him from behind. He wrestles out of it and drops to the ground, out of reach. A flash of metal and the knife is knocked from Yuuki's hand. A fist to Kyle's head. Pain. He rolls out of the way before the second punch lands.

Kyle knows why they're here. Yuuki knows why they're here. Kyle's out of prison, out of isolation, out of their control and they don't like it. They've come to take him back – whether that be to the prison cell or an abandoned garden shed, it doesn't matter. Neither of them are letting themselves or each other be taken.

But they've hit a lemon jackpot: Kyle's not up to his usual strength, both of them are sleep-deprived and they're three on two. And, as they now realise, as well as the random folded up cardboard box that was carried in, these men also have a blaster.

Yuuki screams.

Kyle is distracted long enough for his opposition to get the upper hand. A punch to the gut. Kyle doubles over and the next thing he knows there's two arms wrapped around his chest, pinning his arms to his sides. He's pulled around to face the other side of the room.

Yuuki's on his knees, pressed up against the wall. There's a burn on his right arm. A bad one. The blaster might be a silenced one, but that in no way lessens its impact. Yuuki's other arm is twisted and pinned behind his back, one of the guys holding him there by the wrist and the back of the neck.

Yuuki's eyes meet Kyle's and anger burns in the pit of Kyle's belly. Yuuki's scared to the bone. For *him*.

"What's your problem?!" Kyle shrieks.

The man holding him tightens his hold. "Our problem," he growls in his ear, "is you."

"I did nothing!"

"You were in the wrong place at the wrong time and didn't leave when you were supposed to."

Kyle's eyes widen. The man – no, woman – holding the blaster against Yuuki's already blasted arm is one of the 'guys' he saw at the bar.

"We know you two know things," the woman says flatly, "so spill it before this gets out of hand."

Yuuki grimaces. "What do you mean, 'we know'?"

"The princess. Where is she?"

Kyle struggles to get free but when he does the leader presses the blaster harder against Yuuki's wound. Yuuki clenches his jaw.

"The princess. Tell us where she is now or we'll do it the hard way."

"We don't know about any princess," Yuuki grits out.

The woman scowls. "My name is Deborah. I'm affiliated with Commander Jeff and also happen to be his lead interrogator. Does that prompt your memory?"

Lead interrogator. They don't plan on simply kidnapping the two of them.

Kyle's finding it hard to breathe. "We don't know where this princess you're looking for is and we don't even know *who* she is, so just let us go already!"

"Ain't gonna happen."

"But like I said, we –"

"Here's what's going to happen," Deborah says. "You're coming with us. You're going to cooperate and your friend Takahashi is too. In a moment, you are going to be still and not move. If you do, he gets shot. Is that clear?"

Kyle swallows. He locks eyes with Yuuki's. It's impossible to read what he's thinking beyond fear. Deborah takes his silence and inaction as a yes and gives the guy holding him a nod. Kyle's thrown to the ground. He barely has time to catch himself before there's the sound of duct tape being drawn.

His vision whites out. When rough hands grab his arms, Kyle reacts instinctively and flinches away. Yuuki yells. He's been shot a second time. Kyle freezes. His arms are yanked behind his back. He lands on his face, instinctively moves again and Yuuki's shot a third time.

No...

Duct tape on his wrists, wound tight. Kyle's heart feels ready to explode. He bites his lip when the guy grabs his feet, forces himself not to cry out, not to move, not to react. His ankles are bound as well. Yuuki's crying as he watches it happen.

The cardboard box is prepared. Kyle lets out a sob. The guy bends down in front of him, tears a strip of tape off the roll and presses it over Kyle's lips.

Yuuki isn't shot again.

Deborah's eyes gleam. "Good. Now, here's the deal," she says to Yuuki. "You can go, Takahashi. Kindall can't. If you want him back, you give us the information we want and if it turns out to be true we might be so kind

167

as to consider it."

A business card is dropped on the floor. The guy pinning Yuuki to the wall lets go and Yuuki doubles over in pain. Deborah keeps the blaster trained on his arm.

The two men pick Kyle up. Kyle sobs, muffled this time. He keeps his eyes locked with Yuuki's as he's loaded into the cardboard box. It's cramped. His knees are bent and his fingers are squished between his back and the side of the box, his head tucking in against his chest so that he actually fits. He can't see Yuuki any longer. Kyle's panic skyrockets but he stays as still as he can. The cardboard flaps close over him.

Darkness. The sound of duct tape. The box is taped shut. Kyle whimpers.

There's no more shouts of pain.

The door opens. Kyle chokes on a cry of terror. Avi's soup is no longer so comfortable in his stomach. He's lifted off the ground. The sounds of outside rush to meet him. He's jostled about in the box by the mens' heavy footsteps as they carry him. He tries not to think too hard about what's coming, but it's inevitable. It's not just him he has to worry about, it's Yuuki, too. It's Yuuki who –

Two short, sharp whistles. The men yelp. The box drops and Kyle cries out through the tape as it hits the concrete.

Chaos. There's a scuffle, shouts, familiar voices. The tape sealing the box shut is ripped open.

Sam swears. "Hold on, Kyle. I'll get you out of there."

She brandishes the pocket knife she's got and quickly but carefully cuts through the bindings on his wrists and ankles. She helps him sit up so that he can get his arms back around in front of himself, then braces one hand against his face and pulls the tape off his mouth.

His lips burn. As Sam helps him out of the box, Kyle breaks down sobbing. "Yu-Yuuki's…"

Sam slings an arm over her shoulders, lets him lean on her. "It's okay. Joshua's getting him now."

Kyle's knees are trembling. "No, he – Yuuki, he's…"

"C'mon, Sam, let's go!"

Behind them, Timothy barrels out of the house with a pile of electronics and paperwork in his arms. Kyle recognises Yuuki's laptop and the folder he had sitting on the dinner table.

"Kyle…"

Kyle inhales sharply at Yuuki's voice. Sam's older brother, Joshua, emerges from the house, Yuuki leaning heavily against him. Yuuki's face is dangerously pale, his right arm hanging limply in front of him. The burns are discoloured with internal bleeding and swollen with what is most likely shattered bone.

Before either one of them can be sick, Sam and Joshua get them to the car. It's not Timothy's, and Susan's waiting in the driver's seat, her expression full of fire. When she sees the state of Yuuki's arm, she curses and flings the car door open.

"Tim," she says. "You're driving."

There's six of them and only five seats, but they don't have time to negotiate. Timothy piles the stuff in his arms into the boot and takes the driver's seat. Sam guides Kyle around the car to the rear door on the far side and hops in the passenger seat. She rolls the seat forward as far as it'll go, Susan climbs into the back of the car with a first aid kit and then Joshua's getting Yuuki in from the other side. As soon as Susan's dragged Yuuki across the back seat towards her and Joshua's hopped in and closed the door behind him, they're driving off.

Kyle doesn't see what's become of Deborah and her men. He's too afraid to look anywhere but Yuuki's face.

Susan deftly ties a tourniquet around Yuuki's upper arm. Yuuki groans, chest heaving. Joshua keeps trying to check in with Kyle, talking to him from his crouch between the driver's seat and the back seat where Yuuki's feet are, but Kyle struggles to concentrate on the words being said.

Yuuki's unconscious by the time they reach the motorway, passed out with the overload of panic and pain. Joshua and Susan keep talking, Joshua to Kyle and Susan to Yuuki. Their voices are steady and as calm as being in a situation like this can possibly allow, but Kyle zones out completely to what they say. Something about breathing or him needing to breathe?

Their voices are the last thing Kyle hears before he faints.

18

They're still on the road when Kyle comes to. The city has changed to farmland and remnant patches of bush, and Yuuki's face has grown ever paler.

He turns his head where it rests against the window. Joshua looks stricken. Behind his concern for Kyle is a cold fear. Kyle feels it too. It's evident in Susan's eyes as well. She keeps her gaze fixed on either Yuuki's face or his arm while she runs her fingers gently through Yuuki's hair.

Joshua watches him carefully. "Kyle, are you okay?"

Kyle's too distracted to give any verbal reply. Yuuki's arm…it's bad. The burn is weeping and the skin all around it is an abstract of red, purple, blue, yellow and white that it shouldn't be. Susan dabs a cloth against the wound every now and then, but there's little else she's able to do for him while they're still travelling in the small space of this car.

"It's going to take us about forty-five minutes to get where we're going," Timothy says. He glances at Kyle over his shoulder. "If you need me to pull over, I can do that but we can't stop for long. Cool?"

There's nothing he can think of to say. Kyle numbly realises that, while he was out, someone took off the duct tape that had been still stuck his wrists and ankles. He spies it sitting as a wad of black shoved into the back pocket of the driver's seat, just out of view but not quite hidden enough.

Sam peers around her seat. "How's Yuuki doing?"

Susan presses her lips together, brow creasing. Her hesitation is enough to drive a spear of dread into Kyle's gut. He has to remember to breathe.

"He might lose his arm, Sam," Joshua says tightly. "We might not have the resources to save it."

"It's my fault," Kyle whispers.

Susan looks up sharply. "It is most definitely not your fault. Don't you dare go blaming yourself. It was enough trouble when Yuuki did."

Why Yuuki would feel the need to blame himself for anything, Kyle's not sure. He's always trying so hard to do what is right, to fight for others even when he doesn't know them at all. It makes no sense.

If anyone should've been shot, it's me. Yuuki…he doesn't deserve any of this.

"You heard…Susan…"

The inside of the car falls dead silent. Yuuki's awake.

"D'n't blame y'rrself…" Yuuki murmurs, eyes still closed. "I's not your faul'."

Kyle swallows. "But I –"

"I'll be fine. Jus' glad…glad they didn't take you…"

He opens his eyes then, just a fraction, and stares hard at Kyle for a few seconds before they focus. Yuuki's throat moves as he tries to find the voice to speak but Susan cuts him off with a gentle tap on the forehead.

"Try not to talk too much, 'kay?" she says, frowning. "You two can have this conversation later."

Yuuki doesn't take his eyes off Kyle. He grimaces, jaw clenching tight with pain. Kyle wishes he could do something for him. He can't take hold of his hand because his arm's injured and the tourniquet's probably too tight for him to feel it anyway. Kyle's not one for touch either, so he has no idea how to help. He decides to copy Susan's example and rests a shaky hand on Yuuki's forehead. Something about the physical connection is enough to put Yuuki at ease. He closes his eyes and exhales slowly, the crease in his brow easing but his face losing yet another increment of colour.

"Yuuki," Kyle whispers. "You're gonna be okay, 'kay, so don't...don't push yourself for me."

He doesn't trust himself to speak any louder but Yuuki hears every word he says. Susan does too, and she hums in agreement. "Just focus on conserving energy," she says, "and stay awake if you can."

They watch as Yuuki drifts in and out of lucidity, sometimes fully awake and aware and other times so out of it that he slips unconscious for a minute or two at a time. Kyle keeps his palm resting on Yuuki's forehead and Susan keeps brushing her fingers through his hair.

The last fifteen minutes of the drive are the worst. Sam no longer asks after Yuuki. She only has to look at her brother's expression to know, and the grim silence filling the vehicle is sign enough of Yuuki's condition.

Yuuki's getting worse. Kyle can't bear to look at the arm anymore because of how discoloured it looks. There's no hospital this far inland. While he decides that he trusts Susan's abilities, one glance at Joshua's expression confirms he's come to the same concluding thought: they're not going to be able to save Yuuki's arm.

"We're almost there, guys," Timothy says at one point, his voice betraying how unsettled he is.

They veer off the main road onto a narrow gravel road. Susan adjusts

173

her hold on Yuuki to keep him as still as possible, but it doesn't stop the gravel road from jarring his injured arm. Yuuki whimpers the whole way down. Kyle grits his teeth, stomach swirling. Joshua reaches out and lays a firm hand on his shoulder. To his own surprise, he doesn't flinch.

The place they come to is a simple yet large country house. The weatherboards are weathered and there's a cracked window at the front with cardboard and tape fixed in place behind it. Kyle fixates on it, too hard, too much, but then the car's stopped and people are moving and Kyle is stumbling outside.

"Room's ready, Mrs Harrison!"

Kyle stands where he is, stunned, as his youth advocate comes jogging down the porch steps with a stretcher. *What on earth is Charlie doing here?*

There's little time for any more on that, however, as Susan, Joshua and Charlie work together to manoeuvre Yuuki out of the car. Kyle blanches at the sight of the arm. He staggers towards the edge of the bush neighbouring the property, knowing what's coming. Yuuki cries out. Kyle loses his lunch.

A gentle hand on his back. In his peripheral, the dark green of Sam's shirt. He wonders for a second where her black jacket went, then a comforting weight of warmth settles around his shoulders and he shivers.

"It's a bit colder out here, eh," Sam murmurs.

Kyle doesn't reply. He's too busy trying to distract himself from Yuuki's pained groans and the incoming urge to throw up again.

Susan and Charlie's voices disappear inside the house with along with Yuuki's. A bird sings nearby. Shoes crunch on gravel, one heading into the house also and the other coming over to crouch on Kyle's other side.

Joshua rubs his back. "He's going to be okay."

The rest of Avi's soup becomes garden fertiliser.

"Do you want to come inside? The others will be here soon. They – oh, never mind. Here they are."

Tires rolling down the gravel driveway. Kyle finishes heaving and wipes his mouth with the back of his hand. He doesn't bother hiding the evidence that he's been crying. He's too much a shaken mess to care.

Sam and Joshua help him stand as the car pulls up. Neither of them make him stand on his own after they do, instead each keeping an arm hooked around his. Kyle needs it.

It's a few of his classmates. Laura Smith parks the car and then Logan and Avi jump out, staring at Kyle in wide-eyed concern. Logan has a high-tech rifle slung over his shoulder.

"Man, are you okay?" Logan murmurs. "You look awful."

Avi grunts. "What, you expect him to be okay after all that?"

"You know what I mean."

Laura gets out of the car and shuts the door behind her with enough force to make Kyle jerk backwards. She quickly apologises but his heart is already racing. He's too overwhelmed.

He thought he was going to die in that prison cell. Then he wakes up in a warm house with kind people, after which he's welcomed into Yuuki's home and then almost *kidnapped,* and Yuuki…

Kyle chokes on a sob. "Yuuki…"

Joshua steers him around to the face the open door of the house. "Come on, let's get you inside."

It's not much warmer inside, and the faint smell of cleaning products lingering in the air says that until recently this place wasn't a permanent residence. The furniture, at least, isn't coated in dust, so whoever did the cleaning must've done a thorough job.

They bring Kyle over to an old sofa. It's a little tattered but it's comfy beyond what he could ask for. Sam doesn't ask for her jacket back, but it's too small for Kyle to hide in and the others see that. Laura ducks out of the room and returns with a blanket as thick and heavy as the one from the Harrisons' that Kyle regrets having to leave behind. She takes Sam's jacket, sets it down on the couch beside him and drapes the blanket over his shoulders in its place.

"I'm sorry," Laura says softly, not making eye contact. "I'm sorry for everything that you've had to go through. This happened because of me and I...I suppose I owe you that explanation."

Kyle has no idea what she's on about. The atmosphere in the living room grows tense. Joshua hunts down a box of matches and sets about lighting the fireplace. Logan puts the rifle down by the sliding doors and follows Avi into the kitchen. The jug boils. Sam hangs around nearby.

Laura kneels down in front of the sofa. "Those men...they were never truly after you. They were after me. I believe you heard them speak about a princess the day you were attacked at Village Park. It was me they were talking about."

He can feel Sam watching his reaction carefully, but Kyle is lost. Laura casts a nervous glance at his face when he doesn't respond. Kyle tries to find the words to tell her he doesn't get what she's meaning but they don't come.

"I'm the princess," Laura clarifies. "Princess Amelia."

Kyle blinks. *Oh...*

"I've been in hiding. I wasn't legally eligible to take back the throne from that usurper, Taularh, until a few months ago, when I turned eighteen. But even though I'm of age now, it's far too risky for me to make a move right now and so I've had to lie low. Hopefully…no, it is something that must happen now." Her brow furrows and she looks up at Kyle with a challenge – a challenge to herself – in her eyes. "I *must* make claim to the throne. Kyle…would you be willing to help me?"

Avi cuts in with a steaming cup of tea he brings out for Kyle. "Uh, maybe ask another time, Amelia. Let him recover first."

There's no teabag in the cup, but the aroma the tea gives off is chamomile. Kyle stares blankly at it for a moment before Avi presses it into his hands.

"I'm guessing you don't drink much tea," Avi says, "but this will help. Trust me."

"Thanks," Kyle whispers.

"Be careful. It's not boiling hot but you might want to let it cool down a little."

Kyle nods. Everything Laura – *Amelia?* – just said goes straight over his head. Apparently everything's supposed to make sense now but somehow it doesn't click in his mind. Sensing his confusion, Sam starts talking to Amelia, drawing her away to give Kyle space.

Avi surveys the room with him and sighs. "Is there anything you want?"

Kyle's fingers tighten around the cup. He almost wishes his hands would burn on it, if only to feel anything but *this*. "Yuuki."

"Sorry, what was that?"

"I want to see Yuuki."

There's so many people about, people Kyle sort of knows but kind of doesn't, decent people who have yet to show him anything but kindness…but none of them are Yuuki. Kyle feels his absence like a cold gust of wind.

"They're operating on him now," Timothy says, having come into the room as Kyle said mentioned Yuuki's name. "All goes well, you should be able to see him in a few hours."

A few hours…

Avi pales. "Operating?"

Timothy evaluates Kyle's expression before explaining further. "Susan's working on him now, Charlie too. They…Susan had to make the call whether or not to try to save Yuuki's arm, but the bone's too badly damaged and the nerve and muscle tissue too at risk. If we weren't on the run, we could've taken him to a hospital and it's likely they'd have been able to save it, but…as it is – with what limited resources we have available to us here – we have to amputate the arm."

The sound that leaves Kyle's throat is half a scream, half a sob. Avi quickly takes the cup of tea before he doubles over, struggling to get enough air in, clutching at his arms. Sam wraps her arms around him and doesn't let go. Joshua comes in from the other side and pulls him in close.

"It's okay, Kyle. Let it out," he murmurs. "Let it out."

It's horrendous and it's terrifying. By no means does he intend to make those sounds. It happens anyway. Kyle keeps his head down, hiding behind his hair, so as to avoid having to see anyone's reaction.

Joshua successfully lit the fire, a small comfort to be found in the wake of everything, but it's dying out. He sends Logan to fetch some smaller pieces of firewood from out back – wherever 'out back' is – so he can stay with Kyle while the trauma wreaks havoc on his mind.

It's not your fault, he tries to tell himself. It is his fault, though. If he hadn't moved so much when that lady Deborah's men were tying him up, then Yuuki wouldn't be losing an arm right this very moment.

Don't blame yourself. He should, though. He should be blaming himself...right?

Kyle's chest hurts. He feels so far removed from himself. Who was he before all this? Who was Kyle Kindall before that day Daniel came for him in the park?

The answer is simple: someone he no longer knows.

19

It's five hours before Kyle's allowed to see Yuuki.

As Charlie is finishing cleaning up in the laundry-turned-medical room, Susan's the one to take him. Yuuki's been moved into a single bedroom right at the end of the hallway, the furthest away from all the noise of voices and movement and people getting dinner prepared.

"He's loaded up on pain meds and still waking up," Susan warns him, her face drawn. "But he was asking for you."

Kyle hesitates at the door, anxiousness churning in his gut. He feels the warmth of a gas heater flood out the door when they open it, but it does nothing to stop the wave of cold sent down his spine when he sees Yuuki.

This…this is reality.

Propped up on a mountain of pillows, his right shoulder and chest wrapped up in layer upon layer of bandages, he barely looks like Yuuki – at least, not the Yuuki who came into the detention centre every few days to see Kyle. He has an IV in his hand and a tube running across his face and entering his nose. There's hardly any strength left in him, no confident yet wary set to the shoulders, no concerned furrow in his brow or daring hope in his eyes.

But when Yuuki sees Kyle standing in the doorway, his face softens and a small sliver of light returns to his eyes. "Hey, Kyle…"

Kyle takes a deep breath and walks in slowly, Susan ducking out the door behind him. This time – to Kyle's immense relief – she leaves the door open as she goes. There's a stool sitting by the bed, so he sidles over to it and sits down, fingers digging into the sleeves of his jersey.

It's hard not to look at the empty space at Yuuki's side where his right arm should be. Kyle swallows. "Um, h-how is your…how are you feeling?"

Yuuki blinks slowly. "I don't know."

"I, um…I'm really sorry, for –"

"'s okay. Ju'…glad they didn't take you. I was so scared…think'ng 'bout wha' they might do to you…you…"

Yuuki's eyes lose focus then and the room relapses into silence. To avoid over-apologising, Kyle distracts himself by studying the way the shadows fall over the base of the IV stand.

"Um, so… Joshua was telling me how they rescued us," he says, trying to find a way keep talking to Yuuki. "He said when Sam came over with the soup Avi made, she hid some kind of thermal-sensing-radar tech thing down behind the couch cushions. Timothy thought we might be in danger, but he didn't want to freak us out so he didn't tell us. He said they were monitoring activity going on around the house and they saw…they noticed…"

It's something Kyle's not ready to speak aloud. Maybe with Yuuki, when he's more awake and ready to talk about the near-kidnapping as well, but right now they have an amputated arm and varying degrees of different trauma to deal with. Talking about it all can wait.

"Timothy had prepared in case something like this happened. That's why Joshua's over here instead of at uni. He's the one who brought the tech with him. Sam called her friends. Apparently Logan is in a clay target shooting club. Avi and Laura...*Amelia*...went and helped him on lookout.

"Yeah, so the whole thing about the princess was real, after all. They were looking for her, that's why...that's why they sent Daniel after me. They didn't want me telling anybody anything, in case she heard and got away."

Ironically, Jeff's plan to stop word from getting out there had backfired as soon as Kyle was taken into court. Of all people to have as his youth advocate, it had been Charlie, the man who had taken care of Amelia ever since her parents, the King and Queen, had been assassinated.

Yuuki appears to have drifted off and Kyle can't find the words anymore, let alone the will to speak. He's not sure what was worse – the chaos of his mind going crazy at night in isolation or the chaos of his emotions in the wake of everything that's happened since Yuuki got him out of there. Kyle's almost tempted to wish Yuuki had never carried him out of that cell at all. Maybe then none of this would've happened.

Don't blame yourself.

It's an extremely hard thing not to do.

All of it's too much for Kyle to get his head around. He's still trying to process the reality of being out of prison, among kind people and warmth and hugs and care. It's going to be a few days before he can even try to think again.

When he eventually leaves Yuuki's side for dinner, he doesn't end up eating. Avi's boiled enough potatoes to last them all the next couple of nights and there's a mix of this and that spread out of on the table, but Kyle doesn't have appetite for any of it. He doesn't even get as far as sitting down, not even when Logan offers to trade seats with him so that he's not sitting trapped between the table and the wall. Kyle ends up retreating to the couch, deciding he'll revisit the food later.

After dinner, Logan, Sam and Avi play cards, Joshua and Amelia joining them halfway through the second game. Amelia later shows them to the spare bedrooms for everyone to sort out sleeping arrangements between themselves. Kyle doesn't move from his seat on the couch when they do. He just sits there, knees up in front of him, sipping on the well-cooled chamomile tea Avi made for him earlier. Susan pours him another before she heads off to sleep. Kyle waits until it grows cold before drinking it.

He doesn't sleep. Every time he closes his eyes he feels tape over his lips, hears Yuuki screaming. He loses count of how many times he gets up to check on Yuuki. He wakes Timothy up a couple of times, who's sleeping out in the lounge due to limited space, but he doesn't seem bothered by it either. Charlie and Susan are alternating shifts of keeping a close eye on Yuuki's condition and neither of them object to Kyle's coming and going.

It's a long night, but at least he's not alone.

20

Kyle draws back the curtains and settles back down on the stool. He and Yuuki watch the dawn break together. Stars give way to the brighter light of the sun and the noise of bird song increases in volume. Inside the house, there's nothing but silence.

They're both still raw from yesterday's events. The shadows beneath Kyle's eyes feel permanent now. The loss of Yuuki's arm definitely is. Yuuki saved Kyle from losing himself entirely in that prison cell...but at what cost?

After a long time debating words in his head, Kyle clears his throat. "Thank you," he whispers.

Yuuki turns his head. "Hmm?"

"F-for getting me out of there. Out of prison, I mean."

He waits patiently for Yuuki to find his words, eyes flicking back and forth from the window to his face. Yuuki smiles softly and returns his gaze to the window.

"You never deserved to be in there," he murmurs.

Kyle grunts. "Everyone else seemed to think so."

"They thought wrong."

Down the hallway, cupboards open and close, pots and pans and plates clash. Joshua laughs and says something about Goldilocks.

"How're you doing?"

Kyle glances at Yuuki, frowning. Yuuki's got his eyes closed, but the set to his jaw is still there, so he doesn't look like he's about to drift off to sleep without a moment's notice. He doesn't expect an answer to come immediately, for which Kyle is grateful, but for all the words he has in his English vocabulary, none of them are adequate enough to describe what he's feeling.

In the end Kyle doesn't answer at all. Yuuki doesn't comment; he's feeling the same.

Footsteps. Kyle's heard the weight and pace of that person's footfall enough times now to know it's Susan. He turns as she knocks on the doorframe.

"Avi and Amelia are making breakfast," Susan says, expression tired but friendly. "You're okay with porridge, pancakes or toast? Avi said to say he's happy to cook you up something else if you need him to."

Kyle blinks. "I…I'm not actually that hungry, thanks…"

"You need to eat something, even if it is just a little bit. Or do you want to wait until everyone else is finished, maybe? There'll be things left over and that way you can help yourself whenever you're feeling up to it."

With no appetite whatsoever, Kyle has no idea when that'll be. He says okay anyway.

Susan flashes him a small smile. "Same goes for you, Yuuki," she says, looking past Kyle. "Let me know if you think you're feeling okay to eat."

Yuuki hums in response, not having the energy to answer her in full. Susan lingers at the door a moment longer and then, with her intention for coming to them done, leaves the two of them alone again.

In the midst of the noise of the country house waking up, the room is a refuge for them both. Yuuki sometimes opens his eyes to gaze out the window, other times he closes them and just seems to listen. To what, Kyle's not too sure. He's pretty sure it's not the bird singing in the tree outside the window – his brow is too creased for that.

Yuuki Takahashi. It's strange for Kyle to think how different Yuuki was to him not so long ago. When he'd spoken of second chances and wanting to help, Kyle hadn't believed him. Surely Yuuki doesn't really care as much as he says he does, Kyle had thought.

The whole world had given up on. Kyle had given up on himself.

Why would Yuuki be any different?

Time and time again Yuuki has proved he's different, though, and it almost seems like he'd be willing to do so as many times as it takes until Kyle *knows* it in his heart.

Yuuki had let himself be shot. It's one of the things Kyle had mulled over last night. Yuuki could've tried to escape from where he'd been pinned but he hadn't because he'd feared what would happen to Kyle if he did.

The fear in his eyes. *"Just glad they didn't take you."*

"I'm sorry…"

Kyle looks up, startled. Yuuki's crying.

"I'm sorry you had to go through all of this," Yuuki says thickly. "I wish you didn't have to know what this feels like…this pain, this…"

"Yuuki…"

"You…I know I lost my arm. It's going to take some getting used to. But I'd never be able to live with myself if they'd actually taken you a-and

186

I did nothing. I s-should've done something more, I should've –"

"You're blaming yourself."

Words cut off, Yuuki's sentence falls into choked silence. His eyes widen at Kyle's firm tone.

"Don't blame yourself," Kyle murmurs. "You keep telling me not to. If you say it's not my fault and I say it's not yours, then... it's neither of our faults. I-I know it's not that easy, but..."

With a grunt, Yuuki smiles wryly. "You got that right." He sniffs and glances at him in the corner of his eye. "Thanks, Kyle."

Kyle gives him a small smile. *I'm the one who should be thanking you.*

He stays with Yuuki until the sounds of breakfast in the living room die down. By that stage Yuuki's starting to drift off to sleep, so Kyle quietly takes his leave.

The hallway is dim and quiet. Kyle lingers by Yuuki's room a minute, mentally preparing himself for facing the others. They're not bad, it's just that he's never been part of any of their groups. The Harrisons have each other, Amelia and Charlie have each other, and Logan, Sam, Avi and Amelia are all friends... while Kyle's only got Yuuki. For a good while he had absolutely no one.

If no one had fought for him, he wouldn't have minded. It's not like it would've been a big deal. Kyle can't remember the last time anybody stood up for him besides the few people here who did for his case, so it wouldn't have come as a surprise.

It's with a confusing mix of emotions that Kyle thinks about it now, about how even though he'd given up on himself, Yuuki never did.

He still asks himself why Yuuki would even...

"I don't want the same thing that happened to me happen to you."

"Don't give up on yourself just yet. We're going to get you out of here."

"You're going to be okay, Kyle."

"I was so scared…"

Why would Yuuki care so much? It dumbfounds him. Kyle hasn't done anything to deserve it.

"Because I believe in second chances."

Kyle wants to believe in them too, but hope is a scary thing. He could be robbed of it tomorrow and never see it again. He learnt that the night his father went to his firefighting job and never came home.

But maybe…maybe this time things will be different.

Taking a deep breath, Kyle walks down the hallway and opens the door into the living room.

Riiipppp.

Tape. Logan has tape. No, no, the box – the cardboard box – has tape.

His heart leaps out of his chest. Not breathing, he whirls around and slams the door on the scene in the living room.

Breathe-breathe-breathe, c'mon…

A knock on the door. "Kyle?"

Someone – Logan, probably, judging by who just spoke – tries to open the door. Kyle leans harder against it, pressing all his weight against it.

"Hey, can you let me open the door?"

No, he can't. He can't because the box, the tape, all the people –

Yuuki's voice sounds down the hallway, calling his name. Kyle zones into it, latches onto it like a lifeline. Yuuki. *Yuuki.* His heart's beating too fast. He's dizzy with sleep deprivation and adrenaline, but the second he pushes himself away from the door, he sprints and darts into Yuuki's room before it opens.

"Kyle, just focus on breathing."

Yuuki's wide awake again now. He watches Kyle carefully, pain and concern and empathy and *care* in his eyes, and that's all the invitation Kyle needs to accept the offer of the one-armed hug Yuuki offers him.

Through the bandages wrapped around his chest, Kyle listens to Yuuki's heartbeat, strong and steady. The rhythm of his breathing is a reference point for Kyle's own. Kyle closes his eyes and concentrates hard on trying to slow his breathing down to match it.

"Is he...?" Logan's tentative voice comes from the doorway.

Kyle stiffens, but then Yuuki moves his head and Logan's footsteps are heard heading back down the hallway and he forces himself to loosen his shoulders.

Yuuki rubs his back as best he can while holding him. "You're okay. Just keep breathing."

It's hard to. It's hard to remember how when it feels like there's tape over his lips cutting off his breathing through his mouth. It's hard when his lungs feel like they can't draw enough air in regardless of the flashback.

But Yuuki's warm where the world is cold, light where it is dark. He listened to Kyle when no one else would and fought for him where everyone else gave up on him. It cost him, and he knew it would, but Yuuki did it anyway.

Kyle breathes.

There's no more ripping of packaging tape off boxes, at least not within audible range of Kyle and Yuuki. Yuuki falls asleep with his arm around Kyle. Kyle stays there for a good half an hour before quietly removing himself.

He doesn't go back down the hallway. Instead, after stopping by the toilet and trying not to let the enclosed space trigger another panic attack, Kyle finds the back door and slips outside.

It's cold out, but it's quiet. The sunshine is warm, even if it is intermittent. Kyle walks over to a tree and sits down on among its roots. His shoulders slump. He's exhausted. The lack of sleep is making his knees feel like they're going to buckle at any moment. His head's spinning and the strain of shadows beneath his eyes is beginning to hurt.

He can't bear to think how Yuuki's feeling.

Will there ever be an end to this?

Amelia being the Arkala princess could change everything, but how long's it going to take for that to happen? How much more is it going to cost them – cost Yuuki? They'll be after him, Deborah and that Jeff guy. They'll be after everyone, really, just with Yuuki, Amelia and Kyle at the top of their list of people to take down. It's not a pleasant thought.

If they're being hunted right now, Kyle wonders how long will it be before their hideout at this country house is discovered. How long until they're faced with threats and blasters and corrupt Peace Force officers despising the idea of them starting what will basically be a revolution? Given that it only took just over twenty four hours for them to move in on Yuuki and Kyle, it's probably not going to be long.

Kyle brings his knees up to his chest and hugs them. This doesn't seem like a fight they can win.

"Ah, I thought you'd be out here."

Timothy's voice is gentle enough to avoid making him flinch, but it startles Kyle nonetheless.

"Um, hi," Kyle murmurs. Apparently he forgot that he left the back door open.

Gesturing at an empty space on a large root beside the one Kyle's sitting on, Timothy raises his eyebrows. "May I?"

Kyle watches him warily a moment, assessing, then nods and shifts over a little to give Timothy more space to sit and himself more space between them. Timothy smiles kindly and takes the seat offered.

"You two have sure been through the wringer these past few days, haven't you?" he remarks, looking out into the unmaintained orchard.

Kyle doesn't comment.

"I thought I'd let you know that we've been talking about when we're going to make our first move," Timothy says. "We'll need to act soon. The sooner the better, of course, as I'm sure you'll understand, though we'll be taking into account the time we need to allow for Yuuki's recovery. Charlie and Amelia have enough supplies to last us a while, but eventually that's going to run out and when it does, exposing ourselves won't be an option. Since they're undoubtedly out looking for us, Jeff and his crew, it might not be long until we're found anyway, so the time to act is, at the end of the day, now.

"While we're still figuring out how we're going to that exactly, the others are thinking of starting training. There's inevitably going to be some kind of fighting, so we need to be prepared for that, but you and Yuuki just focus on resting at the moment though, yeah? You've been through a lot and Yuuki's going to be out of action for a good few weeks in the least, so… just focus your energy on healing."

Kyle studies a line of ants running up and down the root by his feet. He frowns hard, mouth twisting in a retort he wants to give but doesn't have the words for. He muses how weird his toes look, pale against the grass.

The anxiety isn't going to be leaving him any time soon. Even the slightest, insignificant noise has him on edge, his skin tingling and awareness on high alert. Yuuki said it himself that Kyle's probably going to be a bit of a mess of emotions over the next few weeks, but it's still unsettling. How's he supposed to heal if he continues to feel like this?

"How are you adjusting to being out of isolation?"

Timothy's question slams into him like a truck. Kyle's not prepared for the churning in his gut it brings. "Fine," he says curtly.

Thankfully, Timothy doesn't press. Kyle doesn't know how to talk about it and he doesn't want to. He's not ready to hear in words how he's feeling. To be frank, he doesn't even know if there are words that can describe it all accurately enough.

The silence that follows is slightly awkward but not uncomfortable. Timothy's got a different aura to him than the reassuring quiet Yuuki's brings, but it's still friendly and patient at its centre. A question comes to Kyle's mind as he thinks about the apparent friendship between Timothy and Yuuki. He spends a long several minutes mulling it over before he works up enough courage to ask it.

Kyle hugs his knees a little tighter. "What was Yuuki like…before…?"

Timothy hums a question. "Before the incident at Ninao?"

"Yeah…"

Risking a nervous glance, Kyle sees something shadowed cross over Timothy's face. It's a painful memory for him, he realises, and one that haunts him every day. He just manages to keep it hidden under that kind expression that is his default.

"Yuuki's always been Yuuki," Timothy says, "but he doesn't smile as much now, not genuinely anyways. He looks a lot more worse for wear on a daily basis, more than I've ever seen him, even on what he used to call a bad day. Inside, he... I don't think he enjoys life as much as he used to.

"He lost his sense of purpose, you know? Once he was able to return to work after recovering from his ordeal in that shed, he found that he couldn't work at all, the prison environment too triggering for him. He worked from home doing paperwork and managing the direction and building of the Trust, but his work output hasn't been of the same quality and he rarely has a productive day.

"It's hurt so much, watching it all happen. It's heart-breaking to see this kind of thing happening to someone with such a heart and passion."

Kyle's tearing up before he can stop himself. "S-so he...he..."

Timothy waits quietly while Kyle fights to regain composure and find the words.

"So when he came to help me...?" The crying is making his chest hurt. He can't finish. Timothy gets what he's trying to say though.

"When I first told him about your case," Timothy murmurs. "I was worried for him, worried I might be asking too much of him. But if you'd seen the determination in his eyes, Kyle... you mattered to him before he even met you. And I'm not just saying that, either. I know it's probably hard to believe in the wake of everything you've been through of late, but you matter, Kyle. That's why we worked so hard on your case."

Kyle drops his head between his arms, shoulders shaking. It hurts. It hurts so bad because he can't understand what reason anyone would have to care about him so much. He did nothing. He's done more to deserve being in prison than he does to be loved.

He hears Timothy quietly ask him if he wants a hug. Kyle wants to say no, wants to stop all this *kindness* and *compassion* and *care* flooding into his heart before it kills him, but when Timothy's arm lights over his shoulders, so fatherly in a way that Kyle hasn't had since his Dad died all those years ago, the dam inside him breaks. He falls into Timothy's side, breaking and exhausted and longing.

Somehow the weight of all the hurt Kyle's been carrying around seems a little less heavy.

21

At least twice that night, Yuuki startles the household awake with a nightmare he doesn't remember having. The first one leaves Kyle shaken to the core. He's heard Yuuki scream like that only once, when he was shot. He knows he should get up to make sure Yuuki's able to calm down on his own, but he's too shaky with adrenaline to be able to move from his spot on the couch. Voices sound down the hall then, however, Timothy's and Charlie's, and the night falls quiets again.

Kyle's in the room later when, two hours after the second bout of shouting, Yuuki starts whimpering. It goes on for a good fifteen minutes before Kyle can't take hearing it any longer. He pushes himself off the wall by the window and gets to his feet, takes a deep breath and reaches out his hand.

He stops. Waking him…probably isn't such a good idea, is it? *By all means, calm him,* Timothy had told Kyle on his way out, *but don't wake him unless you absolutely have to. You don't want to get yourself hurt and I don't think Yuuki wants to remember what he was dreaming about when he wakes up.*

Timothy's words are enough to make him reconsider. Yuuki has enough bad memories already to torment him. Who knows what he's seeing in those dreams?

Kyle does the only thing he can think of that shouldn't be too triggering: he lays his hand on Yuuki's forehead as he'd seen Susan do for him in the car.

Yuuki flinches. It sends a jolt of alarm through Kyle's chest, but before he can take a step back the tension in Yuuki's muscles eases. The whimper turns into a groan, into a small sigh, and then he's still.

It's incredibly weird. He's standing awkwardly by Yuuki's bedside with his palm on Yuuki's forehead while he sleeps. Kyle doesn't know what to think, but it doesn't matter how awkward he feels so long as this in some way helps.

Beneath Kyle's forearm, though, is the empty space at Yuuki's side where his right arm ought to be. It taunts him, accuses him, blames him. Kyle imagines how Yuuki would've been had he not taken on his case, how much of himself he wouldn't have lost had he not promised Kyle that day that he'd get him out of there, out of prison.

He would've still had his arm, for one. Been far less stressed, not have so much to think about…

Don't blame yourself. It's hard not to.

Yuuki's brow moves beneath his fingers. "Kyle?"

Kyle withdraws his hand. "I, uh…sorry…"

"What?"

"I woke you up…"

The hallway light throws shadows over Yuuki's face. The lines beneath his eyes are dark. He blinks and averts his gaze, staring blankly at the wall opposite the bed instead. "No, *thank you*," he murmurs. "Thank you for waking me."

Kyle's tempted to ask what Yuuki was having nightmares about, but the haunted look in his eyes says all Yuuki wants to do is forget about it.

"I keep seeing them," Yuuki whispers. "The men who took me. Two of them were the same guys who were going to take you."

The rawness in his voice cuts through Kyle like a knife, his words even more so. "Oh…"

"That's twice they came for me. First, Joshua and Timothy were with me, then you were…."

"It's not your fault, Yuuki."

"Isn't it?"

Kyle frowns. "All you did was stand up for what you saw was right. Maybe you can't see it now, the hope that brings, but…Yuuki, you saved me. What you did… I thought I was gonna die in that cell. A-and then you saved me and I…"

There's nothing Kyle can say that'll help. The wound in Yuuki's heart is too deep, the emptiness there too dark. Yuuki lost more than his right arm; just as Timothy said, he's lost his confidence as well.

"This keeps happening," Yuuki whispers. "Every time, and it's never just me; whenever I do something, someone else gets hurt because of me. I can't…" He swallows hard. "I don't want to let fear drag me down, but it's…it's hard, y'know?"

"Yeah…I know."

Kyle's too tired to distract him with a random conversation, so he just stands there, shifting his weight from foot to foot trying to think of something he can do to help. Folding his arms across his chest, Kyle leans back into the corner of the room. Being available, being *here*, seems to be the best thing can do.

He stays with Yuuki the remainder of the night. Neither of them sleep. Kyle managed to nap for an hour earlier in the night, but other than that he's had zero sleep and he's exhausted to the bone. The wall is the only thing keeping him upright, his legs soon giving out and making him sink down to sit on the floor.

Light starts creeping in under the curtains. Like yesterday, Kyle goes to draw them back but finds he only has enough energy to reach up and tug the nearest one open. The sky's overcast today and they both feel it. Kyle rests his head against the wall and closes his eyes.

In the quiet before the house starts waking up, Yuuki whispers a confession. "I'm scared."

To that, Kyle has no answer; he is too.

Timothy pulls him aside after breakfast – a late breakfast, since Kyle only goes to get his after the others have finished eating theirs – to talk about the retrial. Kyle sets aside his half-eaten bowl of porridge and follows him outside.

It's cold outside, but again, it's quiet. The shape of the trees surrounding the house blur and tilt a little, but Kyle blinks hard and his vision seems to right itself. He hugs himself and focuses on the conversation at hand.

"I thought I'd better let you know what's happening," Timothy says. "I've written up all the official documents we need, filled out all the necessary forms, but as you've probably figured out, we're not going to be able to hold a retrial at the youth court. It'd be far too risky considering both our situation and yours.

"That being said, we're not just going to drop the case. I've written a couple of carefully worded letters regarding our circumstances, so anyone not involved with Jeff's searching for us will know that there are legitimate reasons why we can't attend a formal court meeting. Hopefully it'll also allude to our reason for being out in hiding.

"Our only problem is getting these documents out there without revealing our location, and that'll mean – … Kyle?"

Kyle sucks in a breath. He's swaying on his feet. "I'm fine," he mumbles, even as his vision goes blurry again.

Out of the corner of his eye, he sees Timothy's brow furrow. "You don't seem like it."

With that extra acknowledgement besides his own, the tiredness slams into him. Kyle feels the blood drains from his face and Timothy sees it. Then the world blurs and all the colours blend and –

He stumbles sideways into Timothy. Hands grasp his forearms, kind, strong hands, and pull him close. Kyle can't tell exactly how upright he's standing, but Timothy steadies him with an arm around his shoulders and the other with a hand on his shoulder.

"Let's go back inside, yeah?" Timothy murmurs.

Kyle can't argue. He trusts Timothy, so he lets him lead him back inside, past Sam tapping away at her laptop and Logan playing a game of cards with Amelia and Avi on the floor beside her. They stare a bit but Kyle can only look forwards, to the couch and to Susan who's sitting there reading a well-read book.

There's no comment as they get Kyle settled down. There's enough room on the couch for him to curl up, back facing the room, without disturbing Susan, and he trusts her enough to let himself be this vulnerable beside her. His head spins as he lies down, but the relief is immense. He's so dizzy.

"'m sorry," he says, voice weak.

Timothy lies a blanket out over him and pats his shoulder. "No need to be sorry. Been a bit hard sleeping, eh? What with everything that's happened..."

"Hmmm..."

"You just rest, Kyle," Susan says. "You need it."

Hearing his name is strange thing. He almost forgets it belongs to him, even though Yuuki calls him by it all the time. The name Kindall, what he's used to being called, is associated with someone no one cares about, so it's hard to reconcile 'Kyle Kindall' as being someone these people care about.

"You matter, Kyle."

He's still trying to process what that feels like.

Voices fade in and out. Kyle's not really sure if he ever sleeps but he's too tired to do anything but lie there with his eyes closed. He's shaking slightly too, probably from how little he's eaten, but he couldn't find the appetite to eat any more even if he wanted to.

At some point while he's drifting, Joshua comes stomping in with firewood. Kyle's blood spikes with adrenaline, but as soon as Susan says her son's name and Kyle reassesses the now-careful footsteps, his heartrate settles again.

The soft roar of the fire that is started both draws on painful memories and lulls him. Every time it crackles, Kyle thinks of the day after his father never came home, strangers forcing him to go live somewhere he didn't want to – with even stranger strangers who never even wanted him in the first place. He thinks about the burn on the side of his hip from a couple of years ago when his foster father pushed him over and into the fireplace, yelling about Kyle's failed grades and how he should be trying harder…

Susan's fingers brush through his hair. He blinks, comes out of the flashback. Despite the low murmur of voices, of easy-going tones of conversation and laughter, Kyle's all tensed up. The fireplace almost sounds like a purr as it warms up the room. Someone's making coffee.

When he doesn't move away from her touch, Susan rests her hand on his head and gently moves her thumb over his brow. However awkward he felt before, when comforting Yuuki, it all disappears in the wake of understanding just how soothing it is.

Kyle's heart fills with a warmth akin to that of the fire. Before he knows it, he's fallen asleep.

"…too risky, but if we're going to…then it's a risk we need to take."

"Well, Sam and I could work something out…"

"…flunk school."

"I'm sure the teachers won't be so harsh on us when they find out why we're not there."

"Avi, you know we *could* go to school. There's nothing stopping us."

"Yeah, but Kyle… I don't know about you, but when I said I'd help I didn't intend on stopping halfway."

"Me neither….but man, our families will be worried sick."

"…encrypt…letter?"

"…can't risk it…"

"… doing okay."

"I've never seen him so *empty*."

"I think it's hitting him pretty bad. You know how Yuuki was at the hospital after the incident, and we were barely hurt. We didn't see what happened inside the house. We had the thermal radar to monitor the movements going on while it was happening, but we didn't see what they saw."

"It was terrifying just seeing what they did to them…"

"Yuuki's not going to be himself for a while. I don't know if he ever will be. If something like this happens a third time, it'll destroy him."

"..'melia?"

"Hnnn, she's been acting a bit strange, huh?"

"Is she still… fact that he's got Arkala'ana blood?"

"Seems like it. If it seems to be affecting Kyle, I'll have a word with her."

Kyle wakes at irregular intervals. When he wakes enough to be coherent, it's to the filling aroma of roasting vegetables and meat. His stomach flips a bit at the thought of eating but growls nonetheless, and he groans with the confliction of lack of appetite and hunger.

"Ah, Kyle. You awake?"

He raises his head wearily, searching for where Avi's voice was coming from. Susan's not sitting on the couch beside him anymore. Kyle finds Avi in the kitchen, just able to see him from here.

"Dinner's just about ready," Avi says, smiling a little too broadly for Kyle to feel comfortable with.

Kyle stares at him a moment longer before deciding how he should reply. "Ahh... I'm not hungry," he lies.

Avi's face falls. "But you haven't eaten all day, though. Surely you –"

"I'll eat later. 's not safe yet." He doesn't realise what he just said until Avi's jaw drops.

"What do you mean... not safe?"

Kyle grimaces. He really doesn't have the energy or heart to talk about the rules of his last foster family's household at dinnertime. He's not there now, he gets it, but there's still a part of him that fears going back. He's not eighteen yet. What if this is all over before his birthday, and everyone goes back to their families, back to the way they lived before all this happened? What if... what if Yuuki decides that taking care of him is too much stress?

No, that is not *what I need to be thinking about right now.*

Too late. He's back in the whirlpool of the thoughts that had plagued him in the prison cell, in those long nights of darkness and cold and isolation. Thoughts telling him he deserved to be there and thoughts telling him that he isn't worth being cared about.

You never deserved to be in there. Yuuki's words.

Kyle swallows hard. He can't bear to look at everyone else's expressions. He sits up, ignoring the way his head spins, and keeping his eyes fixed on the floor directly in front of his feet, retreats down the hallway.

He hates this. Yuuki's going to get sick of him real quick if he's this clingy. He'll shove him away, reject him like everyone else does, and Kyle getting this comfortable with having someone looking out for him is surely only going to make that worse.

But as he leaves the confused whispers and the warmth of the living room, Kyle's thoughts are stilled by a sound he hadn't been able to hear above the crackling of the fire.

Yuuki's crying. Charlie's trying to comfort him with words, but Kyle knows how ineffective words are with hurt that runs so deep. He hastens his steps. He remembers the way Yuuki had reacted when he'd offered to hug him, that time Yuuki had freaked out after coming into Kyle's cell the first time, the way he'd been able to breathe a bit easier after the hug.

He can think himself selfish all he wants for needing Yuuki, but the truth of the matter seems to be that Yuuki kind of needs him too. More than Kyle realises and more than he dares to believe. But what he is coming to realise is that it's not just him needing Yuuki's presence to ground him: they're both each other's anchors.

When Kyle sits on the edge of the bed and hugs him, Yuuki finally lets himself break down fully and Kyle doesn't let him go.

.

22

Three weeks pass both slowly and quickly. Yuuki's arm, or what remains of it, is healing well. Susan took the sutures out a week ago and the residual limb is now wrapped in compression bandages instead of gauze dressings that needed to be replaced twice a day. He's healing well physically, but emotionally...

Yuuki's flashbacks come and go relentlessly. He's shaken up about everything, become more emotional and stressed and fatigued than usual. Everyone, besides the Harrisons and Kyle, keeps relating it back to him dealing with the trauma of losing an arm, but in truth the hurt runs so much deeper than that.

It's not just him dealing with a mind in chaos either. Kyle's been distancing himself from the others, isolating himself. It seems like a cruel twist of fate, to come out of isolation only to feel the need to isolate himself from people all over again. Yuuki did the same though – does the same, nowadays – so he gets it and Kyle doesn't bring it up.

There's bound to be a lot of conflicting thoughts waging a war in Kyle's mind right now, just as there are in Yuuki's. They both need time and space to process them.

Sleep deprivation has become a permanent thing. Kyle sleeps during the day, off and on, and never anywhere without space around him, or Timothy or Yuuki nearby. Yuuki's insomnia and fear of nightmares means that Yuuki's awake for the most part of the night. With Kyle having trouble sleeping too, they are able to keep each other company.

Kyle doesn't eat with the others, only going into the kitchen after everyone's finished. He brings back enough for the both of them and then they eat as much as their appetite allows them. Sometimes finishing a meal is harder than winning a game of chess, but somehow they both manage to get through it. Yuuki drinks slightly more coffee than usual and he's seen Kyle eyeing the plunger, considering.

The two of them become inseparable. They need each other, not in a dependent way but as friends – brothers, even. It's weird to think that only a few weeks ago they were strangers.

Yuuki sighs, thinking about it. He's lost a lot, but if he had the chance to go back in time and tell Timothy he wasn't going to take on Kyle's case, there's no way in hell he'd do it. Getting Kyle out of prison may have ended up costing him an arm, but if he'd stepped back and done nothing, it would've cost Kyle his life.

Yuuki doesn't like to think about how close they came to the latter.

A week ago, Timothy sent the official documents regarding Kyle's release. He intentionally didn't specify a retrial date. He'd had Yuuki, Charlie and Susan read over them to make sure there was no hint of their intentions of exposing Jeff, and when they had found none, Charlie had driven Joshua and Sam into the city to send them.

The drive to the city was a risky move but a necessary one. Timothy took as many measures as he could to make sure they didn't leave a trace of where they were. They can't afford their location to be traced and they can't afford to let Jeff know that they're onto him. He'd already disabled everyone's phone from the network. On the downside that means that if Mitchell's contacted them – or anyone else potentially on their side, for that matter – they won't know it.

Yuuki just hopes that Mitchell has dealt to that Robert guy, the guard who failed to let Kyle out of his handcuffs and failed to report that both the light bulb and the heating weren't working. Yuuki suspects he might have some association with Jeff, perhaps having been the allocated person to keep an eye on Kyle to make sure he stayed shut away as they wanted him to.... but of course, they can't be sure.

Exposing Jeff means acquiring concrete evidence – something that can prove beyond all reasonable doubt that Kyle was set up. If they can do that, they can wipe Kyle's slate clean and stop another situation like Kyle's from happening. They just have to find that evidence.

It's what Timothy's working on now.

Yuuki gets up mid-morning and finds Timothy sitting at the table, shoulders hunched forward. On his laptop screen is a video recording of Kyle's trial. Kyle's asleep in a pool of sunshine streaming in through the living room windows, Yuuki's footsteps not disturbing him in the least.

Susan appears from around the corner, carrying a cup of coffee. "Oh, morning, Yuuki," she says, setting down the cup on a coaster by Timothy's laptop. "I just boiled the jug. Shall I make you one, too?"

"That'd be great, if you don't mind," Yuuki murmurs. "Thanks."

His voice doesn't sound like his own. It's flat, exhausted and devoid of emotion… back to how it sounded in those first few months after Ninao.

He knows both Timothy and Susan have noticed.

Timothy swivels in his seat. He glances over at Kyle and then looks up at Yuuki with his brow furrowed. "I think I finally found something."

With a steady exhale, Yuuki pulls out a chair. He sits down heavily and frowns at the screen, trying to work out whereabouts in the trial it was. Kyle stands with his hands cuffed behind his back, two officers on either side of him and a court full of people scowling at him. The video is paused at a point where Kyle's in the middle of saying something in a desperate attempt to defend himself.

But it's not Kyle who they're looking at. Timothy circles the cursor around a bulky figure standing to the side of the room. He zooms in closer. Jeff has his hands on his hips, a deep frown on his face.

"This is after I gave the final warning," Timothy says. "Before I had to…" *Before I had to stop Kyle from speaking.*

Yuuki raises an eyebrow. "Where am I looking?" He goes to lean an elbow against the table and belatedly remembers he can't – he doesn't have his arm on that side anymore. He shifts in his seat uncomfortably.

"Take a closer look at where Jeff's hands are and tell me what it looks like."

Narrowing his eyes, Yuuki frowns. Something does look odd about the way Jeff's right hand is positioned. It almost looks as though it's twisted sideways, bent backwards like he's reaching behind himself.

There's a pistol in his back pocket.

Yuuki inhales sharply. "H-he was going to…"

"He was going to shoot me."

Kyle's peering over Yuuki's shoulder, the shadows beneath his eyes dark. His gaze flicks to Timothy's, a sobered expression on his face. Susan tiptoes around the three of them to put Yuuki's coffee on the table, then heads outside to give the three of them space.

Timothy pushes his chair back and to the side. He holds Kyle's gaze and nods. "Yeah. He was."

Averting his eyes, Kyle folds his arms tightly over his chest. "I guess I should thank you, then. For shutting me up before I got myself killed." He blinks, shoulders tensing up. "I'm sorry, I-I didn't mean it like that, to say it like that, that is."

"It's all goods," Timothy murmurs. He grimaces. "I'm sorry I had to do that to you."

"It's fine," Kyle whispers.

If they were to hit play and watch the next couple of minutes of the video it would be obvious how much of a lie that is. But it's something that's terribly humiliating for Kyle so they won't talk about it if he doesn't want to. Timothy and Kyle exchange acknowledging half-smiles.

Kyle ducks his head. "So, um… how long do you think we have? Until they find us?"

Yuuki takes a sip of coffee. "I wouldn't be surprised if they already know where we are. We're on an island. It's not like we have many places to hide. They also happen to be good at sneaking up on us."

"So they could come at any time, in other words."

"Yeah."

"They could," Timothy says, "but it won't do you two any good stressing about it."

Yuuki sees Kyle stiffen defensively beside him. His own fingers have gone tight around the cup handle. This isn't general anxiety they're dealing with.

Timothy winces and opens his mouth to apologise when Charlie comes striding into the room. Yuuki and Kyle watch him in their peripheral, on edge.

Charlie stops a metre away from them, right at the edge of Kyle's personal boundary comfort zone. "Hey, Kyle?" he says. "Can I have a minute?"

Kyle's whole body language changes. Knees bent, balancing his weight further over his toes. Shoulders tense, arms tight, eyes flicking from Charlie to the hallway door to the kitchen and then over to the sliding door. It's a subtle shift but it's one Yuuki's learnt to pick up on. The phrasing and tone of Charlie's words makes it seem like Kyle's about to be questioned and Kyle's ready to run. It changes the atmosphere in the room immediately.

Fortunately, Charlie notices. "I remembered I have something for you." He lifts the small bag he's holding up in front of him and presents it to Kyle. "Your, uh, foster family cleared out your things from their house after the trial. It's been on everyone's minds lately that things could get hairy any day now and I don't want you to be without means to defend yourself if it gets ugly."

He probably overheard our conversation, Yuuki thinks tiredly. *So much for a bit of space.*

Kyle uncrosses his arms and cautiously takes the bag. His eyes flash when he looks inside and sees what's in it. He swallows, a mix of emotions passing over his face. He's frozen up – flashback frozen up, eyes wide and unseeing.

Yuuki drinks some more coffee, watching, waiting to decide if he should step in.

Timothy glances between the three of them. "What's wrong?"

The look Kyle throws Timothy is one of apprehension and fear. He takes a step back, and another, then turns with a shaky gasp, slips out the sliding door and disappears around the side of the house.

Something like cold fire churns in Yuuki's stomach. "Charlie, what did you give him?"

"His knife," Charlie says, confused. "It was a gift from his mother, apparently."

Yuuki is out of his seat in an instant. He frowns at the rest of his coffee, decides to save the rest for later instead of downing it right now, and goes after Kyle. He thinks he hears Timothy curse.

Outside, Avi and Sam are having sprint races up and down the lawn. The faint ring of shots can be heard from Logan at the far end of the orchard. Amelia's doing stretches by the driveway. As for Kyle, Yuuki finds him sitting in his favourite de-stress spot on the root of a tree at the back of the house. He has his knife in his lap, resting on the plastic bag in its sheath.

"Hey," Yuuki murmurs, trying not to overbalance with the missing weight of his right arm as he sits down.

Kyle watches Avi and Sam get ready for another sprint. "It's stupid."

"Hmm? The training?"

"What? No. No, me. I freak out about everything."

"It's not stupid. It's just confusing and frustrating."

"Yeah, well...*that*, but...."

"But?" Yuuki prompts.

Kyle pulls the sleeves of his jersey down over his hands. "I keep worrying I'll be sent back there. To prison."

Instinctively, Yuuki goes to reach out a hand to put on Kyle's shoulder but realises with a grimace that he sat down with Kyle on his right. Out on the lawn, Sam does the countdown and then she and Avi take off sprinting again.

"You won't be," Yuuki says firmly. "We'll do everything we can to make sure of it."

Kyle clenches in his jaw. "Right."

"I mean it, Kyle. I'll say it as many times as you need me to – you didn't deserve to be in there in the first place. People would've realised that if they'd listened, and if Jeff hadn't been lurking around getting his way.

"Also… we don't know how rough things are going to get once they find us here, or once we come up with a plan to make our move first. It could get really rough, and if it does…if you need to use that knife, Kyle, then I want you to use it."

The last two times Kyle got in a bad situation and tried to defend himself, he was arrested for killing someone and Yuuki lost an arm. Yuuki's scared that Kyle will hesitate the next time he needs to defend himself, that that hesitation will then get him killed. Since he's still adjusting to only having one arm, Yuuki might not be able to save him in time if that were to happen.

"None of us are going to hold it against you if you need to use that knife," Yuuki murmurs. "If you need to use it for self-defence, then use it. I know that you won't unless it's necessary."

Kyle doesn't answer. There's pain written all over his face, memories he'd rather forget and leave behind. It's hard for Yuuki to think that he might be one of the reasons Kyle struggles, his missing arm and the bandages over what remains of it a constant reminder of what happened back at the house when Kyle's self-defence instincts took over.

He hates that Kyle should be made to feel such a way about his own survival instincts in the first place, especially when he was the victim in both scenarios in the first place.

A distant rumbling catches Yuuki's attention, distracts him. It sounds like a car driving over grave, but as far as he's aware, no one's been out on the road since the drive to the city. Kyle hears it too, ears twitching as he frowns harder. Avi and Sam haven't heard it yet. Amelia hasn't either.

Horror strikes at the exact same moment that Logan comes tearing in from the orchard, eyes wide and yelling, "Evac! Evac!"

Yuuki's blood fills with adrenaline. "*Shoot,* they're here."

23

Everybody races inside the house. They have emergency packs ready in the corner of the lounge. The designated people to carry them – Avi, Sam, Joshua, Susan, Timothy and Amelia – fling them onto their backs. Timothy shoves his laptop into his bag. Charlie helps gather up the USB drives, documents and folders sitting around the table. Logan, still carrying his rifle, takes his jacket and pockets spare ammunition. Yuuki and Kyle get their shoes on and Kyle slips his knife into one of his boots.

Timothy tightens the straps on his backpack. "Alright, out, out! Follow the plan. Stick to your groups. We rendezvous at Checkpoint A."

They file down the hallway, out the back door and run: Logan, Sam and Avi take to the orchard; Charlie, Amelia, Joshua and Susan to the trees at the end of the backyard; and Yuuki, Kyle and Timothy to the bush starting at the side of the house.

There's no waiting around. The rumbling has gotten much closer, tyres on gravel coming nearer and nearer to the front of the house. Judging by the rumbling, there's more than one vehicle on its way. Gravel crunches and a car door opens.

They'll know as soon as they enter the house that everyone was there just a minute ago. They'll know they're close. They'll come after them.

Kyle's face is pale as they duck into the shade of the trees. Timothy leads the way, finding the little trail that he and Joshua starting pathing out a couple of weeks ago. Roots, stones and weeds threaten to trip them up, and more than once Yuuki finds his shoes snagging on plant.

Thanks to Timothy and Joshua they don't have to bush-bash their way through, but it's still a mission when there's fatigue weighing on his body, sleep deprivation sapping his energy and an arm's worth of weight gone from one side and putting his balance off. Kyle's been recovering a little better than Yuuki has been, but he's breathing hard and slightly on the panicky side. Yuuki tries not to let his rapid heartbeat do the same to him.

The checkpoint they're heading for is a small disused hut down in the valley. Avi, Logan and Charlie have been carrying supplies down there over the course of the last two weeks. Yuuki remembers them saying that this way was quite a walk and required a river crossing, something he's not too keen on since he's rather off balance as it is, but they've got to do what they've got to do. At least Timothy knows where he's going, so they won't get lost.

Birds keep singing, some falling silent as the three of them make their way down the trail. The slope starts getting steeper, Timothy and Kyle switching places every now and then to help Yuuki climb down the harder parts. Kyle's not looking too good. His knees tremble every time they pause and his eyes are wild and frantic, but there's no time to stop and ask if he's okay. They have to keep moving.

They've just reached more level ground when noise in the vegetation behind them starts following them. They pick up the pace again but the noise is gaining on them. A voice shouts at them as the river comes into view, just up ahead on their left, growing louder with every stride they take.

The shout comes again. "Halt! This is the Peace Forces!"

Kyle cries out on an exhale. Yuuki's struggling to breathe. Timothy doesn't slow down.

"Halt!"

They don't have enough time; they're going to get caught before they even reach the river. Kyle stumbles. They lose sight of Timothy. As Kyle regains his footing and is off running again, Yuuki does the only thing he can think of to buy them some time and veers off track.

He makes the mistake of throwing a glance over his shoulder as he does so. There's only one officer after them, but it's Commander Jeff.

Yuuki trips. He slams into a tree, his left side taking the impact thankfully, and crashes to the ground. Jeff comes straight after him, taking the bait. Yuuki scrambles to his feet. He can't run fast enough. Jeff weaves through the trees with ease and throws himself –

Kyle tackles him first. "Run, Yuuki!"

The two land in a heap. Kyle twists away from Jeff before he can be pinned down and he and Yuuki take off again.

They don't get very far before they're caught up to again, but it's after they've broken through the trees and are running alongside the river bank when they are. If he can time it right, he could use Jeff's momentum to toss the officer into the –

Yuuki's foot slips. The inside of his boot slides straight down the muddy bank and he's falling.

"Yuuki!"

The water hits him like a cold shock wave. Jeff's heavy footfalls echo in his ears, or maybe it's his heartbeat, or the rushing of water around him. He can't tell up from down, he needs air, he needs *air*. The river's too fast to kick against and he's too weak for the frantic strokes of his arm to have any effect.

Something grabs his wrist. Yuuki's chest seizes up, but the hand's too small to be Jeff's. The fingers lock around his wrist and he jerks to a stop, head breaking the surface.

"..ki! I've got y – "

Under again. Kyle's voice is drowned out by the water.

He can't stay afloat. He kicks but it's to no avail. His boots are too heavy, weighing him down. He's running out of strength and the only arm he has to use to propel himself upward is the one that Kyle is keeping a hold of him with.

Yuuki's lungs burn and scream. He involuntarily gasps for air and chokes on river water. The pain in his chest rips through the muscles in his throat. His thoughts grow fuzzy. Yuuki fights it, desperately tries not to let it get him.

It claims him anyway.

With both hands – Yuuki's wrist in one and the other clutching a rock – Kyle doesn't let go. The strain is tearing at his arms, his shoulders, his chest and his fingers, but still he doesn't let go. He won't.

Yuuki's head is under the water. Kyle fights the current with all his strength, kicking sideways to avoid hitting Yuuki and *pulling* them forwards with his arm, but he doesn't have much of a grip and the muscles in his arms and legs are burning with effort.

It's already been too long. Yuuki's gone limp in his grasp, a dead weight. Kyle contemplates letting go of the rock, letting the current carry them downstream a little more in the hope of finding a better place to get out of the river. If he does that though, he risks them not getting out in time to save Yuuki – or worse, finding a better place to bank only for that place to be more accessible to Jeff.

Not an option. Here the bank is steep and the rocks slippery, but it's their best bet.

When finally, *finally*, Kyle manages to haul them both out of the current, out of the eddies and up an exposed length of stone bed, he's utterly exhausted. He's cold, he's shaking, his chest heaves… but Yuuki's as still as the rocks around them, not even breathing. Pressing two fingers under his chin, Kyle checks for a pulse and finds none.

The adrenaline that washes over him then is colder than the river water and the winter air around them. Kyle crawls around to Yuuki's right side and rolls him onto his left. Water leaks out of Yuuki's mouth. As soon as he's finished pounding Yuuki's back, no more water spilling out, Kyle rolls him onto his back and starts CPR.

He's never done it before. He's shaking terribly. His Dad had taught him first aid but at the time it hadn't really crossed Kyle's mind exactly how scary having to do it could be. Now he knows. He just hopes he doesn't screw up. He can't screw up. He'll lose Yuuki.

There's rustling in the vegetation on the less-steep slope of the bank. Kyle can't see from here if it's Timothy or Jeff. He hopes it's the former because there's no way he fight off Jeff right now, not when he's pouring all of his strength into reviving Yuuki. His heartbeat is loud in his ears, the adrenaline making him shakier than ever. The rustling gets closer as he leans down to give Yuuki breaths, but he doesn't look up. He can't afford to.

Yuuki coughs. Kyle startles, pulling back to turn Yuuki onto his side again instead of starting a third round of compressions. He slips a hand between Yuuki's head and the stones, cushioning the side of Yuuki's face as another mouthful of river water leaves him and his lungs begin to work again. After a few seconds, his brow furrows and Kyle watches with immense relief as his eyes flutter open.

"It's okay," Kyle murmurs. "I got you."

Yuuki's throat convulses. His eyes flick up to Kyle's, then close again. Kyle rubs his back slowly and Yuuki's coughing begins to ease.

"You saved me," Yuuki rasps.

"Yeah."

"Thanks."

Kyle takes a deep breath in and out. "Please don't make me have to do it again."

Yuuki lets out a weak laugh. "I don't intend to."

Now that Yuuki's breathing and not about to die, Kyle's limbs succumb to aftermath of adrenaline. He slumps forward and collapses on his side behind Yuuki, hand still supporting Yuuki's head. The grey-green-blue colours of the trees, sky and river all blend together, forcing Kyle to shut his eyes before he gets dizzy. It's cold, his wet clothes are clinging to his skin and sending a chill down his spine, but he's too exhausted to move.

Somehow he forgets about Jeff.

Boots move from grass to rock to stone, another pair making their way quickly through the vegetation from the other direction. The boots crunch down the bank, getting closer, closer, and then there's two hands on his torso.

Kyle shrieks and lashes out, but Jeff's already got his massive arms wrapped around him and he's not letting go. A knee to the back of his head. Kyle's mind goes blank in the pain. His body won't respond, too fatigued. Jeff carries him off, away from Yuuki and away from Timothy who's just appeared out of the trees.

Yuuki, lying on his back, can only watch in horror. "Ky-!" He breaks into a coughing fit. Timothy arrives at his side and helps him sit up. "Kyle!"

No matter how hard Kyle struggles, Jeff's grip on him doesn't loosen. He kicks at his shins, twists, throws his head back, even tries biting Jeff's arm, but all it earns him is a crushingly tight squeeze that doesn't let up. He sees Timothy get up from Yuuki's side. Jeff sees it too.

Kyle's hauled up the bank onto the grass and then Jeff readjusts his grip so that he's only holding him with one arm. A blaster is pressed hard against Kyle's neck. Everyone freezes. Timothy's expression morphs into fury. Yuuki throws up.

"You're not getting him back," Jeff yells. "He'll be dead before you do."

Kyle locks eyes with Timothy. *Just look after Yuuki.* Timothy's brow is furrowed in a deep 'v'. Kyle swallows hard. *I know you want to help me,* he thinks. *But you've got to think of Yuuki. Jeff will shoot me. He'll shoot me. Yuuki won't be able to handle it if that happens.*

Timothy stays as he is, crouched by Yuuki's side. If he could take down Jeff with his stare he would've done so.

Powering down the blaster, Jeff pockets it and resumes dragging Kyle into the bush. He pulls Kyle around so that he can't see Yuuki and Timothy anymore, kicks him in the back of his knees and picks him up to carry him under his arm.

Spiky bushes scratch Kyle's legs. His feet slam into tree trunks and into the ground below. If there's any good to come out of it, it's that with every hit his right leg takes he feels the solid weight of his knife still tucked safety in his boot. He might be weak right now, but at least he's not entirely defenceless.

Pain explodes in his head. Jeff rams him into the tree again before dropping him and shoving him against the tree with a kick to the stomach. Kyle jerks forward, curling in on himself. Jeff puts a foot on his chest, rolls him over onto his back and pins him there in the dirt.

A backpack is unzipped. Kyle doesn't even remember seeing the Peace Force officer carrying one but apparently he has been the entire time. He's still trying to make sense of what's going on, trying to focus past the pain in his head and chest, when a white sterile cloth falls onto the ground in front of him.

No. It's the same kind of cloth they silenced him with during his trial.

Adrenaline returns at a sickening level. Kyle's vision blurs. A rough hand grabs his arm and loops rope around his wrist. Before it's fastened, and before he can think twice, Kyle reaches into his boot and slips out the knife.

Jeff hisses in pain. "You little –"

The blade slashed his arm. Kyle pushes himself into a forward roll, narrowly avoiding Jeff's hands. The rope slips off his wrist. He pivots on the balls of his feet, brings the knife across Jeff's shin and launches himself out of his crouch before the officer can catch him.

Kyle runs. Energy comes out of nowhere but he knows it won't last. He can hear Jeff running after him. His chest burns as he runs harder, dodges trees, roots, rocks. He realises he's heading in the opposite direction of the hut that is Checkpoint A and it spurs him on.

Good. It'll lead Jeff off their trail. Timothy and Yuuki should be able to get to the hut alright.

Oh man, Yuuki and Timothy. Kyle's running with a knife in his hand. His fingerprints are definitely on it. There's a smear of blood on the blade, too. Adrenaline, anxiety, fear... he's so close to having an anxiety attack, but he can't, he *can't*. His throat constricts. His eyes tear up.

He runs until his body won't let him.

24

Yuuki stares numbly at the muddied hut floor. After what happened to Kyle, nobody's willing to take off their shoes. They're staying here overnight and moving onto Checkpoint B tomorrow, according to Timothy, but everyone is on guard, ready to make a run for it at a moment's notice. He doubts he's going to get much sleep tonight.

His hair's dry now. His clothes aren't. His cheeks aren't. The clothes Charlie pulled out of the storage boxes for him to change into are warm and clean, but all Yuuki feels is cold and tarnished.

"I left him," he whispers. His voice is still hoarse.

Susan rubs his back. "We'll get him back."

Timothy's busy talking to Joshua but he pauses at those words to give his wife a cautioning look.

"I don't care what that guy said," Susan says tightly. "We don't give up halfway in our household. That doesn't change just because we're out in the bush."

Timothy offers her a grim smile. Yuuki feels like a hypocrite.

They fought so hard to get Kyle out of prison and now they're just... leaving him? Who knows what Jeff's doing to Kyle right now, or what he's already done. For all they know he could be dead, something that could've been prevented if they'd gone after him right then and there by the river.

No. Jeff would've shot him.

They've seen how serious these Peace Force officers are. Yuuki's missing an arm thanks to one of them. His thoughts whirl. If they took his arm without hesitation, then they could very well do the same to Kyle if they –

"Yuuki."

He blinks. He's all tensed up, shivering. He's been staring wide-eyed at the floor like it's challenging him to a staring competition. Susan adjusts the heavy blanket around his shoulders, being careful of his freshly bandaged residual limb.

"I know you're scared for him," she murmurs. She surveys the scene before them, the planning and discussion of options. Kyle is at the centre of each conversation. "I am, too. But we *will* find a way to get him back safely, no matter how many obstacles they put in our way. You've done it before. We'll do it again."

Yuuki opens his mouth to say something but finds he can't. He's too angry at himself. Kyle saved his life and then he just *watches* as Jeff takes him away? Timothy said many times on their walk to the hut that doing anything would've been far too risky, that it would've put Kyle in even more immediate danger than he already was, but the thought does nothing to help Yuuki's bone-deep fear.

Images and sensations flood his mind. Instead of the hut, he's bound and locked up in an old garden shed, alone, his mouth sealed shut. Dehydrated. Hungry. Sore. The pain in his arm flares – phantom pain – but it's hard to separate that from the flashbacks and it's only a matter of seconds before he's confronted with another scene.

He sees Kyle forcing himself not to move, forcing himself to let himself be tied up with tape and put in a box so that Yuuki wouldn't get hurt, eyes never leaving his...

Avi holds a cup of coffee out to him, handle facing outwards. Yuuki blinks, lets the aroma of coffee ground him. He mumbles an ungrateful sounding thanks and accepts it. Avi smiles and quietly leaves to join his friends sitting on the bottom bunks.

A clap of hands startles him. Timothy clears his throat. "Can I have everyone's attention, please?"

Amelia trails off mid-sentence talking to Charlie. Sam, Logan and Avi reduce their voices to whispers and then quiet. Yuuki takes a sip of coffee. It's instant. He doesn't care.

"Alright," Timothy says. "As we discussed earlier, no getting too comfortable but get as much rest as you can. We're on the run now and we don't know how long we're going to be out here for. Obviously, our goal is to make it back to civilisation but we're not going to be able to do that if we wear ourselves out too quickly.

"First things first: rules. As soon as it gets dark, we use torches – sparingly. Keep your voices quiet. If you need to go outside for any reason, go in pairs at the very least. That includes going to the toilet. The long drop is, yes, only about twenty metres away, but we still need to be extra vigilant. If embarrassment is what it takes to have each other's backs then that's what we're doing.

"When we move out tomorrow, we're leaving at first light. The sooner the better, as Checkpoint B is further away and harder to access. It's not an easy walk and it'll take us all day, but with any luck we'll throw anybody on our tail off our trail.

"Regarding Kyle…" Timothy hesitates, exchanging a weary look with Yuuki. "We're not giving up on him, just to make that clear, but we can't go putting ourselves at unnecessary… at too high a risk in the process. We have to be careful with everything we do. *Everything*." He lowers his voice. "We also have to consider the possibility that Kyle might be used as a hostage. Under no circumstances act without thinking - not unless the need is dire. They won't hesitate to use him against us."

Timothy falls silent then, letting those words sink in. The atmosphere is heavy, solemn. There's a great sense of uncertainty floating around. A fear that each and every single one of them is trying their best to suppress. They're being hunted, though; it's a hundred percent understandable why that's a hard thing to do right now.

"The stakes are higher than any one of us, yeah?" Timothy says, softer this time. "If we succeed in delivering Amelia to the throne, not just our lives, but everyone else's will be better off. So let's do our best with what we have and let's do it whole-heartedly."

Susan hums in agreement. Logan and Avi nod. Joshua, Sam, Amelia and Charlie look like they're in the middle of playing a game of chess. Yuuki observes, otherwise feeling detached from the whole situation.

Before it gets dark, the backpacks are stocked up with supplies, first aid kits and spare batteries. Timothy's bag of electronics is lined with plastic bags and everything that can be waterproofed is. Joshua boils small pots of water outside, making Yuuki another coffee and everyone else a hot drink if they want one. Dinner comes in the form of biscuits, rice and dehydrated vegetables and meat.

There's not enough bunks for everyone, so they sort out the sleeping arrangement according to who needs it most. Yuuki, Charlie and Susan take the three spaces at the bottom and Amelia, Sam and Logan take the top ones. Timothy and Joshua roll out self-inflating mattresses near the door, Avi doing the same but on the other side of the room. It's not all that comfortable sharing the room with so many people, but the hut manages to retain everyone's body heat, so at least it's not cold.

Yuuki stays huddled in the blanket all night long for lack of a shirt. His clothes are taking their time drying and Susan doesn't want him catching a cold by putting them back on yet. It's easier to breathe this way though, without any jersey collars choking him and making him feel like he's back in the river near-drowning. There's also no sleeve hanging empty beside him to remind him over and over what happened last time Peace Force officers came knocking at their door. Yuuki's mind is reminding him enough.

He doesn't sleep much. It's impossible. The darkness is a canvas for the chaos in his head. It's suffocating. Avi snores. Sam rolls over restlessly in her sleep. Joshua and Timothy trade places in keeping watch. Outside, an owl hoots. In the distance, the river can be heard rushing.

There's not a minute that Yuuki doesn't think about how none of these things tell him about where Kyle is.

Kyle. He should be here with them. They'd let him take one of the bunk beds. If Kyle felt uncomfortable sleeping surrounded by people and in complete darkness, Yuuki would be fine sharing his space. He'd probably be able to get more sleep than he's getting if Kyle were here, though he doubts it would be a significant increase. Total darkness is far too reminiscent of the garden shed at night. Kyle's cell was probably just as dark.

Yuuki tries not to let his imagination run wild but it does anyway. Kyle being tortured. Locked up somewhere. Beaten. Bound. Suffering. Bleeding. Alone or else surrounded by unkind people. Maybe by some miracle he was able to escape, in which case he's probably lost or hurt or…or…

Don't think that. He's not dead. Don't think that.

But how do you know that? asks another part of his mind.

I don't, Yuuki tells it, *but I'm not giving up on him and that's that.*

Doubt is inevitable. It comes and Yuuki fights it. Anxiety fills him. He fights it. Sleep comes and he fights that also, for fear of the nightmares that will take a hold of him, but eventually exhaustion sweeps over him and that's enough to fall into a pattern of napping off and on for half an hour at a time.

The night passes this way, slow and unrelenting.

It's freezing. Kyle doesn't stop shivering. He's curled in on himself as tightly as he can manage, huddled under fern fronds and lying on them. The rocks throw their shadows over him when the moon comes across the sky, the clouds clearing long enough for its light to shine through for a while.

He keeps his knife tucked against his chest, fingers clutching the sheath or the hilt at all times. The temperature drops lower and lower as the night wears on. Kyle hugs the knife closer. He pretends it's a hot water bottle or a blanket or Yuuki's hand. Hopefully Yuuki's warmer than he is right now, at the hut with the others and with food and water and dry clothes to change into. Kyle's have barely dried at all. He wonders if he should be taking them off, but they're all the clothes he has and it's colder without them.

As soon as it's light enough to see by, Kyle picks himself up and starts moving again. He's lost, having run so blindly away from Jeff yesterday that he forgot to take a more descriptive note of the direction he took than 'opposite'. He's shattered, stiff, shaken, and yet somehow he finds the will to push on through the cold and the exhaustion. He has his Arkala'ana blood to thank that he has yet to catch a cold.

Just…get back to Yuuki.

Kyle finds the river as the sun peeks over the hills, lighting up the valley. He follows it downstream, the sun at his back. Checkpoint A is roughly east from Amelia's house, if he remembers the map correctly; if he heads back west, back in the opposite direction of the opposite direction he took yesterday, he thinks he should, by rights, find it.

Thirst overtakes him but he can't risk getting sick from river water. Hunger gnaws at his stomach and saps his energy from him. The only thing Kyle finds to eat is the odd tip of supplejack vine. All of his energy is spent staying upright and keeping on moving if he isn't stopping for a break.

Anxiety fills him more and more the further he goes. He always had a knack for orientation, but when he's this tired it's hard to be confident. He half-expects Jeff to be waiting for him behind every tree, grinning as he watches Kyle stumble along straight back to him.

There is no Jeff, however. There is no one at all. It's just Kyle and the insects, birds and the odd rodent that doesn't hide itself in time.

Kyle reaches Checkpoint A mid-morning. His pace is slow and the trek exhausting with how fatigued he is, but the moment he sees the hut he's able to walk a little bit faster. The sight of it makes him want to cry.

The sight of who's inside does make him cry.

There's no one here. Muddy boot prints, yes. A discarded pair of pants Kyle recognises as the ones Yuuki had been wearing, draped over the top of the bunk closest to the door to dry, yes. But no people. They were here... but now they're not.

Trembling, Kyle closes the door behind him. He sinks to his knees, spies a not-so-muddy spot on the wooden floor boards and lies down. There's fresh water bottled in the corner across the room and there's fresh, clean clothes and packets of food left over in the storage boxes that he should get up to get. But all Kyle can do is lie there staring at the ceiling as his vision swirls, focusing and unfocusing. His muscles burn and ache. The tears give way to pain and then nothing but a hollowness in his chest.

They've gone to Checkpoint B already, haven't they?

He doesn't have enough strength to go after them. Kyle closes his eyes and makes the call to stay here until he's recovered enough energy to make the next trip.

Right now it's hard to imagine when that'll be.

25

"How're you doing, Yuuki?" Timothy asks, falling back in the line.

Yuuki keeps his eyes on the ground in front of him, following the path that Logan's feet take. "I'm alright."

He knows he undoubtedly looks like a mess. Everyone else is looking at least a little bit tired on it, but Yuuki was a walking zombie before all of this even began. Even before he decided to help Timothy with looking into Kyle's case, he wasn't doing so well.

It's been hard keeping up with everybody but he's determined not to slow them down. They can't risk getting caught. If he's got to put in double the effort then that's what he'll do, even if it means he has no energy left at the end of this trek. There will be time to rest later.

"Okay, that's physically," Timothy says, "but how are you holding out inside?"

"I'm not."

Yuuki winces. He wasn't intending on saying that... but it's the truth. Timothy reaches out and pats him on the shoulder. Yuuki grimaces, self-conscious about his missing limb on that side and people moving into the space where it should be.

It's killing him, being separated from Kyle. After everything he did to get him out of prison, now this? Yuuki feels like he failed him. Kyle trusted him enough to let him help, to open up to him, to heal alongside him. He was there when Yuuki thought he couldn't go on anymore, after what had happened back at his house.

All this time Kyle's been supporting him even though he himself is struggling. Yuuki's not sure whether it's selfishness or shame, but he feels like it shouldn't be that way around. He shouldn't have to need that support the way he does.

And yet he does. The words get caught in his throat, but Yuuki forces himself to say them aloud. "I feel like I let him down."

Timothy hums. "I do, too."

There's a raw, bitter anger in Timothy's expression that Yuuki catches a glimpse of. His stomach churns, shame washing over him. It's not until Timothy helps him over a log blocking their way that Yuuki realises he's angry at himself.

"I keep thinking about it," Timothy murmurs. "It keeps replaying in my mind. If I'd been quicker, taken action sooner..." He sighs. "But I know Jeff isn't anyone to mess with. Kyle, he... I could see it in his eyes. He was asking me not to do anything. But that wasn't for himself, Yuuki. It was for you."

Joshua calls from ahead to warn about a slippery uphill slope. Sam and Logan answer him with a tired, drawn out 'okay'. Behind Yuuki and Timothy, Susan turns around to pass on the warning to Charlie, Avi and Amelia who are bringing up the rear.

When Yuuki sees the slope, his heart sinks. *There's no way I can climb up that.* But no matter how much he despairs, he has to find a way somehow.

Even if someone has to carry him up there, they have to keep moving or else they won't make it to Checkpoint B before dark. Winter means they only have so much daylight in a day, and this pace they're going at (thanks to Yuuki) is chewing through it fast.

The only thing keeping Yuuki going is the hope he's clinging to that Kyle managed to escape Jeff yesterday. If he did, Kyle's going to be so lost. Knowing how easy it is to wander off track with the mistake of thinking the path leads a different way, Yuuki worries.

Another thought occurs to him then, watching Sam scramble up the muddy hill after her brother: this is their last chance to go back; by the looks of this slope, once they reach the top of it there's no coming back down again. That means that this is their last chance to turn around and go back in search of Kyle.

"Timothy," Yuuki whispers. "I-I think we should go back. *Someone* should go back, just in case. What if he's there, at the hut, right now as we speak? We can't just leave him there. Someone will find him."

Timothy looks Yuuki in the eye, his gaze fiery and resolute. Yuuki braces himself for the raised eyebrow, the reminder of the risks. He's been tossing up the idea of speaking his thoughts all morning, only he hasn't yet because he knows they can't afford to waste time hanging around when they're most likely being actively hunted.

Instead, Timothy nods and sets his jaw. "Let's do it."

Logan throws him a worried glance over his shoulder as he readjusts his rifle for the climb. He opens his mouth to comment but Timothy cuts him off.

"We've come this far in saving Kyle. There is no way we should be stopping now." Timothy exchanges silent words with Susan and then turns Charlie. "We better go back to the hut. If Kyle's there, he'll have much better luck finding the next checkpoint if he's with us."

Susan nods. She rests a hand on Yuuki's good shoulder. "Who's going?"

"Me, Charlie – if you will – and one of the others..." Timothy frowns, scanning the group. "Avi, can you come here a minute, please?"

Yuuki feels the disappointment like a cold weight settling over him, but he knows the exclusion isn't personal. It's better if he continues on with the others. He doesn't have enough strength to make it all the way to the hut and back this way again, especially if they don't want to be walking in darkness for too long.

"We're going to go back to check that Kyle's not waiting for us back at the hut," Timothy says to Avi. "Now...we don't know what condition Kyle's going to be in and it's going to be a long walk, but if you're able to come with us...?"

Anxiety stabs him right through. Avi's going along in case Kyle's in need of being carried. Yuuki imagines the group coming back with Kyle covered in blood and bruises and swallows. *God, please don't let it come to that.*

Avi realises this too and takes a deep breath. "Yeah, man," he says quietly. "I can do that."

Charlie puts his hands on his hips, his brow shining with sweat. He nods at Timothy and Avi. Ahead, Joshua, Sam and Logan have paused in their climbing. Joshua raises his eyebrows at Timothy in question.

"Change of plan," Timothy says, louder this time so everyone can hear him. "Charlie, Avi and I are going to go back and check the hut in case Kyle's made it there. The rest of you go on ahead. If there's no sign of Kyle, we'll be back before dark. If he's there or something comes up, we'll be back a little later. Don't send anyone after us – just wait at Checkpoint B. Joshua will lead the way."

The atmosphere grows solemn. It's beginning to sink in now, the reality of what's going on. If something happens, there's no going back. If they get caught, that's it – it's over. The only way out of the bush is through victory, arrest or death. There might be a time when they have to make the decision not to go back for one of their own, but as for now and given the choice, no one's getting left behind.

"Can we check our equipment?" Charlie asks. "Let's make sure we're prepared."

Joshua and Sam start making their way up the slope again. Logan hesitates but follows soon after. As Timothy, Charlie and Avi go through a mental checklist of torches, food, water, first aid and other emergency supplies, Susan gently nudges Yuuki towards the slope and gestures with her other hand to Amelia.

"Come back safe, honey," she murmurs to Timothy.

There's no guarantee, of course, but Timothy makes the promise to do so anyway.

Five minutes later, the return-to-Checkpoint-A party take their leave. Everyone else finishes clambering up the slope, Yuuki taking the most time out of all of them, slipping down more often than he's able to gain any traction to pull himself up. Once everyone's made it up to the top, they all sit down for a fifteen minute break.

No one talks. The ground is a common point of interest. Crackers are munched on and water drunk, but other than that it's quiet. Too quiet.

There's birds chirping and the sun's come out a little, but Yuuki's not going to be feeling any better until he knows Kyle's safe. Yuuki's afraid he's getting his hopes up, imagining Kyle coming back at all. He's scared that by hoping he's jinxed it. He can only pray Kyle's at the hut, that Timothy and Charlie and Avi come back as four people instead of three.

Yuuki closes his eyes, grounds himself by concentrating on the feeling of mud plastering his legs and arm, of dirt clinging to his shirt and the hem of his shorts.

He can only pray and hope and hope…

26

It's difficult to get a gauge on how much time has passed. Kyle's been drifting in and out of restless sleep since he drank some water, ate a couple of muesli bars and let the floor take all of his weight again.

The one time he sleeps as opposed to naps, Kyle dreams of Yuuki drowning. Drowning and being unable to save him. Of Jeff grabbing him before he had a chance to dive into the river after him, of watching Yuuki disappear under the water then reappear only to go under again. He wakes even more exhausted than he already was, not to mention sore.

Footsteps sound outside. Kyle groans. Is he so tired he's hallucinating now? But they come again, heavy footsteps like boots, infrequent like they're having to pick their way through the bush.

Kyle's breath hitches. There's two pairs of them, but one of them... he knows an officer who walks like that. *Oh please, no.*

"Check around the back," says Jeff. "Make sure there's not a back door."

"On it."

The second voice is too low and too deep to be Deborah, but the way they talk to each other is enough to say that they're equal ranking officers. Both commanders, then.

Kyle slowly rolls onto his side and crawls on shaking arms to the wall.

He creeps right up to the door, trying to ignore the way his bones and muscles protest. He's trapped if he stays in here. Running is his only option. He's going to have to run for his life, again, and while feeling like this... but it's his only way out.

The second pair of footsteps rejoin the first, rejoining Jeff where he waits guarding the door. There's whispers, probably a few hand signals, and then the door is shoved open.

Adrenaline. Kyle launches himself at Jeff's knees. It's a sloppy dive, and he lands right at Jeff's feet, but his nerves have him slipping out of the way and back on his feet in an instant.

He makes it two and half strides before fire zaps him in the back.

A strangled scream tears through his throat. He falls, shaking. Burning. Pain lances out through his body. A hand on his back. He flinches hard and scrambles to find his footing. He has to run. Somehow he avoids Jeff's sweeping hand as he tries to grab him, but as Kyle forces his shaking legs into motion again he's shocked with the taser a second time.

The second Peace Force officer growls. "Hey. That wasn't necessary."

Kyle struggles to breathe. Jeff's hands are on him as his muscles cramp, snatching up his arms and lashing his wrists together. He keeps a knee digging into Kyle's lower back to keep him pinned.

"Thought you could run and hide," Jeff mutters, ignoring his partner. "Well, you thought wrong."

The rope is tied so tight that it hurts. He's pulled upright, hoisted into the air and flung over Jeff's shoulder. Kyle's head spins. He swallows hard and focuses on breathing in spite of Jeff's shoulder digging into his stomach. He can't afford to throw up; he needs every bit of the food and water he consumed earlier to stay inside of him.

He's carried inside, muscles still twitching. Jeff lowers him down by the bunk beds, only to drop him gracelessly onto the floor. The rope used to bind his hands still has some length left of it, and this Jeff pulls over a rung in the bunk bed ladder. Kyle cries out, his already strained arms straining even more. But Jeff only pulls the rope further, until Kyle's fingers are squished against the wooden ladder. He's then secured there, half-kneeling, half-slumped forward as he is, arms stretched out behind him and his shoulders holding most of his weight.

Jeff finishes tying him in place with an emphasising tug. "No getting away this time."

I think I've realised that already, Kyle retorts but he holds his tongue. He doesn't want to be gagged as well.

"Andy," Jeff says to the other man. "Watch the kid. I'm going to give Deborah our coordinates."

The second officer – Andy – grunts in response as Jeff stomps outside with a radio communicator in hand.

The door stays open and Kyle can hear every word that's exchanged, every breath of laughter. Andy also listens in, though he doesn't share the same reaction to Deborah' jokes as Jeff, instead simply standing where he is by the door with his face impassive. Jeff tells Deborah that he's got Kyle in a stress position, and only then does the full weight of the situation dawn on him.

So that's what this is. I'm basically going to be tortured.

There's a reason why he's tied up. There's a reason why he was put in a box to be kidnapped. Deborah hadn't introduced herself to him and

Yuuki as Jeff's lead interrogator for nothing. His hands are losing feeling and the pain radiating through his neck and shoulders is only getting worse. Kyle clenches his teeth together. Jeff's right: he's not getting away this time.

The call over, Jeff comes back inside. He frowns at Kyle and kicks him in the ribs. A muscle pulls in Kyle's shoulder. He forces himself not to make a noise. Andy glares at Jeff with a raised eyebrow, a deep frown on his face. Jeff glares back, leaves Kyle alone and sits down on the bottom bunk bed opposite the ladder Kyle's tied to.

"So," he says. "My friend will be here in due time but I figure we may as well get started. Where's everyone headed?"

'Checkpoint B' is the answer Deborah will probably end up getting out of him, but Kyle doesn't give it willingly. He keeps his mouth shut and doesn't make eye contact.

"You'll save yourself a lot of pain if you answer me now, Kindall."

I'm already in a lot of pain. What's a little more?

"Kindall!"

Kyle flinches. Jeff's voice booms in the small hut, amplified. He can hear the snarl and impatience in it.

Beside the door, Andy sighs. "Let's just wait until Deborah gets here," he murmurs. "He's not going to answer us."

Jeff tsks. He goes to say something, then hums. "Oh, how could I have forgotten?" Lowering himself into a crouch, Jeff moves right into Kyle's space and grabs his ankle.

The closeness has Kyle's heart exploding and his throat closing up in fear. His arms burn as Jeff pulls his right foot out from under him. He holds Kyle's leg still with one hand and slips the other into his boot, pulling out the knife and its sheath.

Kyle stares at it in Jeff's hands in horror. He jerks his leg back, folding it back under him. His bound hands won't let him move back any further.

He sees now how one of Jeff's sleeves is bulkier than the other at the forearm. No doubt there's a bandage or a plaster on his leg as well. The grin that curls on Jeff's face turns his blood cold.

But before the knife can be unsheathed, Andy strides across the room and snatches it out of Jeff's hands. "Leave him for Deborah."

Jeff almost looks offended. "Who said I was going to do anything?"

"The look in your eyes says it all."

"We're going to kill him anyway. What's the big deal?"

"The big deal," Andy mutters, "is that we'd achieve greater success keeping him alive to use as a hostage."

Kyle wants to be sick.

Jeff gets up and plonks himself down on the bunk bed again. "Then we'll have to carry him around. He'll only slow us down."

"We take him back with us to the vehicles and hold onto him until we need him. How hard is that?" Andy tucks the knife into his belt. "The princess and her friends are going to have to come out of the bush eventually. If we can't get a location out of this guy, then we keep searching and wait until we find it ourselves. If we meet resistance, we offer them Kindall and get them to stand down."

"They don't seem so stupid a bunch of people to surrender that easily."

"Which is why we need Kindall – alive. Alive and well enough to show them."

In other words, they'll beat him up and do whatever they like with him so long as it doesn't result in him dying.

Andy and Jeff stop talking, leaving Kyle to his imagination of 'whatever they like' entails. He's already formulating escape plans as best he can, most simply involving making one hell of a racket and struggling like a fish out of water. He probably won't get far but it's probably the only thing he's got going for him. It's the only hope of escape he's got right now anyways, since he already knows the others won't come looking for him. He knows it'd be too risky for them to do so.

It's an hour and a half before Deborah shows up. Jeff helps himself to biscuits from the food storage. Andy remains expressionless. The ache in Kyle's shoulders grows unbearable. When the noise of boots tramping towards the hut can be heard, Jeff stands up and, almost tauntingly, stretches.

"Took your time," he says, greeting Deborah at the door with a nod.

Andy frowns, acknowledges Deborah and returns his gaze to the window.

The presence of a third person in the room besides himself nearly sets off Kyle's panic. Deborah emanates unkindness and ill intention. She saunters over to Kyle with a gleam in her eye.

"Look at me, Kindall," she says.

Kyle doesn't. He keeps his eyes fixed on the floor so that he can keep all three officers in his periphery. But Deborah doesn't give him the choice, bending down and taking a hold of Kyle's chin, forcing him to look up.

Kyle's vision hones and blurs all at once. The only thing keeping the panic attack at bay now is the fear of what will be done to him if it happens. Fortunately he doesn't have to suppress it for long.

The floorboards creak as Andy shifts, a stick breaks outside and Avi barrels into the room with a shout.

Deborah's fingers are torn from Kyle's face, Avi shoving her to the ground. Timothy steps in front of Kyle, shielding him from Jeff. Both he, Charlie and Andy pull out their blaster guns at the same time.

Andy shoots first.

With a startled yelp, Avi leaps out of the way and bangs into Kyle. An arm muscle tears and Kyle cries out. In front of them, Deborah is shot dead in seconds.

"You traitor!" Jeff yells, whipping out his own blaster.

Timothy and Charlie hesitate. Andy doesn't.

All Kyle's ability to keep it together is lost. Avi, Timothy and Charlie might be here now to rescue him, but there's too much for his brain to process: Yuuki nearly drowned yesterday; Kyle was nearly taken; he spent a night out in the middle of the bush in the middle of winter with his clothes still wet with river water; he finally makes it to the hut that is Checkpoint A and finds the others have already left, that they didn't wait around for him; Jeff came, tasered him and tied him up; and now he's been sitting in a stress position for close to two hours, the woman who came ready to torture him dead on the floor in front of him and Jeff dead now too.

He's safe, but there's no relief to be had. Not yet.

The tears start as Timothy works on the knots tying him to the ladder. He cries hard and silently, his voice caught in his throat. The moment the rope gives, Kyle slumps forward. Avi catches him, holds him up, hugging him as Timothy finishes untying the rope from around Kyle's wrists. Timothy hisses an exclamation and gently as he can manoeuvres Kyle's hands down to his sides.

Kyle's shoulders scream. He can't feel his hands, but as the blood starts flowing to them again they hurt and spasm and shake like crazy. Avi holds him close in a similar way to how Yuuki hugged him when he had two arms, close and protective, strong and warm. Kyle wants to wrap his arms around him but they won't move. Avi doesn't seem to mind though, just holds him and rubs a hand over his back, focusing on massaging the tension and stiffness out of Kyle's neck and shoulders.

"You're okay now, Kyle," Timothy murmurs from behind. Another hand falls lightly on Kyle's shoulder. "Are you able to walk?"

Kyle shakes his head, not lifting his head from Avi's jersey.

"It's alright. We'll carry you back, okay? Are you alright if Avi's the one carrying you?"

He trusts Avi. There's been nothing but kindness in him the whole time Kyle's been around him. Avi's the one he trusts the most after Yuuki, Timothy and Susan. He nods.

"Okay. We're going to get moving. Charlie is talking to Andy here about burying Jeff and Deborah. We'll go ahead of them and wait a little up the track, yeah?"

Kyle's stomach churns. He's too upset to warn anybody, but thankfully Avi senses it coming and moves him so that he's able to vomit on the floor instead of all over Avi. It's disgusting and it reeks, but Avi and Timothy stay with him.

"Hey, Charlie?" Timothy says. "Can you find us some clothes for Kyle, please? His are damp from yesterday still. He'll get sick if he's in them any longer."

Andy adds in his deep voice, "If you guys have any painkillers on you, he'll be needing those too."

"How long…?"

"Almost two hours."

Kyle finishes emptying his stomach of all the food and water he had in there. He groans. So much for keeping it all in.

Avi slips an arm under his knees and lifts him up. "We'll wait outside," he murmurs, and sidles out the open door, carrying him away from the mess.

With the space opening up around him, the fresh air and the breeze blowing across his face, Kyle shudders. There's no bad people out here. Nothing to confine him. Nothing restraining him. Just release.

Timothy follows them out, his backpack slung over one arm while he rummages through it with the other hand. They find a large rock near where Kyle was hit with the taser and settle down there, Avi setting Kyle down beside him. Timothy hands Kyle a water bottle, a box of pain relief pills in his other hand. But Kyle's arms won't work properly, so Avi ends up taking the water bottle and holding it up for him.

After Kyle's washed and spat the vomit taste out of his mouth, Timothy's brow furrows. He looks between Kyle's off-colour hands and the painkillers, then up at Kyle's face questioningly.

"How do you want to…?" he asks.

Kyle's arms and shoulders hurt too much to even try to use his own hands to pop the painkillers into his mouth, which means Timothy will have to do it for him. He's too shaken to be embarrassed, but he has no idea how to ask if Timothy doesn't mind giving them straight to him.

Thankfully Timothy suggests it anyways, and with Avi ready with the water bottle, Kyle's able to get the painkillers down. There's water inside the hut that they can use to top up the bottle with, so Timothy lets him drink as much as needs and can without being sick again.

With a cough, Kyle whispers, "D-do you think we can tru-trust Andy?"

Timothy considers. "Did he do anything to you?"

"No. H-he stopped Jeff from doing anything, though. He was....he was gonna..."

Avi rubs his back again. "It's okay, man. You don't have to talk about it if you don't want to."

Kyle sniffs, ducks his head. His neck hurts. He makes a mental note to make sure he doesn't move too suddenly. "I just...my knife's still in there..."

"The one that Andy had?"

"Y-yeah."

As if on cue, Charlie comes out of the hut with a pile of clothes and Kyle's knife resting on top of them. Charlie sets them down on the rock beside Avi and rubs his forehead.

"Well, Andy seems like a decent guy," he says. "I must say I'm still a little shocked that he'd outright...you know, just kill them like that, but I guess he knows them better than we do." He sighs. "Kyle, lad. There's some dry clothes here for you. A clean pair of socks. You might want to take off your boots too. I think your feet will appreciate some airing out."

Kyle nods. Changing sounds like an absolute mission though, yet another thing he's going to need help doing. But Charlie's right – his feet do feel gross, and he's been meaning to swap his clothes for dry ones since he woke up from his nap. He would've done, if it hadn't been for the unwelcome visit.

He ends up asking Avi to help him, since he's closer in age and he's right here. They head up what's apparently the trail a little bit so that they're not so exposed. Avi helps him take off his boots first, flinging his stinky wet socks off to the side. Once, Kyle would've laughed. Changing out of his jersey hurts badly, as it means having to move his arms, but changing out of his pants is even more of a mission. Kyle can barely stand and Avi has help him with changing underwear as well. Avi doesn't look and Kyle is grateful.

After they find a place to sit down, a bulky tree root jutting out over the path, Avi gathers up the discarded clothing. He calls Timothy over so that Kyle's not left sitting here by himself and then goes to back to the hut to hang up the clothing.

"We'll leave shortly," Timothy tells him, sitting down on the root of another tree. "How are your arms?"

Kyle grimaces. His arms are limp beside him, his hands resting in his lap feeling not much different. Timothy reads his expression well enough and nods, grimacing also.

"Yuuki's the one who brought it up, you know? That you might be back here. I'd been thinking it, but it was Yuuki who turned that thought into an action."

"I-is he okay?"

Timothy grunts. "As okay as he can be, I guess. He'll be a lot better once he knows you're safe."

It's a relief just knowing Yuuki's alright.

Avi returns and the three of them wait quietly while Charlie and Andy get to the hard work. The sound of spade hitting dirt rings through the trees. There's nothing they can do to hide from it. Timothy offers him a part of his sandwich and Kyle distracts himself by nibbling on that. His stomach's settled, thankfully, but he still feels nauseous, especially hearing Charlie and Andy digging a grave or two around the other side of the hut somewhere.

When at last the bodies of Jeff and Deborah have been buried and Charlie and Andy have washed their hands of dirt, the group gathers together in solemn silence and take a couple of minutes to breathe. Andy remains stoic on the surface, but Kyle knows the signs well enough to know that the reason why he's got his arms crossed over his chest is to hide the slight shaking of his hands. When Andy catches Kyle noticing, he averts his eyes. Kyle says nothing.

They head on out. Timothy leads the way, Avi carrying Kyle in a piggyback behind him, Charlie and Andy following behind. Kyle's boots are secured to Charlie's pack and the socks he opted not to wear in favour of airing out his feet are in Timothy's pack. Since Avi's carrying Kyle, Andy carries the backpack Avi had carried in.

The walk is long. Hours pass. They pause to take out their head torches as dusk falls, one break among many that they take. Kyle puts his trust in Avi and naps off and on as they go.

Two hours after dark they make it to Checkpoint B, a small cave that's hidden enough to allow them a campfire. They're probably naught but silhouettes until Timothy in the lead turns off his head torch, but even the shape of five people returning instead of three – one of them carried on another's shoulders – is all the announcement the group needs.

The tense anticipation in the cave dissolves into cheering and clapping.

Yuuki's sobbing in relief can be heard above it all.

27

Avi sets Kyle down near the fire. The second he does, Kyle and Yuuki are pulling each other into an embrace. Yuuki clings to him with all the strength his one arm can muster, crying hard. All Kyle can do is hold onto him and do his best not to break down too. He's too exhausted.

Though he hasn't exactly taken him for granted, Kyle is beginning to understand just how much Yuuki means to him. Yuuki's given up so much to help him. It's unfair and it hurts to see him like this. Apparently it goes both ways though, thinking that; as Timothy and Charlie introduce Andy to the group and Avi gives Susan a report of Kyle's condition, Yuuki's arm around Kyle's shoulders tightens.

Someone taps Kyle's shoulder. The touch is light but it startles him nonetheless and he stiffens, only to turn his head to see Susan kneeling behind him. She murmurs an apology and gestures to a space closer to the cave wall. There's a first aid kit and other supplies laid out on a tarpaulin, unpacked from one of their backpacks.

"Avi said you got hurt a bit," she says softly. "Do you mind if I help you?"

Kyle doesn't answer. He stares at her, unable to think of words and not really understanding what there is to help him with. In a wave of stress, he turns his face back to hiding in Yuuki's jersey.

"Kyle?"

He can't get much strength in his arms, but he holds onto Yuuki a little tighter. He's scared of letting go. It's like he's afraid of what will happen if he does, that Yuuki might be pulled away from him and be shot again, drown or break entirely. Should that happens, Kyle won't have the strength to save him.

Yuuki still hasn't spoken a word. Kyle wonders if he's afraid of the same thing. People keep trying to pull them apart and when they do, bad things happen. They keep happening.

They're afraid for each other.

Kyle knows he should answer Susan, but he's sore and he's tired. It's something he's just going to have to deal with until it passes; it's not like there's anything that can be done about it. He just hopes Susan doesn't mistake his lack of energy as rudeness.

In the end, Susan lets them be and Kyle lets himself relax. There's some whispering between her and Avi and then the cave is quiet of all voices but Andy's.

Kyle considers zoning out, the low roar of the fire and the warmth it brings lulling, but the words being spoken are too solemn: they're talking about what happened at the hut. Without wanting to, Kyle's faced with remembering and the ache in his shoulders, neck and arms renews.

"It was not my first choice to kill them," Andy murmurs, "but if they were still alive, they would only keep coming after you all. Unless you guys want to be killed and have all chances of getting the Princess to the throne taken from you, then we are going to have to take such measures."

The conversation stills, Andy letting his words sink in and everyone else reminding themselves of just how ruthless Jeff and Deborah were. Yuuki's quiet. Kyle's throat constricts.

"This isn't the first time you've intervened, is it?" Timothy whispers. He's close enough to Kyle and Yuuki that they can hear him.

Andy waits for Timothy to repeat the question, unable to hear.

"Ninao? That was you, wasn't it? The anonymous person who leaked Yuuki's location?"

"It was."

Yuuki stiffens. Kyle shifts a little to give him room to breathe.

"I made up a false lead and gave it to Jeff," Andy says. "He wouldn't tell me what his plans with Yuuki were and I found that rather disconcerting. Jeff was so consumed with chasing the lead that I was able to get Yuuki's location out to you guys without drawing attention to myself. It wouldn't have mattered to me if I'd blown my cover, but it would've been a loss of a great advantage to us who don't support Taularh. It's not something I was willing to do if there was another way around it."

Timothy sits down beside Susan with a long, drawn out sigh. "Thank you."

Though Andy chooses his words carefully, it's still enough to throw Yuuki back into the loop of memory. Kyle remembers how the enclosed area of his isolation cell had triggered him. Just like that, Kyle's also thrown into remembering and he swallows.

It'll be a while before they can think about these things without the sensations and the imagery being so fresh and vivid in their minds – a long while.

Yuuki closes his eyes and focuses on controlling his breathing.

"Weren't you also the officer who saw us in the parking lot?" Joshua asks.

Andy hums in response.

"You didn't tell me you guys were seen," Timothy mumbles.

"We weren't sure," Joshua says. "The guy – uh, Andy – didn't come over to question us, so we all decided it was safe to say that he hadn't seen us, or at least not recognised us."

"Well, thank goodness nothing happened."

"What gave you away," Andy says, "was not your appearances but rather your activity. If my job is to be keeping my eye out for anything suspicious going on, then that's what I'll be doing. Two young people messing around with a laptop in the backseat of a car and an older man sitting in the driver's seat looking nonchalant falls under that category."

Joshua winces. "Yeah, I guess it would."

Yuuki's not listening and Kyle isn't really either. They're both exhausted, physically and emotionally, one of them recently nearly drowned and the other having spent most of his energy running from the person who ended up catching him anyway. Kyle's run, swam, saved Yuuki's life, run again, spent the night out in the winter cold with wet clothes, walked, been tasered, tied up and rescued. His mind is still reeling from it all and Yuuki, no doubt, was worried sick for him the entire time.

There's little they can do to comfort each other in the state that they're both in, but somehow knowing that the other is okay is enough. Being able to rest their minds and their bodies is enough. Being able to hold each other…

Kyle's never had a brother. Not a real one and not in a friend. It's been a while since he's known the concept of family at all, what with his mother passing away giving birth to him and his father dying that night at work. No one who hosted him had ever wanted him, a teenager struggling to cope with the ridiculous lack of empathy of society – or rather, in their eyes, a kid with problems, a troublemaker with anger issues.

When he got arrested, he'd almost wished Daniel had killed him, that he hadn't fought back. He wouldn't have ended up in isolation for one, nor would he have had to have the world put on a show for him about how little they cared what happened to him, what he actually did or didn't do and who he is.

Kyle had given up on himself. Yuuki hadn't.

Yuuki by no means *had* to come in and talk to him. He didn't have to be patient and listen. He didn't have to care….but he did. Even if it meant putting his own health at risk, Yuuki was willing to be that reckless for Kyle.

He still asks himself why. He's still bewildered. More than anything, though… he's grateful.

"Thank you," Kyle whispers.

Before he can see Yuuki's confused expression, he's dropped off to sleep.

Yuuki snaps out of his flashback, brow furrowed. *Where did that come from?*

He stares at Kyle's face, trying to work out why he's being thanked all of a sudden and he's still trying to figure it out after the others have settled down for the night.

For worrying about him, maybe? But Yuuki didn't do anything. Kyle had been the one to pull him out of the river. Judging by the bruising ache on the left side of his ribcage, he'd also revived him too. Then when Jeff had caught up to them and taken Kyle, all Yuuki had done was sit there and watch. Kyle had escaped, only to be caught again the following morning at the hut that Yuuki and everyone had left on the presumption that he wasn't going to be showing up anytime soon.

What if they hadn't gone back for him? What if Yuuki hadn't voiced the thought plaguing him that they should go back, just in case? How long would Kyle have lasted, once Jeff had Deborah start torturing him? What would they have done to him?

"Thank you."

Oh. Yuuki's heart stills. *"Thank you for saving me,"* is basically what Kyle was saying. Not just for today, but for the past several weeks. It's kind of strange to think about when only yesterday it was Kyle saving him.

He yawns, gazes tiredly at the steady burning of the fire. With his one arm, Yuuki pulls Kyle a little closer and rubs his hand over his shoulders.

I feel like I should be the one thanking you. You gave me a reason to fight again for what I believe in – to offer people a second chance. You reminded me why I think that's so important.

Even though he's exhausted and Kyle's safe again, Yuuki doesn't sleep well. His mind keeps him awake, replaying over and over things that have happened and taking him through 'what-if' scenarios of all the things that could've happened had they not gotten to Kyle in time. If Andy hadn't been there. If they'd taken Kyle's knife and plunged it into him, made him bleed out, beat him, interrogated him…

Kyle shifts in his sleep. Yuuki's startled back to the here and now. He wonders how long he's been zoning out for, as when he looks to the cave entrance, he can see that Joshua's shape has been replaced with Timothy and Andy's. They're talking softly, Timothy slouched against the cave wall and Andy sitting with his arms around one leg and his chin resting on his knee.

Hearing the familiar warm tone of Timothy's voice, Yuuki finally feels safe enough to try to sleep. Everyone's looking out for each other here, he realises. No one is alone. If someone unfriendly happens to stumble across their little encampment in the middle of the night, they'll have everyone here in this cave to face.

Yuuki closes his eyes to the firelight and the shadows. His mind agrees to let him sleep.

28

They're up at first light and getting ready to move as soon as the sun rises. Everyone's tired. If people aren't moody they're emotionally flat, Yuuki and Kyle falling into the latter category.

Kyle can barely move when he wakes up. He's comfortable, too, snuggled into Yuuki's side, and the fact that he's facing away from the rest of the group is yet another incentive not to move. But Yuuki needs his arm so that he can get ready also.

With a groan Kyle props himself up on his elbow and lets Yuuki have his arm back. He slumps back down, face-first on the tarpaulin straight after.

"Come on," Yuuki murmurs, voice raspy. "We've got to get up."

No matter how hard he mentally wills himself to do so, Kyle finds he can't get up. His limbs refuse to move. His legs feel like dead weights and his arms ache like crazy. His shoulder muscles pinch with every breath he takes. If he stays still long enough he can almost forget about it… the tension headache steadily growing worse, though, not so much.

"Kyle?"

When it becomes clear he's not just being lazy or stubborn, Yuuki ruffles his hair gently. Much to Kyle's humiliation and relief, he calls out to

Susan who's handing out porridge and moments later there's an arm around his back and a hand on his shoulder rolling him into it. Kyle blinks up at Susan, trusting her, as she pulls him upright so that he's sitting up and leaning against her. He's too tired to have the energy to keep his head up.

Susan rubs her hand up and down the side of his arm. "A little sore, huh?"

A grunt is all Kyle manages.

"I've got some anti-inflammatory cream in my backpack. Would you like me to put some on for you?" At Kyle's hesitation, she adds, "Or Yuuki could do it. Whoever you feel comfortable with."

Of course, he can't do it by himself, although that would be the preferred option. The next would be asking Yuuki to do it, but he imagines it would be somewhat difficult with only one arm to rub the cream in properly with Kyle unable to support his own weight. Besides, he feels he already asks so much of Yuuki as it is.

Susan's still waiting for his answer.

"You can," he mumbles. "I don't mind."

She calls Sam over to get the pot from the bag. Kyle feels bad for the lack of interaction he's had with the others recently. It's like he's been avoiding them, and while he kind of has been due to his not being ready for that much social interaction yet, it doesn't make him feel any less bad about it.

Sam was there when he first got out of prison, Logan stopped him from being kidnapped at Yuuki's house and Avi not only cooked for his sake, but also carried him the entire walk from the hut to here. There's also no way Kyle is going to be able make it one step, so Avi will probably be carrying him again today unless someone else volunteers.

Kyle hates how much he has to rely on everyone.

"Do you mind removing your sweatshirt?" Susan asks as Sam hands her the cream.

That much he can do. His movements are weak and sloppy, but he manages to pull it over his head. While he struggles to pull his hands out of the sleeves, Susan inhales sharply. Kyle's confused as to how that could've incurred that reaction when a couple of seconds later, Yuuki breathes out in horror.

"Kyle…" he whispers.

It takes a moment for it to register what they're seeing: the two sets of burns on his back from the taser. He'd forgotten about them being there.

Kyle hunches his shoulders. "It's how Jeff got me."

"He shot you twice?" Yuuki whispers in disbelief, as though he needs verbal confirmation of what he's seeing.

"I think he was angry after I escaped him the first time."

"Andy didn't do anything to stop it?"

Kyle grips his jersey and digs his fingers into the material. He hears Susan unscrew the lid on the anti-inflammatory cream and he's glad for the distraction when she starts applying it. "He stopped Jeff from hurting me," he murmurs, closing his eyes and focusing on the movements of Susan's fingers over his shoulders and the sharp, refreshing smell of mint that follows. "It could've been a lot worse."

His voice is hoarse from having just woken up and it cracks a little on the last few words, betraying his efforts to keep emotion out of his voice. He's ashamed to realise he's still shaken up about what happened yesterday.

He'd thought he'd be feeling better now that he's with the group again, with Yuuki again. But of course that's not the case.

He's just so tired of his mind being so full of chaos. Kyle doesn't know how Yuuki can live with it and not feel like he's falling apart twenty-four seven. It's exhausting.

It hits him then that that is probably exactly what Yuuki feels like. Almost every day. It's hard to think about.

As Susan finishes rubbing the anti-inflammatory into his neck and shoulders, moving on to his left arm and then his right, all Kyle can think about is how if it weren't for Yuuki – if it weren't for every person here in this cave with him, really – he'd mostly likely have ended up with PTSD too. So far it doesn't seem like he has it, although it is hard to tell so early on and with so much recent trauma still affecting him.

At any rate, his life would've been a whole different had it not been for Yuuki. If only he knew how to thank him properly.

After a quick breakfast, the cave starts looking less and less like a campsite as everyone packs up their things and prepares for the hike ahead. Once the cave is tidied so that evidence of their stay is minimal, they set off. They're skipping Checkpoint C today and instead aiming to make it all the way to Checkpoint D before dark. It's another disused hut they've stocked up, and it'll bring them the closest they can possibly get to the palace grounds without risking revealing themselves.

It's a long hike, and since it takes them up out of the valley, there's a decent amount of uphill climbing to do. Kyle feels absolutely guilty listening to Avi's laboured breathing. He even offers to climb a little on his own legs, if just to relieve Avi of his weight for even a few minutes. They both know he can barely walk, however, and Avi cuts him off with a firm no.

Kyle's not the only one feeling like he's not helping though.

"Timothy," Yuuki says from a few paces ahead. "I don't mind taking turns carrying a backpack. I can do it."

Timothy, who's walking in front of Yuuki, shakes his head. "We need you as good as you can be in case we get sprung. You're going to need all the energy you can spare if we run into someone."

"But the others –"

"The others aren't down an arm. And," Timothy says, stopping in his tracks to take a breather and look Yuuki straight in the eye, "the weight you have to carry is heavier than all of our equipment combined. Let us do our part."

The five bags they have are split between Andy, Susan, Joshua, Logan and Amelia today, with Avi carrying Kyle and Sam carrying Logan's rifle along with all their electronic equipment. Yuuki probably feels like he's letting the team down…. Kyle and him both.

Yuuki opens his mouth to argue but is cut off by a warning yell from Andy.

"Helicopter!"

Everyone freezes. Avi hauls himself and Kyle up a few more steps so that he has better footing, but his eyes are wide as looks around for where to go and what to do. Then it reaches them, a distant droning hum growing closer and the tell-tale noise of air being chopped.

It was only a matter of time before the Peace Forces up their search. Andy may have smashed all tracking and communication devices that he,

Jeff and Deborah had carried on their person, but that action in itself was likely to send the search team into high alert.

Kyle, in his tiredness, is confused at why they all take off after Andy, running. Why are they running? The canopy here is still dense enough to hide them from view. Surely they'd be better off freezing than drawing attention to themselves by running around? But then he hears Joshua pass on the message to Timothy about thermal cameras and his heart drops.

They're not safe. Of course they're not safe.

The noise of the helicopter seems to be coming from all around them now. Andy finds a small cave-like dent in the hillside and everyone hurries to cram inside. There's not enough time to think, not enough time to try find somewhere bigger because the helicopter's already passing over the ridge.

Kyle's still clinging onto Avi's back, pressed up against an overhanging rock by the entrance and squished between Yuuki and Avi who are crouched in front of him. He can't breathe. It's too dark. It's too loud. He feels Yuuki's hand on his back, steadying them both, as the helicopter flies and chopping noise echoes through the valley. Kyle's heart won't settle.

All of a sudden he's back in the cell, in the dark, the thoughts in his head louder than the helicopter, his arms trapped at his sides and his hands in front of him because that guard didn't take his handcuffs off.

"Kyle," Yuuki whispers. "You need to breathe."

Avi's looking over his shoulder, panting from the climb and the sudden run. His eyes are alight with concern but Kyle stares past him, unseeing.

He needs to run. He needs to get out of here, but he can't. He can't because he's locked away and there's no way out. The helicopter isn't going away; it's circling. Kyle will be stuck here until he goes crazy. Since Yuuki's in here with him, there won't be any rescue this time.

Yuuki hugs him. It makes the room Kyle has even more restricted and for a moment he can't breathe at all. But Yuuki holds no demeanour of intending to restrain or trap him.

Every breath that Yuuki takes, Kyle can feel. He squeezes his eyes shut and concentrates on it, tries to match his own breathing to Yuuki's.

The helicopter doesn't leave but the vividness of the flashback does.

His sudden claustrophobia doesn't let up but somehow it's a little more bearable.

Kyle's mind threatens to overwhelm him with other images and sensations: the door to the holding cell closing after he'd been arrested; the darkness choking him each night in isolation after the light bulb blew; dying of cold and exhaustion and stress; and the horror of being dumped in a cardboard box, watching the flaps be taped shut over him.

But Yuuki, who found a way to take him out of prison, is here. Avi, who pushed Deborah away from him and carried him away from that hut, is here. All the people who rescued him and Yuuki are here.

The helicopter leaves without finding them.

No one moves. Kyle keeps his eyes closed, desperately wanting out. They have to stay where they are though, in case the helicopter happens to come back around. It's better not to risk being caught out in the open if they decide to keep moving and it does.

They wait until Andy deems it safe before emerging from hiding. It's been a good half an hour that they've been in that cave. Everyone's stiff and eager to get out and into some decent space to move again, but it's

Yuuki, Kyle and Avi who they wait for to get out first. Kyle grits his teeth and swallows hard, begging himself not to cry in relief. Yuuki's hand never leaves his back.

"Do we want to have lunch break here?" Timothy asks as the group comes out.

Andy looks like he's about to advise they move on, but seeing how everyone's weary and in the need for a good stretch, he nods. The general consensus seems to be that people want to stop here. "May as well," he says. "But we'll need to go hard if we're going to make it to our destination in time for nightfall. We're losing time."

Though they took a break an hour ago at the base of the hill, where Checkpoint C was, everyone's ready for another. It's been a tough climb up from the valley these past couple of days, and they've only covered about one-fifth of the way up the hill to Checkpoint D.

Timothy clears his throat. "Okay, guys. It's almost one o'clock. We'll take ten, maybe fifteen minutes here and then we're moving again. We've got about four hours left of daylight and we don't want to be walking on unfamiliar ground near cliffs at night if we don't have to."

There's a few nods and the odd tired vocal acknowledgement. Avi turns around so that he's facing away from the slope and lets Kyle off his back. Yuuki goes off to talk to Timothy, a deep frown on his face. After reassuring Avi he's okay sitting by himself while Avi goes off for a toilet break, Kyle zones into Yuuki and Timothy's conversation.

"I know," Yuuki says. "But it could happen. So if something *does* happen to me…"

Timothy's brow creases. "Hey. It's not over yet. I know where you're

264

coming from and your fear is a hundred percent valid. But Yuuki? We've come this far. Let's not give up the hope that we'll all make it out of here."

"But can you promise me that you'll watch over Kyle if something happens to me? Please?"

It's a struggle, but Kyle manages to push himself to his feet. His legs are stiff and sore, his knees threatening to buckle with every step, but he forces them to take him over to Yuuki.

When Yuuki turns and sees him, Kyle fixes as intense a glare as he can on him. "Nothing's going to happen to you without it getting me too," he grits out. "You've been with me the whole way. I'm with you the whole way. If we go down, we go down together."

Yuuki stares at him, bewildered. "No, Kyle —"

Kyle's legs give way then. Timothy has his arms around him before he falls and Kyle gratefully leans his weight into the man's side. Everyone's watching, listening. Kyle's face flushes as he realises this. He turns his gaze down to study the arrangement of sticks, leaves and stones around his bare feet.

"I mean it," he murmurs. "There's no way I'm letting anything happen to you if I can help it."

Yuuki doesn't answer. He just stands there as if he's astonished that Kyle would want to do such a thing for him, as though it should be Yuuki protecting Kyle and can't be the other way around. After a minute of the conversation going nowhere, Timothy helps Kyle back to where he'd been sitting. Yuuki is still at a loss for words.

With the subject broached, Timothy takes a deep breath and lets it out slowly. "I was talking with Andy while on watch last night," he says, his voice loud enough so that everyone can hear him. "Tomorrow is when we announce ourselves. If we wait any longer, we'll risk getting caught before we get a chance to do so. I think that helicopter just now is sign enough of that.

"We all have to understand that we may not even make it to the meeting. We could be gunned down before we even set foot on palace grounds. If we're not killed, we could be arrested. We could walk into a trap.

"But we've come this far and there's only one way forward. Yes, there's risks, but we'll do whatever we can to make sure we all make it out of there alive and victorious. Is everyone on the same page?"

Nods and hums of acknowledgement. It's hard to know how to feel in a situation such as this. It's too surreal and there's too much at stake. Tomorrow could be the last day their hearts beat. Tomorrow could also be the day they cement the start of a revolution.

If there's any consolation to find, it's that they're not alone in this fight. They have each other, as few a number as they may seem. Anything could happen tomorrow but it's not over until it's over. If they've come all this way then there has to be a way through to the other side of tomorrow.

Regardless of what happens, at least one thing's for sure: they won't be going down without a fight.

29

The group is quiet the rest of the way to Checkpoint D. They're all scared in one way or another, as they should be, but it's starting to sink in just how real and dangerous the situation they're in is. Up until now, it's seemed like it's only Yuuki and Kyle who have been presently in danger's way. Now it's everyone who is.

Kyle feels strangely calm about it all. A part of him wonders if it's because he's already accepted that there might not be any tomorrow for him. There's still a part of his heart that hasn't been released from that isolation cell he'd been locked up in. He half-expects himself to wake up in the morning and be back there instead of out in the bush heading into a life-or-death situation.

The twinge of pain in his shoulders and the ache in his legs are a reminder that this is all real though. Yuuki believing in him, getting him out of that place, listening to him, not giving up on him... that's all real, too. Yuuki believed in a freedom for him that he hadn't thought possible. Though it's hard to in the wake of thinking about tomorrow, Kyle desperately wants to believe in it too.

Sunset has just been and gone when they all arrive at the hut. Avi lets Kyle off his back and groans, flashing Kyle an apologetic smile. But Kyle doesn't blame him for being exhausted. Avi's carried him two days in a row, and today was uphill for at least half the way. That would take a lot of anyone.

"Looks like it'll be a bit cramped tonight, huh" Yuuki murmurs, sidling over to where Kyle is standing. "You gonna be okay?"

Checkpoint D is a smaller hut than Checkpoint A was, with only four bunk spaces and less floor space. Kyle's skin crawls a little thinking about being so closed in with so many people. But it's a shelter at the end of the day and it'll give them better insulation than the cave and the fire did last night.

Kyle shrugs. "It's just for the night. Can't really do anything about it anyway."

Yuuki frowns at the doorway in front of them. Kyle can see he's not looking all too comfortable either, the tension in his neck and shoulders a clear expression of his discomfort. They decide to let the others move around and find a spot to settle inside before they even think about going in.

Beside them, Andy, Timothy and Susan wait as well.

"You guys can have a bunk each if you want," Timothy says. "That way you'll have a bit more space."

Yuuki raises an eyebrow. "There's only four bunks. Who else needs one?"

"Charlie'll be taking one. I'm happy to sleep on the floor, so we can decide among ourselves who will be taking the fourth." He pauses in thought a moment, watching Yuuki and Kyle's expressions carefully. "Would you two rather share a bunk? I doubt anyone's going to look at you funny if you do."

Kyle ducks his head, the thought of being surrounded by people and walls and either a ceiling or another bunk above his head making him anxious. It might not literally be four walls keeping him trapped in one place, but it might as well be.

"How much room is there?" Yuuki asks quietly.

"It would be a squeeze for two people," Timothy says, "if you think about the bunks from the last hut."

"Are we able to sleep by the door, then?"

Kyle swallows hard. He doubts he's going to be able to get much sleep with so many people around, but it would definitely make him less anxious if he could rest with a door at his back – a door that he can get to quickly and go out unhindered.

Apparently the answer is yes, they can do that. They're the last to go into the hut, Susan going ahead of them. Timothy and Andy linger outside to take the first watch and discuss plans for the coming day.

The hut is small. Bags and the couple of boxes of food and water storage they put here take up one of the bottom bunk beds. Charlie is laying down on the other bottom bunk bed, napping, and it seems like the two top bunk beds have now been reserved for Susan and Timothy. Kyle's relieved no one insists on him and Yuuki taking one. He really doesn't have the energy to argue.

With a sigh, Yuuki leans against the wall opposite the bunks and the same side as the door. Everyone's busy preparing food or just simply lying down, staring at the ceiling. Kyle can't stop his gaze flicking from person to person, constantly on guard and assessing everyone for even the slightest hint of ill intention. There's a bit of irritability in Sam's tone and exasperation in Logan's, but otherwise Kyle finds nothing too concerning.

Yuuki's voice sounds too close to his ear. "Would you mind helping me down?"

Kyle startles. Yuuki quickly apologises and Kyle feels shame creep over his face. These are good people who have helped him. He shouldn't be feeling so on edge around them and yet he is. He's not really that nervous about coming out of hiding tomorrow, so it can't be that, and he's mostly recovered from the freak out from earlier in that small cave...

"Kyle?"

He blinks back to himself. "Y-yeah, sorry."

With an arm around Yuuki's back, Kyle lets him lean against him and gently helps lower him to the floor. Yuuki's legs give out before he can fall into a crouch, sending both them both collapsing against the wall. They receive a lot of alarmed glances from around the room.

"I'm fine," Yuuki says. "We're good."

They're not, clearly. Everyone's tired but Yuuki and Kyle are exhausted in ways that none of them can fully understand. It's harder to keep unexpressed now too, with just how deeply tired they are. Everyone can see it. Joshua, Sam and Avi are looking at them with open concern, Susan with a worried frown and Amelia and Logan with raised eyebrows. Yuuki and Kyle can only stare back in unmasked exhaustion.

Tomorrow's going to be fun, Kyle thinks dryly.

While Timothy and Andy discuss their options for a plan of attack outside, the others start getting dinner ready. Bugs start coming in and the air starts getting cold, so they have to close the door, sending Kyle's nerves back on edge. Yuuki on the other hand is too exhausted to notice, eyes closed and lulled by the quiet activity.

It shouldn't be that surprising. Yuuki's been under so much stress lately, on top of his PTSD. It's bound to take its toll at some point. What's worrying is that they've got to walk again tomorrow, maybe even participate in a fight for their lives, and even when he's tired Yuuki never drops his guard like this. This is a new level of tired.

As if Kyle had seen it coming, Yuuki's head drops onto his chest and he slumps sideways into Kyle. He doesn't make any effort to move, only slouches further until Kyle's the only thing besides the wall holding him up. The profound lack of an arm between them has Kyle's stomach churning uncomfortably, but it's not so much the missing limb but the memory of how it happened that gets to him.

Maybe if he hadn't moved so much after Yuuki got shot that first time, Yuuki would still have that arm. It wouldn't have needed amputating if it had only been shot that first time. Possibly not even the second...

But they'd meant to hurt him. A temporary injury is nothing if they can give him a permanent one. Kyle thinks about Yuuki's PTSD and inwardly growls. He doesn't get why people have to be so cruel.

As if they haven't hurt him enough already.

His thoughts are interrupted by the door opening. Timothy enters, head bent wearily. Yuuki jolts awake with the vibrations of Timothy's boots on the wooden floor, pulling himself back into a sitting position leaning against the wall as Timothy closes the door behind him. Andy stays on watch outside.

"We've decided on a plan," Timothy says. "Subject to change, of course, but it's a plan nonetheless."

The people not currently tending to pots of boiling water give Timothy their full attention. Susan opens the side window to ventilate the room while the gas canisters are in use, then comes to sit down by Yuuki and Kyle to reapply Yuuki's bandages. Kyle shuffles over to give her room.

Timothy sits down on the edge of the bunk Charlie's not lying on. "We don't have that many people and we don't have as many people as we'd like, but we're all there is and we're just going to have to make do," he says. "Taularh knows we're coming – without a doubt. While he might not be expecting us tomorrow, he won't be surprised if we show up. Andy reckons there will people there to meet us, namely a bunch of Peace Force officers, so we'll need to do the best we can to avoid them as much as possible, at least until we're in position.

"Now our aim is to bring Amelia to a place where she is able to meet with Taularh safely. Anyone guarding the palace may have been given orders to shoot on sight should they see us. Let's hope that isn't the case. But in case it is, Joshua, you'll go with Charlie and Amelia. Make sure the way ahead is clear and give them cover if they need it."

Avi raises his hand slowly. "Wait, we're splitting up the group?"

Timothy nods. "We have to. We'll be better prepared for something going wrong and have a better chance of survival, should things go wrong, if we're not all clumped together like sitting ducks."

With a nervous nod, Avi lowers his hand.

"Andy will be going ahead of us all and scouting the area," Timothy says. "If there ends up being fighting, he'll also be co-ordinating the men and women in the Peace Forces who are aligned with him. Logan will be able to give us cover fire from the hillside too, so it's not like we're going in blindly and unarmed. Avi, I'd like you to go with Logan and watch his back."

Kyle's heart sinks a little. *If we're splitting up the group, then that means I'm going to have to walk.* He's glad he doesn't have to be a burden to anyone, and that Avi doesn't have to worry about carrying his weight again tomorrow, but he's worried. There's no way he's going to be able to walk that far and have enough energy left to fight or run at the end of it.

From across the room, Timothy watches his expression with the same worry creasing his brow. "Yuuki and Kyle, you two will be hiding. If you go up and find a hiding spot on the hillside – preferably the same hill as Logan and Avi so you don't accidentally get shot – you'll be able to watch what's going on down below. Just be careful not to let yourselves be seen."

Kyle tries to answer with an affirmation but his voice gets stuck in his throat. *Why do we have to be useless when everyone else is doing something?*

Some look must pass over both his and Yuuki's faces because Timothy adds, "The fight might come to you, but unless it does I don't want either of you going anywhere near it. We'll be able to fight better if we're not conscious of the fact that you two might be caught up in it and at a disadvantage. Understand?"

Kyle's lip twitches at being called a disadvantage, but he gets it. This isn't a show of pride. Neither of them have the energy to stand right now, let alone offer a decent ability to attack. If they try to join in the fighting, they'll either be dead in seconds or taken hostages to use against everyone else. They don't want to do that to each other and they don't want to do it to Timothy.

With a glance exchanged with Kyle, Yuuki murmurs a curt, "Got it."

Timothy gives them the thumbs up. "Sam and Susan will be with me, monitoring Taularh's activity and communications.

"We'll have signals. Andy and I have whistles – we'll use them to let you know what's happening on the field. Seven short blows means it's safe enough to emerge and regroup. One long whistle means, if possible, turn around and head back to Checkpoint C, or else here."

"Or run for your life," Joshua mutters.

Timothy grimaces and doesn't argue. "Hopefully that's not the whistle signal we hear. Any questions?"

There's none. Logan asks Avi how long they should boil the dried peas for, but other than that, everyone's quiet.

"Alright. I'm going back outside on watch with Andy. We'll be discussing the different possible happenings and outcomes of tomorrow, so I'll be back in if there's anything else we think of. Joshua, are you alright taking watch after us in a few hours?"

Joshua sighs. "Sure."

"Thanks. In the meantime, you all get as much rest and sleep as you can. Whatever happens tomorrow, you're going to need it."

With his announcement of plans over, Timothy returns outside for watch and further, more detailed planning.

Susan's just finished reapplying Yuuki's bandages. Yuuki doesn't seem to notice. He remains staring at a spot on the floor in front of him, eyes wide and unfocused, even after Susan's got up and moved away.

Kyle frowns. Yuuki's either deep in thought or lost in a flashback. He's contemplating trying to shake him out of it when Yuuki blinks and comes back to himself. His eyes flick around the room in mild confusion.

"You alright?" Kyle asks quietly. "You spaced out for a bit there."

Yuuki swallows, his gaze falling on Kyle. "Yeah…" He looks like he's about to fake a smile and say it's nothing, but he knows by now that Kyle isn't going to think any less of him for being honest, so he drops the acting attempt before it begins. "I was just thinking."

No one's paying attention to them, so Kyle prompts him. "About?"

"Tomorrow. About the sorts of things that could happen and what I could do if they did. I know worrying isn't going to help us, but…"

"You'd rather be prepared than be caught unawares."

Yuuki gives him a painful smile. "Yeah."

Kyle hums. How can they not want to think about things in advance? They have no idea what they're going to be faced with tomorrow. That doesn't make it any easier not to think out scenarios and reactions to them. Something might happen where they don't even have the chance to think.

If things do go wrong, like they have done before, they don't want to be wasting time thinking then what they should've thought about now. It's because Timothy had been thinking ahead, after all, that Kyle hadn't ended up kidnapped that day back at Yuuki's house. It's because he'd thought out an escape plan that they were all able to get away and that Yuuki hadn't been hurt worse.

The two of them are quiet the rest of the night. Kyle keeps an eye on Yuuki in case the spacing out turns out to be flashbacks. They both don't eat much, but they eat what they can, and by the time Joshua heads out the door to take up watch, both of them are lying passed out on the floor.

In the middle of the night, Yuuki jolts awake with a gasp, startling Kyle out of a nightmare of his own. Neither of them get much sleep after that, but it's better than being trapped in their dreams, better than being stuck in scenarios of running for one's life or being caught and thrown back in prison.

Yuuki lies on his back and stares at the ceiling, sighing heavily every now and then. Kyle fixes his eyes on the candle flame burning away in the portable lamp, a subtle yet warm light radiating out from the centre of the room. He tries not to think about how dark the room would be without it.

If only not thinking were less of a challenge.

30

With morning comes the reluctant getting up. Charlie comes in from third watch, waking everyone up with a couple of knocks on the wall. Kyle, who had been dozing, flinches at the sound.

Breakfast is a solemn affair. Amelia is a nervous wreck and ends up dropping her bowl of porridge on the floor, her hands are so shaky. Charlie takes her outside to help her breathe while Logan puts aside his own bowl to clean up and get Amelia another.

Things are packed, the hut is tidied and then the group is getting ready to go.

Susan approaches Yuuki and Kyle with a bag she's prepared for them. Each group is carrying a backpack with them, and since Yuuki will have difficulty keeping it on his back, Kyle's the designated carrier between the two of them. Inside there's enough food and water to last them a day and a half, a first aid kit with an extra roll of compression bandages, a map, a compass, a tarpaulin... and Kyle's knife.

"Yuuki can give you directions on how to reapply them," Susan is saying regarding the compression bandages, but Kyle is too busy trying not to think about the last time he had to use the knife to really hear her.

Yuuki's hand lands on his shoulder. *You're not going to be alone this time,* it assures him. Kyle looks him in the eye and takes a deep breath. He tucks the knife into the side of his boot like he did last time and zips up the bag.

The group set off with the rising sun to their backs. Since Kyle hasn't recovered enough energy to make it up to the top of the ridge on his own legs, Avi offers to carry him at least until the group splits up. Kyle would like to argue but he knows he can't and instead accepts the offer gratefully.

The apprehension is getting to everyone. Avi's quiet. Charlie doesn't smile. Amelia moves between looking like she's about to cry and looking like she wants to hit something. Timothy, Susan, Joshua and Sam stay closer together in the line. The crease in Logan's brow never leaves and Andy glares more than he glances.

Kyle can't help but notice the dimmed light in Yuuki's eyes. It's almost like a part of him is expecting to be shot down today. Kyle feels it too, but just as surely as Yuuki's probably doing every single second, he's wrestling that thought with the hope that their group might somehow succeed.

Maybe Kyle feels that hope stronger since he's only recently been in a place he never thought he'd get out of it. It's different, after all, being the one who was rescued than being the one who rescued.

It's not over yet, Yuuki, Kyle wants to say. He would if it were just the two of them. *It's not over until it's over.* Yuuki's not one to give up easily, but even the most courageous person can lose hope sometimes.

When they come over the ridge, Andy warns everyone to be on the watch for helicopters. The break they take up there is brief. Trees are sparse up here and they're in open view of anyone who could be looking for them. On the plus side, they can see the palace from here – a lone white-stoned building surrounded a decent length of open field. The group is silent as they take in the sight of it.

The way is downhill from there. Kyle uses his own legs to move this time, since it'll be too hard for Avi to keep good balance with so much weight on his back. The slope is steep, too. They can't afford to have anyone falling.

Two thirds of the way down the hill, the incoming air-chopping of a helicopter has everyone scrambling for cover. Timothy pulls Yuuki under a rocky overhang with him and his family while the others take cover under another. Kyle's still out in the open. There's not enough room for another person under either overhang. He's about to panic when Sam grabs him by the arm and drags him in with Yuuki and the Harrisons. They make themselves as small as they can and wait, hearts pounding.

The helicopter flies overhead and keeps going, disappearing over the other side of the ridge they just came over.

Sam releases her death grip on Kyle's arm with a wince and an apology. Kyle just shrugs and tries to hide the fact that he's shaking. He fails badly.

They have to keep moving though, so Kyle has no proper chance to recover. His leg muscles are simultaneously jelly, fire and nerves as he walks. More than once his foot slides out from under him, sending him either crashing to his knees or his side. One side of his leg ends up streaked with dirt just with the first slip.

Now I get why Timothy doesn't want us doing anything but hiding, he thinks in bitter frustration.

Once they've descended to two hundred metres elevation above the palace, the group finally stops for a break. It's not much of a restful one. This is where they part ways. This is where they say goodbye.

The Harrisons stay close. Avi, Logan, Sam and Amelia give each other friendly threats for if one of them doesn't make it out of here. Charlie walks over to a gap between the trees and stands there gazing down at the palace, a distant look on his face.

Yuuki and Kyle sit a couple of metres away from everyone else. There's no words passed between them. No trying to cheer each other up with over-hopeful sentences. Kyle sees Timothy and Susan glancing over at them every so often to check that they're okay, but otherwise they give them space.

Yuuki slings his arm over Kyle's shoulders and Kyle hugs him back. It's about the only comfort they can offer each other in these circumstances. There is a chance they could succeed and there is a chance they won't, the latter being the one of higher probability. They'll find out soon enough which outcome it's going to be. Kyle's just looking forward to it all being over so they don't have such nerve-wracking anticipation hanging over their heads.

After a quick scout, Andy returns and gives Timothy the thumbs up. Timothy nods, quickly finishes off his sandwich and stands. Their cue seen, everyone starts packing up and hugging and bidding each other good luck. Yuuki and Kyle are silent.

Kyle doesn't hear what Timothy says. He's distracted by the sudden thought that, while everyone has families to return to or something to do, he doesn't have anywhere to go after all this.

There's also the matter of his case. Timothy might have enough to clear him, and Jeff's not around anymore to be able to stop Timothy from proving that Kyle's case had been messed with, but...

"What are you thinking about?" Yuuki murmurs, breaking into his thoughts.

Kyle blinks. "What? Oh, it's… it's nothing."

"I wouldn't be asking if I thought it was nothing."

Around them, people are moving. Yuuki withdraws his arm from Kyle's shoulders in order to return Timothy's wave as he leads half of the group away down the hill. Andy has already gone ahead. Now it's just him, Yuuki, Logan and Avi remaining here.

"I was just wondering what happens after all this," Kyle whispers. "For me, if we all make it."

"You're not going back to that cell," Yuuki says firmly.

"Then what happens to me? I'm not eighteen for another couple of months and I highly doubt any foster family is going to accept me."

"We'll probably stay around the palace for a bit, at least until things settle. It'll be safer for everyone to stay together while everything get sorted. I don't know what's going to happen with Taularh, but I imagine that it's going to be quite chaotic from as soon as Amelia reveals herself."

Kyle swallows. "And after that?"

"We'll help you figure out what you want to do and where you want to go."

Kyle takes a deep breath. He thinks of everything he's left behind and the fact that he doesn't have to return to that. Yuuki sounds so sure. Not necessarily sure that there will *be* the opportunity to talk about what options Kyle has available to him, but sure that if there is, things will turn out okay. Kyle wishes he had the same faith.

Logan clears his throat. "Hey, guys? We're going to go ahead. It'll take us a while to get to a good vantage point and we want to be in position before the others are. That okay?"

"All goods," Yuuki calls over his shoulder. "All the best."

"You guys too."

Footsteps and voices fade. In the quiet that's left behind, Yuuki sighs. "I suppose we better get going too, huh?"

Kyle nods. "Yeah."

But neither of them make any effort to move. After a couple of minutes of still just sitting there, they glance at each other and laugh. They take one last drink of water before putting the bottles back in the bag.

Kyle zips it up and shoulders it. "Are we following Logan and Avi?"

"Their general direction," Yuuki says. "We just need to be a bit closer to the rest of the group so we can hear the signals."

Kyle pushes himself to his feet. "Guess we better start making out way over then." He reaches out a hand and Yuuki takes it gratefully, letting himself be pulled up. Kyle notices his face looking pale and frowns when Yuuki staggers a little. "You okay?"

Yuuki waves his hand. "Just a little dizzy. It happens when I don't get much sleep. Are you okay?"

"Yeah," Kyle says automatically, then grunts. "I mean, relatively speaking. I'll manage though."

"Alright then. Let me know when you want to stop. I'm going to need plenty of breaks myself."

Their mood flags quickly. Kyle barely has it in him to walk. Yuuki's finding it harder to navigate his way through the trees and around all the rocks and dips in the slope. They're making good time for how slow they're going, but it's clear they're both running out of energy. They might not make it as far as they would've liked at this rate.

An hour later and the edge of palace grounds are down below them to the right, so close and yet still a decent distance away. They take a number of short minute-long breaks, but it's not enough. They're too tired for this. Yuuki's stumbling more frequently and Kyle's struggling to keep his legs moving.

It comes as no surprise when something happens.

Yuuki's foot rolls. Right behind him, Kyle watches with alarm as Yuuki overbalances and fails to grab a hold of anything to steady himself. He falls right over the edge of a steep incline they've been navigating their way around.

Kyle throws out a hand. "Yuuki!"

He misses.

There's no time to think. He's overbalanced himself now. Sucking in a breath, he launches himself off the ground and slams into Yuuki. He only has seconds to wrap his arms protectively around Yuuki's head and shoulders before they hit the ground again.

Kyle only has a few seconds after that before his head hits a rock and his vision goes black.

31

Twigs and bushes and falling and stones and rocks. Kyle's grip around Yuuki's shoulders loosens abruptly. Yuuki's gut twists at the sharp exhale that comes a split-second before that. He manages to hook his arm around Kyle's back before they're pulled apart.

They roll over and over. The backpack acts like a speed bump, simultaneously slowing them down and slamming them into the ground every turn. Yuuki tenses before each one. Thankfully it's his good shoulder he's rolling onto.

Coming to a dizzying halt, they slide down another metre and then stop. Yuuki's heart pounds like a kick drum in his ears. It's hard to get an idea of how far they've fallen, what with his vision spinning as it is, though past Kyle's hair and the bag on his back, Yuuki can see the top of the slope rising above them.

He dares not move out of fear of sending them downhill even further; gravity could pull them down even further if they're not careful, and Yuuki's dizzy enough as it is from sleep deprivation and exhaustion without adding another tumble down the hill to the mix.

Kyle groans, shifting. It's too late to warn him not to move as he pulls himself away from Yuuki to cradle his head in his hands. Yuuki lets out a shaky breath. Kyle doesn't appear to have a neck or spinal injury by the looks of things.

But as Kyle tries to get up, his elbows buckle and he collapses back into the hillside. His brow creases in confusion.

Concussion, Yuuki's mind supplies as he watches Kyle carefully. Bracing his feet on a tree root, manoeuvres himself so that he's sitting upright. "Hey, Kyle," he says slowly. "Can you tell me how you're feeling?"

They need to get to more stable ground. Yuuki's balance is thrown off from lack of sleep and his still adapting to the missing weight of his right arm; if Kyle starts feeling nauseous and needs to be sick, Yuuki's not going to be able to support him. They're not going to be able to move in a hurry should they need to run or hide for whatever reason if they stay here, either.

But Kyle doesn't look like he wants to move at all anytime soon. A bug flies into his cheek and he doesn't even seem to notice it. He just stares at a leaf in front of him, eyes not even focused on it.

Yuuki's stomach dips. "Kyle? You with me?"

Kyle winces. "Hnnnn?"

"Sorry," Yuuki murmurs, lowering the volume of his voice. "Does your head hurt?"

"Y-yeah…"

"Okay. It's okay. Can you tell me how you're feeling?"

Kyle swallows. A little distressed sound escapes his throat. "Hurts. My…my head."

Yuuki shifts a leg under himself and twists so that he can reach his hand out to lay on Kyle's shoulder. "Yeah. I think you banged your head on something when we fell. Do you remember falling?"

"What?"

"We fell. That's why you're not feeling so good. Do you remember what we were doing before we fell?"

The confusion spread across Kyle's face is concerning. "We were…we were…" his voice trails off, interrupted by a small hiccup. His cheeks pale. "Yu-Yuuki. I'm gonna…"

There's not enough time to get him up off the ground before he starts heaving. Yuuki narrowly avoids getting the mess on him. He grimaces, forcing himself to ignore the sound and the smell before he feels the urge to be sick himself.

"Yuuki?" Kyle whispers when his stomach is finished bringing up its lunch. His eyes water.

"I'm right here."

"I don't feel good." Kyle's words are slightly slurred. They're pitched in a way that punches Yuuki in the gut, and Yuuki can't help but feel Kyle's being scared as his own. All Yuuki can do is keep his hand on Kyle's shoulder and hope it's enough to ground him.

If only I had both arms. Taking a deep breath, Yuuki says, "It's alright. You've just got a bit of a concussion, okay? You're gonna be fine."

"I-I don't think…I can walk, Yuuki. I ca-can't walk anymore."

"That's okay. We'll camp out here. How about we get ourselves off this slope first, and then we can just rest and wait out whatever happens down here?"

"…'kay."

"You're going to be alright, Kyle." Yuuki rubs his hand up and down Kyle's shoulder. "We're going to be okay."

We've just got to find some stable ground. Scanning the area around them, there aren't that many options.

There's a reasonable looking space between a couple of trees a metre or so up the slope, but there's no way Kyle's going to be able to make it up there in his condition and Yuuki doesn't have it in him to drag him up there. Sliding down the hill some more isn't an option either, what with the sharp drop-off only a little further of the way down. Beside that is a fall of at least a hundred metres or so.

Behind Yuuki is a rock with a small patch of less sloped ground. It's three metres away, the closest reasonable place available to them, and there's a few trees in between here and there that can act as foot or handholds. It's not that big of a space, but it's the best option and it'll have to do.

He decides on there. The only problem is getting Kyle over there.

"You're not going….going to leave me, are you?"

Yuuki's attention snaps back to Kyle. He frowns hard. "Leave you?"

Kyle merely blinks. "Ev'ryone does…y-you should, too. Else they'll catch us. Jeff will find me and he'll…he'll find you too. Don't want him catching you."

"Jeff's…not around anymore," Yuuki says. "Remember? Andy took him down at the Checkpoint A hut. You were there."

"Oh…oh yeah."

Yuuki presses his lips together. *This is bad.* "Even if someone was pursuing us, I wouldn't leave you. I'm not going to stop fighting for you, Kyle. Just because your case is over, or will be soon, doesn't mean that I'm going to just leave."

Kyle squeezes his eyes shut, cheek twitching with the headache he's most likely got. "Why?"

"Because you're more than just a case file."

They can keep having this conversation, but it's better that they have it away from the mess, Yuuki thinks. Breathing in the sick that's in front of him can't be helping Kyle in the least.

Yuuki leans over a little further and slips his hand under Kyle's arm. "Are you able to get up? There's a flatter spot where we can rest just a few metres away. You can lie down again over there."

Kyle looks like he wants to argue. He doesn't look uncomfortable lying as he is, but after a minute of consideration, he sighs in agreement. Yuuki helps him not topple over as he struggles to prop himself up on his elbows. He switches his hold to gripping the top of the backpack's shoulder strap, and with that extra support Kyle's able to move himself around the vomit and across the slope to where Yuuki's sitting.

It's slow going, taking them a few minutes just to get halfway over to the designated resting spot, but with careful movements and patience, they make it. Kyle flops down on the rock and lets his head drop with a grunt. Yuuki's eyes widen in alarm, but thankfully Kyle's arm cushions the impact.

With a deep breath in and out, Yuuki leans back against a tree and stares out at the scene before them. The edge of the palace grounds are just below them. Down where forest gives way to field, small navy-clad dots stand in stiff rows. They hold transparent shields in front of them. Sunlight reflects off the blasters they hold in their other hands.

Hopelessness threatens to choke him. The Peace Forces are fully armed. All the get-Amelia-to-the-throne group have is Logan's rifle and Andy's standard issue blaster.

There's a person standing behind the two rows of officers. They're the only one without a shield and the only one not wearing the same dark colours as Peace Force officers.

Taularh.

Yuuki has to squint, but he's fairly sure that's who it is. In the corner of his eye Yuuki sees Kyle watching his expression. Yuuki tries to keep the despair off his face, but it's hard when the two of them are hiding from a man who already knows he's won. It's hard to keep believing in the small glimmer of hope that still remains for them when the leader they seek to remove from the throne is standing out in the open down there, unfazed by the knowledge that he has a challenger heading his way.

Did the helicopters see us coming, after all? Yuuki wonders. *Or is it just that Taularh figured that they'd be on their way, since we were in the forest and since neither Jeff, Deborah nor Andy ever reported in again after being sent after the group?*

"Taularh knows we're coming," Timothy had said. Yuuki can't help but feel like the fight had already been lost to them before they even left the house to make a run for it. Taularh's always had the upper hand, always been one step ahead of them. They're severely disadvantaged as it is.

How are they supposed to –

"'s not over yet."

Yuuki startles. Kyle's still staring at him, frowning hard. Judging by his expression, it's taking Kyle a lot of energy and effort to concentrate.

"We still have each other," Kyle mumbles. "...have each other, so..."

Yuuki sees his flash with the same fierceness they had done so with outside the cramped cave yesterday. It stills the fear in Yuuki's heart, and even if it's just for a moment, he feels courage return to him. His heart warms. "Yeah. We do."

A few minutes of resting later, Yuuki suggests Kyle take the backpack off so he can breathe a little easier. Kyle grumbles at the thought of moving, but decides it's not such a bad idea after all. Yuuki moves from his lean against the tree and crouches down beside Kyle to help him.

They've just gotten his arms free of the straps, Kyle sinking back down to lying down on the rock, when a rustling in the bush startles them.

"Look who we have here!"

Yuuki's breath leaves him. On the other side of the slope they just hauled themselves across are two Peace Force officers. Adrenaline's flowing. They were probably scouting the area doing a perimeter check.

The lady at the front of the pair grins when she sees the way Kyle's arms shake as he pushes himself up to his knees.

"We'll end this now, eh?" the man behind her yells, slipping a blaster out of his pocket. The lady starts moving again and he scrambles across the slope after her. He snickers. "You can die knowing you tried though, if that's any consolation."

Yuuki's on his feet. He uses the tree he'd been leaning against to pull himself up the hill. Before the officers can get to him and Kyle, Yuuki gets to them first.

The lady slips past him, so Yuuki takes on the male officer, throwing himself down onto the slope and kicking the guy's legs out from under him. The guy's arms wheel, eyes widening then narrowing as he lands and fixes his eyes on Yuuki. Yuuki grabs the blaster and wrenches it out of the officer's hand before he can pull the trigger.

"Get away from m—!"

Kyle's shout is quickly cut off. Yuuki kicks at the male officer and glances over in horror to see the female officer grab Kyle by the shoulders and slam him down into the rock. She draws back an arm, hand clenched in a fist, and punches him in the side of the head once, twice – Kyle's efforts to fight back stop – three times.

On the third, Kyle's arms fall limp at his sides and Yuuki's adrenaline spikes. What if those punches fell on the same side of Kyle's head as the concussion?

Yuuki shoves the male officer away from him, rolls over and scrambles back to Kyle's side. He barrels into the lady as she reaches for her blaster, and it's in that moment Yuuki decides that unless he does what he has to, him and Kyle are going to be dead in the next minute.

He plants his feet, one on either side of Kyle, and with all his strength, uses all his muscles to swing his one arm into the lady.

The swing catches her in the neck but Yuuki doesn't withdraw any energy or power from it. The momentum has the lady stumbling backwards. Her eyes widen as her foot meets open air. Anger and alarm are the last Yuuki sees of her before she tumbles down the hillside.

He ducks just in time to avoid getting shot by the other officer.

The male officer levels the blaster at Yuuki's face. He fires and Yuuki dodges, heart beating too fast and his vision too sharp. Yuuki hates this. He hates it, but he has to do it. The officer reaches the less sloped ground, but before he can find any decent footing, Yuuki wraps his arm around a tree trunk, spins on one foot and *kicks*.

He doesn't see his expression; the officer's looking down at the drop that opens up before him as he falls. The officer disappears with a scream that trails off and finishes with a rustling of trees and a thump.

Yuuki's almost too shaken to move. Almost.

There's too much silence. Kyle, as Yuuki sees when he moves back to their spot, is still unconscious, eyes closed and mouth slack. Yuuki kneels down beside him. The rock jars his knees but he pays no heed to it.

With a shaking hand, Yuuki carefully presses two fingers against the side of Kyle's neck, beneath the jaw. There's a pulse. Yuuki leans down and turns his head sideways so that his cheek is hovering over Kyle's mouth. When he feels Kyle's breath light on his cheek, he sits up again and raises his face to the sky for a moment to stall his tears.

Not now, Yuuki. You have to be strong for him.

"Kyle, buddy." Yuuki taps Kyle hard on the collarbone. "Can you hear me?"

It's like that day all over again – that day he found Kyle dying of hypothermia in the cell. Kyle's unresponsive, showing absolutely no sign of having registered Yuuki calling his name. Yuuki bites his lip, the tears spilling involuntarily now. Hypothermia is one thing; a head injury, and possible neck injury, is another.

Yuuki's trying so hard to keep it together, but it's so hard. He's exhausted. Kyle's not waking up. If for whatever reason Kyle requires surgery, he's probably not going to make it.

If they were back at the house and this had happened, Susan and Charlie would've had the equipment to be able to help him. Maybe the palace has the necessary items, but they'd have to get in there in the first place, and that isn't happening unless the signal for victory is given, and even then not until the whole palace has been checked to make sure no one is snuck up upon.

There's also, of course, the option of taking Kyle to a hospital in the city, but the time it would take to get him out there would be too long. It would also mean exposing themselves to any pro-Taularh people out in the public.

Yuuki clenches his jaw. Kyle's survival depends on him, then.

The thought of losing Kyle because of it highlights a loneliness that Yuuki hadn't realised was in his heart. It also shows him, with an overwhelmingly bittersweet realisation, just how much Yuuki had given up the hope that his life could ever have purpose again.

A twitch in Kyle's brow catches his attention. Yuuki watches his face expectantly, waiting for him to wake up, but then his arm jerks. Kyle's whole body seizes, a muscle in his neck jumps and then he convulses. It's not until Kyle's body convulses again and his head lifts and slams into the rock that Yuuki realises what's happening: Kyle's having a seizure.

"No, no, no...."

32

Yuuki hastily slips his hand beneath Kyle's head and the rock. Kyle's arm hits his knees. "Please, no."

He's losing it. Somewhere in the back of his mind he belatedly remembers that he should've been timing the seizure. To the best Yuuki can estimate through his sobbing, it's forty seconds before it stops.

The stillness that takes over Kyle's body is both unsettling and relieving. Yuuki keeps his hand beneath Kyle's head and waits, painstakingly waits, as Kyle comes around.

Kyle slowly opens his eyes. His eyes aren't focused. He blinks but his vacant expression doesn't change. He just lies there and stares at the trees and sky above them.

Yuuki sniffs. If he had his other arm, he could wipe the tears off his face but as it is he just has to let them stay there. "Hey, Kyle," he murmurs. "Are you with me again?"

No reaction. Yuuki's throat constricts. He gently sets Kyle's head down on the rock and takes Kyle's hand in his. He squeezes Kyle's hand and says his name again, hoping, praying that he can hear him. Kyle's fingers twitch and slowly curl around Yuuki's to return the squeeze.

A gunshot rings out across the valley. Yuuki looks to the palace grounds in time to see the figure he previously identified as Taularh topple to the ground. In Taularh's hand is an object that gleams in the sunlight: a gun. Amelia stands a metre before him – still stands, thanks to what can only be Logan's intervention.

"Yuu'…"

Relief cuts through the new wave of adrenaline. Kyle's eyes are locked on Yuuki's face. Yuuki flashes him as much of a smile as he can manage. He gives Kyle's hand a gentle squeeze and rubs his thumb over his knuckles.

"I'm right here," Yuuki whispers. "You're going to be okay, yeah?"

Kyle blinks slowly. "Yu'…Yuu'…"

"Just hang in there."

Down below, the palace grounds are in chaos. An officer – presumably Andy – is hurrying Amelia away from the fight that has just broken out among the Peace Force officers. It's impossible to tell who's on which side. A couple of shots are fired in Amelia and Andy's direction. Taularh hasn't gotten back up again.

"'m… t-tired," Kyle murmurs.

His words are so slurred it takes Yuuki a couple of moments afterwards to understand what he said. Yuuki turns his gaze back to Kyle's face and sees him struggling to keep his eyes open.

Yuuki hums. "It's okay. Just rest."

"D-don't…wan'…want…"

"You're not going to die."

Kyle's eyes slip shut. "…scare'."

Yuuki grips Kyle's hand. "I know." *I am, too.* "But you're going to be okay. You're going to make it. So if you're really tired and you need to sleep, then let yourself do so. I'll wake you up after a while, make sure you're doing okay."

A whimper sounds deep within Kyle's chest, rising in pitch. He swallows hard. A moment later, a tear wells in the corner of his right eye.

"You're going to be okay, Kyle. Just hold on."

Kyle chokes on a sob. "'m s-scared."

Yuuki works his jaw. *Stay strong. Stay strong.* "I know you are. But don't you dare give up. I can't…" He tries to fight his own tears, tries to just focus on breathing, but he can see Kyle doing the same – just trying to breathe – and all of a sudden Yuuki can't take it anymore. "I left my family to come to this country. I never thought I'd find another here. Timothy and Susan and Joshua and Sam…they're like family to me and now you are too. You're like a brother to me, Kyle. You're like a brother to me and I love you.

"So don't you dare leave me, you hear? Not now. Not after all we've been through. Please."

Yuuki can feel it now. The dam he'd set up to keep in the ugly side of his emotions finally breaking. The ability to feel that he'd frozen so that the worst of the pain didn't destroy him. Kyle came into his life and Yuuki learned once more what it means to care for someone so strongly.

He'd thought that taking up the investigation into Kyle's case meant it was his role to do the protecting, but here Kyle is, suffering, because he found Yuuki worth protecting, too.

Ten, fifteen, twenty minutes pass without a whistle signal. The fight appears to have turned into more of a fight based on verbal argument, some of the officers still on the fence as to who they're going to support and the officers affiliated with Andy having to be careful deciding whose word they can trust and whose they can't.

There hasn't been sight nor sound of the two Peace Force officers that found them which can only mean one thing: Yuuki killed them. *What kind of person does that make me?* Yuuki thinks. He's horrified at himself. Another part of himself reminds him that he did what he had to, but…

Is this dread the same kind of terror that Kyle felt when the incident with Daniel Wilson happened? But that had been an accident: Kyle hadn't meant for that knife to end up in Wilson. Yuuki, on the other hand, had meant to push those officers down the slope. He'd wanted them to go down and not come back up again.

To protect yourself. To protect Kyle, he reminds himself. It doesn't make the knowledge any easier to process.

Kyle drifts in and out of consciousness. Despite Yuuki's reassurance that he'll wake him, Kyle's too afraid to let himself sleep out of fear he won't be able to wake up again. Yuuki watches him closely for any signs of deterioration of his condition but so far there haven't been any. If he does get worse, then…

Yuuki doesn't want to think about it.

First aid is all Kyle has available to him at the moment, so Yuuki does the best he can. There's a cut on the back of Kyle's head that's still bleeding sluggishly, on the left side where he initially hit it. The area's inflamed from the impact but the small wound appears to be superficial. Yuuki grabs a roll of bandage out of the backpack, along with some disinfectant wipes and gauze, and does his best to clean and wrap the wound.

It's times like these where the lack of his right arm frustrates him. Yuuki has to manoeuvre Kyle onto his side, head propped up on Yuuki's crossed legs, in order to be able to hold the gauze in place while he haphazardly wraps the bandage around it. Using his teeth to bring the cloth over and then his hand again when bringing it under, he's able to manage, but it's still nonetheless frustrating.

If Kyle's injuries had been worse and required him to use two hands in order to help him…

But that hadn't happened. Aside from the head injury, there's only a few scrapes and bruises to worry about. Yuuki himself has a few scratches on his legs both from the walking and from the fall, but thanks to Kyle he came off rather lightly.

He wishes Kyle hadn't jumped after him. He'd rather take the fall himself than have Kyle die trying to protect him from it.

Don't think that, Yuuki rebukes himself. *Kyle's going to be fine. It's just your anxiety getting ahead of you.*

It's not just anxiety though; it's a legitimate concern. Head injuries aren't to be taken lightly. They're also unpredictable. Given Kyle's age and relative good health, the risks aren't as bad as they could've been, but it's still early.

Anything could happen.

A whistle blows. It sounds seven times, cutting through the atmosphere, declaring. Yuuki hears it but it takes a moment for his brain to catch up to what it means. His heart skips a beat.

Seven whistle blows. They've succeeded.

Yuuki's hand tightens around Kyle's. He replays the sound of the whistle over and over in his head, certain he misheard it or that his mind made it up. Seven whistle blows means there's a tomorrow for them all. It means that there's a future ahead of them.

It means that, finally, everything that Kyle's been through – and all the literal blood, sweat and tears that Yuuki and Timothy have done to fight for him – these last two months wasn't for naught.

"We actually did it," Yuuki whispers. A chill runs through him as those words are given a voice. He's too stunned to move.

Kyle's unconscious, so if he heard the whistle and Yuuki's words, it doesn't show.

The success means they can come out of hiding now. A victory here doesn't mean they're out of danger yet; all it means is that the first step of Amelia taking back the throne has been successful. But it's a much safer situation they're in now than they were even an hour ago, and that's what counts.

Since everyone will be meeting up at Timothy's group's location down below, Yuuki has to find a way to get Kyle down there. He doubts whether or not he can make it that far. He could wait where they are, maybe call out and hope that Logan and Avi hear him or that someone on their side comes and finds them. But there's also the risk that waiting here longer means more time before someone with actual medical knowledge who is able to help Kyle can get to him.

Yuuki takes a deep breath. That means he's the one who has to get Kyle from here to the others. He's exhausted, dizzy and fatigued, but he's also Kyle's lifeline, and that's the thought that gives him the extra burst of energy he needs.

He checks the dressing on the back of Kyle's head. The wound isn't bleeding through the gauze, but that doesn't speak of what bleeding there might be internally. Yuuki can't afford to delay any longer. After several minutes contemplating how best to do it, Yuuki shoulders the backpack and pulls Kyle into a fireman's carry.

It's the toughest exercise he's ever done. Even running a marathon hadn't put this much strain on his lungs and muscles. His legs are burning and shaking with the exertion. Yuuki has to mentally force his knees not to buckle, and every time he slips or loses balance, he has to give it everything he's got in order to get himself moving again.

But somehow he does it. Somehow he makes it to the bottom of the hill and is able to keep walking. Kyle's weight seems to grow heavier with every step, but Yuuki keeps going. He's sweating profusely and his vision's swirling, but he keeps going. His feet start dragging but he forces his legs to keep moving.

When he sees the temporary tarpaulin shelter set up, Yuuki almost collapses then and there. He doesn't have the breath or the energy to call out though, so he keeps going, keeps walking, tears streaming down his face again at the thought of what might happen to Kyle if he can't complete the task of carrying him to the others.

Hands and voices. He stumbles into Timothy who holds him steady and upright as his knees finally decide they've had enough. Joshua and Susan are there on either side of him and then Kyle's weight is lifted off his shoulders. Yuuki sags forward into Timothy's arms.

He isn't even aware of someone taking the backpack off his back. All Yuuki knows is exhaustion, pain and tears of relief that he made it.

Only when he hears Susan speaking reassuringly to Kyle, who must've briefly regained consciousness, does Yuuki let himself go.

33

Yuuki's too worried about Kyle to sleep. Buried deep inside of him is the fear that when he wakes up, Kyle will be gone, and Yuuki can't bear the thought of it. He's awake again soon after he passed out, anxiety twisting and pulling at his mind.

If he weren't so spent, Yuuki would find it funny how even his face feels tired. His head's foggy, there's an ache beneath his eyes from lack of sleep and his face muscles seem reluctant to want to make any kind of expression. He simply just lies as he is and listens.

He's lying on his back, something – probably a blanket of some sort – laid out over him. There's movement beside him to his left, shuffling, hasty footsteps. They retreat, probably on their way to get something. Yuuki focuses his attention a little more and hears Susan's unnerved tone. What chance Yuuki had of drifting back to sleep is gone now.

He opens his eyes for a few seconds and finds her standing with Timothy just a metre away.

"If he has a hematoma," Susan's murmuring, "it can heal on its own. But we'll need to keep a close eye on him for any signs of deterioration. If the clot enters the bloodstream…" Susan presses her hand against her forehead, brow pinched. She grimaces, muttering under her breath, "Let's just hope that doesn't happen."

It's my fault, Yuuki wants to say. *I fell. It was my own mistake. Kyle shouldn't be the one suffering for it.* And yet he still can't help but blame himself.

But Kyle will say it's not his fault. Some part of Yuuki knows it isn't. The worst of Kyle's injuries are thanks to the officer beating him, after all, not from him protecting Yuuki during the fall, and Yuuki's falling over the edge in the first place due to fatigue and dizziness couldn't have been helped.

It's a misplaced guilt, what Yuuki's experiencing, but if the head injury gets worse and Kyle dies, he'll never forgive himself.

Yuuki thinks about how this could've been prevented. About how, maybe if he'd remembered that Kyle had had a knife tucked away in his boot, that he could've grabbed it when the officers came and done more to protect Kyle. Maybe then he would've come away with no more than a concussion.

But it's too late for thinking about that now. That part of the fight is over. The only thing to think of now is how best they can help Kyle get through the worst of the injury and recover.

Another set of footsteps. "Hey, Logan and Avi reporting in. Avi's just over there talking with Sam." A pause. "Are Kyle and Yuuki back yet?"

"Yeah," Timothy says tiredly. "They're inside the shelter. Welcome back."

"What's wrong? Are they okay?"

Susan sighs, murmurs something and leaves.

"It looks like they had a run in with some officers," Timothy explains. "Taularh probably had some guys out on perimeter check. We'll need to wait until Yuuki's had some rest before we find out what actually happened though. Kyle's got a moderate head injury, presumably from having his head bashed, but we're just making that guess based on our observations. So just…maybe let Susan do the telling the others once we have a better understanding of what happened. That okay?"

"Yeah…" Logan trails off, apparently lost for words. "Did Yuuki get hurt, too?'

"Physically, not really. Emotionally, yeah. He carried Kyle all the way down the hill to us. He… looked like he'd been crying a fair bit. I'm guessing Kyle's injury gave him quite a scare."

Lying where he is, Yuuki swallows hard. Scared is understatement. Kyle having that seizure had completely freaked him out and scared him out of his wits.

"Kyle's going to be alright though, right?" Logan asks.

Timothy's quiet for a moment. "We're monitoring him closely. If he needs surgery, I don't know what we'll do. We can't get him to a hospital: it's too risky. We just have to wait and see."

Yuuki forces his eyes open. It takes a lot of effort and energy he doesn't really have right now, but Timothy's hesitation has him unnerved.

Above him, Yuuki sees the blue of the tarpaulin and the slope it's anchored down in. The blue-tinted shade it casts makes it feel like he's lying in a cave, or somewhere protected, and Yuuki almost gives in to the sense of safety and drifts off again.

A soft groan to his left reminds him of why he opened his eyes in the first place. Yuuki turns his head and his stomach dips.

Kyle.

"Avi's about to make food," Logan is saying. "I think he had some instant soup sachet tucked away in one the bag pockets. If we make that up for Kyle, would he be able to drink it?"

Yuuki zones out to the rest of the conversation. Kyle's lying on his back beside him, laid out on an inflatable mattress and his head propped up on a roll of someone's spare clothes. It looks like a mixture of Joshua's and Timothy's t-shirts. There's an emergency blanket covering him like there is one covering Yuuki.

Thankfully, Kyle looks to be sleeping, albeit a little restlessly. There's no crease in his brow and his face is slack, his cheeks are drained of colour. Somehow it all just brings the reality of what happened crashing back down, and Yuuki can't help but feel as helpless as he did up on the hillside all over again.

Kyle will be fine, he tries to tell himself. *Look, he's right there, breathing, still alive. He can make it.*

The bandage Yuuki haphazardly wound around his head is still there, if not replaced. Knowing Susan though, it probably has been done again since she would've wanted to check the wound and the inflamed area on the back of Kyle's head. Yuuki's just too tired to notice anything besides the fact that there's no additional layers of bandage and gauze wrapped around Kyle's head. He hopes that's a good thing.

"Oh, Yuuki. You're awake."

Not too fast, Yuuki turns his head away from Kyle to see Susan coming through the makeshift curtain. The light outside is still bright and Yuuki has to squint. He can understand why they were brought in here, for Kyle's sake at least – privacy and a bit of quiet is one thing, but the last thing they want is to be straining their eyes and risk making Kyle's likely horrendous headache even worse.

Susan crouches down at Kyle's side, a pouch of sports water in hand. As she tears open the pouch, she glances over her shoulder at Yuuki and regards him carefully. "How are you feeling?"

"Scared," Yuuki murmurs. The answer slips out before he realises what he's said, but since his gaze has drifted back to Kyle, Susan understands exactly what he means and what he's scared about.

Susan doesn't answer. Her lips pull into a tight line. Yuuki was there when the accident and the incident happened; no amount of hopeful words such as 'he'll pull through' is going to hide the truth of what danger Kyle is in. Susan might have better knowledge of what those risks are, but Yuuki's no fool and he doesn't need to be given false hope. Thankfully she knows that.

Ever so gently, Susan lifts Kyle into her arms, using her forearm to support Kyle's neck and her hand to support his head. With her other hand she brings the pouch to the corner of Kyle's mouth. After pouring a few of drops of the water and murmuring words of reassurance, she's able to coax Kyle to swallow and drink it.

"How long has it been since we got back?" Yuuki asks. He pushes himself up into a sitting position, ignoring the way his head spins. There's a bottle of water at his right side. Yuuki reaches across himself, grabs it and unscrews the lid with his teeth. "Did Logan and Avi just get back?"

"Yeah," Susan says distractedly. "They stayed up there in position a little longer to keep lookout." She lightly rubs Kyle's throat with her thumb when he coughs. "It's been just over an hour, by the way."

Yuuki frowns at the bottle he's holding. Watching Kyle drink has made himself thirsty, but somehow he can't find the energy to even lift the bottle. It takes a good long minute before he's able to, and by that stage Susan's already lying Kyle back down again.

"We found the bodies of two officers near where you two must've been," she murmurs, moving the emergency blanket over Kyle's shoulders again. "Well, the officers Andy sent to check that area did. Did they find you?"

Yuuki exhales sharply. "Yeah…"

"Did they do this to Kyle?" Timothy asks, coming into the shelter.

Yuuki's grip tightens on the water bottle. "Partially. I-I fell, and he caught me…banged his head on a rock as we fell down the hill. It was just a concussion at first. He wasn't feeling good as it was, and then…" He tries not to think about that officer punching an already concussed Kyle in the head but the memory is too vivid and recent. He has to set the water down before he spills it.

"Then the officers came," Susan finishes.

"Yeah," Yuuki says, ducking his head. "I-I'm sorry. I didn't mean to kill them. I just …I had to get them away from Kyle. They were going to kill us, and one of them, she was punching Kyle – in the head – and then he just …went limp and I…."

Susan puts a steadying hand on his back. "It's okay, Yuuki. You did what you had to."

Timothy hums in agreement. "In these sort of circumstances, sometimes that's the only way we come out the other side – by doing what we have to do in order to protect each other. Even if we'd prefer there to be another way around it."

A wave of exhaustion slams into Yuuki. He slouches forward, hiding his face in the foil of the emergency blanket while he tries to hold back the sob. He's too tired for emotions right now.

"I must've walked straight past them, too," he mumbles. "The officers, that is."

"Then it's probably a good thing that you had your head down," Timothy murmurs.

"Yeah." Yuuki groans and rubs his eyes with his hand. "I'm so tired."

"I'm not surprised. In the last few days, you what? Nearly drowned? Hiked? Barely slept? And that's on top of your dealing with everything your PTSD throws at you." Timothy sits down beside Yuuki and wraps an arm around his shoulders. "The world just keeps beating you down, doesn't it?"

Yuuki grunts. "Guess that's what happens when you keep fighting back."

"Not just that. What happens when you keep fighting back is that people's lives change as well," Timothy says firmly. "People who otherwise wouldn't have been given a voice. People who society gave up on. Those who have lost hope for any kind of future – you give it back to them by fighting for them, Yuuki."

Kyle's presence in the room is even more tangible now. Yuuki knows that it's Kyle in particular who Timothy is referring to, and yet he still doesn't feel like he did much.

"It wasn't just me, you know," Yuuki says. He sits up and looks Timothy directly in the eye. "You stood up for Kyle, too. You did everything you could to ensure he wasn't in danger while you were doing so. Even if that meant judging him to be guilty as a necessary means of protecting him in the courtroom."

Sure, Yuuki was the one who went into the detention centre to talk to Kyle and ask the questions that had not been asked at the trial, but at the end of the day it's Timothy who initiated that further investigation and made sure that Kyle didn't get too hurt in the process. If it had been another judge in Timothy's place, Yuuki probably would've never been given the opportunity to do his part in giving Kyle back the hope and the freedom he never should've lost in the first place.

The expression in Timothy's eyes in a mix of many things. Humbleness, triumph, compassion...and self-blame. It was, at the end of the day, Timothy's own words that put Kyle away. Timothy can't forget that so easily. At Yuuki's words, his face softens a little, but the smile doesn't quite reach his eyes.

"It's not your fault someone decided to screw up Kyle's life for him," Yuuki mutters. "If it hadn't been for Jeff's interference, you probably would've easily been able to prevent Kyle from going to prison. You did what you had to to protect him."

Yuuki stops mid-sentence, realising what he's just said. *I just turned the conversation back on myself, didn't I?* Timothy's smiling in earnest now, as is Susan as she watches over Kyle's condition.

"So you two can stop beating yourselves up now, right?" Susan murmurs. "Seems that sometimes we've got to take unfavourable measures to protect someone. You can't keep blaming yourself for it. We're human; there's only so much we can do."

Timothy and Yuuki nod in unison. They both laugh softly when they realise.

"Alright, alright," Timothy says, grinning. "I'll try to remind myself of that. It would be hypocritical of me to tell Logan not to beat himself up if I'm still doing it, wouldn't it?"

Susan hums.

"Logan was the one who took down Taularh, wasn't he?" Yuuki says, frowning. "Is he okay? He probably hasn't ever...you know, had to kill someone before."

Timothy sighs. "He's a little shaken up. If there's any consolation for him in the matter, it's that he saved Amelia – and likely the rest of us – with that one shot."

"Just as you two saved Kyle and subsequently you allowed opportunity for all this to happen," Susan says, gesturing beyond the curtain of the tarpaulin shelter. "Butterfly effect. None of this would've happened as well as it did if it hadn't been for every action you guys took on your part. It may not have come without a cost, but..."

Yuuki smiles wryly. "I'd gladly lose my right arm all over again if it means seeing a law change... if it means saving Kyle...." His face falls. "I just wish all this didn't have to have cost *him* so much."

"I can't speak for Kyle, but if I were in his position, no friends and family and oppressed, I'd almost be grateful for this bad turn of events if it meant bringing family and friends into my life again.

"I don't mean to say that everything that's happened to him has been good," Susan says quickly. "It's just that, from what I've seen – especially recently – it's that sometimes the things that curse us can warp and twist themselves into being blessings as well. Like how you and Kyle came to meet out of screwed up circumstances."

"Butterfly effect?" Yuuki asks, tilting his head slightly.

"You guessed it."

"I thought you studied medical science, not astrophysics and quantum mechanics."

Timothy grunts. "It's what she does in her spare time."

Susan smiles, pats Yuuki on the back and picks herself up off the ground. She exhales slowly. "I'm going to go see how Amelia's doing. I think she's starting to feel the pressure of what's ahead for her. I'll be back to check on Kyle soon." She nods at Yuuki. "Make sure you get some rest. It's been a long day."

Yuuki and Timothy sit in silence after she leaves. Kyle is still asleep beside them. It's hard to know what to talk about, let alone think.

So much has happened between now and the first time Yuuki ever found out about Kyle's case. Yuuki had been so full of doubt and indecision when Timothy had sent him that letter, but now he's never been so sure about making that decision that he made.

If he hadn't said yes to the taking on the investigation of Kyle's case, Amelia would've still been in hiding, the law wouldn't have had a chance to change – other people's lives wouldn't have had the chance to change, Kyle would likely have died in the cell and Yuuki wouldn't have the brother he has today. It's not as if they haven't suffered loss in all they've gained, but the greatest things in life never do seem to come without a sacrifice.

Yuuki glances over at Kyle, dark shadows beneath his eyes and a bandage securing gauze to the back of his head. He can see a nasty bruise starting to bloom just above Kyle's temple from where the officer punched him. Yet that's only the superficial hurts. It doesn't account for all the damage done inside, the trauma done to his head and to his soul.

If only this all could've cost him less, Yuuki thinks. *He did nothing to deserve any of this…and even if he had, a punishment less than trauma would've been enough. He shouldn't have had to go through all of this.*

Wordlessly, Timothy pulls him into a hug. Yuuki can tell by the line of tension in Timothy's arms that he's been thinking the exact same thing. There are no words to describe what it's like to watch someone get hurt so badly, especially someone who's come to be family. It's hard thinking about how they weren't able to be there for Kyle while he was in prison, while he was hurting the most, but they can be there for him now and be there for him while he heals. It'll be a tough ride, but at least Kyle doesn't have to go through it alone.

At least Yuuki won't have to go through it alone.

Timothy releases him from the hug and lays a hand on Yuuki's shoulder. "I'm going to start getting this place ready for the night. It'll be dark soon, and we're going to want to make sure we've got enough light and warmth in here."

"Where are the others sleeping?" Yuuki asks. The shelter they've got set up here could sleep six or seven people at the most, but with Kyle injured and his condition needing to be monitored, there needs to be room adequate for supplies and moving around.

Timothy tilts his head in the direction of the curtain. "Out there. They've set up just outside there, a few metres away. The shelter's not as good as this one, but we're all too exhausted to find a better place so it'll just have to make do. It doesn't look like it'll rain, thankfully. We'll bring the electronic and emergency equipment in here later just to be on the safe side though."

Yuuki nods. Through the haze that's begun to settle over his ability to think, it sounds like a good plan.

"Susan will stay in here with you two, by the way," Timothy says. "She'll also need someone to wake her up so she can check on Kyle, so Charlie and I will stay here too. We'll take turns keeping watch."

"I want to say I'd like to help, but…"

"You just rest. You need it."

Yuuki grunts. "You need to rest at some point, too."

"I can manage," Timothy murmurs, smiling. With that, he stands up, if a little stiffly and with his feet clicking. The shelter isn't so accommodating of his height and he bumps his head on the tarpaulin. "I'll be back in a bit," he says, shuffling over to the entrance. "Try get some sleep if you can, Yuuki. You look like you're about to turn into a zombie."

If I haven't already turned into one, Yuuki thinks tiredly.

With Timothy gone, the shelter is left in stillness. Noise filters in from outside, conversations and pots clanging and bags being rummaged through, but none of them are all that loud. There's exhaustion seeping into every voice and movement, and the relative quiet after such a long day of walking, hiding, falling and crying is lulling.

Yuuki lies back down. Staring at the tarpaulin makes his vision swim, so he closes his eyes and just lies there, listening. Every so often a small groan sounds in Kyle's throat, making Yuuki's heart skip a beat when he drifts so much that he forgets there's someone else in the shelter with him, but otherwise it's quiet enough to ease his hypervigilance.

Eventually a peace settles in his heart, just before he drops off to sleep.

It's been what feels like a long time since Yuuki's been able to let his guard down like this. It almost doesn't feel right, like the moment he does so, something or someone bad is going to creep up on them. He's afraid to let go just in case something does happen and he's not ready for it.

But Kyle's presence is anchoring and the steady rhythm of his breathing a reassurance. Yuuki focuses on it and before long he's slipping into sleep, decidedly trusting the people around them to take care of them both.

34

Kyle sinks and drowns in pain and confusion. Familiar voices sound nearby. He follows them, tries to latch onto them and drag himself back to consciousness, but more often than not he's swept back into unconsciousness before he can really surface.

It scares him, being stuck in the middle ground of being aware and not being aware. Is sleeping bad? What if he lets himself sleep and that's it – he can't wake up again? What if Yuuki's trying to get him to wake up this very moment and Kyle can't hear him?

His head feels like it's about to explode with every heartbeat. But it's not just his head that hurts – everything hurts. His muscles ache so badly he can't find the energy to move them. Kyle tries to remember what on earth made him hurt like this, but even thinking is a struggle and it only makes his headache worse.

He'd heard Timothy and Susan talking with Yuuki earlier. In his confusion, Kyle wonders if he's back at the Harrisons' home, coming to again after nearly freezing to death in his cell. Maybe they were talking about sending him back there. Yuuki might've been adamant earlier in saying that he wouldn't let Kyle end up back in prison, but maybe he's starting to realise it's for the best. Yuuki's got enough to deal with.

A tap on his cheek. "Kyle?"

The voice isn't Yuuki's. A sudden wave of panic washes over him and Kyle remembers the officer leaning over him. He can't recall what she did, but whatever it was made his head hurt far worse than it already had been hurting.

"Kyle? Can you wake up for me?"

He tries to turn his face away and finds he can't. His head feels like it's been filled with concrete or like someone clamped a vice around it. A distressed cry escapes his throat. Kyle hates how unlike himself it sounds.

A hand grips his. A warm, gentle hand. It's not the grip of someone who wants to hurt him, but rather of someone who cares enough to try to help him past the confusion and the fear of not understanding what's going on.

"Hey, it's okay. You're okay."

Finally he's able to recognise the voice as a kind one, one he knows, and as soon as he's able to place it as Susan's, Kyle's able to breathe normally again.

"There you are," Susan murmurs. "Sorry I scared you a bit there. I just need to check that your head injury's not getting any worse."

Head injury? That explains why the headache's so bad and why he can't think straight....also why he's having problems with his memory.

"Are you able to open your eyes for me?"

Kyle groans. He really doesn't have the energy or the willpower for this. Contrary to his earlier opinion up on the hillside, something he remembers only vaguely, all he wants to do is sleep. He's exhausted beyond what he's ever experienced before in his life.

Somehow he manages to do it. Susan's face is a blur above him. Behind her everything is dark, so it's impossible to make out where exactly he is. It smells like earth, antiseptic and clothes that have been worn for a while, suggesting they're still outside. The amber lamp light glowing to his right somewhere confirms that.

Susan's trying to get his attention, waving a hand in front of his face. "Okay, see my finger?" she says. "Can you follow it with your eyes? Yeah, that's it. That's good."

Kyle blinks. He feels ridiculous doing it but he does as she asks him to. It's hard to keep his eyes focusing on Susan's finger instead of the mix of shadows and light behind her, but Susan doesn't seem to be too worried. Apparently this mustn't be an unusual thing to be happening after a head injury.

"Alright. Can you tell me your name?"

What kind of question is that? "K-Ky...le..."

Susan nods, but her smile is more of a grimace. "And your full name?"

Kyle's stomach churns. Words shouldn't be this hard, right? He knows what he wants to say, what Susan's asking him to say, so why is it taking so much effort to force the sounds to his lips? Susan waits, patiently but grimly, as Kyle fights the frustration threatening to overwhelm him.

"Ky...Ky'le," he grits out. *Come on, you can do this.* "K-Kin...dall..."

Susan rubs her thumb reassuringly over the back of his hand. "That's really good, Kyle. You're doing great."

Not having it in him to smile, Kyle just lies as he is and stares at her. Forcing himself to say just the syllables in his name has sapped his energy, but he's determined to stay awake as long as he can now. It's out of stubbornness and fear more than anything.

The next things Susan checks is his movement and co-ordination. She asks him to move his toes, and while Kyle's glad that means someone removed his shoes for him, he's not sure how much movement he's actually got going into his feet. He's too sore to feel anything but his muscles aching.

Moving his fingers turns out to be easier. He has to concentrate more than he should need to, but he's able to grip Susan's hand without any difficulty. For some reason his right hand feels weaker than his left, even though the worst of the throbbing of his headache is in the left side of his head. Susan notices the difference in strength, of course, and it has her frowning deeply again.

Is there something wrong with me? Kyle wants to ask, but he doesn't have the spare energy for words. Susan's just concerned, right? She said that he was doing well, so there mustn't be anything majorly wrong – besides the head injury, that is.

It's tiring just thinking about it. Without meaning to, Kyle finds himself drifting again. He doesn't even realise he closed his eyes until he opens them again however many minutes or hours later. Susan wakes him up a couple more times, asking him the same questions and doing the same tests. One time he wakes on his own. There's been no change in lighting and no one's there waking him up, though, so he lets himself be pulled back into the torrent of pain and thoughtlessness he currently calls sleep.

When he's next woken, the amber light is gone, replaced by the blue of a tarpaulin and dim lighting. It's relieving knowing that he doesn't have to face the loudness and brightness of outside. He can hear activity outside and it hurts his ears. Susan takes note of his wincing and leaves his side for a few moments to tell the noise makers to be a little quieter. Kyle's more than grateful.

"Wh...where...?" he murmurs, trailing off. Talking costs a lot of energy.

Susan comes back into the shelter in time to hear his words. The furrow in her brow eases. "We're set up near the palace."

The palace? "The f-fight?"

"Yeah," Susan says. Somehow Kyle's efforts to speak make her expression less heavy. "Andy's making sure that the place is secure before we go in. It was too close to dark last night to safely perform a thorough check, so we camped out here overnight."

None of it makes any sense. The last thing Kyle remembers of yesterday is clinging to Yuuki's hand, thinking he was going to die up on the hillside. Kyle doesn't remember any running after that, and if they're not hiding anymore then it must have been safe to reveal themselves.

That can only mean one thing.

"Di-did... we...win?"

Susan smiles, tired but also relieved. "Yeah. We did."

Someone shifts on the ground beside him. Kyle tries to turn his head to see who it is, but it still feels concrete. He doesn't have to push himself, however, as the person sits up and comes over instead, eyes wide as they shuffle over to sit right beside him.

"Hey, Kyle," Yuuki whispers. "H-how are ...?"

Kyle takes a deep breath in and out. Yuuki looks awful. The lines beneath his eyes are darker than Kyle remembers them ever being, and there's a lack of light in Yuuki's gaze. Exhaustion is what it is, as well as a deep-rooted fear and…something else that takes Kyle a little while longer to distinguish: self-blame.

"Not y…y-your faul', Yu'ki," Kyle murmurs. He's still stuttering and slurring, but at least the words are coming out.

Yuuki sniffs. His expression screws up, bottom lip quivering. He swallows hard and covers his eyes with his hand.

"Yu'…Yuuki?"

"I'm sorry!"

It hadn't really crossed Kyle's mind, up on the hillside, how terrified Yuuki must've been. Now that he thinks about it more too, or at least thinks about it as much as his brain will let him, he realises it must've been Yuuki who carried him all the way down to the group.

How on earth did Yuuki find the energy to *carry* him all that way, already exhausted, dizzy, sleep-deprived and stressed? Kyle struggles to fathom how he managed it.

Yuuki's voice is thick with tears. "I thought you were going to die. If not up there, then on the way here, b-because I couldn't protect you a-and I couldn't get you to here quick enough." He leans down, bows down, and hides his face in Kyle's shoulder, his fingers shaking as they curl into the material of the sweatshirt Kyle's wearing. "I'm sorry. You got hurt because of me. I'm always getting people hurt because of me."

Kyle grunts. "What're you…you talking 'bout? Y…you saved m-me."

"I didn't –"

"'m not talking…a-about…just yes'day."

Yuuki sobs. He turns his head away, shoulders shaking. Kyle narrows his eyes and focuses all of his energy into moving his arm at the elbow and lifting his hand to rest on the back of Yuuki's head.

"I didn't...die, Yuu'. Th-thanks to...to you."

And Susan and Timothy and everyone else, Kyle wants to say, but his voice trails off before he can form the words. Speaking is tiring him out fast, and he can already feel the need to close his eyes and rest calling out to him again.

He fights it though, for Yuuki. He'll rest better knowing Yuuki's not hurting himself with blame.

A few minutes later, Susan gently rouses Yuuki with a hand on his back. She murmurs something about changing the dressing on Kyle's head, but Kyle's struggling to follow the words. Yuuki sits up and hastily wipes his face with his forearm.

"Sorry," he says again.

Susan rubs his back in reassurance. "You're okay."

When she's got a new pad of gauze ready, she rolls Kyle onto his side, taking care to move him slowly. The movement makes Kyle's head spin. For a moment he thinks he's going to be sick, but then the nausea settles down again. Yuuki takes a hold of his hand as Susan unwraps the bandage Kyle hadn't realised was wrapped around his head. The missing pressure is both a relief and a headache.

He winces as Susan carefully checks over the wound. She asks him where it hurts the most, but Kyle's run out of energy for words. Thankfully his reactions speak sufficiently enough for him. After pressing the fresh pad of gauze over the wound, the bandages are wound back in place and Susan rolls him back onto his back.

There's a bruise on the side of his head that Susan checks again, too.

Kyle flinches when her fingers brush over it, his heart jumping at the memory of being hit – something Kyle's body can recall but his mind cannot. Susan quickly apologises and Yuuki's hand tightens around his.

The gap in Kyle's memory gives way to sleep.

35

The next few days are a blur, time passing but the pain and exhaustion remaining constant. Andy finally clears the palace safe to enter, and Susan's subsequently able to hunt down some stronger painkillers. Though they don't do too much to alleviate Kyle's fierce headache, they still help to effectively numb it.

Kyle's carried into the palace from the shelter on a makeshift stretcher made of blankets. Surrounded by people who care – Avi's kind voice above his head, Timothy's sturdy shoulders at the other end of the stretcher, and Yuuki and Susan walking on either side of him – Kyle drifts back into sleep halfway across the field. The sense of safety is too overwhelming for him to feel the need to force himself to stay awake for.

He wakes to soft natural light and the white walls of the palace infirmary. Avi comes in to help him change his clothes while he's conscious, something Kyle's extremely grateful for. The stench of sweat is replaced with one of Logan's spare shirts, and Timothy lends him a spare pair of trousers. Once Kyle's changed, Avi helps him lie back down in the bed and pulls the covers over him again with a small smile.

"Hope you start feeling better soon," he says as he stoops and gathers the discarded clothing off the floor. "I'll make you some soup later, yeah?"

Kyle does his best to acknowledge Avi with a smile. "Hmmmm. Your...your soup...soup is good."

Avi flashes him a bright smile. "Aw, thanks Kyle! Glad you like it!"

The soup turns out to be the best food Kyle's ever had. Maybe it's because he's so tired that any good food tastes amazing or that this is the first meal made with fresh ingredients the group has had since they left the house, but Kyle's certain he can taste the love and care Avi's made the soup with.

Sam brings in Yuuki and Kyle's share. When she comes back later to fetch the dishes, it's with a freshly brewed cup of coffee in her hands. Yuuki bursts into over-tired tears at the aroma of it.

Recovery is frustrating. A week since his injury, Kyle's ability to speak is still an issue. Amelia's busy getting settled and the legal means of her leadership established, and Kyle's still having problems forming a sentence without messing up. It's not as bad as it initially had been but it frustrates him nevertheless.

As he's learning though, healing isn't linear. He's able to think clearer but concentration and memory he struggles with. Sitting up leaves him dizzy and nauseous, and he's unable to stay awake for long periods of time. The longest time he's managed to stay awake for is a couple of hours.

Sam and Avi sneak in to see him one night, Yuuki tells him the next morning, but Kyle's out to the world when they come and so they leave before their presence has a chance to wake him.

Yuuki's been napping more often than not, too. He's fallen into a sort of emotional despondency, and it's then that Kyle sees just how far Yuuki's exhaustion goes. Yuuki's too afraid to leave Kyle's side for long, too, to the point that he declined the offer of one of the palace's bedrooms to sleep in so that he could stay in the infirmary.

The same fear grips them both. Yuuki nightmares. Kyle does too. In both their dreams, Kyle's taken back to the cell and Yuuki's restrained from saving him. Sometimes Kyle wakes up to find Yuuki's fingers locked around his, hand clammy and trembling. *Panic attack,* Kyle's mind supplies as he listens to Yuuki's fast and shallow breathing. Yuuki holds onto Kyle's hand tightly and Kyle lets him. One time it helps pull him out of his own nightmare.

The presence of so many officers around has them both on edge. Yuuki startles every time a blue uniform passes by the window. The air inside the room is stifling without the window open though, so the best they can do is draw the curtains.

But that only makes things worse. Being able to see outside and having a visible exit besides the door to the hallway available to them is the only thing keeping the white walls of the infirmary being reminiscent of a cell. Kyle might be recovering well from his head trauma, but healing from emotional trauma is an entirely different matter. He can see now why it's been so hard for Yuuki to heal from the Ninao incident.

Susan comes by twice a day to massage the stiffness out of Kyle's arms and legs. Kyle's shoulders still hurt from pulling Yuuki out of the river and from Jeff catching him the day after. Susan massages them too, working anti-inflammatory cream where the muscles are the tightest. Kyle wishes it would work for his head as well.

"We'll get you up moving around again soon," Susan says on the group's fifth day in the palace. "The sooner the better, even if it's for just a few minutes at a time."

Kyle doesn't answer. Sitting upright is tiring enough. How's he supposed to walk when he's feeling like this? Susan seems to sense his anxiousness and sighs. Kyle winces as Susan's massaging sends a stab of pain through his torn shoulder muscle. She murmurs a quick apology and carries on.

He wonders how much rest she's getting. As well as checking up on Kyle's injuries and managing his recovery, she's also been making sure there's no complications with the healing of Yuuki's residual limb. Then there's also the support she's been offering Amelia, her watching out for her own family while dealing with her own stress...

"Th-thank you," Kyle murmurs. He should've said it a lot sooner than this. "For...f-for helping me."

Susan ruffles his hair lightly with the back of her hand. "It's no worries. I'm just glad I'm able to help you."

Kyle lies awake awhile after Susan leaves. His thoughts have him thinking about how much everyone's done for him and, once again, he's not entirely sure how to react.

Before this, he knew none of these people. Sam had been an acquaintance, Avi, Amelia and Logan no more than classmates. Everybody else had been complete strangers to him, and he a complete stranger to them. And yet here they are, protecting him, fighting for him and taking care of him in the aftermath of it all.

Bewildered is the only word Kyle can think of to describe how he feels about that.

"Yuuki?" Kyle asks, turning his head to where Yuuki's sprawled out napping on the other bed beside him.

Yuuki blinks his eyes open and raises his eyebrows in question.

"C'n...can I as-ask you some...thing?"

"Yeah, of course." Yuuki shifts so that it's easier to talk. "What is it?"

"H-how did you... get me out? Of pr...prison, I mean. I know you and Timothy were...were looking into my case a-and all, but... how did you disprove w-what ev'ryone else said?"

"They had some help."

Yuuki and Kyle turn their gazes to see Timothy standing in the doorway. His mouth is set in a grimace, but there's a proud gleam in his eyes. He finds a seat on a stool at the foot of Kyle's bed and sits down with a sigh.

"I just learned who the witnesses were that came forward after the trial," Timothy explains. "It turns out help was a lot closer to home than we thought."

Yuuki regards him blankly. "What do you mean?"

"Sam went in to the station and gave a statement, on hearing where Kyle had ended up. She told her friends about it, which then inspired Logan to think more carefully about what he heard on the night of the incident." Timothy softens his voice, glancing at Kyle to gauge his reaction. "Logan realised it wasn't Daniel Wilson who'd been the one screaming, so he went and gave a witness statement, too. Logan's family lives next door to the park."

Kyle listens but his heart isn't in it. He finds it hard to comprehend the fact that there were actually people standing up for him.

"You haven't heard any of this yet, have you, Kyle?" Timothy asks, frowning. "They hadn't told you?"

327

If he had, Kyle can't remember it. "No…"

"I suppose you had enough chaos going on in your mind, eh. Too much to have the headspace to think about the details of everything."

"Y-yeah," Kyle murmurs. "I, um…I was afraid t-to ask in case…"

"In case?"

"In…in case you s-said to me it wasn't enough. I-I didn't want to think about…going back there."

Emotion wells up inside of him. It chokes him, constricts his throat and makes it hard to breathe. Yuuki swings his legs over the side of the bed and gets up, coming to sit down beside Kyle. With his one arm, he pulls Kyle up to lean against him. Kyle sinks into the hug and tries to regain composure.

No matter how many times Yuuki says it, Kyle's afraid he's going to wake up one morning back in the cell. Alone, dressed in orange and with nothing but the cold, the darkness and the horrible workings of his own mind to keep him company.

"At the trial," Timothy continues. "Charlie had argued in your defence that you acted in self-defence, but back then we didn't have sufficient evidence to support that. I would've asked further questions regarding that then and there in the courtroom if I hadn't been concerned about Jeff and…well, you saw the video.

"Andy's also got access to recordings of the phone calls and private emails Jeff had been making and sending around in regard to Ninao. While Jeff might not be alive to receive the punishment he's due for everything he's done to you two…I believe it's enough closure for us knowing that he's no longer a threat. He can't screw us around anymore.

"At any rate, what I'm saying is – we now have sufficient evidence to say that the evidence for your case was tampered with. In other words, we now have sufficient enough evidence to prove, beyond any reasonable doubt, that you were set up and the charges against you heavily biased."

Kyle fails to catch half of what Timothy's been telling him and Yuuki. There's too many words and his brain's too tired to really follow. It doesn't, however, fail to grasp the gist of what Timothy's saying.

"So…so that means…?" he asks quietly, but he trails off, hesitating. What if he's wrong? What if he made the mistake of daring to believe, only to find that Timothy wasn't saying what Kyle thought he was saying, and Kyle's a fool to think Timothy would say –

"You're innocent as you claimed to be."

Kyle's eyes stretch wide. He stares at the expression on Timothy's face, compassionate, intelligent, knowing…*sure*. He slumps into Yuuki's side, weak.

A hand rubbing his back, steadying. "Breathe, Kyle. You're okay."

Everything fades out of focus. He's trembling. Yuuki stops rubbing his back to hold him closer, tighter, as the sobs tear through Kyle's throat. The sounds are closer to screams. Kyle clings to Timothy's words, to Yuuki's warmth, to the idea of the slate with his name and 'guilty' on it being wiped clean.

Release is what this is. It's so foreign and freeing that it hurts.

The last two months nearly killed him. So many times Kyle's life was almost stolen from him. But there were people who cared where nobody else did and they never let it happen. What hope Kyle had lost, they gave back to him. What shame he had felt, they overrode with kindness and love.

Another weight settles on the bed as Timothy joins the hug. Yuuki's crying too now, apparently, and Timothy's arms wrap around them both.

"We'll take each tomorrow as it comes," Timothy murmurs, "day by day. You two have a home with us while you figure things out, too, okay? Don't think you have to go forward alone just because we've achieved what we set out for. Susan and I will be glad to have you around, as will Sam and Joshua, I'm sure."

Kyle loses it. What had started off as weeping becomes a full blown panic attack. It's too much. Too much kindness. Too stark a contrast after how he was accused, cast aside and disregarded.

Timothy withdraws from the hug and Yuuki quickly gets Kyle lying down again. Yuuki breathes with him, holding his hand tightly, and slowly, after several minutes of feeling like his heart's going to stop for all the adrenaline rushing through him, Kyle's able to breathe again.

He's not sure what happens after that. His vision goes dark, fatigue sweeping over him. Susan's voice sounds in the distance and then there's a gentle hand brushing the hair out of his eyes.

"It's okay, Kyle," she says softly. "Just making sure you're okay."

In truth, Kyle's not sure if he'll ever be okay. He's been shaken up too badly. The hurts that heal will scar, and the ones that don't fully heal will always stay with him. But if there's anything he knows for sure, it's that he's not alone in this fight against the world anymore.

Yuuki is the very proof of that.

Acknowledgements

Special thanks to Katy, whose heart for those around her is the same as Yuuki's and whose help in editing saved me from burning out from stress; to David who helped me through the process of readying this book for publishing; and to all the readers who supported and encouraged me in the months I was writing this story.

Your support means so much more than I am able to express in words.

The Redemption of Kindall, K.

The story continues in Book Two of the Kindall K series…

The truth behind Kyle's case has had great impacts on the lives of those who unearthed it, and now the Kingdom of Arkala is due to feel them too. But Amelia's authority has yet to be recognised, leaving the group stranded and without the assured safety they'd hoped for.

While they navigate these challenges, Yuuki suffers the consequences of taking on Kyle's case investigation. In a state of restless unease, he finds himself questioning if there might have been another reason behind his kidnapping at Ninao a year ago.

Kyle begins a seemingly futile attempt at finding answers, hoping to help Yuuki find closure and prove that he's worth all it cost Yuuki to save him. The search soon reveals major threats may be closer to home than anticipated.

Published November 2019
ISBN-13 (paperback): 9780473499273 | ISBN-13 (hardcover): 9780473630522 | ISBN-13 (Kindle): 9780473499280 | ISBN-13 (ePUB): 9780473578985 |